CROSSING THE ALLEGHANY.

The cover print is from a painting by Robert Griffing entitled: *A Warning for General Braddock.* It depicts a scene (found on page 151) where Christopher Gist and others evaluate pictographs left by enemy Indians who had camped there in large number the night before.

The "Draft of a Map showing ye Path taken by Christopher Gist – 1750-51" was drawn by Fred Threlfall specifically for this work, using a feather quill pen. Information came from Gist's own map and the "Traders Map" of the same period.

ANNOSANAH

A NOVEL BASED ON
THE LIFE OF
CHRISTOPHER GIST

To Donald
Thanks for your support!

CHRISTIAN WIG

Christian Wig

FIRESIDE FICTION
2005

FIRESIDE FICTION
AN IMPRINT OF HERITAGE BOOKS, INC.

Books, CDs, and more—Worldwide

For our listing of thousands of titles see our website
at
www.HeritageBooks.com

Published 2005 by
HERITAGE BOOKS, INC.
Publishing Division
65 East Main Street
Westminster, Maryland 21157-5026

Cover art by Robert Griffing
Map by Fred Threlfall
Engravings of Gist and Washington from
"Emerson's Magazine and Putnam's Monthly" 1857

International Standard Book Number: 0-7884-3195-1

To My Father

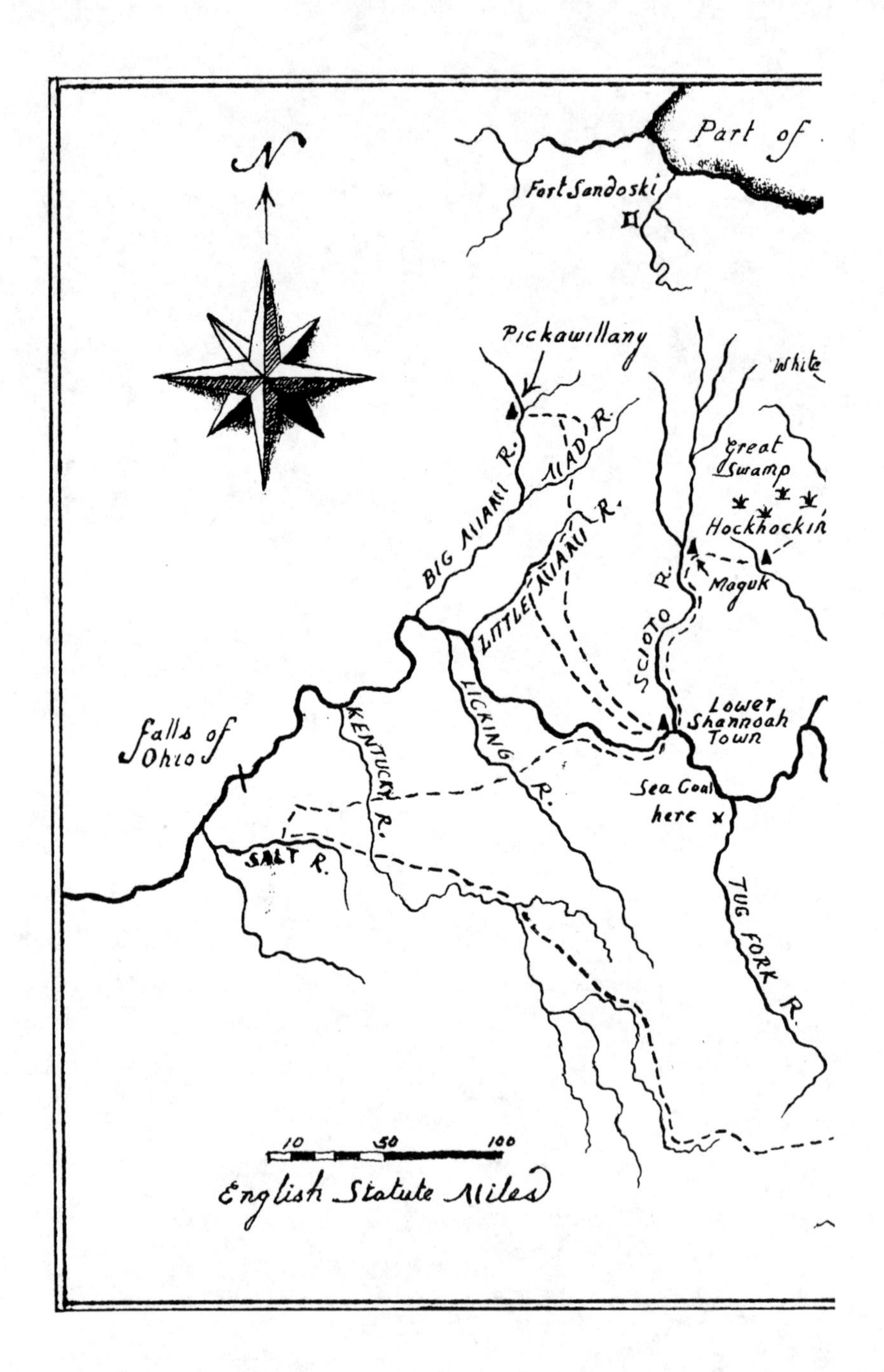

Part of
Fort Sandoski
N
Pickawillany
White
MAD R.
BIG MIAMI R.
LITTLE MIAMI R.
Great Swamp
Hockhockin
Maguk
SCIOTO R.
Lower Shannoah Town
Falls of Ohio
KENTUCKY R.
LICKING R.
Sea Coal here
SALT R.
TUG FORK R.
10
50
100
English Statute Miles

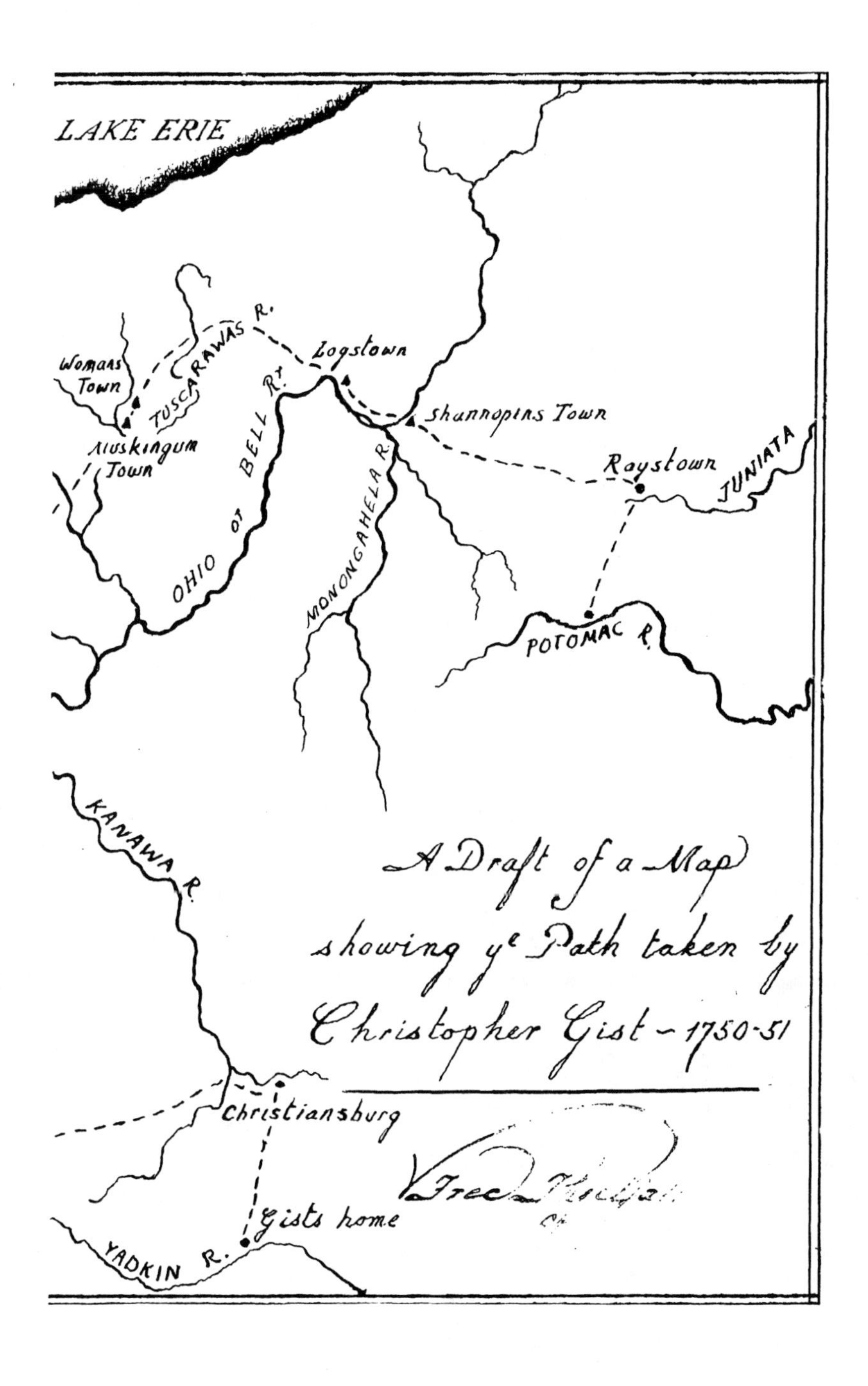
LAKE ERIE
Womans Town
Muskingum Town
TUSCARAWAS R.
Logstown
OHIO or BELL Rr.
Shannopins Town
MONONGAHELA R.
Raystown
JUNIATA
POTOMAC R.
KANAWA R.
A Draft of a Map
showing ye Path taken by
Christopher Gist – 1750-51
Christiansburg
Gists home
YADKIN R.

ACKNOWLEDGMENTS

First, I'd like to thank my father (now deceased) for his unfailing assistance in preparing this manuscript. I would write; he would enter it into his computer. He possessed the unfathomable (to me) ability to type over 100 words per minute.

Of course, I must thank my partner in life, Leslie Heath, for her support and understanding during my quest to complete this work; and for her suggestions for its improvement.

And since family comes first, my brother, Tom, has given his time freely as the computer consultant. Who else can you call at midnight to ask why the printer will not print?

Then there is the first person I met who shared my interest in Christopher Gist – Allan Powell, Professor Emeritus, HCC in Hagerstown, MD. When I noticed he had written his book on Gist, I called him and we have been friends since then. Many thanks to Allan and his wife, Joanie, for their help and encouragement on this project.

And who could imagine I would be able to thank Christopher Gist himself, Fred Threlfall, artist, lecturer and reenactor from Pittsburgh. He portrays Christopher Gist at Fort Necessity and is the visual inspiration for Robert Griffing's two prints featuring Christopher Gist, one of which is on this cover. We've spoken at length during Ft. Ligonier Days about his character and the French and Indian War in which he served. He is, of course, responsible for the map of Gist's first journey.

A heart felt thanks goes to Jerry and Cathy Seymour of Paramount Press in Panama, NY, for our discussions on the history of the Indians as portrayed by Robert Griffing. They introduced me to his paintings and his person and were responsible for obtaining permission to use his print for the cover.

Thank you Robert Griffing for allowing me to use your print for the cover. Your imagery has helped me see the 18th century more clearly.

I would also like to thank my friend Joe LaRose, reference librarian at the University of Akron. Not only did he help me obtain sources, but read parts of my manuscript and offered suggestions.

A fine artist and graphic designer, Dave Brokaw took the print, the specifications and a bunch of ideas, put them together and created the cover design. Many thanks Dave.

Thank you Thomas A. Lewis wherever you are. I had great difficulty characterizing a young George Washington until I read his book, *For King and Country*.

A special thanks to Ron and Chris Wenning of Wennawoods Publishing in Lewisburg, PA, for their reprints of all those old books on Pennsylvania history. They allowed me to have many of my sources on hand at a moments notice. Our conversations have been memorable.

Thank you also to the many folks at various libraries and research facilities: Robert C. Watson, historian and senior researcher at Colonial Williamsburg; Ann Sindelar, research assistant at Western Reserve Historical Society; Leslie Wilson, Inner Library Loan Dept. at the Canton Municipal Library (retired); the folks at the Ohio Historical Society; and librarians at the Carnegie Library of Pittsburgh and the Library of Congress in Washington, DC.

I'd especially like to thank author and instructor John Stevenson of Writer's Digest for reviewing my concept and ideas from the very beginning. He helped channel my energies in a positive direction.

One final thank you goes to my long time friend and fellow rendezvous musician, Dave Neff, who first suggested I write about Christopher Gist, because he was not very well known to the public.

FOREWORD

I used to collect old United States History books that would have been used by my grandmother's generation and hers before that. In the section devoted to the French and Indian War I would often find an engraving of two men on a raft, setting poles in hand, riding on a raging river. One of the men was a young George Washington. The story told how on the way back from warning the French to vacate English territory, the other man, a nondescript figure in buckskins, had pulled from the icy water a young George, who had fallen from that raft. That frontiersman resembled Daniel Boone, Davy Crockett and all our frontier heroes rolled into one. This was Christopher Gist. Now of all the famous men and women who have rated paragraphs and even whole sections in our history books, he got a picture, and deservedly so, because he saved the life of our yet-to-be first president. Every school child in America, up through the early 1900's, knew something about Christopher Gist, even if it were only this one fact – that he saved Washington's life.

Then came the "War to End All Wars" and the world was rocked by so many events, there was no more room in the history books for that picture. Christopher Gist became the "forgotten frontiersman." Simon Kenton and Lewis Wetzel still got some attention, partly because they were Indian fighters. Daniel Boone and Davy Crockett remained in the public conscience with a new layer of merit, largely due to Walt Disney. But Gist, a man of peace and reconciliation, was displaced.

How did this first colonial explorer of the Ohio territory; the man who not once, but twice, saved Washington's life; an experienced frontier diplomat among the Ohio Indians; head guide for the fated Braddock campaign; top recruiter for Washington's army; Deputy Indian Agent for Virginia; how did this man, who did the work of ten men, get forgotten?

The answer is complex. One purpose of this work is to explore those reasons, looking for both the answers to why he was forgotten and why he should not be. The Cherokee and the Catawba mourned his passing, for they admired and respected him. Washington must have missed him. Since their rafting day, he had recommended Gist for every position he had held. A man with Gist's talents and loyalty would have been hard to find. But soon the War for Independence introduced a new batch of heroes; that and the building of a country conspired to leave Christopher Gist behind . . . except for our one image of two men on a raft.

This work will introduce Christopher Gist into the awareness of the reader. My research has led me to believe this is who Christopher Gist was – a man who believed the White and the Indian could live in harmony. The years of warfare would have weakened that belief until, toward the end of his life, his primary job was to keep the Indians away from the white settlements.

The reader will soon notice that, except for the Prologue, all the events are presented exclusively from Gist's point of view. You will know only what *he* perceives; encounter only *his* private thoughts and feelings; only hear *him* reminisce. This will facilitate an unusual intimacy with our forgotten frontiersman. Historic figures of this magnitude are too often heaped with praise, cast in bronze and kept at a distance, lest we discover their humanness. But, having escaped lionization, there are fewer layers to be removed before we find Christopher Gist.

AUTHOR'S NOTE

Annosanah is a work of fiction with an historical base, well grounded in research and documentation. Christopher Gist, the man to whom the Wyandot name, Annosanah, was given, is an actual person in the annals of Colonial America, as are most of the people in the book. The major events are real and my representations of these are gleaned from both period sources and modern scholarship.

Conversation, wherever possible, reflects the thoughts and opinions expressed in letters and journals of the various speakers. Often, though, it is based on probable opinions implied by their actions. Indian oratory is taken verbatim from Colonial records and the journals of Christopher Gist and young George Washington. Needless to say, the words of these various Indians were written down by white men. But, I believe they still give much insight into the way these Indian speakers thought and expressed themselves, at least to the white men.

In addition to the text of the novel, explanatory notes on each chapter can be found at the end of the book. These notes are not numbered, but their reference to details in their respective chapters will be apparent. The novel is intended to stand alone. But by referring to these notes, the reader can acquire additional information helpful in painting a broader picture of the period, relate the location of historic places to today's landmarks, and check sources for confirmation of information. I have also included a bibliography of the sources that appear in the chapter notes.

Christian Wig

PROLOGUE

October 1749

Bright orange flames rose high into the night illuminating a clearing in the woods. Giant shadows of two gesturing human forms danced on a wall of trees. They fed their campfire as men who have nothing to dread but the cold. A wolf howled in the distance, then another. Hobbled horses whinnied a concerned response.

"Weren't long ago we'd a been tendin' a smaller fire," said one of the forms. "Every sooty savage from here to hell and back'll be knowin' our where'bouts. Damn heathen bastards, can't trust em . . ."

"Now Hugh," interrupted the second form lighting a short clay pipe, "you oughtn't talk like that about our red brothers. I've had many a trouble with 'em sure and sometimes I'd swear they're the devil's own spirits in the shape of men. But there's many a good one among 'em."

"True enough, 'til the liquor takes 'em. Why, it weren't but two years ago they tied me to a chair in my own home and was fixin' to scalp me alive."

"I'll not hear your stories 'bout drunken Injens; got enough of my own. If you wouldn't befuddle 'em before you bartered with 'em, you wouldn't have such trouble. And don't you worry 'bout that fire. We're out here to befriend the local tribes for the Company and it don't matter if we find 'em by night nor by day now do it?" Hugh opened his mouth to answer, but was interrupted. "King George's War ended last year, so everyone oughtta be friendly as a whore on payday. We got us four pack horses plumb full of presents for Ohio Injens and our orders is to pass 'em out gen'rously."

"Say Tom," Hugh began, leaning far to the left closing his eyes to avoid drifting smoke from the fire. "We're s'pozed to keep our eyes skinned for good farmland. How'd you tell what's good out here in the woods?" Before Tom could answer, Hugh continued. "Now that never did make sense to me; how farmers'll look all around for land well timbered, cut down all them trees, dig out the stumps and then plant crops. Be a whole lot simpler to just find open land in the first place and save all that work?"

"You sure ain't no farmer, Hugh Parker!" Tom continued, pointing his clay pipe at his companion's face. Every farmer knows big timber only grows on the richest soil. So we look for tracts of flat land with big trees. Simple! Pass me that bottle."

"Oughtta be easy to find," said Hugh, this time leaning far to the right to escape the cloud of smoke. "All the land twixt the ridges of the Appalachians is flat. Plenty of trees." He took a swig and passed the bottle.

Tom knew his friend spoke from experience. For many years Hugh Parker had traversed western Pennsylvania and the Ohio country as a fur trader from Maryland.

"Say Tom," Hugh now leaned backwards allowing the smoke to drift over him, "tell me more 'bout this Ohio Company that's hired us. How'd it start?"

"From the beginnin'?" asked Tom, his eyebrows raised in surprise. He tapped his pipe on a log and a chunk of unburned tobacco fell out.

"Yah, from the beginnin'."

"Well let's see," he scratched his chin as an air pocket in the wood exploded, sending a shower of sparks skyward. "You 'member that strip of land 'bout twenty miles wide claimed by both Maryland and Pennsylvania they was fightin' over back twenty years ago?" He filled his pipe and lit it with a stick from the fire.

"Why Tom Cresap, every man alive knows the story of how you fought for Maryland to have that piece of land. Folks was up in arms for sure. That Pennsylvania sheriff come to arrest you with a dozen men, but you and Hanna shot it out with 'em 'till they burned your house down and hauled you off to Philadelphia in irons. The 'Maryland Monster' they called you."

"You've not disremembered a thing Hugh," Tom took over the tale. "Bloody bastards marched me down the main street to the jail. Hoards of fat little pasty-faced Quakers lined the street as I hollered louder'n an Injen scalp halloo, 'ain't this the purdiest town in Maryland?'"

"That riled them up some I'll wager. Here pass me that bottle. Say how'd you get out of that mess anyhow?"

"Why, I made myself so goddamn ornery and obnoxious, they just couldn't stand havin' me around," He passed the bottle and proceeded to explain how he had then moved to Virginia to let things cool down. While he was there he met the Governor, Thomas Lee and the Washington brothers, Lawrence and Austin. Being in no way intimidated by these gentlemen, Cresap began advising them on the building of "trading houses" for the Indian fur trade and buying land and other frontier subjects about which he had more than ample opinion. "Get the Board of Trade to give you a land grant, says I, 'cause the Six Nations sold all the lands on the Upper Ohio to His Majesty at the Lancaster Treaty of '44." Now according to Cresap they all knew that, but not one of them had ever thought about land speculation before. "Good idea, says they," and that was the last he heard about it for a while.

Cresap interrupted his monologue to stir up the fire. Smoke turned to flame, much to the relief of his friend. "Pass me that bottle," said Cresap. He took a short nip and told how two years ago certain gentlemen of Virginia, being the Washingtons, the Lees, his honor himself Lord Fairfax, the Mercers and thirty other prominent men of means formed the Ohio Company of Virginia. "Just like I told 'em," they had petitioned the Board of Trade for 500,000 acres. The details of how the Company was to obtain use of the land were complicated, depending upon the recruitment of so many families to get the first 200,000 and so on. But as Cresap put it, "the first buck was gutted," and they were now working on the second.

That next step was to invest in goods to trade with the Indians for furs, but they needed a man on the frontier. Each member, now including Cresap, contributed the requisite £100 and a large stock of trade goods was ordered. After this preliminary job of opening relations with the Ohio tribes in the name of the Ohio Company, Cresap and Parker were expected to build a store house at Wills Creek and find the easiest path from there to Redstone Old Fort on Monongahela, where they would construct another such building.

"Now, there ain't no easy path to the Forks," Parker interrupted. "There's seven or eight mountain ridges to go up and over, not to mention impassable swamps, ragin' rivers and every obstacle the devil ever put before a man. Nothin' but privations and difficulties. Here, pass me that . . ."

"Shh!" hissed Cresap, raising his hand to silence. Before they could move, Cresap's "devil spirits in the shape of men" filled the clearing. Wrapped in matchcoats and blankets against the brisk night air, their dark features glowed in the fire light. Swinging ear wheels and bobbing nose pendants cast eerie shadows on expressionless faces. Long, black scalp locks hung down the backs of their necks in sharp contrast to foreheads and faces plucked free of hair. Trade guns pointed toward the woodsmen.

"Shauwanoa, by the looks of 'em," said Parker. "Must be a huntin' party 'cause they ain't painted for war. I count twelve."

"Relax and smile. They just want to know who we are and what we're about."

After several moments of silence one warrior came forward from behind the others. His copper-colored face was disfigured by a long scar running from his nose to where an ear should have been. A dark hole glared at them in the absence of an eye.

"Thirteen," Parker mumbled.

"How's your Shauwanoa?"

"Tolerable."

"Ask him to come and sit down."

Hugh and Tom both rose as the Indian advanced to within six feet of them.

"Welcome, brother Shawano," said Parker in their tongue. "Come, warm yourselves . . ." It was all he could say before the Indian spat out a barrage of words unrecognizable to Cresap. The Indian's good eye gave no hint of friendliness.

"He asks if we're Virginia traders," said Parker.

"Tell him we come bringin' presents to all the Injens on the Ohio from our Governor, their brother, in Virginia." Cresap pointed to the pack horses and the piles of presents laying on the ground nearby. Parker translated.

As if summoned, half the warriors surrounded the presents and began ripping off their canvas covers, passing out the contents to the waiting hunters. Laughter erupted among them as they held up various treasures in triumph. The one-eyed Indian, however, was not amused.

"He ain't interested," Parker noted out loud. He saw Cresap's face turn red, fighting to control his anger.

Again, one-eye began a tirade of hard consonants and vowels that continued for several minutes. His face contorted as his voice grew louder. He pointed at both men, then to their fire and their horses and to the forest. When the diatribe diminished, the Indian waited for Parker to translate.

"He says we are the Great Knives from Virginia. We come to the land of his grandfathers to build roads that'll bring their hated enemies, the Catawba and the Cherokee. He says we come to build a big fort. Soldiers will kill the deer; Shauwanoa women and children will go hungry. Pennsylvania traders, he says, come only to trade for skins. They're welcome, but he says Virginia is not welcome. He says Virginia traders are like the ticks on the deer that come to suck the blood of the land, to cut the trees, build houses, plant fields and raise animals – the white man's cows and his filthy pigs. He did go on about that for awhile. The Pennsylvania traders have told them this."

Scar-face barked orders at three hunters, who sliced the hobbles on four of the horses and led them away. Then he turned to the white men and continued his speech.

"We now have two horses," Parker repeated. "We must go and never come again to these woods. If they find us here, we will see how deep the wolves can bite."

As the Shawnee had come, so were they gone. The lonely hoot of a barred owl broke the forest silence and was answered by its companion. A log shifted in the fire, giving new flame to glowing embers. Giant shadows of two human forms, motionless, poised on the wall of trees surrounding the clearing.

PART ONE

"That their great Men, the Beaver and Captain Oppamylucah (these are two Chiefs of the Delawares), desired to know where the Indian's Land lay, for that the French claimed all the Land on one side of the River Ohio & the English on the other Side."

Christopher Gist

CHAPTER I

September 1750

Twin hounds raised their heads and growled a warning in unison. Their master looked up, grabbed his rifle and hurried to the door. Within seconds he heard the rhythmic thumping of hooves echoing off the walls of his outbuildings. He slid open the porthole to view a young man, perhaps in his late teens, dismount, then fish in his saddle bag. Sensing no threat he pulled back the wooden bolt. Weighing a good two hundred pounds, the three ply oak slab swung on its four iron hinges with nary a squeak. The grain of each ply ran differently to make it nearly impossible for tomahawks to chop through.

"Are you Mr. Christopher Gist?" the messenger asked.

"I am," he replied. "And what might you be doing all the way out here this time of night?"

"I been sent out by Governor Thomas Lee in Williamsburg to give ye this parcel." He handed Gist a small leather pouch. "I been riding eight days straight 'cause they told me to get here quick as I could on account o' you'd want it right away." The courier's speech was beginning to accelerate and Gist was loath to let him continue.

It was at least a 400 mile trip with stretches on narrow paths through dense woods and over rough mountains. To average 50 miles a day was exceptional. Gist praised the young man's efforts and sent him over to the barn where his servant, Gabriel, would help him bed down his horse, fix him a proper supper and fix him a place to sleep.

"I'll have letters for you in the morning. And here's something for your efforts." He took two silver sixpence from a small pouch and gave it to the lad. He knew the Company had paid him, but probably not enough.

"Thank'e sir," his eyes widened as he admired the face of Lord Baltimore on one side and his coat of arms on the other. He flipped the coin in the air, caught it and went to find Gabriel.

Christopher Gist closed the door and walked over to a small writing desk, its finish scratched, edges worn to the wood, a testament to its familiarity with important papers and long journeys. His grandfather had brought it from England nearly a century ago. Writing on the same surface as his father and grandfather before gave him a connection to those ancestors. He was awed by their accomplishments: the founding of Baltimore Town and the establishment of a fur trade with the Indians. If this packet contained what he thought, then perhaps he could begin his own legacy.

The dim light of the tallow lamps cast dark shadows across the puncheon floor as he opened the leather pouch. He unfolded the letter within and skipped to the end to confirm its origin.

Thomas Lee, Esq. George William Fairfax
Lawrence Washington Thomas Cresap
In behalf of Ourselves and the Council of the Ohio Company

His eyes moved to the top of the page where he began to read the script of the document's composer.

Williamsburg the 11th day of September 1750

You are to go out as soon as possible to the Westward of the great Mountains, and carry with you such a Number of Men as You think necessary, in Order to search out and discover the Lands upon the River Ohio, & other adjoining Branches of the Mississippi down as low as the great Falls thereof: You are particularly to observe the Ways & Passes thro all the Mountains you cross, & take an exact Account of the Soil, Quality & Product of the Land and the Wideness and Deepness of the Rivers, & the several Falls belonging to them, together with the Courses & Bearings of the Rivers & Mountains as near as you conveniently can.

You are to draw a plan of the Country You pass thro: You are to take an exact and particular Journal of all Your Proceedings, and make a true Report thereof to the Ohio Company.

You are to observe what Nations of Indians inhabit there, their Strength & Numbers, who they trade with, & in what Comodities they deal: You are also to make an Invitation to all these Nations, that they may come to the Loggs Town in the Spring for a great Feast and a Distribution of presents, to signify Our Desire to Trade with them.

There it was, the appointment he had been expecting. A year ago he received a letter from Thomas Cresap informing him of the Ohio Company of Virginia and its purpose. Because of Cresap's failure with Hugh Parker, they needed another representative, one with standing among the Indians and not openly associated with the Company. The first shipment of goods earmarked for the Ohio Indian trade had arrived from London in March. That spring he and his young servant, Gabriel, traversed the wilderness trails, leading twenty pack horses laden with Ohio Company trade goods; iron pots, lead bars, powder, cloth shirts, needles, knives, tobacco, tomahawks, rum, and all the smaller trinkets pleasing to the vanity of the Indians.

On this trip he met the Delaware, Shawnee and Mingos, the latter being various Iroquois tribesmen who had elected to live in western Pennsylvania and the Ohio country. He was surprised that some older Indians remembered him as a boy accompanying his father, a merchant and fur trader, on expeditions into the interior of Maryland and Pennsylvania. Others recalled him as a young man on his own journeys. His reputation as an honest trader preceded him. They appreciated his calm demeanor, in contrast to the intense haggling of the Pennsylvania traders.

They also liked the low prices: one wool wraparound matchcoat for a buckskin, a wool stroud two yards long for a buck and a doe, a pair of stockings for two raccoon skins, twelve bars of lead for a buck, much less than Pennsylvania's goods.

Also contrary to convention, he allowed no liquor consumption until transactions were complete. After a trading session, when the Indians had warmed themselves with rum, Gist stood before them and awaited their attention. At six foot two he towered well over his audience. Clad in knee britches, boots and linsey-woolsey shirt belted at the waist, he relayed the Ohio Company message. "Brothers of the Delaware, I am come to you from Assarquoa." He used the familiar Iroquoian name for the Governor of Virginia. "I know that a bad bird sits on your shoulder whispering in your ear, saying all manner of evil against us. The road by which we would trade with you has been made foul and great logs are fallen across it. We would have you be strong like men and have one heart and one mind with us and make the road clear, for we have much business to do together."

The speech was simple, yet eloquent in the tradition of Indian oratory. When his appeal was over, an interpreter, with equal emotion, relayed a translation to his listeners. Though Gist could not speak their language, this did not keep the assembly from gauging his sentiment. Years of hearing the white man's speeches had given the Indian a special sense about the speaker's sincerity. They watched facial expressions, body movements, the eyes. They listened to how he spoke, then heard the words. They were pleased. Here was a white man who spoke with neither duplicity nor condescension; here was a white man to be trusted.

After two months, Gist returned to Williamsburg, packhorses laden with furs. While in town, he met with Ohio Company leaders, who were satisfied with the account of his trip and mentioned a possible exploration in the fall.

Now on September 22 he sat, instructions in hand, ready to embark on a new adventure. His mind raced with plans. He needed no one other than Gabriel. They would ride Lott and Spark, two of his best horses, named after favorites he had to sell when he left Baltimore Town. Now how many pack horses would he need? The intensity of his thoughts had not dulled his senses. He heard Sarah's soft footsteps. He turned in his chair to see her standing, outlined by the doorway like a picture in a frame. She was still lovely. Five years on the frontier had dulled the finish on the Baltimore lady, but revealed an undercoating of earthiness more appropriate to frontier living.

"Who was at the door?"

He cringed at the thought of another argument ahead. "An express from Williamsburg come to deliver this letter from Governor Lee."

"I suppose it has something to do with that Ohio Company?"

"Yes. They've asked me to explore the Ohio country for them." He showed her the letter and saw her expression change from sarcasm to sadness.

"And how long will you be gone this time?" she asked in a steady voice, handing back the letter.

He hesitated; several months maybe, less than a year. Neither he, nor the Company members, with the possible exception of Cresap, had any idea how much territory there was out there, nor how many Indian tribes lived on the land. He said as much.

She wiped an eye with her hand, turned, and walked out of the room. He had not often seen Sarah cry.

He thought back to a time when there had been less strife in their life. In Baltimore Town they lived in relative comfort. Son of a prominent businessman and one of Baltimore Town's founders, slaves and indentured servants performed the daily chores. Sarah reared her two daughters in as much "society" as a town of 400 could have.

Their move to the North Carolina had changed all that. During these past five years Sarah had become more vocal in her demands on his time and more critical of his frontier escapades. When he returned from Williamsburg in July, she chastised him for being gone for the planting.

He also knew she was distraught, because the family was disbursing. Sons and daughters were finding their own ways. The many chores were hard, but tolerable as a family. Now, with two children left, they were overwhelming. Christopher and Sarah had discussed these changes. She expressed emptiness; he applauded their independence.

Enough of this reverie! Time to get up from this desk and search for her because of some gut feeling that said this matter must be resolved. Her reaction upset him; he wanted her approval. He found her sitting at the dinner table in the dim light of several wall sconces, wringing her hands.

"Where are Tom and Nancy?" he said, staring down at the wide floorboards. Richard was off looking for land to homestead; Nathaniel was out trading with the Carolina Indian tribes; Violetta had just married.

These two youngest were around somewhere, she answered, again without emotion, but then she turned around to face him with a speed that took him aback. The fire in her eyes surprised him. "It's not right for you to be gone so much! Some of the Indians don't like us here and you know there was that trouble over at Peter King's." Several months ago an Iroquois war party had helped themselves to King's larder, killed cattle and stole horses, while Mr. King was out hunting. "Can't Tom Cresap or any of those other worthless ruffians do it? Why does it have to be you?"

He met her fiery gaze, "Because I'm the only one who can do it right!" He held her stare and continued in a soft voice, "Cresap and Parker are not worthless, but they failed last year and now the Company wants me to try."

"And they could have been killed. What if you don't return this time?"

Back and forth they went, repeating each worn out quibble and quarrel as if it carried new weight. Of course he would come back; he always come back. "I have to do this. It's an opportunity I can't . . ."

"YOU have to do this!" she yelled. "YOUR opportunity! What about me and my opportunity if you never come back. I can't run this place by myself. And who would marry a broken down old aristocracy woman like me? I'll tell you something Mr. Christopher Gist." Her finger aimed at his face. "You've been paying more attention to those . . . those savages, since we came here, than you have to me. Always gone out and done whatever you damn well please with your Indians, and who knows what goes on out there. And those squaw hussies always sniffing around you traders, begging for a proper rogering, and I'll bet you can give it to them!" She stood, hands on hips, defiant, then paced around, gathering more energy for her next strike.

"Nothing goes on out there that shouldn't go on," he yelled back, shocked that she would describe such a scene and accuse him of acting in it. Sometimes it did happen, but it was more often the traders "sniffing" the young maidens. "And I don't lie with squaws."

She looked winded. He tried to explain that his going away had nothing to do with her, but the constricting life of a farmer. He could not just work the land. He need something with more, he searched for the word, "freedom." Could she understand that?

Red-eyed, she raised her head and stared at him. She shook her head. "No, I don't understand. You say you want freedom. Out here in this God-forsaken wilderness you have nothing but freedom, no neighbors, no magistrates or creditors, no one to tell you what to do. Chris, you're forty-four years old, when are you going to grow up and . . ?"

"It's not about growing up!" He shouted, incensed that she should suggest such a thing. It's about boredom. Each morning on the farm he faced the same thing, same work, same place, same land and tomorrow it would be exactly the same. Out in the woods, though, every day was different. The Indians fascinated him. There was always something new, a challenge. He was excited, sensing he had found the right word to describe his passion. She was right. "Freedom" was not the right word. He needed the challenge. His father and grandfather were like that. How could she ask him to give that up!

He could see her begin to relax and as quickly as the altercation began it was over. He sat across from her, looking into her eyes. "Remember when we used to do this for hours?"

"We'd stay up by candlelight and just look at each other like we couldn't believe we were real. We'd both drag around all day from lack of sleep and do it again that night." They chuckled at the memory.

"Look," he said, with softness. "When I went to trade those Company goods this spring, the Indians knew who I was. I won't be in any danger. Besides, I'll take Gabriel again. He can shoot."

She stared at him for the longest time. Then he saw traces of a smile that became wider until it was a grin and then she was laughing and Christopher began laughing until neither could stop.

"The Deuce take you Christopher Gist! You know good and well Gabriel couldn't hit the side of our barn with a cannon!"

They dried their eyes and stared at each other. He stood up and pulled her to him. She did not resist. They clung to each other, her small frame enveloped by his massive body. For several minutes they rocked to and fro.

"This is important, isn't it?" she asked.

He believed so. Men of distinction wanted to settle that Ohio country and they were going to need someone like him to do it. He then told her his plans. His short trip to one small corner of the Ohio territory, between the Monongahela and Youghiogheny Rivers, had shown him thousands of acres of rich land suited for settlement and cultivation. Surely he could regain his family wealth through prudent land speculation. After all, the Company was looking to buy land from the Indians. If somehow he could do the same . . . In addition, there was money to be made in the fur trade. The pelts he brought back were of superior quality and would bring the highest prices. "But it'll take time and you're going to have to be patient."

"I'm sorry . . ."

"Forget it," he said as she looked up at him. He could sense her powerful love and at that moment he did not want to leave her. He sensed how much he meant to her and could not bear to picture her pain if something happened to him. They had been through so much together: the constant humiliation of creditors wanting their money, leaving her family and friends to come out here. And he loved her for it. Yet he knew he had to go. It was the adventure of a lifetime, a chance to see first-hand a whole new land.

"Chris," she said, looking up at him. "Let's go upstairs."

He smiled at her. He was surprised.

"And what might we be doing upstairs?"

"We might be having a tumble together."

"And what makes you think I'd be interested in a broken down old aristocracy woman?" he teased.

She smiled with a bold look in her eye. "Because like you, I'm the only one who can do it right?"

CHAPTER II

October 1750

Indians and traders alike knew many a footpath as a "Warrior Path. But the Great Warrior Path, wide enough for war parties to run single-file through the woods, linked the Iroquois with their ancient enemies, the Catawba and Cherokee. Once, this major thoroughfare lay east of the Appalachian Mountains. The westward movement of settlers, however, had forced a relocation of the path to its present position west of the Blue Ridge.

Such was the path traversed by Christopher Gist and Gabriel. It led from the Carolinas, past Gist's home, 275 miles north to Old Town, Maryland and on through Pennsylvania to New York, home of the Iroquois. Old Town had been a Shawnee village, but was abandoned during their westward migrations twenty years earlier. Thomas Cresap had made his home here for the past nine years. His plantation consisted of a two-story stone house surrounded by a stockade built to withstand an Indian attack. Nearby stood a large barn and warehouse constructed of hand-hewn logs with half dovetail corners and shake-shingle roofs. The barn housed livestock while the warehouse contained Ohio Company stores and trade goods for the Indians. In a rare moment of nostalgia he named his estate "Skipton," after his birthplace in Yorkshire, England. He was not sure of his exact age, only that in his teens he had come to Baltimore Town in 1717. Having entered the fur trade, he moved westward.

Skipton was a popular stopping place. Cresap's amiable disposition and hospitality were known throughout the frontier, especially to the Indians. He kept large herds of cattle and hogs grazing in the surrounding woods and the Indians enjoyed pilfering them. To discourage this practice he welcomed visiting tribesmen by keeping a huge iron kettle full of victuals over the fire. This generosity earned him the affectionate title of "Big Spoon." The Iroquois encouraged his philanthropy by citing the Treaty of Lancaster, wherein English settlers on Indian land had to provide food for traveling bands. Sometimes it took sensitive negotiation to avoid a total plunder of his merchandise. Still, Cresap accepted these risks and maintained a good relationship with them most of the time.

Mounted on Lott and Spark, Christopher and Gabriel crossed the Potomac at the fording place. Cresting the gradual slope of the riverbank, they viewed Cresap's homestead surrounded by a field of rotting tree stumps. Having ridden fourteen days, they were ready for a break in the demands of wilderness travel. The air was cold and damp, heralding the arrival of autumn rains soon to become snow. Gist looked forward to seeing his friend and discussing old times, the Ohio Company and his own present expedition.

As the visitors approached the house, several large, barking dogs of mixed lineage did their best to discourage them. Horses ignored them and walked on. Hannah emerged from the front door.

"Lord-a-mercy," she exclaimed, "why it's Chris Gist. "Thomas," she called louder than her small frame seemed to allow, "Thomas, you come on out here now and see who just rode up! We got us some visitors."

A moment later Tom Cresap appeared from his warehouse. Gist remembered his unique walk with its long strides, gliding along the ground as if he were skating on ice. He was shorter than Gist, but wider and more muscular, with a well-earned reputation for enormous strength. In his younger days he was ever quick to challenge the toughest character in arm wrestling, rock lifting and other feats requiring more brawn than brain. Yet he was quick-witted and possessed a memory for detail to rival any sophisticate of the day. A gigantic black man, who looked as if he were ready for a fight, followed close behind. He smiled though, when he saw the visitors.

"Well damn me if it ain't Christopher Gist," Cresap swore as the riders dismounted. "Right glad to see you, you old rascal." He stepped up, grabbed Gist's hand and shook it like a pump handle. "Damn my eyes if I didn't miss you this summer when you was passin' through, but I was down in Williamsburg showin' them society folks how it's done. By god man how long's it been since I seen your ornery self? Let's see now, must've been five years, maybe six, just 'fore you moved down south."

"Exactly so," said Gist. "It was in Baltimore Town at Payne's Tavern." He turned to include Hannah while describing their last encounter. "Tom here was delivering a load of furs and I was saying goodbye to friends. We stayed until the wee hours of the morning in that fine old ordinary and did wind up a bit fuddled I'd say." He winked at Cresap.

"By thunder," roared Cresap, "we got drunker'n two fiddlers at a weddin'."

"What do you mean we?" Gist shot back. "Who was it carried you to our room and made sure you held on to all that money you got from selling those furs? And who was it nursed you through a good case of barrel fever next morning?"

"Your memory for details is downright embarrassin' Gist. What's your name boy?" Cresap addressed Gabriel, changing the subject.

"Gabriel suh," he replied.

"Goliath," Cresap turned to his man, "bed these horses and then take young Gabriel here and get him somethin' to eat."

"Yes massa Tom," Goliath answered. The two went off toward the barn bantering back and forth like lifelong friends. They made an amusing pair, with Goliath a head taller than Gabriel, who was slight of build and barely able to look his own horse in the eye.

Gist and Cresap slapped each other on the back as they went inside and joked about their last night together. Their friendship was such that it could take up where it left off five years earlier without loss of continuity. Gist, on one of his fur trading excursions twelve years earlier, had lodged at "Long Meadows," Cresap's trading house in western Maryland. They found much in common and became friends over the next three years. Cresap prospered. Then one day a French frigate captured the British merchant ship carrying Cresap's entire shipment of furs. He sold his beloved home to satisfy his creditors and moved farther west. Gist had lost touch with him until that evening at Payne's Tavern.

"It's just 'bout supper time ain't that right woman?" Cresap spoke to Hannah with a wink toward his guest. "Well, by thunder, let's get crackin' and fix us some vittals."

"Fix you some vittals!" Hannah cried in mock disbelief.
"Why, I oughtta just make you eat out of that there kettle over yonder you keep for your Injen friends."

"Damnation Hannah, you know that sorry shit ain't fit for no white man." He turned to his friend. "If you or me was to eat that slop, we'd get sick and most likely die. But them red devils got iron innards. Swear to god, they'll eat anythin'. I just keep addin' bits of this and bits of that, bein' leftovers we won't eat. Keeps 'em happy."

The two sat in what served as the parlor and Cresap pulled a short clay pipe from its holder on the wall. "Have a pipe?"

"No thanks. Never took it up, myself."

"Well, you're lucky. I smoke like a goddamn wet fire; there's a haze followin' me wherever I go, so much smoke I can't see what I'm doin' half the time, nor where I'm goin' the other half. I'm always runnin' out of tobacco and I end up smokin' my own mix of corn silk and died sumac, but it just ain't the same."

"I don't believe I've ever heard you vent your frustration over such a trifle."

"Now Gist, if I didn't air my grief on a regular basis, I wouldn't have nothin' to say. Now can you imagine that?"

Gist said that he could not and steered the conversation to the subject of Cresap's family. In time the topic turned to the Ohio Company and Cresap's position of part owner.

"I guess that leaves me working for you," Gist chaffed.

"Ha! The day I start givin' you orders is the day you can tie me to a tree and use me for a target." Cresap stopped and relit his pipe. "They just sort of gave me this position on account of 'em bein' mostly gentlemen, you won't find them out here much. I'm their frontier representative you might say."

"Then I'll just sit back and listen to your expert advice. By the way, how did you become a member?"

Cresap relayed the same story he had told Parker the year before. "So you see, when Lee got all the partners together, he knew they couldn't do it without me. So there you are!" Cresap continued, "you know, they're gonna settle that land wherever you tell 'em is the best spot. They're aimin' to buy it from the Delaware, or whoever'll sell it, and then have you recruit a hundred families. Then they want you to build a settlement."

"What do you mean whoever will sell it?"

"Well, that gets complicated," said Cresap as he emptied and filled his pipe. He explained that the Six Nations believed all the land in the Ohio Valley belonged to them by right of conquest and they had just been allowing the Delaware and Shawnee to use it. Now at the Lancaster Treaty of '44, the Iroquois thought they were only selling the Shenandoah Valley to Virginia. But that treaty said the Iroquois sold all the lands within the boundaries of Virginia and, unknown to them, Virginia had a "sea to sea" charter from the Crown. Now, Virginia claimed She owned a strip of land hundreds of miles wide from the Atlantic shore clear to the Shining Sea, which of course includes the Ohio Valley.

Cresap paused while Gist let this sink in. The sounds and smells of Hannah fixing dinner began to filter into the room.

"And the Iroquois think they still own it, but since they don't really and don't even occupy that territory, the Company will have to buy land from those tribes who live there, land already given in the grant by the King and bought from the Iroquois."

Cresap looked pleased that Gist understood in spite of his convoluted explanation. He changed the subject. "Now ain't you supposed to be inviting all the Injens you meet to some conference at Logstown next spring?" Gist nodded. "The Company hopes for a big attendance. Then it's gonna be your job to buy that land for whatever they want, plus, a gen'rous amount of presents. You see, the Company's got big plans and you're gonna be right smack dab in the middle of 'em. Oh, I envy you, but I ain't no diplomat like you."

"Being a natural diplomat can be a curse at times; always trying to see the other man's point and never having one of your own. But anyway how do you know all this? They never told me much of anything."

"I attended the last council meeting and asked a lot of questions. Got tired of me real fast, but that brings me to another point. You can't be lettin' them red savages know your lookin' for parcels of land. Them goddamn Pennsylvania traders, those sons-of-bitches, almost got us killed last year by tellin' all them lies about the Company. I still piss pins and needles when I think about it. The presents belonged to the Company, but them four horses was mine and I ain't been reimbursed yet."

"I heard about your run-in with the Shannoah. But don't they already know about the Company plans? The way I hear it, as soon as the Board of Trade approved the proposal, the French and the Pennsylvanians knew the whole scheme."

"I guess there's a good spy network and the Shauwanoa knew about it last year. But among some of the Injens, it's still just a rumor, and not all of 'em have heard it."

The sound of splitting wood filled the silence and provided a welcome break from the intensity of their conversation.

"Now where was I? Ah yes, you just tell them Injens you're invitin' 'em to this conference. Tell 'em their brothers, the Virginians, have a passel of presents for 'em from the King, which is true! Then when you got 'em in the palm of your hand, you buy the land."

"You make it sound so simple."

"Look, I know it ain't, but you're the diplomat," he said with a smile. "Now you know Gist," Cresap got serious, "there ain't nobody knows a goddamn thing about that Ohio country; how many Injens there are; which ones are friendly; even where they all are! Nobody, except them goddamn Pennsylvania traders. Tom Lee and his boys don't have the slightest idea how big that country is out there and they have no notion of what they're askin' you to do. They want you to go all the way to the Falls of the Ohio! Why, all hell would freeze over before any white man could even think about puttin' down roots way out there. Stupidest thing I ever heard.

"Anyway, as far as findin' the Injens, there ain't but one man can help you – George Croghan, Prince of the Pennsylvania Traders, they call him. I met him a few years back and we had us a real nice chat. He ain't like the usual rabble callin' themselves traders. He's more like you, honest and fair towards the Injens. He's out there somewhere trying to undo the damage that French fella, de Blainville, done last year. Ask for him at Logstown. Travels with an Injen named Andrew Montour called the "Interpreter". Oh, and you'll probably run into Barney Curran out trading for the Company. You remember that Irishman who used to be a Pennsylvania trader?"

The call to supper interrupted their conversation. The family sat at the table and Christopher offered the evening grace. The men told stories to the children about their hunting exploits together, exaggerating the number of deer, the size of the bear and ferocity of the wolves. After the meal the two men shared a jug of rum and continued their discussion of Indian relations and other politics of the day. Long into the night the two friends engaged their wit and wisdom and finally retired none the better for the rum they had consumed.

The next afternoon saw them at the warehouse packing supplies for the expedition: several small bags of flour, a cask of salted beef, two kegs of rum, four cured hams, two dozen bars of lead for shot, two casks of gun powder, extra flints, presents for the Indians, strings of wampum, extra blankets and other various and sundry items needed for such a trip, including grain for the horses. Gist would hunt fresh food at every opportunity, but these provisions were necessary for emergencies. They reorganized the two packhorses Gist had brought with him, each horse now carrying the weight of a man in supplies.

As Gist was about to leave, Cresap approached him with a small roll of deer hide that opened into a crude map of Western Pennsylvania. "This here's one of my better artistic endeavors," Cresap boasted. "It shows the stoppin' places along the Trader's Path, mostly Injen cabins and such. I can only help you far as Logstown, 'cause I ain't been no farther. Now, I shouldn't have to tell you this, but whatever you do, don't show your compass. Makes Injens suspicious, like you're surveyin' the land for settlement. Your life won't be worth a tinker's damn!

"And by the way, them goddamn Pennsylvania traders'll be hold up in Logstown. Watch out for 'em, one in particular, Caleb Lamb's his name. He's a knowing blade, that one. Rogues and bla'guards the whole lot of 'em if you ask me. Look well to your flint and steel among that crowd!"

"Thanks for the warning," replied Gist, as he and Gabriel rode off north along the Great Warrior Path toward Pennsylvania.

That evening they made camp by a small brook and had their meal. Gist took out a leather bound notebook and, in compliance with his instructions, began his journal.

> Wednesday Oct 31, 1750. – Set out from Colo Thomas Cresap's at the Old Town on Potomac River in Maryland, and went along an Old Indian Path N 30 E about 11 Miles.

CHAPTER III

November 1750

The gusting autumn winds had robbed the forest of its multicolored canopy, which now lay a foot thick on the ground, obscuring the trail and making a silent sojourn impossible. Still, the travelers passed many signs marking the way. For years Indians had used this thoroughfare and their lean-toes, in various stages of decomposition, were common.

Other trail markers told a tale. Gabriel asked about the red poles protruding from the ground.

Realizing the need for a short break, Gist climbed down from his mount and beckoned Gabriel over to one of the painted poles.

"The Iroquois tie their prisoners to these posts each night," he explained.

"Why dey don just tie 'em to tree?"

"Sometimes they do, but the Iroquois believe the Creator has blessed these red poles to keep their prisoners from escaping."

"Me hear dey make grandee much hurt on dem prisoner."

"For their most hated enemies, yes they have terrible tortures, but often they take them home and adopt them into the tribe to replace others who have died." He ran his hand over a spot of dried blood on the pole. "They make these prisoners run a gauntlet. You've heard about that. All the villagers gather in two parallel lines, maybe a quarter of a mile long." Gabriel's eyes widened as Gist traced an imaginary line off in the distance. "They all have clubs and switches and every weapon you can think of. The prisoner starts running and they beat on him. No matter if he makes it to the end or not, he's given to the women. They heal the wounds and clean them up for adoption."

Very often this was so, sometimes not. But he did not want to scare Gabriel with gruesome stories of torture and cruelty.

"Lookee dere," Gabriel pointed to another sign. "Dat be de story tree. De bark be gone ahn many mans picture painted here." He placed a finger on drawings of little stick figures with bows and arrows where the bark had been stripped. An Iroquois warrior was sneaking up on the enemy over by their fire. The next picture showed a battle and another pictured four prisoners being led away.

"Indians, you see, are fond of making pictures to tell a story. They're also experts at decoration," replied the frontiersman. "They adorn almost everything they make with dyed porcupine quills or beads or woven animal hair. See this neck knife I'm wearing, with this quill design on the front?" He leaned over so Gabriel could see the flower made of quills. "Four different styles of quill work are on this sheath in six different colors." Gabriel admired the artistry. "What say we get moving now? We've got the whole day ahead of us."

A few minutes later they were back on the trail. Unlike most of their journey so far, they had a choice of two routes. Had the season been wet, he would have followed the longest ascending ridge up and over the summit of Warrior Mountain. A lower route led to the east, along its base. The many streams and creeks crisscrossing this lower trail made it impassable in wet weather. Since the season had been dry, they choose the lower trail.

"Lookee dem grandee big tree, massa Gist. Summer time be so dark in dese woods, nobody don see two, tree feet in front him face, even if de sun be shine. But dem tree be six foot one side to de other. Lookee way up where dem many branch grow all together one tangle." Gabriel pointed eighty feet up to where the branches from nearby trees began their interdigitation. "Dey still don be thinner."

This wonderment was entertaining to Gist. These woodland features were just part of the surroundings; he had seen them so often that they were not special. Many people looked upon the dark woods as a place of evil and horror. Not Gabriel. Though he had been in the woods before, he was always excited about them. Gist thought that maybe he was beginning to appreciate them a little more because of his servant's enthusiasm.

Gist rode in front, holding the lead line of the first pack horse, whose tail was tied to the lead line of the second. Gabriel brought up the rear. They kept a slow pace, always mindful of low-hanging branches, dead falls and blow downs.

After four miles their way was blocked by a massive fallen tree that as a sapling must have seen the ancient tribes in their finest war regalia traverse this same path. It lay in decaying majesty, eight feet in diameter and 200 feet long. As a testament to the inexorable continuity of the forest, this sage left a score of saplings to vie for its place over time. Of course, the giant could not die alone. Like a row of dominoes it took out so many of its neighbors that the resulting swath looked like the work of a small tornado. The path had to be rerouted hundreds of yards around the damage.

With obvious difficulty Gist dismounted, staggered to a large boulder and sat down. Gabriel slid off his mount and ran to his master's side.

"You makee friend wit dat ole ague fever, massa Gist?" he asked, hiding the concern Gist knew the young man felt. Gabriel knew the symptoms well, since Christopher succumbed to the intermitting fever yearly about this time.

Gist could feel himself getting weaker as the intense nausea ascended in waves. He knew what the rest of the day would be like. First he would sit naked in a snowstorm, shivering, chattering teeth clicking like a high-pitched woodpecker. Then his fever would rise until he lay in the desert baking like bread. The accompanying headache would be blinding and each time his heart would beat, it would feel as if the top of his head would explode. And the unquenchable thirst . . . Delirium was relief.

"Gabriel," Gist coughed out, trying to mask the discomfort, "go to my pack and get the "bark" and that packet of herbs."

"Yes massa Gist, me know all what to do."

Gabriel returned with the ingredients and a coffeepot, collected small twigs and arranged them in a tepee. From his pocket he removed a bag containing flint, steel and a tin with scraps of charred linen. As he struck steel to flint half a dozen times in rapid succession, several sparks flew onto the charcloth causing tiny embers. This he fed to a pinch of tow and blew on it. The resulting flame he placed within the tiny tepee and allowed it to grow. Placing the half filled pot of water in the fire, he piled several sticks around it and waited for it to boil.

Gist watched amid waves of nausea and smiled at the expertise with which Gabriel built the fire. He had learned this skill several years ago, when they began traveling together. Gist had taught him other wilderness skills – tracking, stalking – and his competence was growing with experience. Even his marksmanship had improved.

On one of his rare visits to Baltimore Town since moving to the Yadkin, he acquired Gabriel from an old family friend. Then but fourteen, he became Gist's personal servant. Gabriel spent hours entertaining the family with stories of his childhood in Guinea, West Africa and even his horrible passage to America. His pidgin English was colorful and at times comical, yet showed a keen perception of his surroundings. He had become an invaluable companion.

"Now you know massa Gist me must have to washee hands. Me faddah back home a Guinea, he say you must have to washee dem hands 'fore you makee de food. He be much plain 'bout dat."

Gist had heard the story of how Gabriel's people were adamant about cleanliness. It was part of their religious practice that emphasized purification.

Gabriel proceeded to pour the herbal mixture containing equal parts of powdered Virginia snakeroot, cloves and salts of tartar into his powder measure until full. This mixture went into the water. He then filled the same powder measure with the Peruvian Bark and added it to the pot. Within minutes the boiling water gave off a sweet-smelling scent of cloves. Gist would drink the tea every hour for four hours. Sometime during the next twelve hours the fever would subside until its next outbreak, one, two or three days later, depending on which type of ague he had.

"Dis here potion must have to boil five minute, Gon cover you many wooly blanket 'cause you be freezin' soon."

Gist said not a word as he watched Gabriel make a bed of pine boughs and dry leaves and cover them with a brown wool blanket. With agonizing slowness he crawled over to his sickbed. Gabriel helped him remove his quilled shoulder bag, shooting pouch, belt and other accouterments. As he lay down, the shivering began and Gabriel piled on the blankets. When the tea was ready Gabriel strained it through a cloth into a cup and gave it to his patient.

The next ten hours were a blur as he passed through the various stages while Gabriel attended to his needs. Gist hated to be so helpless. He knew that if any danger presented itself, he was powerless to react. But he trusted his life to this young man during these times of sickness and Gabriel was committed to the task.

The next morning was clear and cold as Gist, having somewhat recovered, watched Gabriel make breakfast.

"You travel today, massa Gist?" asked Gabriel with a note of concern.

"Yes. The fever left me early this morning and I feel better."

Gabriel needed no instruction, and began breaking camp and packing the horses. From experience he knew Gist would be too weak to help and with neither discussion nor complaint assumed his duties.

About noon Gist pulled himself onto his horse and rode along the giant toward its uprooted trunk. They circumvented the obstacle and returned to the trail. After making six miles, however, his sickness returned and the process was repeated.

Still weak the next morning, Gist decided to continue. With frequent stops along the trail, it took six hours to cover the eight miles to the Juniata River where they spent the night. In the morning they forded the river and intersected the Old Traders' Path. This trail, made wider by twenty years of passing pack horses, led from the settlements in eastern Pennsylvania to the Forks of Ohio and beyond.

After twelve miles of the river path through dense foliage, they entered a thick forest. From colossal oaks, hickories and maples, hung the tangle of a thousand grapevines, the trunks of which were thick as a man's thigh. This contrasted with the sudden grassy plain several miles ahead. Cresap's map marked this hundred-acre clearing, "Shanawa Cabbins."

"This is where we camp," declared Gist.

Gabriel marveled at the size of the clearing and the ruins of several cabins off in the distance.

"This was a Shannoah town twenty or thirty years ago. They built log cabins and cut the trees and planted fields of corn like we do."

"Why dey go from dis place?"

"Well, the Shannoah have always stayed one place for a time, then moved on. Fifty years ago some of them got permission from the Six Nations to settle on the Susquehanna. But the Iroquois considered them subjects and the Shannoah didn't like that much. More white settlers moved into the valley and it got too crowded, so they left for the Ohio. From the looks of things they stayed here awhile."

"Dem Shawana have to make grandee big trip for wood."

"Maybe that's why they left." They laughed and made camp.

Allegheny Mountain was the next obstacle, so steep at times the riders had to dismount and cling to their horses' tails. Other times the path followed one switchback after another. Late on the afternoon of November 5th they descended the mountain by a much more gradual slope and picked a campsite among the rocks at the edge of marshlands. It was marked "Edmund's Swamp" on their map.

Gist looked toward the gray sky. A low blanket of clouds had settled in. "It's going to snow tonight Gabriel and we'd better get prepared. Why don't you unload the horses? I'll hunt us some supper. What would you prefer, buck or doe?"

"Me likee both, massa Gist, but to choose, me choose doe. Be more tender, don you tink?"

"My sentiments exactly," was the reply. "Now when I get back we'll build a lean-to. If you get done before that, start without me," he grinned at his own humor. Gist grabbed his flintlock rifle and disappeared among the trees.

He glided through the woods. Little underbrush could survive under the canopy during the summer and the trees were far enough apart to see several hundred feet in all directions. Without thinking, he noticed certain land marks – a tree with three trunks grown together, a unique rock outcropping – to guide his way home. Every ten feet or so he stood motionless and listened to the sounds of the forest. Hearing nothing of animal movement he continued, being careful to head into the wind. During one of his motionless periods he heard the telltale growling, grunting and thrashing of foliage announcing the presence of his prey. He stalked the sound until he spied a large black bear feeding on wild elderberry bushes at the edge of a clearing. What a magnificent creature, long black hair glistening in waves, even in the pale light of the cloudy afternoon. Muscles rippled as he placed entire branches full of the shrunken, pea-sized autumn berries into his mouth. The branches emerged berryless.

If I were an Indian hunter, he thought, I'd thank the Creator for the gift of this wonderful creature whose life I'm about to take. No reason I can't thank the Lord. He did so, aimed his rifle, and squeezed the trigger. A click, a flash, and an explosion sent a .60 caliber ball spinning toward the small brain of the woodland king. In less than a heartbeat the bear lay lifeless at the base of the bush, having felt neither fear nor pain.

With a hunter's reflex he reloaded the rifle and stood motionless for several minutes, watching for signs of life, listening for the possible presence of a companion or any human sounds. Satisfied of his aloneness, he closed the thirty feet to the bear, rifle poised. When he was sure of the animal's condition, he sliced open the gut with his skinning knife and cut out the heart and liver. He pealed back the skin to reveal the flank, carved off as much meat as he could carry, wrapped the bundle in a section of the bear's hide, and tied it with strips of rawhide. Since he could not carry all the meat, he made several such bundles and secured them in the crooks of nearby trees out of reach of wolves. He would retrieve them later. Shouldering the first bundle, he headed back to camp.

Gabriel had finished their shelter and made a small fire in front. A bed of pine boughs lined the floor and covered the top and sides. He had also unloaded and picketed the horses nearby. A small tree, deprived of its branches, had been lashed between two others. Sawbucks straddled the pole and provisions in their rawhide panniers hung on the sawbucks. All were covered by the same canvas that protected them on the trail.

"You be awful right 'bout de snow, massa Gist," Gabriel said as they looked at the big round flakes beginning to fall.

"This kind will pile up fast," said Gist, as he brought the meat to the fire. "I warrant we'll have six inches by morning."

Gabriel placed an iron pot full of water on the fire to boil. After washing his hands, he cut the heart and liver into strips and threw them into the pot. With several green twigs he skewered chunks of meat and propped them up to roast by the fire.

Sitting under the lean-to, Gist got out Cresap's map and, in the approaching darkness, studied its detail by candlelight.

"Dis be some much beautiful land, don you tink, massa Gist?"

"That it is, Gabriel," he replied, tracing the trail to their next destination, "and I hear it gets prettier the farther west you go."

"Who be de owner o' dis here land?" Gabriel continued.

"Now that's a good question." Gist smiled as he remembered his lesson from Cresap on the very subject. "Pennsylvania says they own this right here." Gist gestured to include their present location. "But they never set a western boundary, though they say it's somewhere around the Forks of the Ohio here," he pointed to the spot on the map where the Monongahela and Allegheny came together to form the Ohio. "Virginia says She owns the Forks and the land from Pennsylvania's western boundary, wherever it is, clear to the Shining Sea and who knows how far that is." Gist then explained about the Iroquois claims. "And the French say it's theirs, because La Salle discovered the Ohio River. Why just last year some French Captain, Celeron, I think was his name, sailed down the Ohio and buried lead plates all along its shores. Some Indians dug one up and took it to Governor Hamilton of Pennsylvania. The inscription claimed the entire Ohio River watershed for

France. He even ordered all the English traders to get off French soil, telling the Indians they could only trade with France."

"Dem Injun be very much mad, me tink."

"Well, Indians, like most folks, don't like being told what to do. Most of them want to trade with us English, because we have cheaper trade goods, better quality too. Now I hear there's a Pennsylvania trader named George Croghan, who's out in the Ohio territory to win back any Indians that might have been frightened over to the French by this Celeron fellow. I'm going to try to join up with him and learn as much as I can, while I'm inviting all the tribes to a conference in the spring."

"Dem Injun come make grandee big noise ahn get much drunk, ay massa Gist?" laughed Gabriel.

Gist smiled. "Oh, many of them will. I suspect there'll be quite a ruckus. Virginia wants a share of the Indian trade and we'll treat them even better than the Pennsylvania traders. Now I suggest we get some sleep so we can leave early tomorrow"

As he lay on a bed of pine boughs wrapped in a thick woolen blanket, Gist thought about the problem of approaching Croghan for help. How much was this trader responsible for the lies told about the Virginians? Could he be induced to help a potential competitor like himself? Gist did not know the answer, but he faded into sleep knowing he would find out.

CHAPTER IV

November 1750

Cotton ball snowflakes fell throughout the night weighing tree limbs to the ground and covering the world in white. Only the campfire escaped. Morning felt the temperature warm just enough for a freezing rain to deposit a sheet of ice on top of the snow. Traveling would be dangerous for the horses; their hoofs would break the ice on the way down, but the sharp ice edge would bruise and slice their forelegs on the way up. So they remained in camp gathering wood by breaking off the lower dead branches of trees, hunting to supplement their supplies and caring for the horses.

Gabriel scraped the snow from the top of the lean-to in preparation for a more waterproof roof of lynn bark. Gist found several linden trees nearby. With practiced precision he made a horizontal slice a foot long near the base and a like cut six feet up. Pealing several inches of the bark upward with his tomahawk, he put the handle under the bark and ripped upward to the higher cut. He continued around the tree until he had six such pieces. Gabriel placed them on top of the pine boughs, weighing them down with more branches.

On the fourth day the rain stopped, leaving their pathway a misery of mud. They had made six miles when another downpour began. Crossing a creek they came upon a rough cabin inhabited by an old Delaware Indian named Kick-ena-pau-lin. Always glad to welcome strangers, he invited them in. He spoke a tolerable English that he had learned from the many traders who passed through.

Kick-ena-pau-lin was of medium height, broad-shouldered and slim-waisted with smooth, graceful muscles. Tattoos of circles and lines in perfect symmetry covered his entire face and body. These were offset by figures of snakes, the head of a bear and other woodland creatures. His scalp had been plucked, according to their custom, except for a spot on the crown of his head about two inches in diameter where his hair was several inches long. This scalp-lock he adorned with beads and a single eagle feather. His long, well-shaped ears were slit, separating the helix from the ear proper, along the edge to the lobe. Silver wire wrapped this distended portion stretching it several inches below the bottom of his ear.

The Delaware were noted for their open-hearted generosity and Kick-ena-pau-lin was no exception. His wife treated them to a meal of roasted venison, boiled corn and beans, and cornbread sweetened with honey. A side dish of melted bear fat mixed with maple sugar served as a dip for the meat. They all sat on the floor in a circle to eat.

After the meal, Kick-ena-pau-lin brought out a long pipe. The smoking of tobacco, while offering comfort to body and soul, had religious significance. Smoke was a gift of incense to the Creator and carried prayers upward to the sky. It also gave the men a way to relax and collect their thoughts before speaking. The Indian had not yet asked any questions, but Gist knew it was time. Gabriel looked on from across the room.

"You come not from Brother Onas," the Delaware began in a pleasant voice, using the Iroquois name for William Penn, founder of Pennsylvania.

Gist thought for a moment about the best way to answer the implied question. Convention dictated a measured response and Gist took his time.

"I bring greetings from Brother Assarquoa. He wishes to trade with the people of the Delaware Nation."

After a brief period of silence Kick-ena-pau-lin replied, looking straight ahead. "Delaware trade with Brother Onas. None left for Assarquoa."

Gist cogitated. The Ohio country was rich in game. Suspecting the Indian was troubled about rumors spread by the Pennsylvania traders, Gist determined to dispel them.

"Bad birds say Assarquoa want to steal the land of the Delaware. They say Virginia want to build forts that will frighten the beaver and the deer. Many bad birds have whispered this in the ear of the Delaware, but it is not so. In the spring Assarquoa will hold a great feast and council at Logstown. Assarquoa wishes for all Ohio tribes to come and receive presents. We have much to trade with the Delaware."

Kick-ena-pau-lin puffed on the pipe and handed it to Gist. "Brother Onas bring too much rum. You bring rum?"

Gist told him of his policy regarding spirituous liquors.

"Delaware know of Kistafa Gis. You good man. We trade with Assarquoa. But you see. The white man want our lands as they have always."

"Would the Delaware refuse an offer of many fine presents for the purchase of land?" he ventured.

The Indian paused, "Delaware have not said no before."

"How will the Delaware answer now?"

He shrugged. "Delaware are many, I am one. Delaware are enemy to France. Will Assarquoa help the Delaware against our enemy?"

Gist hesitated. He had no authority to guarantee this; only a general answer could he give. "If the English and the French are at war, Assarquoa will come to the aid of all his friends."

Kick-ena-pau-lin smiled for the first time since the visitors arrived.

Through blackened, uneven teeth, he ended, "Delaware always listen to wishes of friends."

Gist knew this lone Delaware had no power to speak for a Nation. No Indian did. Yet he was sure he echoed the sentiments of many, if not most of his people. "Then we can be brothers."

"That is so." With the conversation over, Kick-ena-pau-lin showed them their sleeping place and retired.

The sky could not decide whether to rain or snow and the travelers spent another day with their host. On November 11th they left the hospitality of the Delaware chief. But it was slow going. In five days, two of which Gist spent with the ague, they made a mere forty-five miles. Gist knew not from where his strength came, but they forded Quemahoning Creek, climbed the Allegheny ridge known as Laurel Hill and reached the Delaware town of Loyalhanna on the north bank of the river by the same name. Cresap said this name was an Anglicized corruption of the Delaware "Lawel" meaning middle and "Hanna" meaning stream. Their arrival here would mark midpoint on the path between the Juniata River crossing and the Forks of Ohio. Six days later, as they rode into another Delaware camp, Cock-eye's Cabin, Gist's sickness made it hard for him to stay on his horse.

Upon learning of Gist's ailment, the old Delaware, one eye inspecting his guest, the other studying the sky, recommended a sweating treatment in his personal sweat-house. The little hut was an earthen dome five feet high and eight feet in diameter. Small poles, stuck in the ground in a circle, arched to meet in the center. A layer of bark was then covered with dirt. A deer hide protected the entrance.

Remembering how soothing a sudatory could be, Gist could not wait. He stripped and crawled inside. Gabriel made a fire outside, heated the rocks and rolled them into the center of the lodge. A deafening hiss filled the small enclosure when Gist doused them with water. Steam rolled in waves. The hot moisture closed around his body like a giant womb. Sweat oozed from every pore. Eyes closed, he began to relax and let the waves take him. He repeated the effort. New billowing swirls of warm vapors engulfed his form, taking him farther away.

He was a boy again with his father in a Delaware village. Clad in a breechclout, he chased an Indian boy who pretended to be a deer. They played well together and he was happy. The gentle face of his father came into view and spoke, "See what fun you have with these boys? The white man and the Indian can live and play together in harmony. One day it will happen. Have faith, my son, have faith..."

"Massa Gist. Oh, Massa Gist." Like a diver rising from the bottom of a deep, warm lake he emerged from his vision. "You all right in dere? I be worried 'bout cha. You come on out now 'fore you waste all away down to nothin'."

He staggered from the lodge and wrapped himself in a blanket. The standard remedy called for a quick dip in the icy stream. This he did. In and out fast and back into the lodge he went. Twice he repeated the process and retired to a small hut where he slept a death-sleep until morning.

It was noon before they began a two-day trip to Shannopin's Town, a Delaware village of twenty families living in bark-covered huts. In characteristic Delaware hospitality they vacated one for the travelers. Here they stayed four days to allow Gist to recover his strength. Between trips to Shannopin's sweat-lodge, he watched the Indian boys play. He was content like he was meant to be there not as a visitor, but as a native.

As Shannopin spoke English well, he and Gist talked of many things. The Indian shared his knowledge of the surrounding land, its beautiful hills and plentiful streams. But when told of the upcoming Logstown conference and Virginia's desire to trade, Shannopin voiced his complaints about the white traders. "Ten summers ago, I go to Friend's Meeting House in the City of Brotherly Love. Many Lenape come to speak with Brother Onas. We say, 'your traders ask too much for goods'. We say, 'your young white men kill many deers and beavers and we cannot find enough for ourselves.' Then they give us many presents and answer, 'we cannot make prices'. They answer, 'all these things done by traders with no license. If we not buy from them, they not come among us.' But they come anyway, bringing the white man's rum, and we cannot say no. Our warriors become weak with drink and trade away all their furs for trinkets and more rum. We say, 'no bring rum.' In ten summers nothing has changed and now you ask if more traders are welcome. What are we to say?"

Gist pondered his response for several minutes. Time was not a factor here. He knew he could not argue, change the Indian's mind or convince him Virginia would be perfect. He had but to tell the truth. "My heart aches to hear of your troubles. These offences against your people are bad things; they are wrong, and I cannot promise some of these things will not happen with Virginia, but they will not happen as much." He then went into a lengthy discourse on why Virginia's trade goods would be cheaper. Virginia would not use free traders, licensed or otherwise. Instead, only those men who work for the Company, with strict orders about how much to charge, would be permitted to trade; there would be fewer traders. Secondly they had a water route up the Potomac River to Will's Creek, over land to Redstone Old Fort on Monongahela, and up river to the Forks. This journey would take less time than packhorses from Philadelphia and bring cheaper goods. In addition, fewer traders would mean less game killed. Finally they would impose a limit on strong drink. He decided not to go into detail about buying land and building a settlement. Now, gaining this man's trust and friendship was important. Shannopin's word was revered among his people.

The Indian thanked him for his honesty and said he was always welcome at his cabin. He would come to Logstown and hear for himself Assarquoa's speech. If Pennsylvania traders had some competition, Shannopin ventured, maybe they would behave better.

On Saturday the 24th they swam their horses across the Ohio River and headed northwest twenty miles to Logstown. This was an important village built by the French twenty-five years earlier to lure would be Shawnee allies closer to them. Then came the Pennsylvania traders, whose cheaper prices and higher quality trade goods challenged that allegiance. Now the Shawnee shared the town with the Delaware, more recent arrivals from central Pennsylvania. It was the site of several councils and treaties between the Indians and Pennsylvania. Many of the traders, who had spread rumors about Virginia, lived here. Thomas Ward, Samuel Cuzzens, Jacob Pyatt, John Owens and others, some of whom were disreputable in character, were seasoned veterans of the Indian trade. They frowned upon intrusions into what they considered their territory. Gist was the interloper.

Gist and his servant rode in among the crude log houses and approached the longhouse in the center of the village. Seeing no young men, he guessed most of the warriors were out hunting. Women and children surrounded them, seeking any trinkets these strangers might impart. One resident trader approached the riders. He seemed oblivious to the cold, wearing greasy leggings and a long, loose-fitting shirt unsashed at the waist.

"You'd be Gist I'd reckon?" inquired the trader.

"That's right," he answered, still mounted and leading his pack horses. His senses sharpened as he noticed a dozen traders beginning to collect. "And who might you be?"

"Caleb Lamb, sort of the top sawyer around these parts, ye might say. And what bidness might ye be havin' here?"

"My business might not be any of your business," replied Gist with an unfaltering gaze.

"Might not," Lamb agreed, fingering his beard. "But if ye wuz to be tradin' with our Injens, it might. Or if ye wuz maybe huntin' fer land fer that there Ohio Company, then that'd be the bidness of the Governor of Pennsylvania, and that'd be my bidness." The ease with which he spoke could not disguise the mounting tension in the air.

Gist paused to ponder his reply. Pursuing the confrontation would be unwise, since he was outnumbered. He felt sick again and longed to rest here, but his weakness would leave them vulnerable. A partial explanation would, he hoped, be sufficient to diffuse the situation and allow him to move on. "Well Mr. Lamb," he said with a smile, "it seems I have little choice but to acquaint you with my purpose," he nodded toward the group of rough looking traders, now attentive to the exchange. "I'm looking for George Croghan. I bear a message to the Indians from our King, by order of the Governor of Virginia and it must be translated by the Indian interpreter Andrew Montour. I aim to deliver that message."

"I see," said Lamb. "Then ye may consider that Croghan and Montour left here last week fer the Muskingum Town. It might be advisable fer ye to be headin' that way. I'll send an express to let him know ye be comin'. Plenty of daylight left."

"That there is, Mr. Lamb, that there is." The tension passed as Gist and Gabriel rode north out of Logstown along the Ohio River.

Six miles later at Beaver Creek, they came upon Barny Curran, whom he had met earlier that year. Curran and nine other men were camped there hunting for game.

"Why, Mr. Gist, we meet again," said Barney.

"I heard you were in these parts, Curran," Gist returned the handshake, looking at the ten pack horses. "Cresap said I might travel with you."

"Mr. Gist," replied Curran, "ye are certainly welcome to join us. Goin' to the Muskingum Town, we are. Been stoppin' at every village along Traders Road." He made a sweeping gesture to include his fellow sojourners. "Most of these boys is headin' to whatever Injen town they winter at. How'd you fare in Logstown?"

"None the worse for the altercation," replied Gist. "Mighty unfriendly folks though."

"Meet Caleb did ya?" Curran asked. "Well, they don't think much of Virginia hornin' in on their territory, ya know. They don't like me much either fer switchin' sides as they see it."

"That's right," said Gist, "you used to work for Croghan, didn't you? Well, you made the right choice. With the backing of the Ohio Company you'll do better. Virginia is going to trade with these Indians, so they might as well get used to it."

CHAPTER V

December 1750

George Croghan, Prince of Pennsylvania Traders, was a legend. Barely twenty in 1741, he escaped one of Ireland's many potato famines and sailed for Penn's Woods. And deep into those woods he went, applying his ingenuity, wit and charm to learning the fur trade. Within two years, license in hand, he embarked on his own career.

Not much of his success could be attributed to the luck of his nationality. Hard work and resolve were responsible. As a master of merriment and conveyor of conviviality, he won the friendship of the Indians and became a virtual idol among the traders, many of whom were themselves Irish. Practiced in the art of persuasion, he could enlist wealthy merchants to invest in his Indian trade and convince a reluctant Quaker Assembly to give presents to the Indians.

Even as Gist rode the muddy path toward their meeting, Croghan controlled one third of the fur trade in the Ohio Valley. His empire extended from the Seneca village at the mouth of the Cuyahoga River, south to the Lower Shawnee Town. A unique command of Indian dialects allowed him direct communication wherever he went. George Croghan was, without question, the most prominent fur trader and frontier diplomat in the Ohio Valley.

Having spent two weeks on the trail with the crude, lewd crowd accompanying Curran, Gist anticipated Croghan's famed congeniality. The success of his mission depended on Croghan's cooperation. Gist required an interpreter, since he was unfamiliar with the languages of these tribes, and he needed a guide to lead him to the Indian villages. Most of all he needed insulation from anti-Virginia sentiment instigated, he was certain, by some of Croghan's traders. The farther he ventured from home the less his reputation preceded him.

One incident in particular showed him his own vulnerability. In the little Ottawa village of Tuscarawas, a few days back, he met an old Frenchman named Mark Coonce, who invited him to visit his home that evening. Although the Ottawa were loyal to the French, the man was quite civil and spoke of his exploits against the British in the last war. After Gist had returned to his own camp, one of Curran's men happened to mention Gist's connection to Virginia. The Frenchman responded by hurling the disparaging epithet of "Long Knife" across the way, along with an ominous warning to "leave this place before our warriors return!" Gist was unmoved by the threat, but he now knew he was not welcome everywhere.

As the procession neared a Wyandot town on the northeast fork of the Muskingum River, Barney Curran took advantage of a clearing to wait for Gist. "This bein' Croghan's favorite town, we'll most likely find him here. The Wyandot themselves know it as Conchake, but mostly we call it Muskingum. The Delaware say that the elks are so numerous along this river, and so tame, that you can get near enough to see into their eyes." They watched the remainder of the riders file by. "They call the river Moos-king-ung, meaning elk's eye river."

Upon entering the town Gist was struck by its efficient layout and tidy appearance. He followed the traders down what appeared to be the main street flanked by rows of bark-covered huts. A few were round mounds, but most resembled loaves of dark bread with multiple smoke holes, one for each related family in residence. Gist counted thirty such dwellings and guessed there to be upwards of 100 families. Thick columns of smoke billowed from the smoke holes filling the cold, clear air with the pungent aroma of burning wood. As he neared the center of town, he noticed a larger four-family dwelling. English colors hung on a rough standard outside the entrance. This, he supposed, belonged to their chief, though he thought it unusual for an Indian town to exhibit the British flag.

Recent rains had turned village paths to mud. Attempts to cover them with old cornstalks and dry grass made walking hazardous, yet a crowd of villagers braved the tangled muck and approached the line of riders. The few men who were not out hunting stood by and watched the procession. Clad in wool matchcoats and deer skin leggings, their faces registered a range of looks from happiness to disapproval. But the women, emotions unchecked, talked and laughed and waved, one pointing to a fancy rifle, another admiring a quilled bag hanging from some trader's shoulder. A trader called out to a young woman with whom he was acquainted. Unaffected by the cold, young, breechclouted boys ran up to the line of horses, tapping them on the rump or the neck with sticks, pretending to count coup against a superior foe. Mongrel dogs, upturned noses catching every new scent, paced and barked at the parade. A few braver curs rushed to inspect the fresh dung deposited by the passing horses.

Gist nodded and smiled at all who greeted him. He looked around for Croghan's new trading house and saw it standing at the head of the main street toward the far end of the village. The one-story cabin of round logs and a bark roof had a clay and stick chimney dominating one end. Windows looked out on a covered porch spanning the front. As the traders veered left to unload the horses at the adjacent warehouse, Gist headed for the cabin.

Under the Union Jack stood the Prince.

A long black wool cape encircled his short muscular frame as he stood with arms akimbo. Thus was the cape pushed apart to display his manner of dress. Below the waist, he could pass for an Indian. But a white ruffled silk shirt, red wool weskit and black silk neck-stock showed a liking for Philadelphia finery.

"Aye, it's himself!" advanced Croghan in a thick brogue. "We've been expectin' ye, haven't we? And how is it ye are this fine Monday mornin'?" He spoke with a smile on his face and a spark of curiosity in his eye. His clean-shaven face stood out among so many traders with trail growth and displayed whatever emotion its owner required of it. In this case the expression of respect and deference appeared genuine.

"I am, sir," replied Gist from horseback, looking down at the speaker, "quite fortunate to make your acquaintance." He gestured toward the traders with whom he had traveled. "These boys have supplied me with stories of your many exploits."

"Aye, and all true, I've no doubt," Croghan laughed. "Come in, set yourself down and take your rest. We'll be after havin' the noon meal soon and it's a welcome I'll be extendin' to ye."

"Your hospitality is well known, sir," replied Gist, "and I do believe I'll advantage myself of it. What of my boy?"

"Ah yes now, you see I've brought along two of me own servants and the lad can take up with them, that is if ye are of a similar mind?" Croghan tilted his head sideways, questioning.

"That'll be fine, Mr. Croghan."

"Arrah now, the Injens refer to me as their Brother the Buck, but ye can call me George. The 'mister' be too formal for the frontier, don't ye agree, Mr. Gist?"

"Then you must call me Chris."

"Aye, now that's settled, follow me inside."

After Croghan sent one of his servants to locate Gabriel and help him with the horses, he and Gist repaired to the fireplace and sat on opposing benches. A servant brought two flagons of hot buttered rum. Both men drank – Gist waiting for Croghan to begin, Croghan grinning from ear to ear at his guest.

"'Tis certainly a pleasure to be drinkin' with such as yourself, a man acquainted with some of life's comforts." He spoke as though familiar with Gist's past. "Sure 'tis that most of 'em have never seen the inside of a proper house," he gestured toward the traders outside. "Nor can they converse about anythin' more engagin' than the arse end of a horse, which they see plenty of in a day's work. And you, comin' all the way from the Logstown with those rogues of the forest, methinks ye must have been a bit uncomfortable at times."

"Well, George, comfort is a relative thing. It's true I've spent some time in the city, but my father took me among the Indians at a young age and I've been dealing with them and traders ever since. What surprises me though is His Majesty's colors flying over an Indian village."

"Arrah now! Ye might expect that in a time of war, which it's not, not yet mind ye. But 'tis barely three weeks since the French arrested the free trader, John Patten, and took him to Fort Detroit. Tradin' with the Twightwees at Pick Town, he was, when he gets hisself a message to go to the Cross and trade with those Injens there."

"What's the Cross?"

"'Tis a wooden cross surely big as the one on which Christ hisself met his fate. I've seen it, halfway twixt the portage from the Little Wabash to the Maumee where the voyagers worship. Well, when Patten got there, the Injens told him that the French at the Miami fort requested his services. So he makes the forty miles to the fort and when the poor bastard gets there – clank!" Croghan clasped his thumb and forefinger around his opposite wrist to indicate how they threw him in irons.

Croghan called to his man for a refill and continued. "'Twas the bastard Celeron de Blainville, commander at Detroit, what gave that order, sure as I'm Irish. He's the devil hisself, or one of his bosom favorites, I'd swear. And him invadin' the Ohio last year, claimin' all this land for France. Did ye ever hear such blather? Tried to turn all me Injens against me, he did. Took the better part of three months to win 'em back. I wintered with Old Britain among the Twightwees and that's where I'm headed now, in a round about way. The Assembly, bless their pious little pacifist souls, has condescended, after I had a little talk with 'em, to grace the Twightwees with £700 worth of presents to assure their continued loyalty."

"Sounds like you've foiled the French."

"Aye, I've been more persistent than a good case of the piles," Croghan exclaimed as he took a long swallow of the rum. "Why, they call me le grand interprete Anglois pour les sauvages," he said in an Irish-accented French. "There's a bounty of £500 for me own scalp this very minute," a sharp nod of his head signaled a pride in his infamy.

"Any takers yet?" Gist joked.

"Why, half the Injen nations and the angels of hell would come to me aid if they was to try," Croghan laughed with the confidence of a general. He rose and went outside. Gist followed. They stood for a moment overlooking the Wyandot village. Children were playing on the main path, one rolling a grapevine hoop along the ground, while several others were shooting short arrows from small bows through it.

"Before I came to this village," Croghan said, "they was tradin' their skins to the French. Lord, and don't ye know, they paid dearly for poor fare. And without a blacksmith, what broke stayed broke. I'm after givin' 'em better prices, higher quality, and Tom Burney, the blacksmith, now stays here most of the year. Half the village has switched allegiance, includin' their king. The Union Jack flies to remind the other half from whence their prosperity comes."

"It would seem a simple choice for the Indians to make," said Gist. "Inexpensive, well-made goods, where's the rub?"

"Aye, it's not so simple, for ye must know the Injens don't like to align themselves with one to the exclusion of the other. Then along comes a chief, who hates the French like Satan hates angels. Two years ago Orontony of the Sandusky Hurons, we call him Chief Nicholas, moved half his warriors to this town. No longer was they happy to be Huron under the French. Nicholas left with a flare though; burned the Sandusky village to the ground, he did. After he moved here he tried to sway the rest of the village to the English side. Then I came along and together we continued. Poor bastard died September last. Final words on his lips was, 'never return to the French nor allow their Blackrobes to come among you.' Hell of a thing to up and die like that."

"What happened to the rest of Chief Nicholas' town?"

"Moved to the French fort at Detroit, they did. We'll meet 'em in battle I'll wager, and it'll likely be soon."

They re-entered the cabin and filled their cups with rum from a small keg. The afternoon light was growing dim and Croghan had his servant light several candles.

"I've sent runners to all me traders in the Ohio country, tellin' 'em to come here for their safety. The Injens have sent for their important chiefs at other Wyandot towns. When they arrive, a general council we'll be havin'. And if I was yourself Chris, I'd be preparin' for another of His Majesty's wars. Why, at Logstown on the way here the Delaware told me they wanted the English to build a fort on the Ohio to protect 'em. They're expectin' war with the French in the spring."

Gist's ears perked up at these remarks. The Virginians did not know how the Indians would react to the proposal of a fort in their territory. Though the Ohio Company did not themselves want to pay for the building and upkeep of a fort, this was his first clue that one of British construction may be acceptable. He doubted there would be another war. The treaty of Aix la Chappelle was only two years old. Had it not ended King George's War and settled the rivalries between France and England?

He turned the discussion to the safety of his own mission. "You are aware, of course, that Pennsylvania traders made it difficult for the Virginians last year." Gist hesitated. "Is that always the way it's going to be?"

"I've heard that no trouble came to yourself, tradin' your company's goods with the Injens," Croghan answered. "Perhaps inexperience was their problem."

"Cresap and Parker are not exactly beginners," Gist said, looking down at the quilled vamp in Croghan's moccasins. He eyed Croghan and asked, "how do I know you won't tell the Indians my true purpose?"

"Arrah now! Chris, ye do have a direct way about yourself," Croghan smiled, pointing toward the big frontiersman. "To be sure, these savages would do anything I say. I could rid meself of the likes of ye, and the Pennsylvania fur trade would be the better for it. But surely 'tis not me own desire to cause anyone harm, especially to one so esteemed as yourself. Perhaps we can work out an arrangement that would benefit the both of us."

"I have heard of your several partnerships and I would choose not to involve myself in one."

Croghan bristled at this. He had many investors in the fur trade and amassed a considerable debt. Last year, the year of the locust plague, had yielded few hides and English creditors had received no remittance. Croghan's reputation as the trader in whom to invest was in question. A momentary frown returned to a grin as he continued.

"May the patience of Job be with ye, while I show ye somethin'," Croghan said as he disappeared into another room. He returned with a scroll of parchment that he unrolled for Gist's inspection. "See here," he pointed his finger at a particular sentence and began to read, "'The Six Nations, in appreciation of his constant attention to the preservation of peace, and as a testimony of the sincerity with which they desire its continuance, of their own free will and without any application on the part of the grantee," he stopped to clarify, "that would be meself." He continued, "'in the year 1749 in public council at Onondoga, do make this grant to George Croghan.' It amounts to 200,000 acres around the Forks of Ohio. And it's been confirmed by the western Indians at Logstown."

"I see," Gist said, "but how can this benefit both of us?"

"Well. Are ye not to search for the finest land around to satisfy the King's grant? If that be anywhere around the Forks of Ohio, methinks ye could see that your Ohio Company grant doesn't overlap me own gift from the Iroquois. And are ye not also out here promotin' trade for Virginia? I can make that easy for ye..." Croghan left the sentence hanging.

Gist was amused. Here was the King of the Traders with power over all the Indians and whites on the frontier, making a rather reasonable request in exchange for a guarantee that his own mission would be successful. Well why not? He had not yet picked the Ohio Company land. He could find out where Croghan's grant lay and avoid it. Surely with the millions of available acres there was room for both grants.

"A rather thinly veiled threat George, but I'm a practical man. I'm sure I'll have little trouble choosing land for the Ohio Company that does not interfere with your grant. You have but to show me its extent and I'll simply avoid it."

"Chris," spoke Croghan, "I do believe we will work well together. Soon as I get meself a full description I'll acquaint ye with it. But while we're waitin' for my conference why not stay here. I've plenty of room, which'll offer ye a bit of privacy, and I'll gladly acquaint ye with a complement of bed to warm ye on these cold winter nights. What d'ye say to that?"

"I am in your debt sir," replied Gist. He certainly did wish the privacy of a room and a comfortable bed. But he politely refused the night's companionship. Although the host tribe on the frontier sometimes offered female comfort to travelers, Gist had not indulged himself in the custom since he had married Sarah. He did not want another woman. He loved Sarah and would share himself with no one else.

"As ye wish." Croghan spoke as he smiled and winked at the frontiersman.

"Massa Croghan, dinner be on de table," announced one of his servants.

"Are ye ready now for a hearty meal me friend? I have the finest cook on the frontier among me servants."

The two men rose from their benches by the fire and walked to the table.

CHAPTER VI

December 1750

Christopher Gist waited for his "Brother the Buck." For two days the town expected traders and Indians to answer Croghan's call. Of these days, Gist wrote, "Saturday 15 & Sunday 16. – Nothing remarkable happened." Then the Evans brothers arrived bringing bad news. A band of sixty French and Indians had captured Joe Faulkner and Luke Erwin, two more of Croghan's employees, confiscating seven horse loads of furs. The feeling of alarm among the traders intensified. Croghan voiced his concern, hoping his remaining traders would arrive without incident. His kingdom was eroding.

Besides boredom and bad news, one event lifted Gist's spirits. Returning from the woods one afternoon, he saw Croghan talking with an Indian wearing a most colorful outfit – brown broadcloth coat, scarlet weskit and white, ruffled shirt. A broad band of red paint encircled his face. Brass arm bands, bracelets and a large silver gorget composed his assortment of jewelry. This could only be the renowned Seneca interpreter, Andrew Montour.

In his thirtieth year, Sattelihu, as the Iroquois knew him, was respected by whites and Indians alike. He was an honorable translator of each other's ideas, speaking ten Indian languages.

"I have heard of you, Mr. Gist," Montour said in flawless English, the four-inch twisted brass earrings jangled as he shook hands. "George tells me of your desire to go with us to Pick Town. We can use another rifle the way things are lately." They walked over and sat by the fire. "Since these Ohio Indians have come over to the English, they're constantly being threatened."

"What do the French hope to gain by terrorizing these Indians?"

"To get them to move back to the Wabash," answered Croghan.

"Closer to the French," added Montour. "Their King, Old Britain, told them he would move back in the spring, but everyone knew it was just to appease de Blainville. Old Britain believes that along with English trade comes English protection."

"Arrah now, the Twightwees have asked me to send 'em more traders, but I can't get no more to go. Fourteen have been killed or captured in the last six months. When I tells the right Honorable Governor Hamilton," Croghan spat the name, "he says it's up to the Injens themselves to, and I quote, 'preserve the road safe and commodious.' The Twightwees will get no protection from French harassment and you know the devil'd go blind before that bloody Quaker Assembly will appropriate money for a fort. Not the devil himself nor all his forefathers could've cooked up a finer scheme against His Majesty's traders."

"What's Pennsylvania doing about trading spirituous liquors to the Indians?" Gist asked.

"Aye, the situation's worse now than when the law was passed thirty years ago. A trader can't take but five gallons at a time into the woods. And if an Injen was to find a stash in the woods, he's to smash the kegs," Croghan laughed. "Talk about a wolf guardin' the sheep. The wise, old chiefs have pleaded many times with the Assembly to enforce that limit, but it's all for naught. Who'd there be to enforce it?"

The conversation continued long into the night, moving from the political to the sublime, hilarious to risque. Somewhere in the middle of risque, Gist left and walked into the bitter night air to gaze at the stars. He soon met Gabriel, whom he had seen little of since arriving.

"Looks to me like you've got a following." He had noticed some subtle interplay with several young Wyandot women. His black skin intrigued them and they would come just to touch him.

"Why, massa Gist, me have grandee much good time."

They walked through the village to a path leading toward the fields. Together, they gazed up at the Milky Way arching overhead.

"How all dem stars get up in dat sky, massa Gist?"

"Now it just so happens that when I was with the Cherokee several years ago, I got a touch of the ague. Once, when the fever broke, I was staring up into that same Milky Way and the old medicine man who cared for me told me this story. It goes like this:

"A long time ago when the sky was black, an old man and his wife lived by beating corn into meal and trading it for meat. One day they discovered that something had been stealing their cornmeal at night. They looked around and found the tracks of a giant dog. They were afraid of such a mighty animal and couldn't decide what to do.

"The next day they held a council. One by one the warriors rose to suggest some violent act against the cur. Always, the family disapproved, for fear of hurting this animal.

"One wise chief suggested that everyone should bring noise makers and hide. Then when the dog came to eat, they would jump out and beat their drums, shake their rattles and shout. This would scare away the dog.

"That night when Sister Moon had traveled half way across the sky, they saw the dog approaching from the west. He was magnificent, coat shining like silver in the moonlight. When he reached the corn meal, he began to devour it in great gulps. The hidden villagers jumped up, surrounded him and made a terrible racket. The beast was terrified and confused. He ran around in circles looking for a way out. Blocked at every turn he took a giant leap straight up into the night. The meal, pouring out of his mouth, made a white trail across the sky and that trail is what we see up there. Cherokee call it Gil' Li Utsun' Stanun'yi, or 'where the dog ran.'"

The two looked up in silence, each imagining the size of the dog required to drop enough meal to form a band of countless stars stretching across the heavens. "You b'lieve dat story be true, massa Gist?"

Gist knew of many such stories that explained to the Indians why things were. "Well, they believe it's true. If I were Cherokee, I'd believe it."

"But we know God created dem stars."

"The Bible says God created the stars, yes, but it doesn't say exactly how," he chuckled. "To the Cherokee He gave that answer." Gabriel seemed satisfied and they bid each other goodnight.

As Gist walked toward the cabin he saw Croghan and Montour still in the midst of animated conversation. Several other traders had joined them around a roaring fire. All were fuddled with drink. As he approached he could hear a dull murmur of voices interrupted from time to time by a hideous laugh that fell back into the dull murmur. This gathering was a curious phenomenon that had a life of its own. Not wanting to interrupt its flow, he determined to retire.

"Hey Long Knife!" shouted one of the traders in a muddled slur. "Ain't ya got yourself a squaw-woman?" The circle fell silent. "Whassa matter, them squaws ain't good 'nuf fer yer fancy Virginny short-sword?" The voice erupted into that hideous laugh he had heard a moment ago. Gist did not recognize it. The weeks with Curran's men had familiarized him with everyone's voice and laughter. This must belong to one of the new traders who arrived. What were their names now? Evans, that's right. Gist had pegged them as uncouth rogues, slow but troublesome. He decided to ignore them.

"Hey Long Knife!" the voice persisted. "I'll bet that nigger boy o' yourn gittin' some an' you ain't?"

Several traders were trying to hush him. Gist again ignored the insults.

"Hey Long Knife!"

The man must be a fool. How could he still be alive out here on the frontier where some would kill you for looking cross-eyed? Drunkenness can excuse a lot, but you can go too far.

"How 'bout that white woman over t' White Woman's Creek? She good 'nuf fer yer fancy Virginny short-sword?" He was referring to a nearby white woman, who was captured as a child and grew up among the Indians.

Gist turned around and walked to the fire. On his face was a frozen grin, but no smile graced his eyes.

"I don't believe I've made your acquaintance." Gist was amiable. "Gist is my name, born in Maryland, recently from North Carolina. Long Knives, you see, are from Virginia, so does not apply to me."

With a mischievous grin, the crusty trader looked around at the others. "I'm Jabez Evans from Pennsylvania," in direct mockery, after which his voice broke into that repulsive cackle.

Gist read the man as one who would do anything for a fight because he loved to fight. Avoiding a tangle was nearly impossible, unless you were prepared to back down.

"Well, Mr. Evans, it looks to me like you're a fighter."

"That's right, Mr. Long Knife."

"And I'll bet you win most of them, don't you?"

"Yer goddamn right I do. I win all of 'em," he smiled and nodded to all the others.

"Well, I wouldn't want to spoil a perfect record, would I?"

The traders were having a good time watching.

Gist continued, "Now, I've been out in the woods for several hours and I could stand something to warm my blood. Boys, hand me that bottle you been passing around and go get another. Mr. Evans and I are going to have a few drinks, isn't that right Mr. Evans?"

"Ye wouldn't be tryin' t' get outta that fight now would ye Mr. Long Knife?" Evans slurred speech spoke to his condition.

"No, Mr. Evans from Pennsylvania, we can still have our fight. Here have a sip." Evans took a long swallow and handed it to Gist, who appeared to do the same, but did not drink. Oh, he was not afraid of a scrimmage, but brawling was for a younger breed with something to prove. Gist had proved it years ago. It was more of a challenge to avoid the fight.

"Mr. Evans, while we're warming ourselves for our fight – here, take another – just look up at that Gil' Li Utsun' Stanun'yi."

"The what?"

"That up there, the Milky Way," he pointed to the sky and Evans' eyes followed. "Now how do you suppose all those stars got there?"

"I don't know. I never thought . . ."

"Well, let me tell you. You see, long, long ago – here, have another sip – when the sky was black . . ." Gist proceeded to repeat the tale he had told Gabriel earlier, but with great embellishment. On and on he talked, describing every Indian, the village, the weather and all the different plans each villager had for meeting the crisis. Constantly he coaxed Evans to upend the jug and soon the story neared its end. "They beat their drums and shook their rattles and..." Gist stopped as he watched Evans, in a perfect sitting position, slowly slide backward off his seat to rest with his back on the ground and feet on the log.

Gist stood, looked at the sot and shook his head. He bid goodnight to the circle of surprised sutlers and headed for the cabin.

As he went inside he heard someone ask in dismay, "well . . . well what happened to that dog? How'd them stars get up there anyway?"

CHAPTER VII

December 25, 1750

A week had passed with no renewed challenge from Jebez Evans. His salutations even included a hint of respect. It was now Tuesday morning and Gist missed his family. He was not very sentimental. Many times he had left them on one trading excursion or another without much thought. But he could not remember ever being gone over Christmas.

This day had special significance for him. Sarah would read the Christmas story from the New Testament and he would recite excerpts from the Homilies of the Anglican Church. The first date in his copy was 1547 and attributed to King Edward VI. This set of twelve sermons covered every subject from church doctrine to proper moral behavior and he was rarely without it. It helped him keep in touch with certain aspects of his faith. He resolved, therefore, to play his customary role and read selected passages to whomever would listen.

He felt much better now, sensing that his decision to do a familiar thing in an unfamiliar setting would render him less estranged from it. He threw off his bear skin blanket and went outside to inform Croghan of his plans.

"Ah! It's himself," announced Croghan. "And a Merry Christmas to ye, Chris."

"And to you George."

"And how is the Long Knife this mornin'" inquired Croghan. The men often greeted him this way since the encounter with Jebez.

"Is that name to follow me from now on?"

"Don't fret yourself, Chris. These boys look up to ye for your handlin' of Evans that night. A walkin' whiskey keg he was, with as good a case of gallon distemper as I've has ever seen. But old Mark Coonce may have given ye a name that'll stick like a burr."

"Well, I guess we'll see. By the way, it being Christmas Day, I was hoping to hold a little informal service and read some sermons and such. How do you think that would be received?"

"Arrah now, ye have posed a prime question, haven't ye? Will the boys be wantin' to go to meetin'? I'm afraid to say that few of 'em are inclined to hear any good. But ye are welcome to try."

Gist then went about asking the traders if they would attend his proposed gathering. All refused. He was about to give up when a small soot-covered Thomas Burney, the blacksmith, approached him along with half a dozen traders and several Indians.

"Mr. Gist, sir, we heard ye was ta preach a sermon, so we thought we'd come over ta listen," he announced, having removed his narrow-brimmed hat that revealed a white forehead and smashed-down hair. "But some of us be Romanists an' some be Anglicans an we don't none of us want ta receive poorly on account of our convictions."

Their interest appeared genuine; their request sincere. "Well, gentlemen, I have no design or intention to give offence to any particular sect or religion. The Doctrine of Salvation, Faith and Good Works is only what I propose to speak, as I find it in the Homilies of the Church of England. Is that acceptable?"

"Aye, it is with me," answered Burney.

"Then follow me to the fire and we'll begin."

Gist pulled out his well-worn missal and flipped to the pages he so often read. In his deep baritone he began the first sermon on Salvation.

"Because all men be sinners against God, therefore can no man by his own acts, works, and deeds (seem they ever so good) be made righteous before God."

He did not read every word, but skipped some to maintain continuity of thought. He was used to doing this when reading to his children each Christmas. And since the attention span of most of his small congregation was not much greater than that of his children, he saw no reason to change. The crowd began to grow as he read now from the sermon on Faith.

"The first coming unto God is through faith, whereby we be justified before God."

He read certain passages with a flare common to brothers of the cloth, rising on his toes and gesturing with his free hand to emphasize a point. From the third sermon on Good Works he read the final passages.

"Cast in your minds how you may do good unto all men and hurt no man. Obey all your superiors and governors; serve your masters faithfully and diligently. Oppress not, kill not, beat not, neither slander nor hate any man; but love all men, speak well of all men, even your enemies that hate you. Take no man's goods, but content yourselves with that which ye get truly; and also bestow your own goods charitably, as need and care requireth. Flee all idolatry, witchcraft, and perjury; commit no manner of adultery, fornication, or other unchasteness, in will nor in deed, with any other man's wife, widow, or maid, or otherwise. And travailing continually during this life thus in keeping the commandments of God, you shall not fail, as Christ hath promised, to come to that blessed and everlasting life where you shall live in glory and joy with God forever: to whom be praise, honor and empery for ever and ever. Amen."

His congregation had multiplied to twenty traders and more than a hundred Indians. Andrew Montour paraphrased a translation and added that Gist was of the same faith that the English King recommended to all his people. The Indians flocked around, thanking him for his message.

Then their Principle Chief motioned for silence. He walked up to Gist and spoke in a loud, scratchy voice that attested to many years of addressing his people. After he was done, Montour translated for all the traders to hear. "I have heard your words, Long Knife, and they are true words. From this time on you shall be called "ANNOSANAH". It is the name of a good man who once lived among our people. This must always be your name. I have spoken."

When the chief departed, the crowd cacophony resumed, each member shouting out his question. Montour tried to translate each one for Annosanah's reply.

"Will you live among us?" asked one.

Gist replied, "I'm honored by your request and would choose no other village for my home, but I don't know whether the Governor would give me leave. And if he did, the French would perhaps come and carry me away as they have done to other Englishmen."

"Then you must bring great guns and build a fort to protect us from the French, for we have now gone over to the English side," shouted another.

"We wish to be shown the principles of Christianity."

"Yes, we like you and want you to marry us in the Christian manner."

One man said he would never desire to return to the French or have their priests come among them. "We love the English, but we have seen little religion among them. Will you help us?"

As the crowd began to disperse, several of their important warriors, wives and children following behind, approached. They spoke in soft tones and motioned to their children to come stand in front of them. Through Montour they said that he must be a minister of the Gospel and would he baptize their children?

"Tell them I am not a minister, but a mere layman. I have not the authority to baptize, but I will speak to the Governor about sending a proper minister to care for their needs."

The last Indian stepped up to Gist and Montour with a smile on his face and a book in hand. Contrived for him by the French, this book marked the days of the week, so that by moving a pin every morning, he could keep an accurate account of time and thus observe the Sabbath Day.

After all had gone Montour and Gist stood, each reflecting on the morning's events. Gist was awed by the unexpected reaction to his reading, like a small window had been opened letting in a flood of light.

"Annosanah has distinguished himself today," said Montour. "These Wyandot people love you. Annosanah is a name worthy of honor."

"Thank you, Mr. Montour. I've read these homilies every Christmas Day since I was married twenty-two years ago."

"It is a good thing to read to them," said Montour. "More whites should do so." Almost as an afterthought he continued. "I will tell you a story. My mother, Madame Montour, was the daughter of the Governor of New France, Count Frontenac, and a Huron woman. They raised her on the stories told by the French Blackrobes. When she was ten, the Seneca captured her and adopted her into the tribe. One day the great Moravian missionary, Count Zinzindorf, was reading the story of our Savior's birth and His life here on earth. My mother burst into a flood of tears. The Blackrobes had taught her that Bethlehem was in France and the English had crucified the Christ. That is one reason I hate the French. Do you understand?"

"That I do. I've heard of these perversions spoken by the Jesuits to win converts. They fuel the fires of hate against the English. Better they hear no religion than the wrong one."

"Annosanah has again spoken the truth."

"Annosanah – it sounds like an Iroquois name."

"That is because the Wyandot are Huron, who moved from the northern shores of Lake Erie down to Ohio. Long ago Huron and Iroquois were one people. Their speech has many similarities. Annosanah means 'speaker of truthe words.' It is a fitting name, Annosanah."

Montour walked away leaving Gist with his thoughts. He spent the rest of the day alone in the woods under the pretense of hunting. In the past several years he had become melancholy after reading the sermons. They humbled him, because they said that all his good treatment of the Indians amounted to nothing without faith in his God. And he was doubting that God. Or maybe he wasn't doubting God, just his Anglican teachings. How could God judge these Indians so harshly?

The Anglican Church regarded Indians as pagan savages who only needed conversion to Christianity to become civilized. But civilization required people to stay put, produce, govern, and a whole host of activities unknown to the Indian. The Church cared not for their other qualities of love, tenderness, compassion. He knew them to be just as loving and kind and charitable to those of their own family as whites were of theirs. In fact, these characteristics extended to the whole tribe, where the same could not often be said for a white community. The Anglican Church did not view these attributes as necessary for a good Christian life. Salvation was the key.

He wondered about his Indian name – Annosanah – speaker of true words. How could he be a speaker of the truth, when he did not know the truth? He sensed what was false, but truth?

The next day was as dispiriting as Christmas had been uplifting. Gist sat at Croghan's table by candlelight reading what he had just written in his journal.

> Wednesday Dec. 26. – This day a Woman, who had been a long Time a Prisoner, and had deserted & been retaken and brought into the Town on Christmas Eve, was put to Death in the following manner: They carried her without the Town and let her loose, and when she attempted to run away, the Persons appointed for that Purpose pursued her, struck Her on the Ear, on the right side of her Head, which beat her flat on her Face on the Ground; they then stuck her several Times thro the Back with a Dart, to the Heart, scalped Her, & threw the Scalp in the Air; and another cut off her Head; There the dismal Spectacle lay till the Evening; & then Barny Curran desired Leave to bury Her, which He and his Men, and some of the Indians did just at Dark.

What about white accusations of Indian cruelty. This terrible act highlighted the savagery of the Indian. But were the whites less barbaric? In his youth he witnessed a man, accused of some crime, being tarred, feathered and ridden out of town on a fence rail. He saw the man later. The hot tar had scorched his skin, leaving ugly scars on his head over which no hair would grow. The sharp rail had broken his pelvis, torn the thigh muscles and rendered him crippled for life. Which people were more barbaric?

CHAPTER VIII

January 1751

Early January was uneventful. A trader named Michael Teafe came in from near Lake Erie and reported that the Ottawas were aligned with the French. The other villages of the Wyandot Nation, he said, would desert the French and join their brothers on the Muskingum. Several days later two more of Croghan's men brought news that French Indians had captured another English trader.

It was time to go. On January 12th Croghan made preparations for their departure. The packhorses went south toward the Lower Shawnee Town with other traders. Croghan, Montour and Gist stayed behind that evening to attend Croghan's council, but it did not look promising. Few of the Wyandot wise men from surrounding villages had come. Others were disordered with liquor and the council was dismissed.

Two days later it reconvened. A hum of energy flowed through the chief's house as the men filed in. It was soon clear that not enough sachems were present for a consensus. The grand assembly that Croghan had expected did not materialize. The problems of protection for his traders and French allegiance for half the Wyandot Nation would remain unaddressed.

But Gist still had an invitation. "Brothers of the Wyandot," announced Montour as he translated for Gist, "we are here to acquaint the King and council of this nation with a great event. These four strings of wampum signify that the great English King over the water, your Father, has sent under the care of the Governor of Virginia, your Brother, a large present of goods, which is now landed in Virginia. Assarquoa sends Annosanah to invite the Wyandot to come and partake of their Father's charity to all his children on the branches of the Ohio."

The chiefs adjourned to consider the invitation. Half an hour later they returned. One of their chiefs stood and gave the reply. "Our King and all of our chiefs wish to thank their Brother Assarquoa for his care. We thank Annosanah for bringing us news of gifts awaiting us in Virginia. Whether we will travel in the spring to receive them, we cannot give you an answer. We must hold a general council of the several Nations of Indians and our many

Wyandot Brothers in the spring." After several formal amenities and much shaking of hands, the meeting adjourned.

Later at Croghan's cabin, over a flagon of hot buttered rum, Gist confessed his disappointment. "I was expecting more from this conference."

"After the treatment the Wyandot received from Pennsylvania," Montour volunteered, "it is no wonder they do not accept so willingly. They asked Pennsylvania for help to resist the French and none was given. Since Chief Nicholas died these people have had no leader and cannot agree on anything."

"I understand that, but they have treated me with such deference, I was hoping for a more enthusiastic response. Surely, they must realize another trading partner is in their best interests."

"Arrah now, another trading partner it is, to be sellin' your Company's goods for less than me own and perhaps puttin' me out of business?"

"No, George, to keep your men honest, force the reprobates out, and control the flow of liquors. With Virginia as a partner, the Indians can achieve all that."

"Aye, and the Ohio Company will be doin' all that, will it? It's a fight we'll be havin' then – Pennsylvania against Virginia."

"Come on George, don't you think there are enough Indians out here to keep two trading establishments busy for a lifetime."

"Not unless the French stop capturin' my traders," he said, got up and walked outside.

Gist raised his eyebrows at Montour. "Our brother the Buck is losing his empire."

"I understand that, but it seems to me that another trading firm with honest men to run it will bring more Indians to the English side. Side by side we'll rid ourselves of the French threat without a war."

"Annosanah," Montour interrupted, "you do not speak as though you would consider Indians as partners. You call them 'children' of the English King, but they are not children of any king. They are warriors who have killed in battle, suffered the pain of wounded bodies, hearts and souls; they care for their families. Annosanah, they are men!"

Gist was taken aback. "You are right, of course," he answered, "but the English have been calling them that at treaties and meetings for many years."

"And the Indian cringes inside each time the treaty-maker calls him a child. He endures it because he needs the white man's trade and during a treaty ceremony, where there are many important men, he has little choice. But out here, despite your name Annosanah, they do not have to listen."

"Sattelihu, your words are true, and I will allow that I've spoken those words many times, not realizing their implication. But I cannot change the way the English treat the tribes."

"You cannot change what has been, Annosanah, nor can you affect the white man's way. You can only change yourself."

Annosanah awoke to bright rays of sunlight creeping through the gaps in the chinking of Croghan's log cabin. He felt good. It was hard to believe they had been with the Wyandot a whole month, but the easy life had allowed him to regain his strength and he was anxious to leave. Three and a half months away from home, he still had far to go. Croghan's itinerary pointed southward to the Lower Shawnee Town, for which he carried messages from Governor Hamilton, then north to Pickawillany. Some of the Irishman's employees were taking the packhorses of presents directly to the Twightwee town. Gist accompanied Croghan to take advantage of his protection.

The villagers at Conchake had presented him with many gifts since his sermon of Christmas Day: a pair of deerskin leggins, a beaded breechclout, a buckskin hunting shirt. These he had worn around the town to show his gratitude. For the coming trip, though, he rolled them up in a blanket and donned his old knee-breeches, grateful to be rid of the drafts on certain parts of his body unaccustomed to exposure. One elderly woman presented him with a pair of elk-hide moccasins, lined with blanket wool. Attached to the shoe part was excess hide that wrapped around the ankle up to mid calf and tied with a thong. His familiar elk-hide hunting frock, with its frayed lining of brown wool, gave him the warmth he needed for winter travel.

At midday they rode west from Conchake for five miles to White Woman's Town, on the north branch of the Muskingum. This village of several Wyandot families was the home of Mary Harris. Croghan explained that when she was ten years old, almost fifty years ago, the French Mohawk Cahnawagas captured her in a raid on Deerfield, Massachusetts. In time she took a Cahnawaga husband, by whom she had several children.

Croghan rode up to a gray-haired woman carrying two buckets of water suspended on each end of a stick across her shoulders.

"Ah Mary and how is your charmin' self this fine afternoon?"

"Me charmin' self be none the better for the seein' of thee, George Croghan," she mimicked his Irish brogue. "What hath thee brought me this time?" She put down the buckets and straightened up, showing a dark, leathery face and clear, blue eyes.

"Mary, Mary, growin' to appreciate me little contributions, are ye?" He turned to Gist, "she knows I bring her a little somethin' now and again." Turning back to Mary, "this time I've brought none other than Christopher Gist, now called Annosanah by the Wyandot."

Mary eyed Gist, who nodded. "More than the Wyandot now call thee Annosanah. The story of thy Christmas message spreads far across the land. I remember how very righteous were they back in New England. Many's the time I've wondered how the white men be so wicked as I see them in these woods. 'Tis good for such as thee to visit, Annosanah. Where thee be headin', George," she redirected her attention to the Irishman.

"Arrah now Mary, ye know I can't be tellin' such as yourself of me wanderin's. Ye'd likely let it slip to your Frenchies and they'd be out after me scalp, they would."

"George Croghan!" she cried. "If I wanted the bounty on thy Irish head, I'd shoot thee myself and carry thy bloody scalp clear to Detroit. Now, get thee gone, that I may finish." Directing herself to Gist, she added, "Annosanah, I would request thy presence at my home this evening."

With Gist's affirmative reply, the traders rode downstream a hundred yards and made camp.

"Meanin' no offence here Chris, but I'd be watchin' what I told the lass about your travels. Never know to what red Injen she'll let slip your plans.

After a meal of boiled venison and sweetened chocolate, Gist walked over to Mary's domed hut and announced himself. The fire warmed them as they sat across from one another on bear skin floor covers. He admired the intricate quill design on a knife sheath and shoulder bag hanging on the wooden frame. Several bowls and an iron kettle sat by the fire. A powder horn and French trade gun stood near the door.

Mary was curious about life in New England. Gist could not supply many details of the northern Colonies, but found her intelligent, inquisitive and well mannered. He told her some of himself, his family and his exploits, avoiding any mention of the Ohio Company. She, in turn, related her life among the Cahnawagas.

"The forest be heatin' up," she looked deep into Gist's eyes. "'Twill not be long 'fore tomahawks run red with the blood of the French and the English. These eyes be too sad to see it happen again. My husband likes the French. We'll not stay here long."

"I bid you good luck, then, Mary Harris," said Gist as he turned to leave. "May God go with you."

"And with thee, Annosanah."

The five-family Delaware village of Hockhockin, three days and sixty-five miles farther along the trail, greeted them the afternoon of the 19th. Men and women alike came to see Annosanah, about whom they had heard so much. The town was too small to warrant a council, so Gist relayed an informal invitation to the chiefs. Andrew Montour translated. After the presentation, Montour approached him.

"Annosanah, come with me. There is something you must see."

Montour led him along the main path toward a bold rock eminence ahead. The abundance of trees made the view difficult, but soon a small clearing revealed an awesome towering monolith of solid rock. Like an island in a dried up sea, it rose 200 feet above the surrounding forest. At its base, half a mile long, a tremendous pile of fallen boulders, rock rubble and forest debris sloped upward to meet a precipice of fissured, furrowed sandstone descending from above.

"Ach-sin-sink," Montour broke the silence. "Standing Stone, a place of the Creator. Come."

Gist walked to the base of the woodland monument, awestruck by its size, silenced by its beauty. With youthful exuberance he followed Montour up the narrow winding trace on the south side, carved in the stone by an ancient people. The treacherous path led to the summit, a rolling, rocky plain one hundred yards long and fifty wide, scattered with malnourished trees and underbrush. At irregular intervals, large flat boulders jutted out into space. Here were the ashes of countless fires, kindled in the offering of prayers. Endless piles of flint chips spoke of generations of warriors, who hefted chunks of the obdurate stone up the tower to sit and knap arrow and spear points in the presence of the Great One. From one of these overlooks they viewed the valley of the Hockhocking River to the west.

"Five miles north," Montour pointed, "the river shapes itself like the neck of a gourd. The Delaware word for this shape is hock-hock. It is from this they take the name of the river and their town." He then gestured toward the flat land in the distance.

Gist saw the many open spaces where the trees no longer grew and the soil was dark.

"They burn the land each spring. New growth brings the deer and bear to feed. In this way, the people have not far to hunt."

"They must also plant some of that burned-off land," said Gist, "judging by how close it is to their town."

"Corn, squash and beans, yes. This is a wonderful land. Since the white settlers have pushed them west, the Delaware are much happier than they were during their time in Pennsylvania."

"Who can blame them? I, myself, am much happier where I live away from the cities and the settlers."

"And you took Indian land and built your house on it." Montour said without malice. "And your Ohio Company sends you out to look for the best land on which to build a settlement, and you will sell that land until it overflows with white people who will crowd out the Indian. I believe you are a good man, Annosanah, but you know not what you do."

Gist was surprised at this confrontation and he did not know how to respond. His first reaction was to take umbrage. In the treaty of 1744 the Six Nations had sold all the lands east of the Appalachians. He felt he had taken no Indian lands. Yet he had not gained his reputation for diplomatic discretion by flying off on the defensive handle. He suspected Montour had this discussion in mind earlier.

"My father," Gist began, "believed that the Indian and the white man could live together in peace. I believe this also. The Ohio Company wishes to buy Indian land, not take it."

"Madame Montour believed as your father. For many years she was an interpreter between my people and the English, but she and the Indians knew what the whites do not yet realize. When the English need the Indian trade, there is cooperation. That is the condition for peace. But when the English want land, it is different. My people do not understand how the white man can own the land as I own a horse or a gun. This land was given to the Indian by the Master of Life for their use while they live. No man owns the land and no Indian can sell what he does not own.

"In the time of my grandfather, when the English traded many presents for a parcel of land, the Indian reasoned that they just wanted to use it. But the English divided that parcel among his white brothers, built many houses and put up fences. My grandfathers could no longer hunt there.

"Now, when the English trade presents for land, the Indian has no choice. He must have powder, guns, lead and the blankets to survive. But deep down in his heart he knows he has sold off another part of his future for the need to live today."

"Sattelihu," Gist used his Seneca name, "can the Indian ever refuse?"

Montour paused. "Annosanah, on the chase, have you ever tracked a wounded animal to a place from which it could not escape?"

Gist nodded. "It was a bear, who turned to fight."

"One day the English will ask to buy the Indian's last remaining parcel of land. Trapped, like a cornered animal, what do you think he will do?"

Annosanah thought he knew the answer.

The next morning they traveled fifteen miles southwest, to the Delaware town of Maguck, at the north end of an extensive grassy plain. From a small mound in the center of the plain, they saw a slow-moving river to the west.

Montour explained that the Wyandot who used to live here named it Scionto – place where the deer are plenty. The Shauwanoa call it Wee-la-athar-theepe, or hairy river. The deer, being so many, leave the water thick with their hairs when they come to drink.

Three days at the Maguck Town allowed the weakened horses to graze on the rich, green stems of wild rye sticking out of the snow. Then it was south to Win-daug-halah's Town, a Delaware village of twenty families on the Scionto. Win-daug-halah, a wise and venerable chief, was gracious and invited them to stay in his house. He ordered his black servant to tend their horses. Pleased to meet Gabriel and Croghan's servant, they relieved the animals of their burden and took them out to graze. Because of Win-daug-hala's influence and his commitment to the English, they agreed to a general council.

The town awoke to six inches of new snow. Village chiefs stepped high through the layer of white on their way to the chief's house for the meeting. It began with the silent smoking of the pipe while minds prepared for the coming exchange.

At an appropriate time, Montour stood and introduced Annosanah, repeating a brief account of how he acquired his honorable title. Gist made his invitation as before. Croghan told them of his Pickawillany mission. He emphasized the English commitment to their brothers, the Twightwees, long time friends of the Delaware. After some cautions regarding the French, they relinquished the floor to await a reply.

Several minutes of silent meditation passed until Win-daug-hala, holding four strings of wampum, stood and spoke. "Brothers, we the Delaware return to you our hearty thanks for the news you have sent us. We assure you we will not hear the voice of any other nation, for we are to be directed by you our brothers, the English, and by none else. We shall be glad to hear what our brothers have to say to us at the Logstown in the spring. To assure you of our hearty good will and love to our brothers, we present you with these four wampum."

That night, Gist was happy to write in his journal the proceedings of the first village council to accept his invitation. He finished with additional information he thought the Company would want to know.

> This is the last Town of the Delawares to the Westward – The Delaware Indians by the best Account I could gather consist of about 500 fighting Men all firmly attached to the English Interest, they are not properly a Part of the six Nations, but are scattered about amongst most of the Indians upon the Ohio, and some of them among the six Nations, from whom they have Leave to hunt upon their Lands.

"I suspect," said Gist as he penned his last sentence, "the reason we got such a good response is because the Delaware have been close to Pennsylvania for so long."

Montour replied, "for over a hundred years, the Lenape and Pennsylvania have been brothers – during their movement from the Atlantic Sea to the Delaware River, then to the Susquehanna, through western Pennsylvania to Logstown, and now out in the Ohio country. But the farther they go from the English, the more their eyes are opened and their ears will hear. Even the Lenape can learn to say no to the English."

"Whose side are you on, Montour," Gist had turned to face the Seneca, "ours or the French?"

"Sattelihu is on the side of Sattelihu. I am Seneca," he said, hardening his voice. "But Sattelihu has eyes that see. The French are like the trees, but the English are like the leaves that cover the trees. They will be here long after the French are gone. I help my Indian brothers understand the English so that the Covenant Chain of Friendship does not bind too tight and the wounded animal is not so easily cornered."

CHAPTER IX

February 1751

Five miles down the River Scionto, at its confluence with the Ohio, lay the Lower Shawnee Town, principal village of the Tshil-i-kau-thee sept and known to them by that name. The path led through fields cultivated during season and past rows of wegiwas, the homes of individual families, much like those of the Delaware and Wyandot.

"Here's somethin' for your journal, laddie," Croghan said to Gist. "There be nigh on to one hundred of these wegiwas on this side of the river, and at least half that on the south side. Now I've not been to the west side of the Scionto, but I hear there's about thirty or forty wegiwas from several different tribes, Wyandots, Painkashaws, Weas, and maybe a few Mingos. To be sure, all these towns be growin' like ivy."

The party being small and without packhorses of trade goods, the usual tide of welcoming villagers did not appear. Instead, Croghan led them to the principal chief, Neu-che-con-neh, whose house was in the shadow of a small fort.

"Kro-Gun wel-kom," said Neu-che-con-neh in a familiar greeting. As he spoke no English, Croghan exchanged amenities in his best Shawnee and they agreed on the importance of a general conference for the next day. He introduced Annosanah and the chief expressed prior knowledge of the white man, who reportedly spoke true words.

"Now where d'ye suppose he's heard about the likes of you?" Croghan wondered aloud.

Gist winked at the Irishman, not knowing himself.

Several village chiefs escorted them to the river, whereupon they fired their guns in a prearranged signal to Croghan's traders on the south side. Gunshots sounded in reply, heralding the speedy arrival of six canoes, each two towing a large log raft. Horses and men were ferried across to the trading cabin and storehouse, much like the one at the Muskingum town. Montour wandered off, leaving the two traders and Croghan's servant to unload their horses and move into wegiwas kept vacant for their use. Gabriel, having arrived earlier, soon appeared, showing Gist the whereabouts of their packs and horses and seeking permission to accompany a Shawnee hunting party. Gist gave it and Gabriel disappeared into the bustling village.

Croghan's employees, whom he had sent ahead from the Wyandot town, drifted in from various parts of the village to begin the involved task of categorizing goods, taking inventory and the myriad other jobs required of them. Now that the boss had arrived, leisure time was curtailed. The work lasted as long as daylight, when they locked the door and returned to their recreational pursuits.

The numbing cold of the clear January night kept most people inside. Gist, however, welcomed his aloneness and walked about the village admiring its cleanliness. Dogs with thick winter coats lay in the snow chewing on discarded bones or frozen balls of horse dung. The many outdoor fires smoldered, their makers having moved inside. As he passed the houses, he could often hear a single suspenseful male voice amidst occasional oo's and laughter of a small audience. He suspected this to be a story teller engaged in an entertaining narrative. Some wegiwas emitted sounds of excited cheering, followed by moments of intense silence, during which a clicking noise was heard. Every Indian tribe he knew played some sort of dice game with pieces of antler or bone.

There were also the low-pitched male tones mixed with the giggles and the unmistakable breathy sounds of lovers loving. In his past, he had walked through camps of soldiers and heard many of these same sounds. How much alike were the whites and their Indian brothers – story tellers, gamblers, lovers. He had often been amazed at how people could seem so different, yet be so alike. He turned the corner and headed for his assigned wegiwa.

The sound of passion had awakened in him feelings of desire for Sarah and the memory of their last evening together. Contented he would be to stoke up his fire, lie back under his bear skin and drift off dreaming of their reunion. As he approached the hut, he could see the golden glow of a tended fire. Gabriel would be gone for a week or more. He looked around to assure himself he had the right dwelling.

Curious, he pulled back the deer hide door and stepped in. Across the fire sat a most beautiful figure of a young woman, wrapped in a buffalo robe. Though she was no more than fifteen, her teacher had spared no effort instructing her in the female art of allurement. The light of the flames illuminated her long black hair, flowing down and mixing with the brown hairs of the robe that parted to reveal small, copper-colored breasts. Her legs were tucked underneath, but a pair of knees, reddened by the heat of the fire, protruded from the edge of the robe.

The depth of the situation was not lost on Annosanah. She was a gift to him from an important chief and his refusal of her might bring offense. Then the girl's feelings had to be considered. Rejection might cause her humiliation. Kicking her out was out of the question. He felt his own heat rising, but his personal convictions would not allow a union with this gift.

"Do you speak English?"

She shook her head no. Oversized, brown eyes studied him.

"Delaware, Wyandot?" he could do well in the former and could manage some words in the latter, having learned at the Muskingum Town.

Again she motioned no.

"I am Annosanah," he said, indicating himself. Pointing to her, he said, "You are?"

For the third time she shook her head. He continued to talk, explaining how she was very beautiful, but he already had a wife and was very happy. He knew she did not understand his words and maybe he was voicing them to bolster his resolve as much as anything. But when he was able to make her understand that they would not be intimate, he thought he detected a look of relief in her eyes. Then, as if on some prearranged cue, she began to cry. He expected this and made no move to comfort her. With the understanding of a concerned father, he bid her to lie down and cover herself. Grabbing his own bear skin, he retired to a spot near the door and curled up facing the wall. Several times he awakened to hear her placing wood on the fire, but in the morning she was gone.

Annosanah had little time to eat before a delegation of village chiefs, dressed in their finest attire, arrived to guide Gist and Croghan across the river, where stood the fort and council house. The stockade was a larger version of Thomas Cresap's, enclosing an area 200 feet in diameter. Inside stood the council house ninety feet long and thirty wide. A pole frame faced with elm bark supported a gable roof twelve feet high at the peak. Seating was arranged in two parallel sections separated by a line of fires every ten feet.

The white traders were the first to be seated around the center fire. They admired their surroundings in silence. Three beams spanned the width of the house, each resting on two wooden pillars carved in relief with the figures of animals: rattlesnake, turtle, various birds. On the middle pillars, exaggerated human faces looked down at the assembling crowd. A twist of tobacco hung above each figure.

"Each animal represents a different clan of the Tshil-i-kau-thee tribe," Montour explained. "The faces are those of the Grandmothers. The medicine men offer her twists of tobacco before each official gathering."

It took an hour for the meetinghouse to fill, as the pride of the Shawnee Nation filed in and sat cross-legged on the dirt floor. As Montour or Croghan recognized certain warrior chiefs, they pointed them out to Gist.

"That warrior with the red piping on his leggins is Nic-ki-phock and next to him is La-wack-a-mic-ky," said Montour.

"Arrah now, there's one I've not seen for a spell, Coy-ca-do-len-ne, himself, over there with the gray hair. He was vice councilor at Logstown when I first arrived there in '44. Went over to the French, he did.

"See scar-face with one eye just now walking in?" Croghan continued.

"That be 'The Pride,' the English call him. He's the one entertained your friends, Cresap and Parker."

"There walks the son of a great man among these people. Loa-pee-ka-way, King Opetha's son. Remind me to tell you about him later," said Montour.

Their command of Shawnee names and faces was indeed impressive, but Gist could commit only a few to memory. Each had decorated himself in the various silver pieces; scalp-locks adorned with eagle feathers; leggins edged with ribbon and beadwork; quilled neck knives. The smells of wood smoke, bear grease and smoked leather permeated the air.

"And now, you see one of the greatest captains of war. He is their speaker, Mi-the–meatha-quotha, called Big Hominy by the English. He carries the calumet and will begin this council by lighting it," Montour whispered to Gist.

At last the house was full and the meeting began with the passing of the first pipe. Nearly 100 attendees passed several pipes among themselves and talked in low tones.

"Guess who's not here," said Gist in a whisper to Croghan.

"The big chief himself, Neu-che-con-neh, I know. Now why d'ye suppose that is?" he asked more to himself than to Gist.

As was customary, when the smoking was through the ones who called the assembly spoke first. Croghan stood and delivered speeches from Governor Hamilton, telling of Pennsylvania's pleasure at having the Shawnee number among its friends and trading partners. These messages Croghan spoke himself in an imperfect, yet impressive display of their language. Then he motioned for Montour to stand and the tone became more serious. Montour translated.

"Ye all know the English trader and gunsmith, John Frazier, now at Venango on Allegheny. Two of his traders, Turner and Kilgore, were captured during the last Strawberry Moon by French Indians." A moan of concern filled the room. "Now, we have good news. On the path from Detroit to Montreal, they escaped from a French guard during the night and went to the English fort at Oswego."

Gist could see from their expressions that they were all delighted the French had been foiled, if in a small way.

"These two men bring word that the French will pay £500 to anyone who would bring meself, George Croghan, Prince of all the Pennsylvania Traders, alive to them, and £200 for the Seneca interpreter, Andrew Montour."

The house exploded in a roar of surprise at the large sums being offered. Croghan allowed the noise to subside.

"Brothers of the Shawonese, I ask ye to remember that it's meself, who has supplied ye these past seasons with the best trade goods ever to come from the King. The £500 any warrior would receive for me scalp would only be squandered and meself gone. Now if I be gone, how can I continue to supply the Shawonese and their Injen brothers? And how would ye be sure to know the words of your English brothers without Sattelihu to warn ye if they dance around the truth?" Croghan winked his eye at his audience, grinned and danced a little jig, much to the enjoyment of the Shawnee, who hooted and howled at the jest.

"Brother Shawonese," Croghan continued, gesturing like a Sunday preacher, "the French are like bad birds which sit on your shoulder and whisper all manner of evil against the English. These same French have threatened you and your Wyandot brothers with war in the spring. Our soldiers have seen ten of their canoes laden with stores for a new fort at the place where the White River flows into the Lake of the Eries. Ye know several of our traders have been taken and we advise you to keep your warriors at home 'til we know what the French will do."

Croghan sat while Gist rose to have his message translated by Montour.

"Brothers of the Shannoah Nation, I am Christopher Gist, now called Annosanah by your elder brothers, The Wyandot. I have come among you to tell you of a large present of goods sent by the King, of Great Britain. This gift is now under the care of Assarquoa and is for all the people of the western tribes. I am come to invite you to partake of Assarquoa's generosity at Logstown in the spring. We hope you will clear your ears of all the evil said against Virginia and open your eyes to see a good road between us."

Mi-the-meatha-quotha rose and took in his hand several strings of wampum, holding them high for all to see. "These are the speeches received by us from your great men," he said, addressing Croghan and Gist. Montour continued translating. "From the beginning of our friendship, all that our brothers, the English, have told us, has been made good, for which we return our hearty thanks."

Taking up four additional strings of wampum in his hand, he continued. "Brothers, I now speak the sentiments of all our people. When first our forefathers did meet the English, our brothers, they found what the English told them to be true. We are but a small people and it is not to us only that you speak, but to all nations. We shall be glad to hear what our brothers will say to us at the Logstown in the spring, and we hope that the friendship now subsisting between us and our brothers will last as long as the sun shines or the moon gives light. We hope that our children will hear and believe what our brothers say to them, as we have always done. To assure of our hearty goodwill toward you, our brothers, we present you with these four strings of wampum."

Big Hominy walked over to Annosanah and handed him the wampum. There was some talk of an escort to Pickawillany, but nothing came of it. A hand shaking ceremony ended the council.

"Well," Croghan remarked, "Chief Neu-che-con-neh didn't show himself.

I'll not believe he was sick like they said, but that's why we could get ourselves no escort."

"And let us not forget," interrupted Montour, "that Neu-che-con-neh led Chartier's band of Shauwanoa to join the French not five years ago. Big Hominy was with them, and Loa-pee-ka-way, and Coy-ca-co-len-ne, and La-wack-a-micky and half the warriors in that room. It is true that they returned three years later and begged forgiveness from the governor, but they are like the grains of sand that go whichever way the wind blows."

"And I presume," said Gist, "the French will try anything to win them back, including force?"

"Arrah now, make no doubt the French'll be usin' every way they can to bring all the Injens to their side. But I think that these Shawonese are so well grafted in ye English interest that they'll not be so easily moved."

Gist and Croghan walked to the riverbank lined with dozens of elm bark canoes and dugouts. They picked one and shoved off for the lower village. Bright sunshine shone across the surface of the water, revealing a complex pattern of conflicting currents.

Croghan broke the silence. "I hear that ye have again distinguish yourself among the Injens."

"And how's that?" Replied Gist with no hint of his meaning.

"To refuse the affections of Loa-pee-ka-way's daughter would be unthinkable to such as meself, fearing, as I would, to cause the ire of one so great. King Opetha's son he is. Opetha was King of the Pickaway Shawonese. Years ago he led his people from the South to the Lower Susquehanna. Many stories of his bravery in battle they be havin' and mind ye I'll bet most of 'em's true. So what does he do one day but give up his throne, he does. If anyone knows why, they've not told the likes of meself. But he had a followin' he did, and they built a town back thirty years ago, where that fellow Cresap lives. They stayed there awhile, 'til they was attacked by their ancient enemy, the Catawba. Aye, fought like Kilkenny cats, they did, and when the dust settled, King Opetha was dead. Loa-pee-ka-way led them to the Logstown and now he's here."

"You have wandered from your point, George."

"Aye, now I have at that. Well, as I was sayin', there's not been a trader to refuse a chief's daughter, nor any other squaw for that matter, in their memory. Loa-pee-ka-way is of the opinion that you are, how did he put it, blessed by the Grandmother with power to control your body's desires. And out of respect for that power," Croghan said with a wide grin, "he's givin' ye the use of his daughter for cookin' and keepin' things tidy. That's for the remainder of your stay. Oh, and just for the sake of convenience, she'll be stayin' in your wegiwa."

Gist turned around and glared at the Irishman, who had begun a hearty laugh.

"I don't suppose there's any way out of this?"

"Not unless ye leave tomorrow and you'll be better off waitin' for me. The Assembly's instructions to me, as they could not see fit to extend the proper presents to the Shawonese, are to gauge their sentiments and exert me overwhelmin' powers of persuasion. That, me friend, could take awhile," he smiled.

"I see. At least you might tell me her name. I asked, but she wouldn't say."

"Aye, now, that's because they don't believe in the tellin' of their names. When asked, they say they don't know."

"Do you know her name?"

"Why, every eligible male knows her name and would like to marry themselves to the likes of her. She be called Wau-thee-wee-la, meanin' 'bright horn' or 'She-who-shines-in-the-night'. I'll bet her name-giver dreamed of a magnificent buffalo with horns shinin' in the moonlight on the night she was born."

"Lord Almighty, George, what am I going to do with a child on my hands."

"Chris, me good friend, I'd be more'n obliged to trade ye places, but me advice on the matter's pretty much what ye'd think it'd be, comin' from one such as meself."

CHAPTER X

February 1751

While Croghan's traders were busy trading, he made his famous merriment with the chiefs of the town. Important war chiefs, lesser village chiefs, it did not matter. Croghan said that the Shawnee commitment to his personal safety, the growth of his business and their loyalty to England would be won in small doses. It all required a mixture of sincere friendship, entertainment, flattery, competition and bribery. Gist and Montour held their share of interviews, treated guests to spirituous liquors in moderation, lavished compliments and allowed themselves to be challenged in shooting matches and other contests. Croghan dispensed presents at his own expense.

They were rewarded, one day, by an invitation to an unusual dance festival. It began in the evening with a proper official, similar to a town crier, walking through the streets, heralding the upcoming event.

"He says," Montour explained, "that all those who wish it so, are dissolved of their marriages as of now. A public feast, to start tomorrow, will continue for three days, after which time the women will again choose husbands."

Gist's eyebrows raised. He had never heard of this custom.

Morning began early for the participants as they ate their first meal. Near the fire a wrinkled old man sat cross-legged before a log drum, striking a slow beat, his high, singing syllables calling the women to the dance. Others soon joined him until four musicians thumped and sang a steady rhythm. From out of the crowd the women gathered in a circle surrounding a crackling fire. They began rotating, first to the right and then to the left. During the first hour the circle broke hands to admit new arrivals until seventy women were dancing. Blankets tossed aside, their accumulating body heat warmed them.

For several hours this continued while the men stood by wrapped in blankets or matchcoats. They smoked, laughed, pointed, cajoled and jeered until it was their turn. One by one the women receded while men took their places. They too shed winter protection and assumed a figure eight around two fires. Watching women behaved in much the same way as the men. The spectacle continued, as the women now replaced the men. On toward dusk a plentiful feast awaited the participants, after which they danced the whole night through. Many pranced along until they dropped in a heap where they remained until revived by the cold. Some crawled away; others rose again.

Gist watched as long as he could, but grew tired and craved the warmth of a wegiwa. He walked down to the river, grabbed a canoe and set out toward the south side. Icy wind darts stung his face. His eyes watered. He smiled as he tried to imagine a ceremony such as this among his own people, who reputedly stayed married for life, whether they were happy or not.

The next afternoon Gist returned to the ceremony to find the situation much changed. The women were again dancing, but slower than before. Clothing was in disarray; bare limbs and feet were oblivious to the cold. Muddy were the dancers' paths that once had been frozen ground. A few had passed out, the remaining circle having to step over them. Some could barely stand. A chant emanated from the hearty as the drum continued its beat. Gist approached Montour, who was also watching.

"Looks like they're about dead."

"They look this way now, but on the third day they get energy from Kohkumthena, the Grandmother. You will see."

"What are they saying?"

"They sing about being women and all that they must do. The chorus says, 'I do not fear my husband, I will choose what man I please.'"

True to Montour's prediction the energy level of all dancers on the third day was phenomenal. One hundred men danced in wild gyrations, jumping as high as the flames, sometime in long lines and other times in a figure eight. They marched around the outside of the fort and through the council house.

On toward evening the women lined up as the men filed by. When a certain woman wanted one of the men passing by, she stepped in and joined in his dance, taking hold of his clothing. Thus they continued in the dance until all the women had made their choice. With the festival over, the happy couples retired.

Montour explained that although some couples did dissolve their marriages, most of the women chose the same partner as before. It was a time to reaffirm marriage vows and celebrate their union.

It was during this time of entertaining the chiefs that Gist grew to appreciate Wau-thee-wee-la. She made his fires, cooked his meals, and kept the wegiwa clean. In return he supplied their food. Their main activity together was an exchange of language. Each evening, they showed each other various items and relayed their names in English and Shawnee.

Gist removed his knife from its sheath. "Knife," he said as he held it in one hand and pointed to it with the other.

"Mar-nee-thee," she answered.

He picked up the iron kettle sitting by the fire and called it by name.

"Oh-kee-ak-wa."

Rifle was pa-am-kau-taa-kee; blanket was huk-wee-waa; shirt, pee-tenee-kar; dog, wee-shee; and so on. He noticed how many more syllables the Shawnee words had than their English equivalents. She learned much faster than he. By his time to leave, he had command of about one hundred words. By placing the new words into English word order, he was able to make simple sentences she could understand. He could not, however, follow much of what she said, but it was a start.

Now he was finding it more difficult to curb his feelings of desire for Bright Horn. To his people she was but a child. Among the Shawnee she was a woman, ready to marry, bear children and set up a wegiwa of her own. Several times he looked into her eyes and saw an affection that unnerved him. He would look away and make an excuse to go outside. Nights were most difficult and he found himself taking long walks in the cold to avoid the warmth of the wegiwa and thoughts of her.

Gabriel returned after ten days with the hunting party. He had learned much from the other young men and walked with new confidence. But as Bright Horn was there, he did not require Gabriel's services, so Gist gave him leave to dwell among his new friends.

"Gabriel," said Gist, "I want you to stay here and take care of the horses and provisions while I'm gone."

Gabriel was not at all disappointed.

"Croghan informs me we'll be leaving tomorrow for the Twightwee Town. Croghan and the others will then go back to Muskingum. I'll return here to get you and head for the Falls of Ohio."

That night in his wegiwa Annosanah and Bright Horn began their lesson. It was halted, however, when she began to cry. He asked what was wrong, to which she replied that he was leaving tomorrow and she was very sad. He would be back, he said, in several weeks and they could continue their schooling. Again she began sobbing. He moved to her side and put his arm around her in an attempt to comfort. She buried herself against his shoulder and sobbed. Her warmth pressed against him as he ran his hands over her coarse, black hair and down her back. Her fingers began to knead his arm muscle. She stopped crying. A familiar feeling rose from deep within him, as he pushed her far enough away to admire her beauty, face dusky and smooth with youth, eyes dark and desirous – those eyes, filled with naive trust and thoughts only of now, this time, this place. What did she see in his eyes – lust, hesitation? This woman-child could not know that once the passion was gone, the feelings remain. But he had let it go too far. Now nothing else mattered. She, the one without experience, without guile, had taken him to her place and time. One tender kiss sent him to a realm of sensation he had not known existed.

When he awoke, it was dawn and she was gone, as he knew she would be. He felt contented as he lay reliving the night. How different she was from Sarah, how primal and without inhibition. But what was that, a thought of guilt? Something from his revered Homilies about adultery was pulling at a corner of his bliss. He cast it aside like an old moccasin. Besides, how could anything so beautiful be wrong?

As he dressed, he was thankful this was his last day. To stay longer would be awkward, as he was not sure what his expectations regarding Bright Horn would be. He knew she and the Shawnee got from him what they wanted. His essence would now be added to the collective spirit of the people. He guessed he could understand that. He felt humbled by the great compliment.

Gist knew he must visit her father before leaving, and asked Montour and Croghan to escort him to the house of Loa-pee-ka-way. They were welcomed inside and seated around the fire where they exchanged greetings.

"I do not have the words to express my gratitude to you and your daughter, Wau-thee-wee-la. She has shown me the spirit of the Shannoah people."

Montour translated and the chief smiled at the compliment. Lao-pee-ka-way then spoke several phrases.

"He says she should be your wife."

Gist considered his reply. "Tell him she would make a good wife, but it is custom among my people to have but one."

"In the days of my grandfather," the chief replied, "one wife was also customary. Now, more than one is admissible. It is true, not many men have two wives, but each man is permitted to keep as many as he can support."

"Tell him," said Gist with a grin, "perhaps his grandfathers were wise. My wife would not take kindly to a second one."

Lao-peek-kaway smiled and spoke.

"He says," Montour translated, "that having two wives is like having two rifle-guns, an old gun and a new gun. The new one wants much shooting, but the old one is already broken in and very reliable."

Gist bowed his head toward the chief in recognition of the clever metaphor. After the audience, Annosanah, Sattelihu and their Brother the Buck walked to their horses, where Croghan's servant waited. They crossed the river on the log ferries as before, this time allowing the rafts to flow with the current to the western shore of the Scionto. Here they disembarked, circumvented the small village and made ten miles along a path heading northwest toward Pickawillany. No one spoke, a fact that Gist found pleasing, as he was in no mood for conversation. He thought about his continuing trip, the Ohio Company's plans for their land grant, and his own part in the recruitment of settlers of that land. But his thoughts kept returning to Wau-thee-wee-la.

CHAPTER XI

February 1751

BOOM! BOOM! BOOM! BOOM! The retort of the guns continued for a quarter of an hour, scaring up flocks of birds and sending the woodland creatures scurrying to their usual hiding places. Such was the custom of the Twightwees when welcoming important visitors. Croghan by himself would have rated this welcome, but the added visit of Annosanah was special cause for celebration. After Croghan and his traveling companions crossed the Great Miami River, twenty traders and more than a hundred Indians greeted them with excitement. They asked if any of their compatriots had been captured, whether the Assembly's Indian policy had changed, and in what new mischief the French were involved. Croghan cajoled them, answered their questions and raised their spirits with a string of invective against the French.

"Why, should any of ye worthless buggers be taken by the Injens, we'll be marchin' up to the Miami Fort and fry them Frenchie bastards like they was bacon," Croghan exclaimed. His audience roared in approval, adding their own insults.

Without warning, the crowd hushed and parted for the King of the Twightwees. Six feet tall and light skinned, the elder chief welcomed the new arrivals, paying particular attention to Annosanah, and inviting them to his log house.

"He is Unekenemi," Montour told Gist as they approached the leader's house, "chief of the Piankeshaw tribe of the Miami Nation. He is a bold fighter and friend of the English. Three years ago he led a revolt against the French at the Miami Fort and burned it to the ground."

"What brought him here?"

"Chief Nicholas, longtime friend, told him of this abandoned Shauwanoa village called Pki-wi-le-ni, and even asked permission from them for Unekenemi to settle here. For his loyalty to the English, he is called Old Britain. He first brought sixty families here. Now, there are over 400."

"Quite an impressive town," said Gist, as he looked around at the twelve-foot high stockade amid the countless log cabins and bark-covered huts. "But there is one section with similar houses and then a different area with another kind."

"Aye, different tribes make different houses," Croghan added. "Whole villages of Weas, Wen-augh-tan-neys, Piankeshaws, and other Miami tribes have come from the Wabash to be closer to the English – meself in particular. These Twightwees be a very numerous people. 'Til last year all these tribes was under one king, Le Pied Froid. But his whole village, and others along the Wabash, up and left him to come here. Now that was the breakin' up of the most powerful Injen nation west of the English settlements."

Gist looked at Montour, wondering if the Seneca would let this statement go unchallenged.

Croghan continued with a gentle nudge in Gist's side. "Why, their strength be far greater than the Six Nations and their legends contain many stories of how they gave them Iroquois a proper thrashin' and chased 'em clean back to New York."

"The Twightwee have these legends, it is true," Montour countered. "But we of the Six Nations have true accounts of courage in battle, as we fought to push them from our hunting lands back to the Wabash."

"I would've expected ye to say somethin' like that. If what ye say be truth, why do the Iroquois allow the Twightwees into the Chain of Friendship?" Croghan was serious now.

"The Six Nations reach out the hand of friendship to all those who hate the French and love the English."

"Spoken like a true diplomat, eh Chris?"

As the procession reached the chief's small house, Gist thought of how Montour had evaded the real reason the Six Nations accepted the Miami alliance. For several years the Iroquois' influence and control over their claimed territory had been eroding. Once, tribes had asked the Iroquois for permission to hunt or live on their land. Now these same tribes were challenging the limits of that dominion. Too many of the Western Iroquois, notably the Seneca, were sympathetic to the French and the Onondoga Council no longer ruled as before.

When they were seated inside, the pipe was passed. Assessa-pansa, son of the King and war chief in his own right, placed wood on the fire at regular intervals to maintain the warmth and comfort for his aging father. At one point he attempted to pass the pipe to Unekenemi, who did not reach for it. Assessa-pansa waited with the pipe extended for ten minutes until his father awoke and took it. No apologies were offered and no impatience registered.

Montour requested an audience with all the chiefs of the village that evening. They decided that everyone should retire to prepare for the council. The travelers decorated themselves and Gist wore the leggins, breechclout and moccasins made for him by the Wyandot at Conchake.

Evening approached as one Wea, appointed for the task, toured the village to announce the beginning of the congress. Events proceeded much the same as in their many previous councils, with one major difference –

Montour spoke none of the Miami dialects. True, both Montour and the King spoke French, as did many Miami chiefs. Yet in matters of state, they preferred the subtleties and nuances of their native tongues.

Montour began in French, "Brothers the Twightwees, as we have been hindered by the high waters and other business with our Indian brothers, no doubt our long stay has caused some trouble among our brethren here. Therefore, we present you with two strings of wampum to remove all the trouble from your hearts and clear your eyes that you may see the sun shine clear, for we have much to say to you. We would have you send for one of your friends that can speak the Mohican or the Mingo tongues well, that we may understand each other thoroughly, for we have much business to do."

After Montour delivered a message of good will from the Delaware and Wyandot, the short council was over. This gave Gist time to tend to his journal that he had neglected on the route from the Lower Shawnee Town. By candlelight in one of the trader's log cabins, he began writing:

> All the Way from the Shannoah Town To this Place (except the first 20 M which is broken) is fine, rich level land, well timbered with large Walnut, Ash, Sugar Trees, Cherry Trees &c, it is well watered with a great number of little Streams or Rivulets, and full of beautiful natural Meadows, covered with wild Rye, blue Grass and Clover, and abound with Turkeys, Deer, Elks, and most Sorts of Game, particularly Buffaloes, thirty or forty of which are frequently seen feeding in one Meadow: In short it wants Nothing but Cultivation to make it a most delightful Country.

Croghan entered the cabin with an armload of wood. He placed several logs on the fire behind Gist and turned to view the journal.

"Arrah now Chris, ye wouldn't mind if I was to see what ye be writin' would ye?"

"Of course," replied Gist. "There's nothing but my observations. Uninspiring, I'd say."

Croghan leaned over Gist's shoulder and read what he had just written. From his weskit pocket Croghan pulled a short clay pipe, which he lit, and began puffing until a cloud of smoke filled the small room. "Ye underestimate yourself, Chris. Your writin'll be read by them with the means to change this territory." Gist continued writing while Croghan walked around the table to sit across from him. Croghan went on. "Now did it ever occur to ye that this was already a delightful country without cultivation?"

"What's your point, George?" said Gist, a little irritated.

"Are ye not aware that cultivation will put an end to the fur trade in these parts? Folks'll be movin' in and critters'll be movin' out. What d'ye suppose will happen to traders such as you and me?"

Gist looked up from his writing. "And I might ask you what you plan to do with your 200,000 acres around the Forks?" Before Croghan could answer, Gist continued. "I'll tell you what you're going to do. You'll pick the best spot for a home and when the settlers start coming, you'll sell the rest.

"Let me tell you something," Gist continued. "Six other companies have petitioned the Board of Trade for land this side of the mountains. I'll warrant that within ten years they'll all have settlements in the Ohio Valley. Those people will pay for that land and those who own it first will make a tidy profit. My being in on the beginning of such a plan can't do me any harm."

"Tryin' to get back to where ye once was, ey Chris?"

"Well, let's just say I'm tired of farming."

"I don't blame ye. Tell me now, how is it ye landed in North Carolina of all places?" Croghan asked.

"Well, now I don't talk about that, but I guess there's no harm in it." Gist began a brief account of his path to the present. In 1722 he was seventeen, working for the London Fur Company. They would front him the trade goods and he would go out trading among the Indians and bring back furs. His warehouse was situated down on the Baltimore docks. One night the storehouse burned down, just like his father's had several years earlier. It was no coincidence. He had his suspicions all right, but could not prove a thing. The Fur Company had little choice but to set a judgement against him for £10,000.

Croghan whistled at the figure.

"Everything I could do to pay them back, I did. Surveying jobs; I was the Baltimore County Coroner; and the whole time I was a ranger in the Baltimore County Militia, I was out hunting and trapping furs to sell. For that they brought me up on charges several times."

"So, ye were one of the Maryland Rangers?" Croghan's bushy eyebrows rose in admiration. "Aye, many's the fine tale I've heard of their fightin' and diein' to protect the settlements."

Gist smiled at the recognition. "Well, you know how much resemblance a tale has to the truth. Many a time I found myself alone with an axe, keeping the trails clear for when the militia was called. Every once in awhile, we'd get the chance to chase after a Seneca raiding party. Sometimes we got them and sometimes not. Mighty slippery, those Seneca."

"Montour'll be glad to hear that," Croghan replied.

"Then my father died and, me being the eldest son, I inherited his holdings. When the London Fur Company found out about that, I didn't have them very long. They sent a representative, you know, one of those plump clerks with pink cheeks and a powdered periwig. Said if I wanted to avoid debtors' prison, I'd sell those holdings and pay the company. I didn't see that I had much choice."

"Did that get ye close to paid off?"

"No no, I still had a ways to go. Thirteen years I spent working to pay off that debt and much of what I paid was from my father's estate." Gist shook his head in disappointment, still not quite able to believe his own story.

Gist continued, "But I had an idea. I took my brother in as a partner and we bought £2,000 worth of trade goods on credit using Nathaniel's good name. I went out among the tribes and traded for furs to ship back to England. We would have doubled our money and in two years I'd have been out of debt." Gist looked Croghan straight in the eye. "And don't you know that ship, carrying a whole year's worth of pelts, the finest deer and beaver hides you ever saw, that ship sank in a storm off Barbados."

Too many years had passed for Gist to be upset at his misfortune. But the irony of his situation always amazed him. No man had worked harder to extricate himself from financial disaster, but this last tragedy was more than he could handle. Not only had his idea shoved him farther down the line of indebtedness, but his brother had been ruined in the process. The Gists, with Christopher as their patriarch, sold their estates and moved south, through the German settlements in the Shenandoah Valley, to North Carolina on the very edge of the frontier, 500 miles from their troubles.

"Now that's quite a story. Don't suppose ye get up to Baltimore much anymore do ye?" Croghan asked with a gleam in his eye.

The comic relief was just what Gist needed and he threw back his head and laughed as he had not laughed for a long time.

For the next week, while the traders replaced the many decaying logs in the stockade, Croghan distributed Pennsylvania's presents to the chiefs and held various councils. Gist repeated his invitation to Logstown. But one event in particular allowed him to witness first hand, the commitment Unekenemi was making to the English.

On the morning of February 24th four Ottawa Indians came into town under French colors. The village chiefs assembled and escorted them into the longhouse. Unekenemi was flanked by Croghan, Montour, and Gist on one side and a Mingo interpreter on the other. Assessa-pansa and two other Twightwee chiefs, Aquen-ackqua and Navecqua, sat close by. The Ottawas sat across from the King in the place reserved for guests.

After the pipe smoking one of the emissaries presented Unekenemi with two kegs of brandy, about seven quarts each, and a ten-pound roll of tobacco. Their speaker stood up, took two strings of wampum, and began in French.

"Brother Miamis, what we have to deliver to you comes from our father, the King of France, and he desires that you hear what he has to say to you." He laid these two strings down upon the kegs and took out four others. "Your father, remembering his children, has sent you two kegs of milk and some tobacco. He has now made the road clear for you to come and join him." With a fifth string in his hand, he continued. "Your father will forget all the little differences that have passed between you and him, and desires that you should not be of two minds, but let him know your minds freely this one last time. Our father will send for you no more."

Several minutes passed, whereupon the Piankeshaw King stood and gave his reply. His voice was cool and cutting. "It is true that our French father has sent for us several times, saying the road was clear. But I say it has been made foul and bloody by him. We have cleared a road for our brothers, the English. Your father has made it bad and has taken some of our English brothers prisoners, which we look upon as having been done to us. We will no more listen to our French father!" Unekenemi walked out.

For two days the people of the Pickawillany talked of their chief's behavior toward the Ottawa messengers. No Twightwee in anyone's memory had been so rude to guests. This serious breech of custom could only be justified by Unekenemi's intense hatred for the French.

An ominous aura surrounded the council house that afternoon, but did not temper the words of the speaker. The Captain of the Warriors, Aqua-lack-qua, held four strings of black and white wampum in his hand. His voice was harsh. "Brothers the Ottawa, you are always differing with the French yourselves, and yet you listen to what they say. We will let you know by these four strings of wampum that we will not hear anything they say to us, nor do anything they bid us."

Aqua-lack-qua then pointed to a pile of goods containing six strouds and two matchcoats, and held up a string of black wampum. "These clothes are in return for your presents to us. Now you desire that we may speak our minds from our hearts, which I am going to do. You have often desired that we should go home to you at Detroit or the Miami Fort, but I tell you it is not our home, for we have made a road as far as the sea to the sun-rising and have been taken by the hand by our brothers the English and the Six Nations and the Delaware, Shauwanoa and Wyandot. We assure you it is the road we will go. You threaten us with war in the spring. We tell you that if you are angry with us, we are ready to receive you and resolve to die here before we will join you. That you may know this is our mind, we send you this string of black wampum." After a short pause, looking at the dark belt of beads as if to remember one final point, he added. "Brothers the Ottawa, you hear what I say. Tell this to your fathers the French. This is our mind and we speak it from the heart."

"Sounds like a pretty heavy commitment," Gist stated as he and Croghan walked through the village back to their quarters. Children darted across their path, yelling the scalp hallo; two young women turned to admire the visitors.

"Aye, to be sure," said Croghan as he returned their gaze and winked. "But you just watch. Soon there'll be another council and they'll be wantin' more trade goods and a blacksmith and just more attention in general."

"Ah, but this is just what we want, whole tribes loyal to the English and trading with us for their necessities, hey Croghan?"

"Arrah now, that may be so, but it'll just means more work for meself. I'll have to write Governor Hamilton and convince him to liberate more presents from the Assembly or head for Philadelphia and do it meself, and I'll have to persuade Tom Burney to move from Muskingum, out here to do their blacksmithin'."

"That'll not be easy. Burney's comfortable where he is and with a Wyandot squaw and a young one on the way."

"Aye, but I happen to know he'd practically turn hisself inside out to get away from his in-laws," Both men laughed.

"Well, if he's so anxious to go, why do you have to persuade him?"

"Why laddie, he's Irish! Ye've got to argue with him."

They were still chuckling, when they came upon the Ottawa delegation shouting angry words at Aquen-ackqua and Assessa-pansa. One Ottawa stopped his abrasive voice, held out his hands and lowered his head. His spoke in low, mournful tones. Another pointed to Gist and Croghan, accusing them of something.

Montour stood nearby, arms crossed, watching the scene. He told Gist and Croghan how one Ottawa warrior was berating the Miami for aligning with the English, while the other was lamenting the expected destruction of their nation. "They cursed the English, and pointed to you," Montour nodded toward Croghan, "for placing a log in the eye of the Twightwee people. The French, they say, will sweep down upon them like a fire in the forest and burn their village, kill their men and scatter their bones over the land where their souls will remain forever."

"Will they do it?" asked Gist.

"I believe their threat has teeth," Montour replied.

"Aye, as do I," said Croghan, "and we can do nothin' but sit by and watch. Hamilton'll not lift a finger to protect 'em," his voice echoed in the fading sunlight.

CHAPTER XII

March 1751

Icy wind blasted across the snow-covered meadow, forcing the traveler to retreat further into the fur of his buffalo robe. It was a magnificent, hairy hide, rendered soft and supple by hours of constant rubbing on the "breaking stick" as it dried from submersion in a mixture of water and the animal's brains. Une-ken-emi's wife and daughter had presented it to him on his last day at Pickawillany. He wore it with the fur side next to his body for maximum warmth. It wrapped around his husky frame, covering all his accouterments. In his arms he cradled his rifle, primed on half-cock. The gentle swaying of his horse and the warmth of the robe made it difficult to stay awake, much less alert.

When the trail south from Pickawillany crossed the Mad River, Croghan's team said their good-bye's and headed southeast back to Conchake. But Gist had to return to the Shawnee Town to finish his Ohio Company assignment. Believing that French Indians might lie in ambush for him somewhere along the way back to the Tshil-I-kau-thee town, Annosanah rode south ten miles to the Little Miami River and followed it to the southwest, away from his destination. His plan was to travel in that direction for several days and then cut back east through the woods, intersecting the same Pickawillany path he had taken to the Miami town two weeks earlier.

As Spark followed the well-worn trail, the frontiersman gazed across the mile wide prairie to view a herd of buffalo feeding on whatever grass protruded above the snow. He stopped counting at fifty and noted at least another ten or twenty scattered about. As a boy visiting Indian villages with his father, he recalled the story tellers weaving tales of vast herds of these beasts in the endless grasslands west of the Mother of all Rivers into which the Ohio flowed. These buffalo, numbering in the millions, were enough to provide every necessity of life to those people. Yet this magnificent animal was too sparse to provide for all the Indians in the East. In this land the deer provided those same requisites. To the Indian these were gifts bestowed upon them by the animals themselves.

Yet, this largess from the forest had long since been replaced by the white man's trade goods. The Miami had worn the calico shirts of the French for years; rarely was deer skin clothing found, except for the leggins. Of course the trade gun replaced the bow and arrow; thread was substituted for sinew; wool blankets displaced beautiful robes of hide like the one he now wore. The Indians' old way of life, respected and revered in tribal histories, was being supplanted by the very goods they now needed to survive.

That was the way it was, Gist reasoned to himself. English society had demanded furs since before his grandfather's time. The trader ventured into the wilderness, enduring hardship and privation, to barter with the Indian for those furs. They brought what the Indian needed to support his family and to continue the chase, as they called the task of hunting. The system worked well, until traders administered spirituous liquors without scruples. This happened often on the frontier, much to the dismay of the tribal chiefs, who could see the decadence in their warriors. Many times the Indians had petitioned the colonial governors for liquor regulation. Assemblies had passed laws, but with no means of enforcement. Conscience, or a lack thereof, ruled the trader in his dealings with the Indian. Gist was growing angry with the thought of someone like Caleb Lamb rendering the Indians raddled with rum and taking their skins for a token.

These events led to a progressive evolution away from the old ways, when the Indian was self-sufficient, to a dependency upon the white man. Gist knew he was part of that change, both as a trader and as an agent for the Ohio Company. The copper kettles, the powder and lead bars, the clothing and thread, beads and trade silver, knives and tomahawks – all these goods that he brought to the Indians – continued to encourage that dependence. He knew he could think about this situation for hours and not find the right or wrong of it, except for the liquor.

As the path curved to avoid a frozen swamp, Gist forced his thoughts to a more pleasant subject – his last days at Pickawillany. Pictures of the Warrior's Feather Dance filled his mind. A capacity crowd had stuffed itself into the longhouse; the sights and smells of bear grease and leather, tobacco and wood smoke, filled every space. Drums pounding in cadence invaded the human chatter, while a solo monotone called for silence. Three dancers, painted in brilliant blue, white and vermillion bands carried long poles with the feathers of swans and other birds woven into wing patterns at each end. They jumped about, dove up and down and waved their wings in perfect time to the music. A shining, breechclouted warrior stepped forward and struck the post with his tomahawk. Music and dancers ceased while this actor recounted his many exploits in battle. After he threw some article of appreciation to the musicians as payment, the sequence repeated itself until no more warriors rose to recite.

Gist could still hear the drums pulse on into his thoughts of the assembly on their last full day. Assessa-pansa smiled in good faith, his rich, soothing voice aimed at the white visitors. "You must now send us a blacksmith to mend our guns and hatchets. We promise never to give heed to what the

French say, but always to hear and to believe what you our brothers the English say." The drums faded as the Articles of Peace and Alliance between the English, the Wa-waugh-tan-ney and Piankeshaw were signed.

As with so many other ceremonies, the shaking of many hands marked the conclusion. Emotions, often restrained in the presence of white men, were unfettered. Faces smiled. Joy flowed like water and the whole town felt as if a damn had burst, releasing the pressure of apprehension. To be welcomed into the Covenant Chain that the English shared with the Iroquois, Delaware and a host of smaller tribes, was an honor.

It occurred to him in his fogged condition as he rode along that he had not been alone since before his journey began. Oh, he had taken brief jaunts to hunt for food, but here it was March 4th and he was a solitary figure in the wilderness.

The silence was refreshing. Much of the time in his fur trade business he rode from one Indian village to another. He enjoyed the company of others. Yet, there was something exhilarating about being companionless in a primeval woodland. You did not have to think or talk – just be. He was one with his surroundings; actions and reactions well rehearsed from years of experience in frontier travel. He was cautious, quiet, forever alert...until now.

Spark, however, was attentive. Ears perked, head high, she caught a new distant sound. A resulting tension in her muscles awakened him. The faint echo of a far off muzzle blast reached his ears and he reined to a halt. Both listened to the sporadic rumble of gunfire to the south.

"Must be a hunting party," he whispered, rubbing her neck. "Probably shooting at a buffalo herd. Might be friendly, might not, but we can't afford to find out, can we girl? Guess we'd better go another way."

He led his horse along the edge of the woods, looking for an opening in the low branches, brush and pricker bushes. A recent deadfall, having crushed the natural barricade to the forest, allowed him to slip through. Now, not only was he alone, but without a path. The going was difficult at first. Often he had to dismount to negotiate circuitous routes, consulting his compass at every turn to maintain a southeasterly direction. As he penetrated the depth of the forest with its pillars of bark and roof of intertwined branches, travel was easier. The big trees were twenty feet or more apart and visibility was good for a long way. A journey through the wilderness was safe this way, because not even Indian travelers varied from the paths.

Try as he might to think other thoughts, his imagination focused on Wau-thee-wee-la. What forbidden door had she opened in him on that last night? Dare he anticipate another? Nothing could be gained by it – nothing but a fleeting pleasure and another memory. He knew it for what it was – mere animal passion, the carnal sin, the disease for which faith in God somehow provided the cure. He must resist the temptation. Still, he could not escape his increasing expectation as he neared the town.

After three days he intersected the Pickawillany Path about thirty miles above the Shawnee Town, where he arrived that night. To a welcoming crowd of Indians and traders, he gave a short speech about the recent peace concluded between the Twightwee and the English. Hundreds of guns echoed in honor of the treaty.

Of course Miami runners had preceded him, informing the town of the recent events. Annosanah's reputation was enhanced when they learned that it was he, who had written the words of the treaty on the white man's paper. Croghan had dictated that treaty, but Gist's role earned him a place of honor in Loa-pee-ka-way's lodge.

Gist sat across from the chief as Wau-thee-wee-la served them boiled venison with a sauce made from bear fat and honey. Conversation was sparse, because of his marginal command of the language. Wau-thee-wee-la could not assist; he was on his own. But by using hand signs and the words he knew, Gist could relate the highlights of his journey. He noted the many buffalo he had seen grazing in the large meadows south of Pickawillany.

"Buffalo have great happiness close to their Indian brothers," said Loa-pee-ka-way. "They make path through the forest."

"I have heard of great herds on the big meadows toward the sun-setting," replied Gist, pointing to the west with a great sweep of his hand. "It is said that these buffalo are as many as the blades of grass."

"I too have heard this. Our brothers from that land have visited us. Many of their tales are hard to believe: spouts of boiling water as tall as the tallest oak that shoot up from the earth; empty land where painted rocks bake in the sun and nothing grows; mountains that reach to the sky and shine with the light of the sun."

Their conversation continued to focus on the wonders of nature each had seen or heard about. As the light of the fire dimmed to glowing embers, Loa-pee-ka-way, with apologies, announced a necessary errand and left the warmth of his bark-covered house. Wau-thee-wee-la appeared with several small logs that she placed on the coals. She knelt where her father had sat and gazed at the lambent tongues of flame encouraged by the new arrivals. Her dark shadow danced on the wall behind her. Straight black hair reached the floor.

He was enjoying the mood he felt sure she was trying to create. Her mild flirtation excited him and he ached to hold her again. "Annosanah is speaker of true words," she said, raising her head and looking him in the eye. "Is it true about the many buffalo and the land of the shining mountains?"

"I have not seen it," he replied, "but I believe it is so." He knew she was just making conversation and he answered several more questions like this. Her brown eyes watched him and widened at his response. She giggled at a humorous comment and rocked to and fro sending her shadow gliding in tandem behind her. He fought to keep from reaching for her.

With some sense of the need to gain control of the situation, Gist spoke, "I have not heard about your mother," embarrassed at not having asked before.

"She is dead of the white man's pox," she lowered her head and stared at the fire.

Gist knew she meant smallpox. "I'm sorry."

"Will you stay with our people long?" she raised her eyes for his answer.

"No, I must leave soon. My journey takes me to the Falls of Ohio and then home to my people."

"Your family," her eyes returned to the fire, "your woman?"

"Yes."

"Will you come to our people again?"

"Knowing the future is hard, but I believe I will be part of this land for many seasons."

With no warning she blurted out, "I cannot come to you tonight, Annosanah. My father says it was right at first, but now if I cannot be your woman, it would be wrong and I do not understand." Tears glistened on her cheeks.

Gist's heart sank. He contemplated his response and wound up saying, "your father is wise. I cannot take you as my wife and there is no future in our union now."

The spell was broken as Loa-pee-ka-way entered, as if he were listening outside and picked that moment to enter. His daughter left the fire without a word and retired to the deeper recesses of the hut.

"We have sorrow to see you go, Annosanah."

"I will keep the memories of this visit in my heart," Gist replied, placing his right fist over his heart.

"Tomorrow I will take you to a Mingo chief, who has just returned from the Falls of Ohio. He can advise you on the safest way to go."

The two men bid each other a goodnight and Gist retired to his assigned sleeping house. Fresh pine boughs lay under a buffalo hide, giving him the softest bed he had known in weeks. Sleep was almost immediate, relieving him of thoughts about Bright Horn.

Gist spent the next several days preparing for his continued journey. The Mingo chief informed him of a hunting party of French Indians at the Falls. "If you go there, they will kill you or carry you off. They now have heard of Annosanah and would consider it a great honor to take you."

In spite of the warning, he continued his preparations. Perhaps the hunting party would be gone by the time he arrived; he was prepared to follow the Company's instructions. He had a long way to go, with greater difficulty than he had encountered so far. The Mingo told him that the land south of the Ohio held few people, meaning fewer well-worn paths. The hills were so steep and vegetation so dense, that travel was a formidable challenge.

Yet, Gist was anxious to be the first white man to explore this expanse of untamed land. He sensed the importance of this honor, one he was determined to deserve.

On this last night before his departure, Annosanah lay under the buffalo robe thinking thoughts of the journey ahead and his obligations to the Company, trying to suppress fantasies of Wau-thee-wee-la. This could be the last time he visited this place; or if he could return, by that time she would be married. He was not ready to live with the Indians, take a wife among them and leave behind the white man's world. He could not be Annosanah all the time.

He heard soft footsteps right before the deerskin door to his we-gi-wa opened and Bright Horn stepped in. She said not a word, but went straight to the fire and knelt, head bowed, back arched. Christopher looked at her from under his buffalo robe and blanket. The room had grown colder as the fire faded and she put on more wood. Her eyes remained downcast, as if unsure of her welcome. As he raised the corner of his robe, she accepted the invitation and snuggled in beside him. For a time none of it mattered.

On the morning of departure, Wednesday, March 14th, Loa-pee-ka-way brought Annosanah a small token of friendship – a full-grown Paroquete. He was a foot in length, body in multiple shades of green, head a bright, canary yellow. Although they were wild and plentiful along the river, this one's yellow-tipped wings were clipped. It even mimicked a few short Shawnee lines about being hungry, thirsty and when someone was coming.

So, on a westward reaching river path, rode a more seasoned Gabriel, followed by two pack horses and a weathered Christopher Gist with a Paroquete on his shoulder.

CHAPTER XIII

May 1751

"Hey old man!" Gist called to the stranger, who was hurrying toward one of the homes in the settlement near his plantation. At first the man did not answer, but Gist cantered his horse a bit until he was nearly on top of him. "Hey you, stop!"

The man stopped, forcing Gist to ride on by and make a turn to face him. The man showed fear at first, but then beamed a smile of recognition. Gist saw that it was deaf old Delaney.

"Top o' the mornin' Gist," he yelled. "Heard ye was gone a spell. Made it back, did ye?"

"Mr. Delaney, where's my family?" Gist yelled back just as loud. "I've just been to my home and no one's there."

"No one there, eh? Well, not surprised. Injen trouble this winter, ye know? Killed five near here, they did. Didn't know 'em though. Terrible what they done to 'em . . ."

"Mr. Delaney, where's my family?"

"Yes, yes, well, frightened away by that, they was. All went to Rowan Court House. Most of us did for a time, ye know. Just got back myself. Lotta repairs need tendin . . ."

"Thanks for your help. Give my best to the misses."

"Oh, she's not about now, poor thing. Lord took her this winter... yes...sure are a lotta repairs need doin' when you been away awhile. Ye know, I can't find my . . ."

Gist left the old man in self-conversation and struck a path for Rowan. He was anxious to find his family and the rest of his kin. Late in the night, at the little settlement of Rowan Court House forty miles southeast of his home, he found Sarah, daughters, Nancy and Violetta, and youngest son, Thomas. The next day the extended family came from whomever's home had taken them in. Laughter and gaiety went on into the night, as Gist and Gabriel sought to best each other at telling the most entertaining story of their journey. Gabriel won with his tale of the drunken trader and the Milky Way.

Gist then told of their trip home from the Falls, which they did not get to see. As they neared the Falls, the hunting party of French Indians was still evident. Guns fired, recent moccasin tracks abounded and freshly set traps were everywhere. The risk of capture seemed great. Remembering what Cresap said about the feasability of settlements there, Gist decided, with regret, to leave exploration of that area for another time.

He and Gabriel set out easily for the first few days, ascending the nearest mountains to determine the best course. Still, it was a grueling passage. The banks of the many streams were so steep they had to follow them for miles to find a crossing. They spent entire days cutting through the dense entanglement of laurel thickets. Scarce food in barren sections of the mountains weakened the horses and incessant rains made the trails slippery.

On one precarious path Gist's horse fell, pulling down the packhorse tailed up with it. Both horses were bruised, but the poor Paroquete plummeted from Gist's shoulder and tumbled down the mountainside until he rolled up against a rock. By the time they could reach him, he had spoken his last Shawnee word. It had taken them two months to fight Kanta-Ke wilderness south of the Ohio and now on this May 19th they were happy to be home.

When at last the party ended, Christopher and Sarah walked alone under the moonlight and the Milky Way.

"Where did you hear that story about the Milky Way?" she asked, holding his hand and swinging it back and forth.

"It's a Cherokee legend. Is that where Nathaniel is again?"

"He spends more time among them than he does his own kind." She sounded annoyed.

"How old is that boy again, I can never remember? Is it eighteen or nineteen?"

"Nathaniel turned nineteen a month after you left."

"Well, I feel fairly proud of him. He's better at being an Indian than I was at his age. He picks up the Indian speech quicker than a dog does fleas. I've always had trouble there myself."

"Tomorrow we should move back to the Yadkin. I'll need to be in Williamsburg by the middle of June to deliver this journal. Until then I must make a map of my journey, and if I know those Ohio Company boys, there'll be more to do."

Gist remembered what Cresap said about a settlement on the Ohio Company land grant and recruiting families for it. Then the Logstown conference, to which he had invited the Ohio Indians, loomed somewhere in the future. It was already past spring and he wondered how long it could be postponed. Still, he felt it prudent to avoid a lengthy explanation until he had more details. He did not want to upset Sarah on his second night home.

With two wagons loaded full of personals and food stuffs, they spent several days relocating. In fact the whole clan was on the move. When it was over and Gist and Sarah were alone, she asked the question, "Chris, what did you mean when you said those Ohio Company boys will have more for you to do?"

So he told her what he knew – the plans relayed to him by Cresap so many months ago. For a brief period, when he would return to lead his people to the Promised Land of the Ohio Country, he and Sarah would be together. Beyond that . . .

"I understand," she began, "that this venture with the Ohio Company is what you want. What about what I want?" She swung around to face him and continued. "How can I put any more work into our home here, when I know you'll just come back some day and take us to another place where I'll have to start over again for the third time?" She trembled, "and what if you don't come back? How will I manage this plantation with all my children gone?"

Christopher pulled her to him, "shhh," he whispered, rubbing her back. It felt tense, more bony than he remembered. "I'll return to take everyone."

"Christopher Gist!" she interrupted, pushing him away to arms' length. "You promise me! Promise me you'll come back for me. Don't leave me out here to die!"

He held her, surprised at her plea. "I have no intention of leaving you here. I promise you I'll come for you." How much taller she was than War-thee-wee-la.

The week flew by as Gist divided his time between his journal, the map, and his family. Soon his inner voice was calling him to Williamsburg. Once more he and Gabriel packed their horses, said goodbye, and rode away.

The Ohio Company reviewed his work with satisfaction, but the lands he recommended west of the Ohio would not do. Too far away, they said. The Company wanted more information, and on July 16th provided him with another set of instructions. Again he was to draw from Cresap whatever horses and supplies he needed for a second trip. This time his journey would begin by finding the most direct route from the Company storehouse at Will's Creek to a landing on the Monongahela by the mouth of Redstone Creek. Secondly, he was to explore the land south of the Ohio River, down to its confluence with the Great Kanawha.

Furthermore, he would continue inviting any Indians he might see to the same Logstown conference he had invited them to during his first trip. George Croghan had already held his meeting with the Iroquois and chiefs of the Delaware, Shawnee and Wyandot. "Our brothers of Pennsylvania have kindled a fire here at Logstown and expect our Brother, the Governor of Virginia, to send his speeches here," they said. Virginia had sent presents but no representative. The Company thought it better to wait until it had decided on which tract of land it wanted to buy. It was Gist's task to let the Indians know their invitation had been accepted. The new date was set to coincide with the month of the planting moon, May, the following year.

On November 4, 1751, pursuant to his instructions, Christopher Gist left from the Ohio Company storehouse in Frederick County, Virginia opposite the mouth of Will's Creek. Besides Gabriel, he was joined by his son, Nathaniel.

March 1752

The trio had spent the last four months hunting and scouting the proscribed territory. Not wanting to pass up the opportunity for profit, they carried a sizeable number of furs on their way home. Their last assignment was to find the best path from Redstone Old Fort on Monongahela to Will's Creek. Amid the ruins of an ancient Indian earthwork at the mouth of Redstone Creek, they made camp. The Gists took advantage of Gabriel's cooking and continued their conversation.

"Now, let's just face facts here, Nate. You've been lounging around too much in those warm southern winters with the Cherokee and can't take a real winter up here. That's why your feet got frostbit back in December." Gist teased his son.

The tiny fire was encircled by three small pots anxiously awaiting their water to boil. Hot cocoa would be a welcome treat on this drizzling evening. Earlier that month at one of the Delaware hunting camps they visited, Gabriel reported overhearing threats to their safety. Since then the travelers kept their rifles always nearby and maintained a low profile.

"Well, that's a might be," continued Nathaniel, "but lest you be doubtin' my skills as a woodsman, might I remind you who it was shot that elk at 150 yards?"

"Ye gads son, I don't know how you could have missed. There were thirty of them."

"Massa Gist," Gabriel wispered.

"I know," said Christopher. "I've been hearing him for a while. An Indian who makes that much noise wants to be heard." Just the same, he reached for his rifle and put the hammer on half-cock.

"No shootin' me now," called a voice from the darkness. "Joshua comin' in now."

Gist recognized the English-speaking Delaware, whom he had known for several years. Back in December, they met him at the camp of another Delaware chief, Oppa-my-luca, not far from their present location. Gist told them about the conference and had Joshua deliver the same message to Tamaque, the Beaver, as the English called him, an important chief among the Delaware.

"Joshua, come in and warm yourself by our fire," Gist extended the invitation.

After the usual amenities, Joshua got to his assigned task. "Annosanah, two of our great and wisest chiefs, Tamaque and Oppa-my-lucah desire to know the answer to this question. The French claim all the land on one side of the River Ohio and the English claim all the land on the other; where does the Indian's land lie? It is the same question asked by Oppa-my-lucah earlier and you did not answer. Oppa-my-lucah wishes to know your answer."

Gist looked at his son and his servant and ran his thick fingers through his graying hair. Joshua could not have asked a more difficult question. How could he answer? He was scouting land the Ohio Company planned to settle, thus assuming it was company land on which to do so. The first settlement west of the mountains was his responsibility. But had not the Wyandots at Conchake invited him to come and build a fort and bring guns to defend them against the French. Besides, the Ohio Company was willing to pay the Indians well for the half-million acres granted to them by the King. Was that not recognition enough that the Indians owned the land?

But it was premature to reveal these plans to the chiefs. The words of his father came to mind. He was an admirer and acquaintance of William Penn, the first Quaker Governor of Pennsylvania, who applied Christian principles in dealing with the Delaware and other tribes. He was much loved and respected for it. Gist's father often quoted Penn. What was it he used to say?

"Joshua, my friend," Gist began in a relaxed tone, "we are all one King's people and the different color of our skin makes no difference in his subjects. You are his people as well as we. If you will take land and pay the King's rights, you will have the same privileges as the white people have. And to hunt, you have liberty everywhere, so long as you don't kill the white man cattle and other domestic animals."

"Annosanah." Joshua said after having listened, "I will take your words to my chiefs. At the end of two days, I will return to this place on Monongahela and tell you what they say." Then, he was gone.

No one wished to break the silence. The fire crackled, an owl hooted in the distance.

"Massa Gist," Gabriel ended the silence, "One time I asked de same question 'bout who own dis land. Why you don just give him de same answer?"

"Well Gabriel," Gist said with a deep sigh, "the Delaware chiefs already know the answer. Many times they have said it is their land, given to them by the Creator. Had I said that, they would have laughed. Indians know that white men don't believe such things and we could have been in serious trouble. Neither would it bode well for us if I had mentioned Virginia's sea-to-sea charter. So, I had an idea."

He told them about his father's beliefs that Indians and whites could live together in harmony, and how his father quoted William Penn, when it came to Indian policy. Penn's famous treaty with the Delaware included a passage similar to the words he gave Joshua.

"Indian memory being what it is," Gist continued, "their chiefs will recognize the similarity of my words with those of Penn. We should be safe.

I've been worried at times, whether the Indians would challenge us for collecting so many furs these past months. If they accept my answer, I won't concern myself any longer."

He knew they would accept his answer. And he felt a faint pang of guilt at having contrived his answer to fit the situation. Was he not Annosanah, speaker of true words? Yet true words could sometimes get you killed.

He could see the problem. Being the first settlement across the mountains might be acceptable, if the whites were willing to behave as his father and William Penn did. Yet Gist knew this was unrealistic. Maybe he could control the people recruited for his settlement, but no others, and there would be others. More villages would mean many pioneers and among them, people who hated Indians.

On the evening of the second day Joshua returned as promised. As before, they sat around the small fire as Joshua told them of his journey. He was happy to announce they were all quite safe.

"Annosanah, you may come and live among us or along this river, or wherever you please. The great chiefs like you. You answer them true, for we are all one King's people sure enough."

But Gist knew it was a lie. William Penn may have believed it and Richard Gist may have been sincere, but he, himself, no longer believed it possible for Indians and whites to live together in harmony. There would just never be enough people on the frontier who felt this way; not enough to make a difference. They would not be "all one King's people." His own feelings aside, he had to face the fact that the members of the Ohio Company were motivated by profit and naught else. What had before been complex was now quite simple. If the displacement of these Indian People were the target, he was the point of the arrow. Sure, the Indians had moved away from the white man in the Colonies in the past. That was why they were here. But it was all supposed to stop at the mountains. Now he knew it would not.

CHAPTER XIV

May-June 1752

Three canoes, English colors flying from their bows, approached the landing. Blasts from a hundred rifles announced the arrival of Cono-gar-iera, the representative from the Onondaga Council, appointed to guard the Iroquois interests in this, the Logstown Treaty. Then came the Mingo chiefs from the various Iroquois tribes that had relocated to the Ohio country. They disembarked and moved toward one of the many rough-hewn log cabins that gave the town its name.

The most dignified among them, though, was not the Onondoga chief, but another, taller, wearing a lace-trimmed tricorn. He strutted along, allowing the others to plow a row through the crowd to the opened door. Tanacharison, Half-King, the Oneida chief sent by Onondaga to watch over the Ohio Indians, had arrived. He had, no doubt, planned this dramatic entrance to occur well after the Virginia commissioners had arrived. Four days earlier, along with the Virginians, came £1,000 worth of presents. Perhaps these would assuage the anger many Indians felt toward the colony.

Christopher Gist, the only Company member to sit at the council, had preceded the commissioners by several weeks, making sure to meet Andrew Montour well before this conference. A new Governor Dinwiddie, recent Ohio Company member, was unable to guarantee its interests. Joshua Fry led the commissioners appointed by a Virginia legislature unsympathetic to Ohio Company goals. In fact two of the commissioners were opposed, because of their connections to competing land companies. They all wanted land. Gist was there to insure the Company got its share.

His first task was to learn Indian sentiment toward the goals of the conference. Those were the confirmation of the Treaty of Lancaster in 1744, and permission to build a settlement beyond the bounds of the current white population. To confirm the Treaty, the commissioners had to tell the Indians what the Six Nations had signed eight years earlier. At that time the Iroquois believed they were ceding to Virginia only those lands peopled by Virginians west to the Blue Ridge, where lay one of the warriors' paths. Virginians beyond this line, those in the Shenandoah Valley, must leave, or be willing to share their bounty with passing Iroquois war parties.

The colonial delegates, on the other hand, had different words. Their deed recognized the King's right to all the lands that are or ever shall be within the Colony of Virginia.

Virginia also wanted permission to build a settlement. When the Board of Trade first received the Company's application, England was still enmeshed in a war with France. Their grant was contingent upon the erection of a fort for the protection of the settlement. Peace now prevailing, the Company had asked for relief from that proscription.

Because the Company could not be sure of the commissioners' success, it gave Gist private instructions:

> If you find the Commissioners do not make a general Agreement, you are then to endeavor to make purchase of the Lands to the Eastward of the Ohio River and Allagany, and procure the Friendship and protection of the Indians. You are to engage Andrew Montour the interpreter in the Company's Interest and get him to assist you in making purchase of the Indians' Lands, and as the Company have great dependance and confidence in the said Montour, they hereby promise to make him satisfaction for the trouble, and let him have a handsome Settlement upon their land without paying any purchase money.

The Indians held discussions among themselves for five days after the arrival of Tanacharison. The Commissioners waited. Messengers called on various Delaware, Shawnee and Wyandot chiefs for consultation. The commissioners waited. On the 10th of June, much to everyone's relief, the Indians appointed a delegation of sachems to treat with the Virginians.

Virginia's presents were piled high. Colorful wool blankets, ribbon-edged breechclouts, calico shirts, kegs of powder, kegs of rum, smooth bore trade guns, lead bars, copper kettles and a host of other goods upon which the tribes had become dependent – all made an impressive array in front of the longhouse. Governor Dinwiddie's instructions were specific about displaying the gifts at the onset. Passing them out after a conference was normal, but here, a good look before hand might soften Indian resolve. The array sat surrounded by several lean-tos, their roofs of green leafy branches contrasting with the browns and grays of the log buildings. These provided some relief from the heat for the delegates. Spectators crowded the sunny spaces between and around the lean-tos, their collective voices filling the air.

"Sachems and warriors of the Six United Nations," began Joshua Fry with sweeping arm gestures to include those Iroquois and Mingo chiefs sitting in the shade, "our friends and brethren." With these last words he nodded to the contingents of Delaware, Shawnee and Wyandot, who comprised most of the crowd.

Each faction had its own interpreter. Andrew Montour repeated Fry's first words to the Iroquois sachems in their native tongue. Fry continued. "We are glad to meet you at this place to enlarge the council fire kindled here by our brethren of Pennsylvania, to brighten the chain and renew our friendship, that it may last as long as the sun, the moon and the stars shall give light, to confirm which, we give you a string of wampum."

As Montour translated, one of the commissioners scribed the proceedings. Gist sat next to him, thankful it was not his job to write the account. He did not mind writing those journals for his two trips into the Ohio territory. Yet, keeping up with a translator, remembering what was said, listening to the speaker, was more than he cared to do. Now he could focus on the speakers, their mannerisms and facial expressions.

"Brethren, at the Treaty of Lancaster in the year . . . " Mr. Fry went on to explain what the deed actually said. Gist thought of the wisdom Fry showed in acknowledging the debt to Pennsylvania. On the day of the commissioners' arrival, George Croghan called the Indians and whites alike into the longhouse. In his speech he recommended that they welcome the "brethren of Virginia kindly." This was a change, considering that the Pennsylvania traders, many of whom were in residence at that very moment, were the "bad birds" whispering all manner of evil against the Virginians. Gist wondered at Croghan's sanction.

Fry droned on. "Brethren, it is the design of the King, our Father, to make a settlement of British subjects on the southeast side of the Ohio, that we may be united as one people by the strongest ties of neighborhood and friendship, and by these means be able to withstand the insults of our enemies."

It sounded good, Gist had to admit. Fry was using all the right words, saying all the right things. Yet, Gist thought he detected a lack of sincerity. His gestures seemed a bit too stiff. If he felt it, the Indians would also.

"Brethren, be assured that the King, our Father, by purchasing your lands, had never any intention of taking them from you, but only that we might live together as one people and keep away the French who would be bad neighbors."

Although this concept did not make any sense to the common English settler, Gist knew it did to the Indians. To them, the whites had purchased the right to use the land. In a reality all too familiar to the Indians, land once sold became forfeit. He doubted whether the Indian delegates believed Fry's statement. He tensed for their reaction.

When Montour finished translating that sentence, some of the Indian delegates looked at one another. Tanacharison appeared unaffected by the remark.

Fry continued. The English monarch was not like the French King, who planned to take possession of their country. Did he not send an armed force to bury lead plates claiming all Ohio land for France? That was just three years ago. Had not the French threatened the Shawnees and the Twightwees in an attempt to weaken their alliance?

"We earnestly exhort you not to be drawn away by the empty, deceitful speeches of the French, the peculiar talent of that cunning people, but in all their attempts to shake your duty to our common father, think on what real acts of friendship have been done by the English and what by the French. Weigh these things in your mind and then determine who best deserves your esteem and regard, for it is not by vain, unmeaning words that true friendship is discovered."

For another fifteen minutes, Fry dragged on about the first meeting between Indians and whites and how they took hold of the English ships and tied them to their strongest trees – steadfast and loyal friends forever.

Sweat ran down Gist's forehead past his bushy eyebrows into his eyes. He unknotted the scarf from his neck and wiped his brow. He feared the commissioners had failed. Now what chance did he have to negotiate for the Company, after Fry's patronizing disposition. Then again, perhaps the Indians were so accustomed to this scenario, that they expected such treatment. He would await the Iroquois reply.

After Joshua Fry finished, the presents were distributed. Warriors appointed for the task removed them. Within minutes not a single trade good was visible.

Tanacharison stood beside the Interpreter. Raising a ten-row belt of wampum above his head, the audience voiced its awe and approval. He lowered the belt and turned to face Montour. Croghan stepped up to translate for the commissioners.

"Child, remember that you are one of our own people and have transacted a great deal of business among us. You are employed by our brethren of Pennsylvania and Virginia as interpreter between us and our brethren, which we are well pleased at, for we are sure that justice will be done on both sides. But you are not interpreter only, for you are one of our council, having equal right with us to all these lands. You may transact any public business on behalf of us, the Six Nations, for we look upon you as much as any of the chief councillors. To confirm what we have said we present you with this belt of wampum."

The Half-King now stood beside Croghan, and held a string of wampum. "Brethren, it is a great while since our brother, the Buck, has been doing business between us and our brothers of Pennsylvania, and we understand he does not intend to do any more at this time. So I now inform you that he is approved of by our council at Onondaga, for we sent word to them of how much he has helped us in our councils here. We wish to let you and him know that he is one of our people and shall help us still and be one of our council. I deliver him this string of wampum."

He turned to face the Shawnees and produced a tomahawk from his belt.

Holding it aloft with a long string of black wampum, he told them that he was taking the hatchet from them and was tying them up with strings of black wampum. They could war no more against the Cherokee. Turning toward the Delaware, he did likewise. "I take the hatchet from you," his voice boomed so everyone could hear. "You belong to me and I think you are to be ruled by me. And I, joining with your brethren of Virginia, order you to go to war no more."

One issue remained. Some years back, the Six Nations had complained that the traders brought in too much spiritus liquor and charged an exorbitant price for it. Conrad Weiser had answered by delivering a belt of wampum and telling the Indians to pay no more than five buckskins for a keg. The traders all agreed on this price.

"Since that time," Tanacharison continued, "there has been double the quantity brought out yearly and sold as formerly. We have made our complaints since to try to stop such large quantities from being brought in, but as there has been no action taken to prevent it, we believe Mr. Weiser spoke from his mouth and not from his heart and without the Governor's authority. So, we think it proper to return this belt."

The restlessness of the crowd signaled the end of the day's conference. As the shadows lengthened, participants retired to their respective camps and lit their cooking fires. Soon the sweet smell of roasting venison filled the air as Montour, Croghan and Gist discussed the day's events.

"And why d'ye suppose Andrew, here, gets a ten-row belt, while meself must be satisfied with a string of beads?" Croghan nudged Gist while pointing to Montour.

"My guess," Gist answered, "is he took you down a notch or two and rewarded you in the new position."

"You trade with the Ohio Indians," Montour interrupted, "and make it possible for them to keep their independence from Onondoga. This makes it hard for the Half-King to influence them. He is an important sachem to his own people, but here, among these tribes, he is like a shadow that must have its sun to be seen."

"You mean he has no authority, except that derived from Onondoga," Gist said.

"Arrah now, to the English, he be half a king, and to Logstown, even less. He resents it, so he diminishes me with the string."

"And what do you make of him taking away the hatchet?" Gist asked.

"To be sure now," answered Croghan, "he's making spectators out of 'em."

"He wants something, I'll wager," continued Gist. "He knows how much we want his consent for that settlement, especially since, according to Fry, Britain has no intention of taking the land we bought."

"He may figure we'll go around him and negotiate with the individual

Ohio tribes. The Half-King makes himself whole by diminishing the Ohio Tribes," Montour remarked. "The Shauwanoa and Delaware who live there, now have no voice."

"Will the Half-King confirm the Treaty?" asked Gist.

"Aye, we'll not be knowin' till the morrow."

Another sweltering day greeted the conference; participants assumed their positions. The Half-King had exchanged his tricorn for an elaborate gustoweh, a traditional headdress with feathers and spikes protruding from a wool hat decorated with quill-work.

"Brother Assarquoa," he began. "You acquainted us yesterday with the King's right to all lands in Virginia as far as it is settled and further from thence to the sun setting. We are well acquainted that our chief council at the Treaty of Lancaster confirmed a deed to you for a quantity of land in Virginia which you have a right to. We assure you we are willing to confirm anything our council has done in regard to the land, but we never understood, before you told us yesterday, that the lands then sold were to extend further to the sun setting than the hill on the other side of the Allegheny hill, so we cannot give you an answer now."

Gist sat in the same spot with another day's worth of sweat beginning to accumulate. He listened to the Half-King just say the Lancaster Treaty could not be confirmed at this time. Yet in view of last night's discussion, perhaps he would bargain.

"We are sure the French design nothing else but mischief. We therefore desire our brethren of Virginia to build a strong house at the forks of the Ohio to keep such goods, powder, lead and necessaries as shall be wanting."

Well, Gist thought to himself, at least they're granting us a stockaded trading post complete with arsenal. It was a start.

The speeches ended early, raising more questions than answers. In response, the Virginians requested a private audience that evening to clarify the notion of whether a strong house might include a settlement of people. Tanacharison, however, said it did not. They appealed. At a settlement they could make and trade goods to the Indians far cheaper than what could now be obtained. He would not be swayed.

At the end of their meeting, Tanacharison added, "It must be remembered that I always speak the sentiments of others and not my own." Montour translated while the Half-King walked away, leaving the puzzled listeners to wonder at his meaning.

"He is telling us," said Montour after the others advanced their theories, "that he must say certain things because of the presence of Cono-gar-iera."

"How can we give him a reason to grant us a settlement?" Gist asked. "Montour, you know him best."

"Annosanah, you already know how. Your British officials always offer certain incentives to Iroquois chiefs to promote negotiations. Unlike Englishmen, however, we do not desire these things to accumulate wealth; we value them for the prestige they bring us among our people."

"I see. Then why not approach Cono-gar-iera and the others in private and offer them large tracts of land within the Company's grant. Montour, you're the only one who can do this. Ask him for another private audience, but this time with just you and the Iroquois sachems. Suggest to the chiefs that they could sign an agreement to be confirmed by Onondaga later."

"That means another conference," said Montour.

"The Governor has already planned another one at Winchester next summer," Gist replied. "I say we try it. We don't have much choice. This whole thing revolves around land. I'll bet that's why you're assisting us with such enthusiasm, ey George?"

"Arrah now, Chris, I'm on me way to financial ruin this very minute. The French and their bloody Indians have forced all me traders out and captured me trade goods. By God, if the Irish luck don't change soon, I'll be settin' foot in Philadelphia just to see the innards of debtors' prison. So ye see, all I have now is that land grant I showed ye. If ye can get the sachems and Montour a grant, maybe ye can help me keep mine."

"If you were to come and work for Virginia, perhaps that could be arranged," Gist said with a smile.

Croghan waved the statement away. "There be one more minor detail ye might be overlookin'. Ye can get approval from all the Iroquois in the world, but it'll not be them that's livin' here," Croghan reminded them. "Delaware and Shawonese'll not take too kindly to settlers."

Gist addressed the question to Montour. "Will the local tribes abide by Onondaga?"

"Eight years ago, yes," Montour replied. "Now it is hard to say. Neither tribe has a strong leader, nor have they openly complained about having the hatchet taken away. So maybe they will listen."

"Again, I say we have no choice," Gist said. "We have to tell Fry and the commissioners. The Ohio Company can't grant that acreage, without their knowledge and approval. I'll tell them at once."

Montour acknowledged the plan and went in search of the sachems.

Two days later Tanacharison addressed the commissioners. "Brothers, we have heard what you said in regard to the King's design of making a settlement of his people on the waters of the River Ohio. You likewise told us that you had a deed for those lands signed by our council at the Treaty of Lancaster. We assure you of our willingness to agree to what our council has done, but we have not the full power in our hands here in Ohio. We must acquaint our council at Onondaga of the affair and whatsoever they bid us do we will do."

"In regard to your request of building a strong house at the forks of Ohio, you told us it would require a settlement to support it with provisions and necessaries. It is true, but we, ourselves, will take care that there shall be no scarcity of that kind until we can give you a full answer."

Tanacharison gave Fry three strings of wampum to emphasize the last point. After translating this, Montour asked the Half-King for a private meeting. He agreed. Montour led the procession – Tanacharison, three Mingo chiefs, Cono-gar-iera, and the three commissioners – into the longhouse.

Crowd noise intensified as many speculated upon the outcome. Delawares and Shawnees would resent a white settlement, but the Half-King had taken away their voice. Both nations complained of the Iroquois selling their lands in Pennsylvania, often forcing them to relocate. And, as always, the Iroquois sachems lived far away and would be little affected.

A half-hour later the delegates returned. As they regained their lean-tos, Montour told Gist that they were satisfied in the matter and willing to sign and seal the writing. The commissioners produced the document confirming the Lancaster Treaty. Tanacharison guaranteed that the tribes would not molest settlements on the southeast side of the Ohio river and would protect the British subjects therein. After all the representatives had signed or marked the document, Tanacharison made a final speech for all to hear.

"Brethren, we have traveled through a long and dark way to meet you at this council. We have now completed our business with pleasure and satisfaction, both to you and us and as we now return back, we do so in the name of the great King, your father, as also in the name of your brother, the Governor of Virginia, remove all obstacles out of the way and make clear the road between us."

Countless amenities and much pumping of hands signified the end of the treaty. Both the Virginians and the Ohio Company got what they wanted. Gist had no time to rejoice. He did what he had to do and he could not rest. His list was endless: find the exact site of the settlement; survey it; begin building; transfer his family; recruit more families; improve the road from Wills Creek to the settlement; and it went on.

At that moment Christopher Gist could say he was happy. He was in his element, with tasks to perform. Those daily hardships he endured on the frontier, he perceived as challenges to be overcome. Gist chose this life over a more civilized existence. Potential conflict between Indians and whites because of the settlement was far in the future. What was not a short term concern was long range and he could not worry about it. He was ready for the next phase in the Ohio Company Plan.

"Might I ask where ye be off to now?" Croghan's inquiry did not surprise Gist. He knew the Irishman would report to Pennsylvania's governor on the progress of the Company.

"Philadelphia, I think, to recruit settlers for the Company lands." What could it hurt to tell him the truth. The Pennsylvanians would find out soon anyway. "Then back to survey a settlement and begin building. Sure you don't want to come along? I can get you a letter of license to protect you from your creditors."

"Aye, thank ye no, but I will invite ye to me Pine Creek land, bein' the Iroquois grant, just south of here by a few miles. Then I must away to me home at Aughwick for supplies."

"I declare George, you have as many estates as the King of England."

"Arrah now, I did, if ye include me tradin' houses at Conchake, Pick's Town and Shawonese Town. But I fear they be lost for some time."

"Perhaps, but the Ohio Company settlement and strong house may alter the balance and keep the French at bay. Your trade would be restored then." He hoped he was right about that. A fort and settlement would show the French and Indians that Colonial resolve to defend their land was alive.

They traversed the ten miles to Pine Creek. Here Croghan delighted in showing his house, out-buildings, pastures with contented grazing horses and ten acres of cornfield complete with fencing.

Two weeks later, as Gist prepared for his Philadelphia journey, a young warrior, christened "Powell" by the whites arrived with news from Pickawillany. Sixteen days earlier, he said, a force of 300 French and Indians – Ottawa and Potawatomi – led by Charles de Langlade, had descended upon that village. They burned the town, killed the resident English traders and many of the Miami inhabitants. As punishment for his defiance, Unekenemi was killed, his body cut into pieces, boiled and eaten by the conquering tribes.

They stared in disbelief as Powell told of the horrific deed. Gist remembered Old Britain's anger, his refusal to listen to the French emissaries, the ominous Ottawa warning. Was this a prelude to a grand conflict between the English and the French, or just a local score the French had to settle with a recalcitrant Piankeshaw sachem? Gist knew that his side had to gain a victory soon. It need not be a battle. A reasonable show of force and resolve would even the scales.

PART TWO

"As to the Summons you send me to retire, I do not think myself obliged to obey it; whatever may be your Instructions, I am here by Virtue of the Orders of my General; and I intreat you, Sir, not to doubt one Moment, but that I am determin'd to conform myself to them with all the Exactness and Resolution which can be expected from the best Officer."

Legardeur de St. Piere   Commandeur sur
La Riviere au Beuf

CHAPTER XV

November 1753

"Fathers, I am come to tell you of your own speeches; what your own mouths have declared. Father, you in former days, set a silver basin before us, wherein there was the leg of a beaver, and desired of all Nations to come and eat of it in peace and plenty, and not be churlish to one another, and that if any such person should be found to be a disturber . . ."

They crowded the marquis tent. Christopher Gist sat cross-legged on the ground. Two candles, each in their own silver candlesticks, sat on either side of his knees illuminating his writing paper, inkwell and feather pen. He scratched the speech with the speed of a bug darting across the paper, ink specks flying as he jerked the pen from it's well, blotches here and there. Here he was doing exactly what he hated; writing fast to keep up with a translator and having to remember what was said.

"Now Fathers, it is you who are the disturbers in this land. We kindled a fire a long time ago at a place called Montreal, where we desired you to stay and not to come and intrude upon our land. I now desire you to dispatch to that place, for be it known to you that this land is ours and not yours."

The speaker stopped and looked at Tanacharison, who then continued his story in the Oneida tongue. He sat motionless with eyes closed in total concentration, recalling the speech he had made to the French commander just three months earlier. Gist bet he was quoting verbatim. At length the Indian stopped so that John Davison could translate. He made ready his pen.

"Fathers, if you had come in a peaceable manner, like our brothers the English, we should not have been against your trading with us as they do. But to come and build great houses upon our land and take it by force; this we cannot allow."

Again, Davison ceased and Tanacharison began. Gist reflected upon the young major in the Virginia Militia, for whom he had acted as a guide these past three weeks before arriving here at Logstown. He was glad the man had placed himself at the Indian's level by also sitting cross-legged in front of him. This aristocratic novice had managed to offend every Indian he had met, before Gist could advise him on proper protocol. And when he could give counsel, it was often ignored.

"Fathers, both you and the English are white. We live in a country between. Therefore, the land belongs to neither one nor the other. The Great Being above allowed it to be a place of residence for us. So Fathers, I desire you to withdraw, as I have also desired our Brothers the English; for I will keep you at arms length. I lay this down as a trial for both, to see which will have the greatest regard for it. That side we will stand by and make equal shares with us. Our brothers the English have heard this, and I come now to tell it to you, for I am not afraid to discharge you off this land."

Davison was quiet for a moment. "Major Washington, sir, Tanacharison says this is the end of his own speech to Gen'ral Marin at Fort Le Boeuf. He gave the Gen'ral a wampum belt of all of his major points. Next he'll tell ya the Gen'ral's reply. Sir, he'll actually become the Gen'ral."

At this point, Tanacharison, whose tone had been one of a controlled orator, became angry and loud. With trance-like verve, his eyes closed and his face twisted in vehemence. Three pairs of gigantic, silver earrings jingled a punctuation to each sentence. His words were hard and cutting. The black tattoos of lines and symbols on his face stretched into shapeless designs.

When Tanacharison had finished, Davison looked at his comrades, shrugged and commenced with the translation.

"Now my child, I have heard your speech, but it is my time to speak now. Were is my wampum belt which you received in Montreal? That is the true record of our agreement. This wampum, which you have discharged me off the land with, I do not know. But you need not put yourself to the trouble of speaking, for I will not hear you. I am not afraid of flies or mosquitoes, for Indians are such as those. I tell you, down that river I will go and build upon it according to my command. If the river is blocked up, I have forces sufficient to burst it open and tread under my feet all that stand in opposition, together with their alliances, for my force is as the sand upon the seashore. Therefore, here is your wampum! I fling it at you! Child, you talk foolish. You say this land belongs to you, but there is not the black dirt under my fingernail that is yours. I saw that land sooner than you; before the Shauwanoas and you were at war. Lead was the man who went down and took possession of that river. It is my land, and I will have it. If people will be ruled by me, they may expect kindness, but naught else."

When he was done, all were silent. Gist could not believe that a French general would speak to an important Indian dignitary in such a manner. He knew many whites felt this way about the Indians and their land. He suspected Washington of similar opinions. But to belittle a potential enemy to his face was unconscionable. The French commander had since died, Tanacharison said, but the sting of his insults would not abate.

The Half-King then told how the French had built two forts, one at Presque Isle on Lake Erie and the other on French Creek about fifteen miles south. A new wagon road connected the two. This report was the first confirmation of the rumor upon which the English had been forced to rely.

The next day Major Washington called a council in the longhouse. He requested an escort by some of the young men to the nearest French fort. Tanacharison promised a guard of Mingo, Shawnee and Delaware to demonstrate the love and loyalty they felt for the English. Since they did not know Washington was coming and could not have planned ahead, they would send runners to call in various chiefs and dignitaries appropriate for such a mission to the French. They required several days.

"By God in Heaven Gist, just who do these savages think they're dealing with?" demanded the young Major, pacing back and forth within the confines of his small marquis. Four steps each way was all the room allowed. Gist stood just inside the front tent flaps watching the young officer, every bit as tall as he, beside himself with fury. John Davison, familiar with the many Indian dialects in the region, crouched in the corner.

"The miscreants," Washington continued, "desire me to wait three days for more of their kind to arrive here and form our guard. Three days! My orders are to make all possible dispatch, and waiting here is contrary to those orders. Let this Half-King fellow deliver his French speech belt at his own convenience and not hinder the business of the Crown!"

"With due respect, Major," spoke Davison, "that's three nights includin' tonight, and considerin' the importance o' this here journey an' all, I should think it worth the wait."

Washington, his pocked face lending a look of ferocity beyond his experience, spun around in mid stride to glare at the interpreter he had hired there. At that point Gist felt it prudent to interrupt, knowing the Major did not appreciate being corrected.

"Major," he asserted. "The Half-King does understand English. It will do no good for him to know you think so little of them and their errand. He told you himself how the French commander insulted him. You must ride to the nearest French fort to deliver the King's demand that they vacate British territory. Tanacharison must use this opportunity to give back his people's French treaty belts. He is waiting for a delegation of Shannoah and Delaware to do the same. We will sorely offend him if his advice goes unheeded."

"You Davison," asked the Major, "I have heard you grew up a captive among these barbarians. What say you of these matters?"

"That I did, Major," Davison spoke with the confidence of one who knew the Indians. "but I'll not be tellin' that now. What Mr. Gist said is true. Tanacharison'll not like havin' hisself questioned. However, I've two notions that bear a listenin'. The first bein' that the Six Nations sent Tanacharison to watch over those of their people who moved to the Ohio, Mingos, we call 'em. But these Mingos are more of their own mind with each passin' moon. Tanacharison is like a voice in the wind to them; sometimes it is heard and sometimes not. He is neither king nor half of one, but a big brother who tattles on his little brothers."

"For heaven's sake Davison, spare us your metaphors and make your point," Washington cried.

"As you say Major, I grew up among barbarians," Davison said with slight hint of sarcasm. "Point is, the Six Nations'll take neither the French nor the British side and Tanacharison cannot control Mingo allegiance. But he's been insulted and his honor's at stake. By influencin' the Delaware and Shauwanoa to deliver up their belts, his honor will be restored."

"You mean we wait just so this savage can feel better about himself? Hm! What's your second point?"

"Simply that every Injen with a French fusil fin from here to the Lake of the Eries is hopin' to catch hisself an Englishman and sell him to the French. A warm body or a cold scalp, they care not. Your only hope to deliver that message is by havin' Tanacharison with ya. All Injens know he is an Oneida council chief and out of respect, he and his'll not be harmed. So to insure the success of your mission, you'll pretty much have to help him . . . feel good about himself."

"Hm!" Washington breathed. "Then we wait."

In the early morning of the third day, the Major, Tanacharison and Monacatoocha met. Neither Shawnee nor Delaware chiefs had appeared with their speech belts. Another day was requested and given. That same night they learned there would be no grand expedition to protest French aggression. Still, the chiefs had not arrived. One Delaware sachem, King Shingas, sent word that he could not come because his wife was sick. He assured them, however, that the Delaware speech belt would be delivered up by its custodian, one Custologa, now living at Venango.

"King of the Delawares!" scoffed Washington, using the title Tanacharison had given Shingas the year before at the Logstown Conference. "Me thinks Shingas behaves in a cowardly manner. How can he command the respect of his people if he will not confront the French?"

"Now Major, I was present at that conference and witnessed the so-called coronation," answered Gist. "It seems the Governor requested the Delaware to choose one of their wisest councilors and present him as a king. Well, they hadn't done it yet, so Tanacharison says that he thought it proper to name Shingas as their King to handle any business between the English and the Delaware. Funny thing, though, when the ceremony was to take place, Shingas wasn't even there. His brother Tamaque, the Beaver, stood proxy for him and received the suit of English clothes tailored for Shingas. You know how short Shingas is? So when Tamaque, who's several inches taller, put on the suit, it looked like it'd shrunk."

Smiles erupted all around as each man pictured the sight of an Indian in a shrunken suit of white man's clothes. The subject lost its humor as Davison spoke.

"You know Major, Sir, that namin' him a King is of no account. Shingas could no more be a King than I could. He's a major chief of the Turkey Clan to be sure. But accordin' to ancient custom the head sachem must be of the Turtle Clan, like Tamanend, who made the first treaty with William Penn years ago."

"Well, that may be," said the Major, "but it does not change the character of him. I want no more to do with the likes of him, who will not face . . ."

A loud banging on the front tent pole forced an abrupt halt to the conversation. Tent flaps spread to admit Tanacharison, who asked John Davison to translate. He began his monologue.

Davison turned to Washington. "He says our escort will consist of four: a Delaware messenger, Jeskakake, who recites the speeches on the wampum strings; Old White Thunder, a Delaware medicine man; and a young Seneca hunter named Guyasutha."

"Ask him about his promise of a large contingent."

After the exchange in which Tanacharison answered without hesitation, Davison replied. "He says that a greater number might make the French suspicious of some evil and cause them to treat us all rudely. It's better now to be small."

"Tell him we will leave at first light."

When Tanacharison had gone, the first to break the silence was Gist. "Now Major, I do believe he's about as good as any fur trader at talking himself out of a promise. It appears to me he just plain can't get anyone else to go."

"Hm!" was Washington's retort. "First light gentlemen."

CHAPTER XVI

December 1753

"Where are those cursed Indians?" demanded the Major of no one in particular. "It's nigh on eight o'clock. My design was to leave over an hour ago. I will be detained no longer by a . . ."

It was the last morning in November. The men Washington had hired at Wills Creek – Barney Currin, John MacQuire, Henry Steward and William Jenkins – had begun before dawn to tear down the Major's tent, he being the only member of the party to have one, and pack the horses with supplies for the journey. Grumbling at the early call, they drank coffee as they sat close to the fire to await departure. Jacob Van Braam, the former Dutch officer whom Washington had engaged as his French interpreter, sat by himself. His aristocratic demure did not mix with their frontier nature.

"Yes sir, Major," replied Gist, knowing that maintaining a positive relationship with this demanding young officer would be prudent. "I'd say they have a different timetable in mind. Before a long journey like this, they need some time to prepare."

"Prepare what? There are four of them! They have no tents, no supplies, no . . ."

"I understand, sir," Gist interrupted, "but it's more mental than physical. They'll be praying for a successful journey and smoking the pipe." Seeing how disturbed the young Major was becoming, he offered to try and speed up the process. "I'll just get Davison. We'll find the Half-King and see if we can't hurry him along."

An hour later Tanacharison and his three companions led the way north along the path to the Delaware Indian village called Venango. Davison explained that the name was a perversion of "winingus," the Delaware word meaning "the place of many minks."

After five days of cold, wet weather, where one all-day downpour kept them from travel, the entourage entered the town at the mouth of River au Boeuf where it flowed into the Allegheny. A small contingent of resident Indians, having been informed of their approach hours earlier, met and guided them past ten stick houses that lay in an egg-shaped pattern surrounding a longhouse. One rough-hewn log cabin stood close by. French colors flew overhead. This had been the cabin of the gunsmith and trader, John Frazier, who had been ousted by the French earlier that year.

Washington, followed by Van Braam, rode up to this cabin and dismounted. A surprised French officer opened the door and stood, mouth agape, not knowing what to say.

"Les inviter dans," said a voice from the darkness of the cabin. "Il semble nous avon invités."

Van Braam leaned over and whispered to the Major.

The French officer who offered the invitation stood and came forward to greet them. "Je m'appelle Capitaine Philippe Thomas Joncaire. Je suis tout à vous," Gist heard him say as the door closed. Several Delaware residents welcomed Tanacharison and his three companions and they all disappeared into one of the stick houses. This left Gist, Davison and the others to pitch Washington's tent, build fires and make shelters for themselves.

The noise of laughter and loud talk filtered outside. "What d'ye s'poze they be a doin' in there?" asked Barney Currin. Having renewed acquaintances with Gist from prior travels, the two shared a lean-to. Gist was writing in a leather bound journal, his quill pen scratching the details of their trip from Logstown. The fire provided just enough light by which to write.

"Well, I suspect they're doing what officers do when they get together – drink liquors and boast of past campaigns," Gist answered.

"Donno 'bout that," Currin continued. "Major seems mighty taken with hisself; far too serious minded to be gettin' fuddled with the Frenchies. Besides, he has no campaigns to magnify."

"True," Gist stuck the quill in the small clay inkwell and looked at Currin. "Just between you and me, I've heard about the Major from my daughter, Nancy. While she was staying at Belvoir, the Fairfax estate, young George there," Gist pointed to the cabin, "came to visit her. She says he acted the fop just like that young William Fairfax; too fond of clothes and the way he looks in them. And he's quite well acquainted with the gentleman's liquor, though I'll bet he's no match for the trader's whiskey."

"Not well adjusted to these parts, I take it."

"Well now, I haven't heard him complain once. In fact, I've heard more grumbling out of you four this morning than I'll bet I hear from him the whole journey."

"Ah now Chris, you know we'd all be complainin' if it was middle o' summer an' we could sleep 'till noon."

Gist smiled. "I will say, though, the man has no patience with Indian ways and he doesn't ask me for any advice. He just expects everyone to do as he commands."

"And don't he just excite so when them Injens have other plans," Currin laughed. "By the by, what'll ye be doin' when yer ink freezes?"

"Guess I'll be remembering everything, won't I? Actually, you can just put it by the fire . . ."

They were interrupted by the cabin door opening to liberate Washington and Van Braam. Both headed toward the tent.

"Mr. Gist," Washington spoke as he passed near their lean-to. "A word with you?"

Davison had made it a point to tend a fire in front of the tent in anticipation of the Major's return. Gist joined them. Washington looked even more somber and serious than normal.

"And how did it go in there, Major?" Gist broke the silence with a quick smile and raised eyebrows toward Davison.

Washington appeared not to have noticed the levity and began. "My impressions, and I'm sure Mr. Van Braam will agree, are that we have little time to complete our task. Captain Joncaire and his officers, under the influence of copious amounts of wine, I might add, revealed that it is their absolute design to take possession of the Ohio, and by God they would do it! They know we English could raise two men to their one, but they say we are too dilatory to stop them. They pretend to have an undisputed claim to the river by right of discovery made by one La Salle some sixty years ago.

"It is the purpose of their expedition to prevent our settling the Ohio lands. They have heard some families have already done so. That must be your settlement, Mr. Gist. They revealed their number of forts, their locations and the garrison at each. The commander who gave such rough usage to the Half-King has died and the bulk of their men were recalled to Montreal. We already knew that. But when the river thaws, they will return. It requires but four weeks in large boats to make passage across the lake."

All were silent when Washington had finished. Gist noticed that the amount of detailed intelligence this young novice had obtained was indeed impressive. Then it dawned on him that this might be why the French officers had been so loose of tongue. To them Washington was a joke, an amusement posing no threat. Perhaps the French officers believed no one would take him seriously because they did not. And what if the English did listen to him? Inter-colonial bickering and slow reaction time would render the British impotent. The French had no fear, so they told him everything. Maybe the Major's approach merited more respect than he was at first able to see. But he must still try to anticipate possible blunders toward their Indian escort. Such breeches of protocol could jeopardize the mission.

"So what is our next heading?" Gist inquired.

"Captain Joncaire says he is unable to accept the letter from the Governor. We must, therefore, proceed another sixty miles to the first French fort where a general officer commands." A gentle rain put a finish on their conversation. "Gentlemen, we leave," Washington checked himself as if he were recalling a previous experience. "We must leave as soon as possible tomorrow. Mr. Gist, you and Davison prevail upon our escort to ready themselves rather early."

"We'll do our best, sir," replied Gist.

The rain continued all night and all the next day, preventing further travel. It was, however, unlikely they would have continued even in fair weather. That afternoon, Tanacharison and his Indians held council with the Delaware chief, Custaloga, to whom King Shingas had awarded possession of the French speech belt. Gist and Davison attended. They looked on as the Half-King tried to prevail upon Custaloga to relinquish the belt. If this were done, the Delaware would be renouncing their friendship and cooperation with the French. Custaloga replied to Tanacharison in a calm manner.

When he finished, Davison translated. "You say rightly that King Shingas is a great chief of the Delaware and his will should be done. Still, he could not come and he has sent no speech, which is necessary to deliver up such a belt. As I cannot pretend to make a speech for a King, it shall have to await his person." The irony of the situation was obvious, as it was the Half-King who had declared Shingas "King" in the first place. Tanacharison was, for once, speechless.

With the council over, Tanacharison was the first to emerge from the longhouse, followed by his three companions. A French officer rushed up to invite them to Joncaire's quarters, whereupon the Captain embraced them. Joncaire's ingratiating words were retold by Davison to Gist and Washington.

"Joncaire apologizes for not greeting them earlier, but he didn't know they were here. The Major did not tell him."

They watched as Monsieur La Force, commissary of the French stores, produced a carafe of some liquor and poured flagons for Washington's Indian escort. With much boisterous talk they were soon rendered incapable of resisting. Washington shook his head in disgust and returned to the warmth of fire and blanket.

"That is precisely why I did not tell Joncaire they were here," he said to Gist. "I knew this would happen."

Later that evening the discussion turned to the day's events. "I know you said Shingas was afraid of the French," spoke Davison to the Major as they hugged another campfire. "And Custaloga has an excuse for not returning the Delaware belt. But I be tellin' ya there's naught of fear in their hearts."

"That's right," agreed Gist. "We believe neither Delaware chief will allow Tanacharison to tell them what to do. They challenge the Half-King's authority again."

"Besides," added Davison, "Tanacharison can return home to Onondaga anytime. These Delaware and Shauwanoa now must live off the French, who have driven away all the English traders. Neither can afford to give up their French treaty belts."

"What you are saying is that no loyalty exists to Britain among these savages," Washington surmised.

"Very little, I'd say," said Davison.

"They see another war coming and they're hedging their bets," Gist observed.

"Well, I for one have no stomach for these heathen savages who will not declare allegiance to the country that has befriended them and treated them well for over a hundred years." That was Washington's final word on the subject and he retired to his tent already filled with the snoring of Van Braam.

In spite of valiant attempts by Washington to discourage another council, they witnessed Tanacharison try to return his own French speech belt with the shapes of four towns on it. His oratory was much the same as the one he had given General Marin. The result was also the same. Monsieur Joncaire would not accept. The commander of the next fort was the man to see.

The French offered no liquor on this night, but the Major took the precaution of having Davison stay with the Indians. "Don't let them out of your sight," he ordered. "Remind them of their obligation to the Crown and to us."

Earlier that day Washington had sent the other men and horses a short way up the creek to a fording place. This left the Major, Gist, Davison and Van Braam with their own horses to follow the next morning. Gist lay in his blanket under the lean-to watching Davison slide some of the many long tree branches into the fire. They radiated outward from the fire like the spokes of a wheel and when one end burned down to red coals, he shoved it further in.

"D'ye think this letter the Major be carryin'll scare the French into runnin' away?" asked Davison.

"You'd be hard pressed to find a more futile mission to send an emissary upon," Gist remarked. "This letter says to the French, you will leave,' and they, of course, will say 'no we will not' and then there'll be another war. It's like two gentlemen exchanging pleasantries before a duel."

"Except that this duel has been going on for years and no one ever wins."

"Well said John, and except for certain periods of peace here and there, it's been war for fifty years or more: King William's War, Queen Anne's War, King George's War, and all the Indian attacks in between."

"So why d'ye s'poze they bear the names o' royalty?"

"Probably, because royalty always starts them. Now I suggest we get some sleep. We have to gather our Indians tomorrow."

CHAPTER XVII

December 1753

The dark fort loomed, sinister, silhouetted against the field of snow that stretched hundreds of yards in all directions. Countless stalactites of pointed tree trunks pushed up through the white blanket. A heavy snow had begun at sunset. Now, several hours later, the expedition stood across what Washington called "French Creek" and viewed the fort on the opposite side.

The building of the fort and the need for firewood had laid bare the forest that formed its massive wall in the distance. Four block houses stood at each corner with connecting stockaded walls twelve feet high. They could see the roofs of two log cabins inside, perhaps for the commander and officers. Other cabins outside the fort probably housed the enlisted men.

Every pine tree in the vicinity must have been cut and hauled to the river shore for the construction of the many bateau that lay about. Gist counted 170 finished and many others in various stages of completion. Over fifty birch-bark canoes were pulled up on shore. Was this the flotilla for the spring invasion of the Ohio?

The French officer, La Force, and the several soldiers who accompanied the emissaries from Venango, hailed the fort and the gates opened. As before, Tanacharison and his three companions found warmth among the Indians camped outside the fort. Among other log buildings within the four bastions was a chapel; this was given to Washington and his men. They moved the benches against the wall and lit a fire in the fireplace. Excessive rain, sleet and snow for most of their journey from Venango left everyone wet and chilled. After a month of miserable weather the little chapel was a welcome refuge.

Gist awoke to the rustling of the Major dressing in his finest uniform of the Virginia Militia officers corps, white knee breeches, red weskit and blue coat, wrinkled though they were from confinement in his pack. Van Braam stood in waiting, dressed in an officer's uniform Gist did not recognize.

"I shall return upon completion of my task. You are in charge here Mr Gist." He spoke with the total conviction of a man on the most important mission of his young life. He showed no humor, no contemplation, just a consuming focus on one job – the delivery of Dinwiddie's letter.

Gist smiled. Perhaps it was just the enthusiasm of youth. He hoped so. He had known men too full of themselves – tax collectors and creditors – with whom he had had too much experience. Gist knew that men of focus and determination were necessary to get things done. Yet, tragedy resulted when men were so sure of themselves that they allowed no advice or consultation from others more seasoned. That, Gist observed, was the problem with Washington. But with nearly half the mission completed, he was beginning to like the determined young man and hoped he could push that negative trait in a more positive direction.

Washington returned near the dinner hour. Gist listened as he spoke. "The letter is delivered and translated into the French for St. Pierre, the commander of this fort. He says tomorrow he and his officers will hold council to draft a response. In the meantime, we are free to roam at will. They seem unconcerned that we may collect intelligence of the place."

"I suspect," replied Gist, "they think we can do no harm. So we count a hundred men. By spring a thousand or more will come from Montreal. We count the boats and by spring there'll be a hundred more. What intelligence could we possibly gather that would hurt them?"

"I do see your point Mr. Gist. But we shall gather what we can and find out what there is and report it anyway. Governors are always impressed by exact numbers."

"Yes sir, of that you may be sure," replied Gist. Maybe there was hope for the Major. That statement showed a keen understanding of why sometimes a meaningless task must be done; not because the particular information was so valuable, but because people in authority were impressed by exact numbers. "I wouldn't tell the men that, sir."

Washington acknowledged.

The next day they did just that. While the French officers were engaged for hours in their council, Washington and his men counted soldiers, guns, cannon; re-counted the number of bateau and canoes; figured the height of the bastions; and determined the use of each building in the fort.

Besides the information collected, an unforseen benefit soon appeared. The morale of the men rose to new heights. What had been a miserable trip with nothing to do but follow orders and plod along, now had meaning. A certain unchecked excitement prevailed. Even Gist was affected. He had two men assigned to each task and, when completed, listened to them argue over numerical discrepancies, sending them out again until they could agree. The consensus among the men was that they were doing something that might eventually hurt the French, even though Washington and Gist were skeptical. If any of the other men thought the gathering of information was unproductive, no one mentioned it. The day concluded with all the information written in Washington's journal. A genuine feeling of accomplishment lifted their spirits and calmed the feelings of discontent.

On the 14th of December the party awoke to a heavy snowfall as the temperature dropped. They held a discussion after a scant breakfast. Their horses had little food and daily grew weaker. Washington decided to send Barney Currin and two others with all the horses back to Venango before weather conditions became treacherous.

"I have the offer of several canoes and I desire to float down French Creek to Venango and on down Allegheny to the Forks and then to Frazier's at Turtle Creek on Monongahela," explained the Major.

"What if the rivers freeze, Major?" asked Currin.

"If that happens we'll go as far as we can and meet you at Venango We'll then go the rest of the way by land. But I must leave post haste; my business demands it."

That being settled, men and horses disappeared into the forest leaving the others to await the French reply. Gist knew they did not have much time for a water route. The temperature during the day was around freezing, but dipped well below that at night. The rivers would soon freeze over. They made preparations to be under way at a moment's notice. Washington called a meeting with Tanacharison to communicate these plans and make sure his Indians would be ready to travel. The Half-King, in turn, pressed St. Pierre for an audience that evening. The Englishmen were not invited, but Tanacharison relayed the details.

"St. Pierre," Davison translated, "will not accept the speech belt of the Mingo's living on the Ohio, saying the peace was never meant to be broken between us. He made us many promises of love and friendship. He said he wants to live in peace and trade well with us. As proof of this, he will send to Logstown some goods along with an officer and some men to deliver them."

One of the French officers interrupted the meeting. St. Pierre requested Washington's presence. Motioning Van Braam to accompany him, the Major departed without a word, leaving Gist and Davison to make apologies to the Half-King.

"Does the rude behavior of this man never cease?" asked Tanacharison. "Perhaps a bad bird sits on his shoulder and tells him we Indians are human beings in form only and unworthy of polite treatment. We reserve bad use for our enemies, but give our friends good use. If this Major of Virginia is our friend, why does he act in this way?"

Of course, though Gist, Tanacharison had pinpointed the problem. So many whites felt that Indians were unclean, base, gross, vile, uncivilized and unworthy of respect. And young Washington, coming from his semi-aristocratic background, seemed to share those feelings.

"I'm sure you have in your tribe what we call headstrong youth who do not listen to their elders and behave rudely. Is this not so?" Gist asked the Half-King.

Tanacharison considered this a moment and then answered. "It is true. We do have this kind of young warrior among us. But we do not make him a sachem of peace. We wait until the flint and steel strike many fires of experience and bring forth the light of wisdom."

"We are indeed watching flint strike steel in this one," Gist continued the metaphor. "But he is not a sachem of peace. He is beginning his trial as a war chief and we shall see what light of wisdom shines forth."

Tanacharison turned and walked away without comment. Davison gave a worried look at Gist after translating the last phrase.

"Do you think the King is convinced?" asked Gist.

"No," said Davison, "he sees through the Major, I think. Still, you said the right things and you had no choice. Perhaps Tanacharison will continue to help us because you express faith in Washington."

"I hope so, because we're not out of these woods yet."

An hour or so later the Major returned to the chapel with St. Pierre's reply. Wrapped in an oil cloth packet and tied with leather thongs, it was waterproof. While he was putting it in his pack Gist entered. "Davison," he commanded, "leave us."

Gist was mad; he was sick and tired of the ignorance and stupidity of this young officer. Washington stood up.

"Major," he scolded. "I just spent half an hour smoothing Tanacharison ruffled feathers after you abruptly left him without so much as a by your leave." Gist was getting angrier as he spoke. "I've watched you offend the Half-King many times just by omitting courtesies so common to the English, that by doing so can only be on purpose. These Indians respect civility and good usage and your continued rudeness threatens this mission."

Washington began to turn away, but Gist grabbed his shoulder and spun him around to look him in the eye.

"I will not let that happen," Gist hardened. "The Half-King thinks little of you. You could change that by showing him some consideration. If you can't do that, I'll tie you up and carry you home laid across the back of a horse. We need the Half-King to get home. Without him we fall prey to any French Indian with a gun and scalping knife. Do you understand me?"

Washington was silent. He stared back at Gist. He stared for the longest time and then cleared this throat. "You are right, of course. I just have a hard time dealing with these people and their petty excuses and delaying tactics. I don't understand and I get so mad that I can't see straight."

"Major," Gist calmed, "you just relax and let Davison and me take care of it. We realize the importance of your mission. You follow our lead and we will get you back to the Governor.

"I shall endeavor to be more patient and, as you suggest, more courteous. As you say, we do need them to get back. You see, I have just asked the commandant by whose authority the French have made prisoners of several of our English subjects. This country, he says, belongs to the French. No Englishman has a right to trade on the Ohio or the waters of it and he has orders to make everyone a prisoner who tries."

"So we must keep the pans primed on our way home and all I ask is that you keep your promise. If you find yourself at a loss for what to do or say, just ask me. It's no crime to ask. Only the fool blunders on without a clue."

"Yes, Mr. Gist, I'll do that. Your advice is much appreciated."

So there it was. His first open confrontation with the Major had gone well. He would not have taken him home laid across a horse, but what he said worked, at least for now. Why he had not been so firm with him earlier was hard to say. Perhaps he did not care before. Maybe now he saw that this young man was destined to become part of the frontier and so decided to influence his education. Or maybe he felt the danger increasing and he just wanted to improve his own chances of getting home. In any case he would see how well the young man listened.

"Mr. Gist," Washington called from outside the chapel.

"Yes Major," Gist answered as he stuck his head through the doorway.

"Just look at the Half-King and the commandant laughing and carrying on. What do you suppose it means? I'm ready to go now and Davison has told him this."

"Davison," said Gist, "why don't you saunter on over there and find out what's going on?"

Sometime later the interpreter returned with a troubling report. St. Pierre was using every ploy, from presents and rewards to promises and flattery, to delay Tanacharison's departure until after Washington left, thereby rendering the emissaries without escort. The commander had ordered several kegs of liquor and some provisions to be placed in Washington's canoes, perhaps to buy their compliance. And at any moment they expected French liquor to render the Indians incapable of leaving.

"Please come with me Davison. Mr. Gist," Washington said. "We cannot allow this duplicity."

With Washington in the lead, the three marched up to Tanacharison. "Tell the Half-King," said the Major, "that I wish to speak with him. It is a matter of grave importance and cannot wait." St. Pierre and his officers looked on.

This was translated and the Half-King waited for the Major to continue. "Brother," Washington began, "twenty-one days ago I called upon the sachems of the Six nations to inform you of my mission and to ask your advice and assistance in proceeding by the nearest and best road to the French."

Gist was impressed. The Major was repeating part of the speech he had given the Half-King upon their first meeting three weeks ago. That had been a well-thought out oration and had impressed the chief.

"Brother, you promised to conduct us and provide our provisions along the way. You said that you could not consent to our going without your protection, for fear some accident should befall us.

"Brother, my mission, which I told you was to deliver a letter from the Governor of Virginia, in which he told the French to vacate this land, is only half over. Now I must bring the French answer to my Governor. I only require you to honor your promise and guide and protect us back to Logstown from whence we came."

I was a good speech. Gist mentally commended the Major for his choice of words and the respect with which it was given.

After Davison's translation, Tanacharison addressed the Major. "Brother, it is true that we promised as you say and we intend to be your guard on the way to our home. The commander here has begged us stay until the morning to discuss some business. Because he has used us so well, we are obliged to honor him in this way. We shall be ready to leave in the morning as the Major wishes."

Washington inquired of Davison, "You speak French, is that right?"

"Yes sir, enough to get by."

"Kindly accompany me to the Commander."

The two walked over to St. Pierre, who stood with some officers a short distance away.

"Legardeur de St. Pierre, sir, as we have concluded our business, your promise was to forward my return journey as best you could and not detain the Indians, as they are part of my company. I respectfully request, sir, that you conduct your business with them so that we may both fulfill our obligations."

"Major Washington," St. Pierre replied with an air of condescension, "I assure you I have no knowledge of their reason for staying. They may leave anytime. I shall even provide an escort for you as you have chosen to go to Venango by canoe. Monsieur Joncaire is in need of some supplies."

"You are too kind. We shall leave first thing in the morning." Washington bowed to the Commander and turned toward the chapel. "Davison, please inform the Half-King of our imminent departure on the morrow and secure his promise that nothing shall hinder them."

Sometime later, Davison returned to the chapel where he found others sitting about, performing various tasks necessary to frontier life – cleaning rifles, patching holes in clothing, melting lead into ball molds. Gist was mixing a cup of hot chocolate; the Major was writing in his journal.

"Why don't you read us some o' that journal, Major?" Davison asked. "We'd be obliged t' hear a few lines concernin' our journey. It'll likely make ya famous one day."

Washington considered this. "I will read some of what I wrote about today's events.

"Dec. 15th The Commandant ordered a plentiful store of liquor, provision and etc. to be put on board oar canoe, and appeared to be extremely complaisant, though he was exerting every artifice that he could invent to set our own Indians at variance with us to prevent their going 'til after our departure; presents, rewards and everything that could be suggested by him or his officers.

"I can't say that ever in my life have I suffered so much anxiety as I did in this affair. I saw that every stratagem that the most fruitful brain could invent was practiced to win the Half-King to their interest and that leaving him here was giving them the opportunity they aimed at."

"Well," interrupted Davison, "that be the truth o' the matter, which ain't over yet by no means. Tanacharison did vow to leave in the mornin', but I just learned that the French promised him a present o' guns, powder an' ball, horns an' pouches an' other possibles."

Gist was more comfortable that night than he had been in awhile. He had spoken his mind to the Major and given him an ultimatum without losing his temper. The young gentleman had listened, at least this time. It was a start. He hoped the Major would open his mind to more suggestions on how to cope with Indian ways. Maybe this Washington was destined to spend a considerable amount of time out here on the frontier in one capacity or another. The more he knew about Indians, the better it would be for everyone, whites and Indians alike.

"Damn the French bastards," swore the Major the next morning. "Am I never to pry our Indians from the French grip? What can I do? First they will accept the gifts, then drink a toast and remain another day. Mr. Gist, I'll gladly take you up on some of your advice."

"Well Major," Gist reasoned, "let's try looking at this from Tanacharison's point of view. No offence sir, but all you've given him is a matchcoat, a twist of tobacco and some strings of wampum. And we are his friends. Now, his enemies, the French, have gotten him drunk several times, given him many trinkets and now they're giving guns and powder. What would you do?"

Faced with the undeniable logic of the situation, Washington could say nothing.

"What you can do is just what you did yesterday. You appealed to his honor and it got his attention. If St. Pierre hadn't promised those guns, Tanacharison would have gone with us today. So you say the same thing today in different words. Davison can help you in the translation. If it doesn't work, we'll have to go without them and take our chances."

CHAPTER XVIII

December 1753

As promised, the French brought guns and other accouterments to Tanacharison. True to form, they offered a drink of liquor "to warm their blood in preparation for the journey through the cold December day," they said. The Indians milled around the French Commandant, thanking him for his hospitality and presents. At a wink from Gist, the Major and John Davison approached the Half-King and demanded his attention. Washington relayed much the same appeal as the day before, but with a stronger emphasis on the Half-King's obligation. In fact, he applied so much pressure that, much to Gist's surprise, Tanacharison refrained from drink and agreed to leave at once.

They were soon on their way, with the five white man in one canoe and four Indians in another, Tanacharison in the lead. Presents for Logstown, provisions for Venango, two officers and four common soldiers occupied the four French canoes that followed.

The three parties traveled at different speeds, Indians outdistancing them all. Freezing temperatures having lowered the water level, they were often forced to disembark and guide their canoes over the shoals. At one point every canoe was portaged a quarter of a mile because the thick ice could not be broken. It was here that they all caught up with one another. One French canoe had overturned, causing the loss its cargo of powder and lead. That night they bivouacked in three separate camps twenty miles above Venango.

The trip was tedious and tiring. Comic relief, however, eased the tension the next day when a French canoe ran upon the side of a steep shoal and overturned. Three of the men fell into waist-deep water and watched as several casks of wine and brandy floated away. The remaining soldier, who managed to stay dry by landing on the shoal, ran splashing to overtake the casks. One was all he could catch.

The Indians were hysterical; Washington and his group took their turn in laughter and finger pointing at the Frenchmen's expense. The French soldiers shook their fists and called out what the Englishmen assumed to be obscenities, but could not understand. As Washington's party ignored their plight and turned to the task of guiding their own canoe along, one voice prevailed above the others.

"Sacré bougres. Allez vous faire foutre!" it called.

"What did he say, Van Braam?" asked Washington.

"Vell Major, mein knowledge of vulgar Frans is neet too goot."

"Bloody bla'guards, he called us, sir," Davison spoke up. "Then he told us to . . . well . . . commit an unnatural act that is physically impossible."

"Timid are we Davison?" Washington asked. "I think we've all heard it before."

The canoe containing Gist and Washington put to shore at Venango and was met by Barney Currin and the other servitors. Now that all were united, they spread out to share the four lean-tos they had used before. They stoked the fires and lit new ones to keep the bitter cold at bay. The Indians landed close behind, retiring to the lodgings of fellow Mingos as before. After landing, the French went straight to Captain Joncaire's headquarters. The Englishmen listened, expecting to hear a loud voice that would signify a reprimand for losing two canoes and most of the liquor. They heard nothing.

"My boots," cried Major Washington, "where are my boots?" As they were well frozen, Washington had placed them on sticks by the fire, along with his frozen stockings, to thaw. When he awoke to nature's call, the boots were gone. He hobbled barefoot through six inches of snow to a secluded spot. Upon his return he sat in his bed and stuck two red feet as close as he dared to the fire. "I'll bet those bloody Frenchmen took my boots to get even, damn their blood. Van Braam, you must register a complaint with Captain Joncaire and get me my boots back. A joke is a joke, but . . ."

"Oh Major." Gist, having heard the complaint, walked back into camp at that moment carrying winter moccasins and leggins. "By the way, I took the liberty of trading your boots to a big Frenchman for two pair of moccasins."

"You what! Those were my best riding boots."

"I know, sir, but look. The horses are very weak and will not carry us much longer. So we'll have to lead the horses and you can't walk far in those boots. We'll be in deeper snow and your feet will freeze. So this is what you do: you put these leggins on first, then these smaller moccasins; you can wear your stockings. Then you put this larger pair on over the other ones. You line them with grass, or moss; line them all around, top and bottom. Now you tuck your leggins inside the moccasins, wrap this extra leather around your leg and tie it off." Gist pointed out the details on his own outfit.

"Here," Gist handed the things to Washington. "They're made of elk hide and rubbed with bear grease – much warmer than your boots. I'll go get you some moss."

The Major looked like a different man in Indian dress, at least from the waist down. He still wore the wool sleeved coat of the Virginia Militia, along with a large black wool cape and his tricorn. Davison had set up a meeting with Tanacharison to find out whether he would accompany them.

"Tanacharison says White Thunder has injured himself in a fall and is unable to walk. They'll remain here several days until he's better and go by canoe down to Logstown."

"I see," said Washington. Facing the Half-King, he stuck out his hand; the King returned the grasp. "Tell him that Monsieur Joncaire will employ every scheme to set him against the English, as he has done before. Say that I hope he can guard against this flattery and let no speeches influence him in their favor."

Davison then relayed the Indian's reply, "Do not be concerned, for I know the French too well for anything to engage me on their behalf." Tanacharison continued. Davison hesitated, but at the Major's insistence, he shrugged. "You are brave and strong. When he sees you again, he hopes you will have cleaned the moss from your ears, that you may hear Indian brothers, for there is much they can tell you."

Washington reddened; whether from embarrassment or anger, no one could tell. His reply was even tempered with no sign of either. "Tell him I will consider his words of wisdom and may the next time we meet be under more pleasant circumstances."

CHAPTER XIX

December 1753

Gist awoke on Christmas day and snuggled deeper into his blanket as he contemplated their predicament. For the past two days the return expedition had spread itself over a quarter mile along the path, with Gist in the lead. Each of the eight men rode while leading a pack horse. Within the first few miles it was apparent that the horses were too feeble and the baggage too heavy. They were soon walking, having divided the baggage among all the horses and themselves. The woods were silent, but for the passing caravan and an occasional icy gust of wind. Snow piled higher. Frequent stops to correct shifting loads and clean compressed snow from horses feet made progress agonizing. As the blanket of snow obscured its direction, Gist often had to scout the path ahead just to determine where it went.

Without much thought he abandoned the idea of his customary devotional readings. It would be the first time in years he would not read from the Homilies on Christmas. Washington was aggravated at the slow pace and he knew time would not allow his indulgence. What the men needed now were snowshoes. Several additional inches of snow had fallen overnight making them a necessity. And three of the men had frostbitten feet.

The Major saw the advantage of the snowshoes and sent the men into the woods to collect pine boughs. Rawhide and leather strips, common articles in every woodsman's supplies, were collected and construction began. Within several hours they made the shoes, ate a meager breakfast and reloaded the horses.

After a day of travel in this manner, Gist could still sense Washington's frustration. At last the Major came to him with an idea. "Mr. Gist, at this pace how long do you figure it will take us to get to Wills Creek?"

"Well Major," Gist answered as he scratched in his head, "that's hard to say. The horses can only move about half speed, so I'd say about twice as long as it took us to get here on the way up – another three weeks, maybe longer."

"And how long by foot, that is if we . . ."

"Now Major, you're not thinking of . . ."

"Just tell me how long if we cut across country through the woods by the nearest and straightest way to the Forks."

"Less than half that time," Gist answered with reservation. "Major, I must strongly advise against this. With all due respect sir, you're an excellent horseman, but we'd be walking for many a mile."

"Mr. Gist, you know how important this mission is. The Governor must get this reply most expeditiously. If we are to challenge this French invasion in but a few months time, I must get to Williamsburg post haste. I shall place myself in your charge, as you are the more experienced in matters of foot."

Gist could offer no rebuttal. Besides, the vigor of youth was on Washington's side and would perhaps atone for his lack of fittness. "We will, of course, be more vulnerable to unfriendly Indians, just the two of us."

"I have thought of that. I will be under your command should such an occasion arise."

"Fair enough Major," Gist was encouraged by the young man's readiness to acknowledge inexperience in matters about which he knew naught. "May I recommend a matchcoat in place of your cape. It'll be less cumbersome and not so prone to getting caught on briars and such."

Both men donned matchcoats and backpacks, along with their leggins, double moccasins, and improvised snowshoes. From a distance they looked very much alike. Mr. Van Braam was left in charge of the horses and men. They were to make the most of their situation and return to Will's Creek as soon as possible.

Leaving the others behind, Washington and Gist set out on the day after Christmas along the path to the Murdering Town. Gist set a fast pace to test the young Major, who neither complained nor requested a slower stride. At no time did Gist have to wait for him to catch up.

After eighteen miles with few breaks, they stopped at a vacant Indian cabin made in the Shawnee fashion – a rough stick house wrapped in bark. Washington almost collapsed on the dirt floor. The remains of an old fire lay in the middle and he stared at it as if his eyes could make it glow.

"Major, may I suggest that you go through our packs and find us something to eat? I'll get some firewood."

Within an hour the cabin was as warm as it would get and chunks of venison boiled in snow water; the creeks and small runs were frozen so thick, they could not break the ice.

They went right to sleep without conversation. Gist awoke every so often to keep the fire burning, but as far as he knew, Washington did not stir. After a few hours Gist awakened him to resume the trek. The new moon was barely visible, but by the position of the stars Gist made it to be several hours after midnight.

Early in the morning they reached the Murdering Town and stopped to rest. Few of the inhabitants were astir, but Gist was able to trade for parched corn and dried meat with the same Delaware woman from whom they had bought food on the way up. While they were partaking of the fruits of their trade, a Delaware man approached them. He spoke a tolerable English and Gist thought he had seen him at Venango, but was not sure.

"Annosanah," he said to Gist, "good see you again." He shook Gist's hand and turned to the Major, "and Wassinton, you good man too."

"Why you go by two on foot?" the Indian asked. "Before, you were many, with many horse and Tanacharison your chief." He continued to question them; when had they left Venango; where did they part with their horses; how soon would they join them again?

Before he gave any answers, Gist drew the Major aside and explained that satisfying this man's curiosity was unnecessary. The mere fact that he was so inquisitive was enough to arouse suspicion.

"Maybe so," Washington said, "but if he can guide us to the Forks, we can get there faster, since he may know the exact way."

"I'd advise against this, Major."

"Speed, Mr. Gist, is of the utmost importance." Then Washington turned to the Indian and said, "we must travel the nearest way to the Forks from here. Can you show us the way?"

"I glad to go. When we go?" the man asked.

"Now," replied the Major.

"You tired," the Indian said to Washington. "I take you pack, no?"

Washington handed him his backpack and they set out at a brisk walk. The woods were silent, except for crunching snow and an occasional popping tree. The going was tiresome because of the many small hills and valleys. The pace set by the Indian was taxing, even for Gist, who adjusted his matchcoat to admit more of the cold air on his chest. He had removed his mittens some time ago to keep himself cooler.

At the next small run he stepped onto the ice, knelt down and began chopping at it with his belt axe. It was like hacking at a rock, but as he chipped away, water seeped into the hole. He scooped up the frigid liquid in his hands for a refreshing drink and moved out of the way for Washington coming up behind.

"Major," he said, "you're sweating too much." The edges of his collar and neck stock were damp. Drops of sweat slid down his temples from under his tricorn.

"When we stop for the night, you'll freeze in your own sweat." He did not have time for an in-depth explanation so a bit of exaggeration would hammer the point home. "Open up your blanket and take off that neck stock and your mittens. All that is necessary in camp, but on the trek it just makes you too hot."

Washington complied without comment, indicating to Gist that he was already tired. Their guide appeared and urged them on. They kept a fast pace for several miles until Gist thought he detected their guide leading them more to the east than south. It was hard to tell under such a cloudy sky. He figured the Forks lay about thirty miles south of the Murdering Town, but traveling in a straight line was impossible. At one point Gist stopped under the pretext of answering nature's call and checked his compass. As suspected, their heading approached due east.

He found a large log and, after brushing off six or eight inches of snow, sat down, watching the young Major several yards behind. From the way he was walking Gist could tell his feet hurt. This was not surprising considering the Major was used to boots with a heel; the long distance walk, flatfooted in moccasins, would stretch his calf muscles to the point of pain.

"Mr. Gist," the Major, breathing hard, stopped and leaned on his rifle, "I suggest we encamp somewhere close by."

The Indian saw them resting and retraced his steps to their log. "You tired," he said to Washington. "I take you gun, no?"

The guide began to reach for the muzzleloader, but its owner moved it, "thank you no! I am perfectly capable of carrying it myself. And please return my pack to me. I can carry that too."

"But you go fast now," replied the Indian. "Ottawa here in woods." He gestured with a wide sweep of his arm all around them. "Scalp, kill; we hurry now. We go my cabin, be safe."

"Is that why we're heading east, not south to the Forks?" asked Gist.

"You can hear a gun to my cabin. Hurry, we go, eat, be safe," clearly avoiding the question.

"You go on ahead a bit and we'll follow," Gist said to the Indian. When he was beyond earshot, Gist confessed his distrust of the fellow. "Major, I don't see much point in continuing to follow him. He's going the wrong way and may be leading us into a trap."

"I am aware of that Mr. Gist. But if he does have a cabin close by it sure would be a comfort to rest for a while and warm up some. Maybe I could dry out some of my clothes since I have sweated so much."

Gist saw the logic in that and against his better judgement they continued for a mile or so. When their guide steered more to the north, Gist called a halt and inquired again about the distance to his cabin.

"Two whoops to my cabin. Come, we hurry."

"I don't like this Major."

"I know, but let's give him a chance. How far is two whoops anyway?"

"Oh, the way they can yell I'd say about half a mile or so, maybe more."

Washington called a halt two miles later. "I agree with you, Mr. Gist. Let us stop at the next run. We will get water, send our guide on his way and resume our journey."

They summoned the Indian and told him of their plan. No facial expression revealed his feelings. Assuming he was leading them to the next small run, they followed him from the woods into a large open meadow. Gist stopped at the edge to allow his eyes to adjust to the brightness of the snow-covered field. It happened almost too fast for Gist to react. The Indian, not fifteen paces out into the field, turned and aimed his gun at one of them. Gist, not sure which one, shoved the Major one way, himself falling the opposite just as the hammer hit the frizzen. The ball whizzed close to his head, as he saw the guide run for cover behind a huge white oak at the edge of the meadow.

"Are you shot, Gist?" Washington called out.

Gist had already begun to rise. "No – get him, now!" he commanded, and hurled himself toward the oak like a shot from a cannon, Washington close behind. Gist rounded the tree and caught their assailant just as he was aiming. Gist was quicker. He knocked the rifle aside with his own and with his greater height and weight, ran over top of him, knocking him down. Dropping to his knees on the Indian's chest, some two hundred pounds of Gist forced air from the Indian's lungs while a knife headed for his throat.

"Gist" Washington yelled, "No!" and grabbed the knife-wielding arm.

Gist, still breathing hard, relaxed his grip on the knife and turned to look at the Major.

"Do not kill him. We can not kill him. Maybe he is leading us into an ambuscade, I don't know. But if he is, killing him will just make it worse for us. This is a peace mission and I do not want possible accusations of murder on my shoulders."

Gist sheathed his knife and climbed off the Indian. He said not a word, but grabbed the Indian's gun as well as his own and stood looking down at the man fighting for breath. Then he motioned for the Major to come away from the recovering Indian for a consultation.

"Well then," Gist said, realigning his accouterments, "as you'll not have him killed, we must get him away and travel all night ourselves to avoid another encounter with him or his friends. I have an idea. Just play along."

Gist went over and helped the Indian up, brushing the snow off and straightening his clothes. "I'm sorry to hurt you. It was a mistake. I suppose you fired your gun because you were lost and were signaling others to come and find you?"

"No lost. Cabin this way," he pointed to the northeast. "Very close now. You come. Shooting gun big mistake. I sorry."

"Yes, well, we understand. You build us a fire here. Then you go on home. We're very tired and will follow your tracks in the morning."

As the Indian made the fire and prepared to leave, Gist spoke to him. "Here's your gun. It's still charged, so see that you don't fire it by mistake. And here's a cake of bread for you. We thank you for guiding us here. Go now and when we arrive tomorrow morning you can hunt for us and give us fresh meat. We have no more."

The Indian hurried away. Gist waited several minutes and followed his path. An hour later he returned, satisfied their former escort was making a beeline to somewhere and not intent upon returning, at least not yet. They moved their camp about a half mile away. By a small fire they melted some snow for drinking water and ate several handfuls of parched corn.

"Chew some jerked venison on the way, Major, and let's go," Gist said in an unkind tone. He was irritated at Washington for changing the stakes by letting the Indian go. He could have killed him and hidden the body. But they would have been heading south anyway as fast as possible at night until they dropped. So he guessed it did not matter. What irritated him was that this young tyro gave him a command in the heat of battle, so to speak, against his own judgement, and he listened. He could not believe he had listened. He was not cold blooded and he did not enjoy killing the few times he had had to do so. Nevertheless, he felt this situation had dictated it to assure their safety. If they had indeed cheated an ambush of its prey, the predators would pursue. He and the Major could only push hard and pray for snow to cover their tracks.

Food was going to be a problem, he thought as he chewed a bite of jerkie. Both he and the Major were down to a small portion of corn and meat. It was twenty miles or more to Shannopin's Town over hilly, difficult terrain that no straight course could traverse. The risk of shooting game was too high, given a probable pursuit. He was not sure their rations were enough. In fact, he had never been in a predicament such as this. Stranded in several snow storms for days at a time with little to eat, yes, but this was not the same. By now they had been awake and traveling for nineteen or twenty hours, except for a few hours at the Murdering Town and several breaks. And they would have to go all night. However long a man could go without sleep or food, they might just find out.

Hours passed. They no longer attempted a brisk pace and plodded along under crescent moonlight. Of all the days and nights it had snowed on their journey so far, it would not do so now, when they needed it to cover their tracks. Washington kept a few paces to the rear, though where his strength came from Gist could not tell. Conversation was nonexistent; the young Major followed the seasoned veteran.

And it was cold. With a starry, cloudless night above and a foot of snow below, stopping was out of the question. A fifteen minute rest would have frozen them in their tracks. They ate on the move and shifted their rifles from shoulder to shoulder and then from one hand to another, trying to disperse the weight that grew in proportion to their fatigue.

CHAPTER XX

December 1753

It was not an impressive sunrise. No clouds refracted the sunbeams to spread color throughout the eastern sky. Nevertheless, it was a wonderful sight after a long night of frozen visions and frigid thoughts – and the sun was on their left. The many hills and valleys had made it impossible to maintain one steady direction. Gist's occasional use of the compass guaranteed their heading. Still, it was a surprise to be going the right way. He had to wonder how much of the night they spent actually going south.

To check the compass was a cooperative effort. Washington held the two-inch diameter disc, ready to take the reading. Then Gist would strike a spark to some char cloth and light a small nest of tow he used for cleaning his rifle. The flame he held in his cupped hands lasted only five seconds before it was too hot to hold. Each time he checked the compass he was off track, and he knew that for hours at a time he had ceased to focus. No matter now, for it was a brand-new day and he was drawing strength from the sun.

Piney Creek, at least he thought it was Piney Creek, was frozen solid and he could do nothing to break it. Pulling a dead branch off a tree, he handed it to his companion. "Major, sir, why don't you start us a fire while I get some more wood. We'll cook some hot chocolate and have us a proper breakfast."

Washington attended to the task at hand with sloth, but without complaint.

"I hate to stop now but I think we have no choice." Gist took Washington's rifle, emptied the powder from the pan, cleaned the touch hole and re-primed it. Doing the same to his own piece, he recovered their locks with rawhide protectors.

"Got that fire going yet, Major? Come on, talk to me!" He was hoping the cold had not dulled the young man's mind.

"Damn it Gist," he sounded sharp and angry, "curse you for talking me into leaving my cape behind. I near froze to death last night with this matchcoat and one bloody blanket and I have not seen one damn briar bush. If I ever get out of this . . ."

"Now Major, don't get so excited," Gist said as he scooped up a potful of snow to melt. "I'm trying to make a woodsman out of you. Besides, nobody wears a cape. Everyone, Indian and white man alike, takes a good stout wool blanket like these. At least you have your coat on under this blanket. That's more than any Indian would have. No wonder you were sweating so much."

Washington grabbed Gist's matchcoat and opened the front to reveal an elk hide hunting jacket over top a linsey-woolsey shirt. A woolen undershirt showed through the opening around his neck, overall, an outfit no warmer than his own. He looked into Gist's eyes and then turned away to dump another hand full of snow into the pot. It hissed as some of it missed the pot and hit the fire.

He was not worried yet about the Major. His eyes had revealed a determination and a defiance that would replace warmth at least for awhile. He took a small brick of chocolate and part of a cone of sugar and threw them both into the pot. "I don't see how we can stop here, do you Major?"

"No, I suppose not. Where are we?"

"If this is Piney Creek, it goes south right into the Allegheny River about two miles above Shannopin's Town. Don't know exactly how far, but can't be more than ten miles. I spent several days there recovering from the ague about three years ago on my first trip for the Company. Shannopin, himself, told me much about the area."

"Chocolate is done," Washington said. He poured half the hot brown liquid into Gist's tin cup.

It was sweet and chocolaty and the best he had ever tasted. Gist got out another brick of cocoa and more sugar and plopped them into the pot, along with two handfuls of parched corn. "This will make a good chocolate mush. By the way, how much food do you have left?

Washington did not answer.

"Let me see your pouch."

Washington glared at Gist as he untied the cloth pouch from around his waist. It was about a foot long by three inches wide and flat, except for the last inch.

Gist stared at the Major, who lowered his eyes.

"Guess we'll have to ration this better," Gist said without accusation as he produced his own pouch half full. He poured some of his parched corn into Washington's bag.

"One small handful every several hours is all you need. Hell, an Indian can get along on half that.""

Washington said not a word, but retied his food pouch around his waist. They doused the fire. Gist spread the ashes around and covered the spot with snow as best he could. If it snowed soon, no hint of their presence would be seen.

Warmer, but no less fatigued, they continued their winter ordeal up the countless hills and down the numerous valleys. None were difficult, but easily served to double the mileage as they were channeled along the windings of the creek. Gist kept his focus, looking for signs of Indians. Washington was never more than a few feet behind. He now ate whenever Gist ate. Although he sometimes appeared to be fighting for every step, he never asked for a rest. It was as if he knew his chances of survival depended on Gist's every move.

Afternoon turned to dusk as Gist came upon Indian tracks crossing their path. "Hunting party for Shannopin's I'll wager," said Gist.

"How do you know?"

"Snowshoe prints are deep. Also, they're not all in a straight line. They carrying a heavy weight, like maybe an elk carcass, and stagger sometimes when the ground is uneven. A war party would travel light with shallow steps."

"So if they are Shannopin's, they are on our side, right?"

"I wouldn't bet on it, Major. These days it's hard to tell who your friends are, especially in the dark." Gist had Washington look ahead several hundred yards over the snow-covered forest. The huge trees were sparse and it was easy to see in all directions. "See that outcropping of rocks? You head toward there and find a place to hide. I'm going to follow these tracks a ways. I'll meet you by those rocks." Gist turned to leave.

"And what if you don't return?"

"Then I guess you can tell any stories you want, because there'll be no one around to say different," he smiled.

Gist followed the tracks to no avail. They were several hours old and as it was well into another frigid night, he felt they were safe. He met Washington at the rocks, a large gathering of well-worn boulders strewn about. The Major had collected a small load of firewood in preparation for a fire.

"I hate to say this, Major, but I don't think fire is a good idea. You can smell a fire for miles in the woods on a cold night. I didn't follow the tracks very far."

"I see." Washington tried not to show his disappointment; he was starting to shiver.

Gist motioned him over and felt his sweat-soaked shirt that Washington agreed to remove. He cut some low hanging pine boughs and made a palate between two large boulders. Washington wrapped himself in his blanket and lay down with the wet shirt on top. His companion then spread the woolen matchcoat and his own blanket over him and finished with a few pine boughs.

Gist treated himself in much the same way, except for the shirt problem he did not have, nor the extra coat. His rifle was pressed up against his body ready for possible action. He fought sleep to calculate that they had been awake and moving for forty-five hours.

Morning came early – too cold not to get up. Gist spent several minutes listening to the surrounding woods for signs of human activity, but all was silent. He went over to shake Washington, beginning to show signs of life. A quick, cold breakfast of parched corn had to suffice.

Several miles separated them from the Allegheny River, which they reached without incident. They talked of the temperature being so low that the river would be frozen over by now and they could just walk across. But when they saw it, they stopped in their tracks, dumbfounded by disappointment. The river, being over a hundred yards wide at that point, was frozen about fifty yards from each shore. The middle was an angry flow of ice chunks driving toward the Forks several miles downstream.

"I guess we have to make a raft," Gist commented as he looked on at the almost noiseless passing ice, some flat, others jutting into the air at odd angles to a height of several feet. He knelt to remove his makeshift snowshoes.

"You intend to cross that on a raft?" Washington pointed in disbelief at the frozen projectiles streaming along.

"Major," Gist said in a voice reserved for meddlers with negative opinions, "we have no choice, unless you want to stay here until it freezes solid. By then we'll be statues." Gist pulled out his belt axe and began looking for smaller trees. "We want them about six inches thick." He extended the hatchet to Washington. "This will keep you warm. I'll spell you now and then."

Washington looked at the axe without taking it. "But what about the shallow crossing at Shannopin's Town?"

"Major," there was tension in his voice, "that's two miles away and we are here and we have to cross this river. There's no other way."

"May I remind you, sir, that I am still in command."

Gist looked the young man in the eye for what seemed the like minutes. He saw fear – fear of the river, the cold, not completing his mission. He knew from experience that it was difficult to reason with a man in fear. He withdrew the axe from Washington's reach and went over to the nearest qualifying tree. Kneeling in the snow, he chopped.

"What are you doing, Gist?"

Gist did not answer. Wood chips kept flying.

Washington moved closer and grabbed the axe at its zenith, demanding, "I am in command here and I say . . ."

Gist grabbed the nearest foot and jerked, sending an astonished Major on his rear. "Major, Shannopin's Town is two miles away," Gist said as he retrieved the axe, "and there's no guarantee the river will be any different there. Besides, not every Indian there will be friendly, you can be sure. I'd just as soon avoid it altogether. So I am building myself a raft to cross this river. Now, you're welcome to come along or not." Gist went back to chopping.

Washington sat for a while watching the raft take shape. First, one log was chopped to an eight-foot length and then another. But Gist was tiring fast. Exposure and lack of food had taken their toll on his strength. He rested and spoke to the young gentleman.

"You know Major, I could use some help here." They looked at each other for several seconds. Washington crawled forward and extended his hand for the axe.

The little raft was eight feet long with a dozen, six-inch logs lashed side by side with strips of grapevine. Two smaller diameter logs were laid across at both ends over and under the raft for rigidity. Two straight poles, each about fifteen feet in length were cut for setting poles to push them across the ice infested water.

A dwindling reserve of energy slowed their pace. Every movement was an effort and every effort became more painful as afternoon approached evening. Amid the trees of the forest, they were not troubled by wind. But the icy river with its high, shore-lined trees provided a frigid corridor for the wind to blow through. Breathing was difficult and watery eyes hindered their vision.

They finished just after sun-setting. Gist tied their rifles and snowshoes to the logs and together they dragged the raft to the shoreline and across fifty yards of rough ice. As the frozen fragments flowed by, water spilled over the edge of the ice creating a slick, glassy surface for the last six feet.

"We'll put one end in the water and then you jump on," he instructed the Major. "We'll try to push ourselves across with these poles. Ready?" Washington nodded.

Water and ice pulled at one end of the raft, gently at first as Washington crawled on. As Gist inched the raft farther out into the flow, it grabbed as the power of the river slid it off the ice. They stood up and grabbed the setting poles, jamming them through the ice chunks to touch bottom. They made little progress as they tried to coordinate their efforts on one side to push the raft across while the ice flow sped them down river.

They were inside a giant jigsaw puzzle – jagged ice segments separated by lines of black water; the whole sequence, moving with the current, was surrounded by a shiny, unbroken icy border. The thin crescent moon, reflecting off the white ice, barely illuminated their destination. Yet before they crossed half way, the raft rested against a larger mass of ice traveling at the same rate of speed. Stuck, they could go no farther across the river.

"How about if I just slow us down so that chunk goes on by?" Washington said and without waiting for an answer, jammed his setting pole down to the bottom of the river right in front of the raft.

Before Gist could yell, "No!" the force of the current had thrown the raft against the pole that bent and catapulted Washington out into the dark water between the plates of ice. Gist could do nothing. The raft was moving too fast. It was impossible to go back, get to shore or stop. He was a prisoner and Washington was out of sight.

But as soon as he had thought the thought, Washington's head appeared among the ice chunks with a hand outstretched to catch an approaching log. The raft was upon him. The protruding hand caught a corner and grabbed on, avoiding the direct path of the raft. There he clung, dragged along, unable to muster the strength to pull himself up. The weight of both men at the corner being too unstable, Gist helped him work his way along to the side. Gist pulled him onto the raft where he sat with knees under his chin, arms hugging legs. He shivered and the icy wind pulled at his wet clothes.

Gist was busy. Washington's stunt had indeed slowed the raft enough for the huge plate of ice to move on by, but there was another problem. An island loomed ahead and he could not move the raft over to collide with it. The alternative was unthinkable. They could not stay on the raft.

"Island coming up on the right, Major. Get ready to jump and run on the count of three." He helped the shivering Major to his feet and untied their guns and packs. Washington said not a word and tried to ready himself. The raft approached the island. It looked as if they would pass about six feet to starboard. Gist threw the packs on shore.

"Ready, one, two, three," Gist yelled. He let Washington jump first so their combined weight would not be placed on the edge at the same time. Gist followed carrying both rifles. They landed in several feet of icy water and waded ashore as the raft continued its journey down river.

Gist knew he had to work fast if he were to save the Major from frostbite or something worse. Washington just stood in his tracks not quite knowing what to do. Toward the interior of the small island, Gist led them. No outcroppings of rock or huge trees offered them protection, but at least they were out of the direct path of the arctic wind. Gist then had Washington remove his matchcoat, military coat and shirt exposing bare skin above the waist to the elements. Gist removed his own matchcoat and blanket and wrapped them around the Major's white torso. His skin felt frigid.

Next, he wrapped Washington's blanket around a tree and twisted the ends over and over to wring out as much water as possible, the same with the coat. They were already quite rigid and getting stiffer as the remaining water froze.

"Why don't you gather some fire wood Major, while I make us some shelter?"

Washington acknowledged, shuffled toward a tree and began breaking off the low hanging branches. Before long Gist had made a lean-to. From a few small pine trees on the island, he obtained branches to cover the roof, sides and floor of their shelter. Time to check on the Major.

Gist found him walking around carrying a small pile of wood as if unsure of its purpose. This was serious. Though not quite delirious, he was not exactly lucid. The Major had to be warmed, and fast.

He started a fire close to the mouth of the shelter and fed larger and larger sticks until it was blazing. "Gotta take your leggins and breeches off and dry them out, moccasins too."

"What am I going to wear? You can't do that. I won't have any clothes."

"We'll just wrap you in wool like before, you'll see."

The lean-to helped reflect the fire's heat. Together they removed the freezing clothes and laid them in a pile. Washington's body had taken on a blueish tint. He had the Major lie on some pine boughs by the fire and he piled on the wool. Gist took the now frozen blanket, stiff as rawhide, and laid it over the reclining Major.

The ground was too frozen to drive in sticks, so he made little tripods on which to hang the wet clothes. All around the fire they sat, exuding trails of steam as the water warmed and evaporated. Their survival that night depended on a hot fire. Despite the possible presence of unfriendly Indians, he felt safe because they were on the island. Gist collected piles of wood and chopped up the larger pieces to create a larger bed of coals. Over by the river he found several large, waterworn rocks to heat by the fire. These he placed between Washington and himself as they lay in the shelter.

Now it was time to tend to his own feet and fingers that had been numb for hours. Peeling off his frozen double moccasins and placing them by the fire, he could see his feet were pale and cold as ice. He rubbed them with snow and then held them as close to the fire as he dared. They burned without being consumed, excruciating and continuous. At times he would slump forwards and close his eyes, but he could not stay for long. With Washington wrapped in all the blankets, he could not get warm. He thought of Sarah and the warmth they had shared over the years. Then the passion of the Shawnee girl would flood his mind. Out here in the frozen dark of night, shivering, unsure of his deliverance, closer to his God than ever before, the guilt grabbed him by the throat and squeezed.

Somehow, he dozed. Waking with a jerk, he listened to the silence, wondering what had startled him. A barred owl hooted close by, answered by its mate. Maybe that was it. He turned all the pieces of clothing around on their tripods and continued to encourage the blaze. He dozed in a sitting position much of the night. As the gray light of morning emerged from the darkness, so too did he unfold and greet another chance to get home. He prodded his prone companion. "Cloudy this morning, Major. I think we'll get that snow we've been wanting."

Washington crawled around collecting his warm, damp clothes.

Gist handed him a cup of hot chocolate. The Major took a sip and made an objectionable face at the bitter warm liquid.

"No more sugar, but at least it'll warm you some."

"What happened to your fingers?" Washington asked, eyeing them as he took the cup. The tips were red and raw with little white blisters here and there.

"Frostbite," he said, looking at his hands. "I've had it before. You lose a fingernail now and then."

"Toes too?"

"Yep."

"Does it hurt?"

"Only if I allowed myself to think about it. Let's see about getting off this island." Gist changed the subject, not wanting to be reminded of the pain he had experienced at the thawing of those digits by the fire during the night. It was true that he had been frostbitten several times before, but never this severe. He wondered whether he would lose some toes this time, but he could not worry about that now.

With both men dressed as before, and new padding in their moccasins, they set out to survey the river. To their surprise and delight, the severe cold that night had frozen the river hard enough for them to pass over to the opposite shore. They resumed their journey across country, heading straight for John Frazier's cabin. Ten exhausting miles later, on but one last handful of parched corn each, they arrived at the trader's cabin.

CHAPTER XXI

May 1754

A weary Christopher Gist rode toward Winchester, after having left Lieutenant Colonel Washington's camp at Great Meadows; the hundred miles he had traveled without sleep. Washington felt it imperative that he make haste to reach Governor Dinwiddie, who was waiting in Winchester for an expected Indian conference. And by coincidence, the Governor had requested Gist's presence. Because of his contribution at Logstown, his expertise was needed. While he was there, he was to inform His Excellency of supplies, uniforms and every other necessity for Washington's virgin, vagabond army. Washington had communicated these deficiencies by letter several times without satisfaction. In fact, the Colonel felt ignored. Perhaps a personal appeal was necessary. Washington also took the opportunity to make Gist the personal purveyor of bad news from the frontier; the French had overrun Gist's Settlement and a large force was marching toward him.

Gist reflected as he rode along, that ever since the Fort Le Boeuf mission, nothing but disappointment had emerged from the west. Upon their return they had met a young Ensign Edward Ward, brother-in-law of George Croghan, leading seventeen pack horses and as many men loaded with tools and supplies – destination, the Forks of Ohio – to build Fort Prince George. Soon after Gist returned to his settlement, he received orders from the Governor; proceed to the Forks and lend a hand. Captain William Trent arrived on February 17th, after completing a storehouse at the mouth of Red Stone Creek on the Monongahela. With him were twenty frontiersmen and traders, whom he had recruited. Gist's old friend Cresap was there, Tanacharison and a half dozen Mingo warriors, all engaged in the task.

On April 13th the fort builders received word from John Davison that a thousand French soldiers were on their way and due to arrive within days. The news lit a fire under the builders, who redoubled their efforts to complete the fort. Conditions could not have been worse. After two months of backbreaking work, poor hunting and meager supplies, they were down to their last several handfuls of corn. Expected provisions and reinforcements had not arrived and Captain Trent had gone to Will's Creek in search of both. Their second-in-command, Lieutenant John Frazier, was busy at his trading post on Turtle Creek and would not take charge.

What happened next, Gist vowed he would never forget. Five days after Davison's warning, just as the last entry gate to the fort was being hung, he and the other builders watched in amazement as the French flotilla snaked towards them. Hundreds of canoes and batteau in neat rows extended up the Allegheny as far as the eye could see. Several hours went by as one by one the vessels beached at the point. Men and cannon formed ranks and marched within one hundred yards of the fort. Claude Pierre de Contrecoeur then demanded of Ensign Ward his surrender. The forty Englishmen were permitted to return to Will's Creek with all their possessions and weapons.

One amusing anecdote emerged from the humiliating event. Gist smiled as he remembered Contrecoeur trying in vain to purchase Ensign Ward's complement of carpentry tools. The sum rose higher with each refusal. Ward, having no use for French currency, only relented when reminded that Contrecoeur might just confiscate the tools and leave him with nothing.

While this was happening, Gist later learned from an officer in the Great Meadows camp, Washington had recruited a force of 160 men from Alexandria and tried to reinforce the builders. The Governor had given him the authority to requisition wagons and horses from local inhabitants along the way and he had done so. In fact, one Winchester resident, forced to contribute to the cause, had complained to the sheriff, who then issued a warrant for Washington's arrest. When the constable was confronted with 160 hostile gun barrels, he reconsidered his duty. Gist laughed. Knowing Washington's respect for law and order, he could just imagine the paradox created in the young man's mind at having to defy an officer of the law in the service of His Majesty the King.

Gist walked his horse along the path widened by Washington's woodcutters several weeks before and thought about what this little episode implied. He knew, having been in Williamsburg, that many were unconvinced of the danger of French aggression. Others felt the Governor was overreacting to the French, because of his personal stake in Ohio Company lands now being threatened. Whatever the reason, few settlers were willing to relinquish their possessions to an army they perceived as unnecessary. Nor did the sight of this pathetic force inspire confidence. Many of Washington's recruits were either teenage farm boys enlisting against parental wishes or derelicts without adequate personal clothing.

Gist soon tired of considering these recent events and turned his thoughts inward. Time for that was rare. Continual occupation with current jobs and future tasks had not allowed him personal plans or evaluations. Nevertheless, as he walked his horse toward Winchester, he thought about his situation, not that of England or Virginia or the pitiable frontier army, but his own. And he was not happy.

First of all, he was still employed by the Ohio Company, but had received no compensation from them in months. Then he was not sure whether he went to aid the fort builders in the service of the Company or the Colony of Virginia. Furthermore, "Gist's Settlement," as it had been called by Indians and traders, had been funded by the Company. All that he owned were his personal effects brought by the family from the Yadkin River farm. Even his second home at Opeekon, near Winchester, was built on Company land. True, he and his sons had hewn the logs and built the small two-story home, but without owning it, the land it was not his.

Two years earlier while in Williamsburg, he had applied to the Board of Trade, along with Andrew Montour and Thomas Cresap, for an 80,000 acre parcel of land to adjoin that of the Ohio Company. This was in part to fulfill the Company's obligation to Montour for his role in the Logstown Treaty. It was also for his own benefit – land he could build upon or sell. The request had not yet been granted. These things, he knew, took time, but his anxiety was growing. It was difficult, having done so much for the Company and Virginia and the Crown, not to feel you were entitled to a few amenities.

As if this were not depressing enough, his move from the Yadkin River to frontier Virginia and his frequent journeys to Williamsburg and Philadelphia had stirred the pot of past creditors. Rumor was that debtors' prison awaited him in Maryland should he return.

Overall he had not much to show for being the first Colonial explorer of the Ohio country, the first settler west of the Allegheny Mountains and the man who had made it possible for Washington to be where he was now. His own journal of that first journey among the Ohio Indians received little attention in England. He had spent considerable effort editing it for public readership, but it was never printed in the Colonies. He did not receive the recognition he had hoped. Then along came that motivated Major Washington, whose life he had saved twice, who turned his journal into a booklet with one day's notice and became a hero. Oh, he did not begrudge Washington his due. Considering his upbringing and lack of experience, he had performed quite well. At least Washington's booklet started many Colonials talking about the French and their threat to the west, even if they could not quite believe it.

And what of his wife and family? Why, he had barely seen Sarah during the past four years. Aside from his two journeys for the Company and one as Washington's guide, he had been to Philadelphia twice to recruit families for the settlement; traveled to Williamsburg several times to deliver his journals and discuss plans and procedures; blazed a path from Will's Creek to Red Stone Creek along with a local Indian named Nemocolin; surveyed and laid out a town and fort on the Ohio at the mouth of Chartier's Creek several miles north of the Forks; abandoned that, according to Company instructions, in favor of a fort at the Forks that he then helped build; built his home at Opeekon; constructed a more elaborate house and out buildings at the New Settlement; attended two major Indian conferences; led his family and relatives from North Carolina to Opeekon and then to the New Settlement, and countless other tasks required by the Company.

He thrived on being busy out on the frontier. Sarah did not. She was unwell and resting at the Opeekon home, attended by Violetta and other family members. It had happened suddenly, or you might say that circumstances accumulated over the last several years and resulted in sudden sickness. The few times Gist was home became unpleasant as tension between them grew. When Fort Prince George was overrun, most of the settlers at Gist's Settlement retreated to Winchester leaving the Gist family and relatives. But when a voice from the past, one Captain La Force – now second-in-command of the new French Fort Duquesne at the Forks – called upon him one morning in early May, he knew it was time to leave. The next visit by French soldiers might not be so amiable.

When he informed Sarah of their need to leave post haste, she flew into a rage. She railed against the French, the Ohio Company, the Indians and Gist himself for bringing her into the horrible situation. Who could blame her? It was the third time she had been asked to move in three years. She sank to the floor sobbing uncontrollably. Not being able to comfort her, he sent Violetta to attend her. Their journey back to Opeekon with but one wagon load of household possessions was uneventful. When he had last left Sarah, she had not recovered. She was silent with a fixed stare, refusing both food and communication. He felt sick to his stomach about this most recent development, but knew not what he could do. So he hardened himself against his thoughts and returned to the settlement for another load.

On the afternoon of May 26th he arrived home to find that La Force and a detachment of fifty soldiers had been there again. Their intentions had been unclear, but the two Indians guarding the house managed to dissuade the invaders from killing his livestock and breaking up the contents of his home. He followed their trail to within five miles of the Great Meadows, where Washington had established his camp several days before. The next morning Gist had reported his reconnaissance and that was when Washington dispatched him to Winchester. His plan to bring another wagon load of belongings to Opeekon on his way to the Indian conference had been foiled.

So now, as he walked his horse among the sixty odd log cabins of Winchester, his mood matched the gray day and the decrepit condition in which most of these structures found themselves. He was not, however, too engrossed to notice what was unusual for an Indian conference – there were no Indians. A treaty of this size should have merited a hundred or more camps on the field adjacent to the Governor's temporary residence. Traders would also have been set up to conduct business. None were present. One militia encampment sat to the rear of the house; two soldiers guarded the door. Gist dismounted and tied his horse to a post. After greeting the guards and introducing himself, he was admitted. At a large table in the center of the room sat Governor Dinwiddie amid stacks of papers, books and ledgers. A white quill pen jerked to the rhythm of its scratching tip. With a flourish he penned his signature and blotted the ink dry.

"Oh, Mr. Gist, good of you to come." He stood and walked around the table to offer his hand. Gist liked the Governor, because he was not pretentious and would make the effort to help the commoner feel at ease. Gist shook the hand and sat in the chair offered to him. The corpulent Dinwiddie sat back down, his ruddy complexion even more flushed for the effort. His smile was pleasant, but Gist noted the bloodshot blue eyes from either lack of sleep or the consumption of wine. His reputation for overindulgence was only exceeded by his esteem as a shrewd businessman.

"I've been expecting you any day now for this conference," he said as a well-dressed black man brought what Gist guessed to be a brandy. He declined the offer for a libation. "Damn few Indians though. But come, come, what news from the western country?" He asked, "and kindly speculate as to where are the Indians."

Gist remembered the first time he heard this Governor speak. Knowing his Scottish roots he had expected a heavy brogue, not the refined English speech he heard. Later he learned the gentleman was raised in Dumfries along the English border and had attended the University of Glasgow. Being a Lowlander, his accent was much closer to that of a London merchant than a Highlander, so many of whom had migrated to the colonies after the Jacobite rebellion.

Gist relayed the points Washington wanted him to cover and then answered the Governor's question. "It would be my guess the tribes are waiting to see what happens between us and the French. We didn't impress them at Fort Prince George and the new French fort there looks pretty inspiring, so I've heard. Those Indians are choosing sides and it appears that most of them have picked the French."

"I thought as much," replied Dinwiddie. He sat back in his chair, sipped his drink and sighed, "Oh me, Mr. Gist, what am I to do?"

Gist interpreted the question as rhetorical.

"I cannot get the burgess to appropriate an adequate sum for our defense without it being so clogged with unreasonable regulations and encroachments. They demand that control of its expenditures reside in a committee of their own choosing. I fear I must soon give in lest our entire frontier be compromised."

Gist now knew he would be there awhile as a sounding board for the man's complaints.

"And of course you've heard the burgesses are refusing to sanction my fee of a mere pistole for affixing my royal seal to a patent for land. I tell you Gist, I've said it before, that the people here are too much bent on a republican spirit. I should propose that Parliament pass an act to force all colonial assemblies to obey the laws of the Crown. By God, that would do the trick." By now the Governor was pacing back and forth. "I assure you, Gist, I am heartily fatigued and quite weary of these obstinate Virginians, so full of their own opinions and completely deaf to arguments and reason on every proposal for their general betterment." He stopped and looked about as if self-conscious about his own tirade. Then he resumed his seat and picked up a broadside. "Listen to what they have written about me.

You promised to relieve our woes,
And with great kindness treat us;
But whorf; awaw! Each infant knows
Your whole design's to eat us.

And that is just one verse, and all over an insignificant pistole." He threw his hands upward in disgust.

Gist thought it prudent to refrain from laughing. He had read the whole poem before and passed it off as just another of the political verbiage often thrown to the public. He also thought it best not to offer his opinion on the subject, as he was inclined to side with the burgesses on the pistole issue.

"As if matters weren't bad enough, " Dinwiddie continued, "I have here another letter from our young commander in the west." He held up a thick sheaf of papers and let them drop on the desk.

Gist remained silent.

"His subalterns have submitted a formal complaint. Their pay being less than equal officers of the British regulars and their daily rations no more than a common soldier's, they have threatened to resign en masse. And our young commander cannot decide whether to join them or not, for he would rather," at this point, Dinwiddie retrieved the letter and read verbatim, "'serve voluntarily, then I will with the greatest pleasure in life devote my services to the expectation without any other regard than the satisfaction of serving my country; but to be slaving dangerously for the shadow of pay, through woods, rocks, mountains -- I would rather prefer the great toil of a day laborer, and dig for a maintenance, provided I were reduced to the necessity, than serve upon such ignoble terms . . .'"

Dinwiddie tossed the letter upon a stack of papers and stared at Gist as if looking for an answer.

"Verbose, I'd say," said Gist, "but he is a passionate young man, your honor. For all his inexperience and bullheadedness he might be precisely the man you need out there right now. He has no preconceived ideas of what can't be done." Gist could not believe he was defending Washington, but the Governor was in such despair that he felt a few well-placed words might help. This was not the time for an objective discussion of Washington's attributes. "Would that we could borrow that passion every now and then, don't you agree, sir?"

"I know your tactics Gist, and they'll not work on me," Dinwiddie cautioned. "You cannot elevate my mood with a positive characterization of that bothersome Colonel." He sat back and smiled. "Does have a persistent nature about him and I confess it has rubbed me raw at times.

"That brings me to the reason I called you. Though I cannot deliver on all the Colonel's demands, I can see that he gets more assistance. Because of your knowledge of the situation, your years of experience in difficult circumstances and your relationship with Washington, you can help him perhaps better than anyone else. You can make his task easier. The young man has complained ardently of hardships, inadequate supplies and conveyances, not to mention the lack of power to hang deserters. I have countered that these misfortunes do attend the military life and are looked upon rather as opportunities for glory than objects of discouragement. Be that as it may, the present commissary, John Carlyle, is inadequate by himself and that is why I am appointing you, along with George Croghan, as assistants to Carlyle. Together you will obtain the provisions this young officer needs to properly vent his passion in the right direction."

Gist was dumbfounded. The absolute last job in the world he wanted was that of commissary – the man everyone blames when there is not enough salt to cure the beef; not enough wagons to carry supplies; when the flour is gone. And judging from what he knew of Washington's problems, improving the situation would be impossible.

The next day Croghan and Montour arrived for the conference. Croghan was no happier than Gist at the appointment. Montour was quite satisfied to be an adviser and interpreter to Washington. The three held a joint meeting with the Governor, who had just received news from the frontier.

"Mr. Gist," Dinwiddie began, "it appears you left our young Lieutenant Colonel too soon, as I would have been obliged for your assessment of this event. On the eve of the day you left, an Indian messenger named Silverheels, if you know him, came to the Colonel from the Half-King saying he knew where a body of Frenchmen were hidden. Washington took forty soldiers and a dozen Indians and tracked the French to a hollow, well concealed among the rocks. He surrounded the soldiers, gave the command and fired. Fifteen minutes later ten Frenchmen lay dead; one escaped. One Englishman was killed and one wounded. Their commander, one Jumonville, has been killed. His second, named Druillon, and Monsieur La Force, with whom I believe you are acquainted, were captured. Twenty-one prisoners will arrive here shortly."

"This is good news," exclaimed Montour. "Our young commander has vanquished his first foe."

"Perhaps," the Governor replied, "but the French maintain they were ambassadors on a peaceful mission to deliver a letter to the English commander to leave French territory. Such a letter was found among Jumonville's papers."

"If this is true," said Gist, grasping the implication, "it would be the same as if the French had attacked us on our mission to Fort Le Boeuf. And that would have been an act of cowardice and murder."

"Arrah now! So how does young Washington defend hisself?"

"Washington claims they had several days to deliver their missive to him, but kept scouting his camp, sending runners back to Fort Duquesne, spying on his movements under the guise of a diplomatic mission. This is what he writes, but his tone betrays his lack of confidence. The one who escaped will most assuredly relate the diplomatic scenario. It matters not who is right, for within several months the whole world will think Washington the cruel murderer of a peaceful diplomat."

PART THREE

"These savages may, indeed, be a formidable enemy to your raw American militia, but upon the King's regulars and disciplined troops, sir, it is impossible they should make any impression."

General Edward Braddock

CHAPTER XXII

May 1755

Incredible how the Indians can sustain their scalp halloo – that piercing, pulsating, penetrating yell that pained the ear, curdled the blood and raised bumps over the entire body of the listener. The pitch rose and fell as each warrior sought to best his brother. How that cry in all its forms had struck fear into the very marrow of man and beast along the frontier. Gist felt the air move as its ululating intensity tried to overwhelm the rhythmic beat of the drum. Showers of sparks from two huge fires carried the resonant sounds upward into the black night.

Brown, tattooed bodies, their beaded breechclouts flapping like wings, leaped to impossible heights and bent to unimaginable lows in the motions of battle. Painted heads of red, black and yellow, crowned in scalp-lock and feathers, blurred in rapid movement.

Gist stood beside Croghan admiring, attuned, mesmerized like everyone else: soldiers, camp followers, General Braddock himself.

"Arrah now," Croghan leaned over toward Gist, "they all live with me at Aughwick, but I don't see a war dance every day."

The volume of the drumbeat diminished as two lines of ten warriors faced off. As the rows charged each other, the beat increased, reaching a crescendo with a mock battle. Fighting pairs pantomimed their fray. When the skirmish was over the warriors melted to the side leaving one lone warrior dancing in the center – Monacatoocha. Tall and rangy, half his body was painted black; the other red. The tomahawk carved in his chest was outlined in the opposing color; its head of red against the black background dripped blood. Likewise were the crude bow and arrow engraved in each cheek of his face contrasted.

Older and slower of movement, the drums matched his cadence as he began singing in a high, scratchy voice. He sang of his thirty battles, of wars and raiding parties, of killing seven men and taking eleven prisoners in one battle alone, of vision quests, his love for the English and hate for the French. On he sang of renewed allegiances, reiterating his promise to fight for Britain.

Earlier that very afternoon these same Indians had congregated in front of the General's marquee outside the gate of Fort Cumberland. With long colorful metaphor, facilitated by Croghan's creative translation, they agreed to take up the hatchet against the French and march to Fort Duquesne. Braddock vowed to be their staunch ally and never lie to them. He then lead the contingent over to the artillery, where soldiers fired in succession three howitzers, three 12-pounders and three cohorns into the woods. After the display that elicited hoots and howls from the Iroquois, they returned to their camp and celebrated by feasting on a bullock furnished by the General.

Now, as Monacatoocha danced and sang on, Gist inquired of Croghan, "have you heard from the Delaware and Shannoah?"

He motioned for Gist to follow some distance away where there was less noise. "Not yet and that disturbs me. But I'd say the General's treatin' all our Injens quite well, don't ye think? Rumors of that must be circulatin' by now. Think we're bein' watched?"

"I do," replied Gist. "I just hope we're not stuck here too long or we'll lose the interest of your friends. You can see your Indians are ready to go to war tomorrow and we're not likely to march till sometime next month. Here it is May 19th and Braddock's been here nine days with no sign of leaving."

"Arrah now, that young Shirley seems to think we can be ready in a fortnight," Croghan said, referring to the General's secretary, son of the Massachusetts Governor.

The two continued to discuss the lack of supplies promised by Pennsylvania and Virginia, spoiled beef packed without pickle by Thomas Cresap; sour flour packed in green wooden barrels by his son, Michael. And where were 200 wagons, 2500 horses and 500 beeves promised by Governor Dinwiddie?

"Aye, 'tis our misfortune that the General did not land in Pennsylvania and build a road to this fort from there instead of goin' through Virginia. 'Tis shorter and much more settled with farms where the army could buy wagons and supplies."

Gist glanced at Croghan, disappointed that his friend would bring up such a sore subject.

"Now George, we've heard this before. It would have taken an extra month to cut a twelve-foot road from Pennsylvania to here."

"Aye, and isn't that the very month we're gonna be spendin' right here waitin' for the supplies we could have had from Pennsylvania?"

"But at the time, we didn't know Dinwiddie would have so many problems," Gist countered.

Croghan continued. "Gist, every man knows what the Virginians'll not be admittin'; that the only reason this road goes from Alexandria instead of Philadelphia is the Ohio Company. Whoever has the road to the Forks at the end of this war will own the fur trade."

"You seem, sir, to imply our Company somehow misrepresented its case to the General to influence his decision to go through Virginia." Gist bristled.

"Now, take it easy Gist," Croghan mollified.

"Let me remind you who would not appropriate funds for a fort at the Forks, even after the Indians requested one – Pennsylvania. Virginia built it instead. And who would not appropriate funds for this war – Pennsylvania. Virginia voted £20,000. So don't go preaching to me about Virginia's faults."

Gist turned and walked away, angry with himself for getting angry and angry with Croghan for making him so. But Croghan was right about the fur trade. Besides bringing British trade goods up the Potomac to Will's Creek and on to the Forks, the Ohio Company wanted to bring regular shipments of wagons loaded with raw materials to a factory at the Forks, where trade goods could be produced at low cost. This would further outmaneuver Pennsylvania's system of licensed individual traders. However, this plan required a road, which Virginia and the British military were building. And with the fort to protect the factory, there would be a settlement and more land to purchase from the Indians to sell to settlers. There would be fortunes to make, and his would be among them. That was why he was here: to continue where he had left off – was forced to leave off due to the damn French invaders – so he could get on with making that fortune while he was still young enough to enjoy it. And Hell's fire to anyone who would stand in his way!

General Braddock looked happy and well fed on the luxurious gourmet meal served by his two chefs. Gist could smell the left-over baked ham wafting in from the cook tent nearby.

"Quite some entertainment the other evening, I say," said Braddock. "If our Indian friends put as much energy into the fight as they do the dance, we have nothing to fear." Gist and Croghan nodded in agreement, as their audience with the General began.

"Our Delaware visitor the other evenin'," Croghan commented, "spoke of a reinforcement of 900 Frenchmen expected at Fort Duquesne, but with this drought, there's no water in the river. They cannot get there."

"I agree," said Braddock, "but even if remote, I can't afford that possibility. If what he says about a garrison of fifty is true, we must march as soon as possible. I've received from Winchester a draft of Evans' new map of Virginia and Pennsylvania." All three men stood looking at the black outlines of rivers, mountains and colonial boundaries on ivory colored parchment. "As you can see, a route by way of Shippensburg would have been shorter than our route through Will's Creek. Too late now. But Governor Morris says he'll have that road done by the first of July. It'll run from here," he pointed to Shippensburg, "to here at Turkeyfoot." He moved his finger across the map to a spot where the Youghiogheny River and Laurel Creek joined to form the likeness of its namesake. "It'll be our supply line from Pennsylvania, especially if we have to lay siege to the fort. I can no longer depend on Virginia."

The General had given Virginia two days to send the promised supplies or he would march back to Alexandria. Braddock no longer trusted Dinwiddie's promises and determined to buy his supplies from a more cooperative Pennsylvania. He sent Washington to Williamsburg to bring the Crown's £4000 sterling out to the fort. Coincidentally two days later ninety-one well-built Pennsylvania farm wagons arrived, courtesy of the new Postmaster General, Benjamin Franklin. He had placed ads offering to pay for their rental, the cash being supplied by Braddock. Eleven of them, along with twenty packhorses, were loaded with food and other gifts for the officers – a present from the Pennsylvania Assembly. Gist mood sank as these presents continued to make Virginia look bad. And this was the third such string of packhorses from Philadelphia.

Gist, however, had no time to brood over the situation when the next day Richard Peters, secretary to the Pennsylvania Governor, rode into the fort. His mission was to check on the progress of the new road. Peters stayed four days and on the last day visited the Iroquois camp a quarter of a mile away. Gist, Croghan, Montour and Monacatoocha were there. For the secretary's benefit, the outspoken Monacatoocha launched a diatribe against the General, who, he said, held war councils without consulting the Iroquois. Furthermore, both officers and enlisted men had been propositioning their wives and daughters, plying them with frontier whiskey and trinkets, luring them into their tents and debauching them. This led to fights among the men and quarrels with the Indians. Peters, an ordained minister in the Church of England, observed this licentious behavior and registered his abhorrence with Braddock. Gist and Croghan were again called in the next day.

"Gentlemen," the General began, "Mr. Peters has advised me that I should end this lasciviousness by sending the Indian women back to Pennsylvania. This will unburden the troops with thoughts of fornication and render discipline more tolerable. Now I don't begrudge a soldier his due now and then, but the situation has gone quite too far."

Gist and Croghan looked at each other with concern. "Sir," Croghan was first to speak, "if ye be sendin' home their women, I can guarantee the men will follow and ye'll loose 'em all."

Braddock listened.

"As you yourself have requested, sir," Gist added, "the Iroquois have already promised to scout for the army, and to send home their women when we march. We cannot travel with impunity through these woods without Indian scouts."

"And what about the 400 Cherokee pledged by your Governor. Is that promise to be as empty as the others?"

"My son, Nathaniel, has been sent on that mission and should arrive any day now." God, he hoped he was right. A boon like that would guarantee their success.

"You'll forgive me Mr. Gist," said Braddock, "if I reserve judgement until I see them. Meanwhile I shall have to order all sutlers to cease the sale of liquor to any Indian, including your friends Montour and Monacatoocha, who can suck up quite too much of it. Furthermore, the Indian women are forbidden from the soldiers' camp, likewise soldiers and officers from theirs. I expect a degree of bawdy behavior among so many men, but this intermixing has caused such a decline in discipline I can no longer give it my countenance. Keeping them separate must do for now." Braddock dismissed them.

"Well, there ye have it," remarked Croghan after leaving the General. "I wondered how long 'twould take for him to start layin' down the law."

"You'll hear plenty of complaining among the soldiers now, I'll wager."

"Arrah now, soldiers is always grumblin. 'Tis in the blood. Why, if they was garrisoned in London's finest brothel with unlimited whisky, they'd be complainin' for lack of sleep."

Gist laughed.

"Glad to see you're in a better mood now."

"Not really," Gist said.

"With that new Pennsylvania road completed, maybe there'll be a bit of friendly competition after this campaign."

"Not so friendly, I'll wager."

"Arrah now, once upon a time ye told me there was room for everyone out here. Have ye changed your mind now?"

Gist could not answer before three Delaware chiefs, who had just arrived, shouted their demands for an audience with the General. Their voices rose as they learned Braddock was unavailable. Gist and Croghan rushed over to them with the proper greetings and apologized for the General's lack of time. Tomorrow, Croghan said, would be a better day.

The next morning Braddock interviewed the three sachems escorted by Gist and Croghan. They asked when the General would begin his march against Fort Duquesne. When Braddock responded by saying within several days, the Indians smiled. They vowed to return to their homes, bring their brothers and meet the army along the way.

"They be spies, or me name ain't George Croghan," he commented while walking away from the General's tent.

"My thoughts exactly and I don't know that I'd have given them those presents the way the General did."

"Aye, ye can bet he's wise to their rouse, but also wise in the givin' so's not to arouse their suspicions."

"Silly though, sending spies," said Gist. "They're sure to be observing us from atop Will's Mountain and can tell by our preparations we're almost ready to leave."

"Aye, and we'll be out of here so dreadful slow their spies be back an' forth to the fort a dozen times 'fore we get there."

"So I guess we can assume the Delaware and Shannoah have gone over to the French."

"Well laddie, who can blame 'em? They've seen us get nothin' but a beatin' from the French since we was forced to leave the Forks. And how long ago was that?"

"April last. So what'll we do now about Indian scouts?"

"Don't know, but I think we'll be findin' out soon. Yonder rides yer son, Nate, and he's alone."

Nathaniel rode over to his father and dismounted. Tall and well-built, he looked like a twenty-year-old Christopher Gist.

"Well. Nate my boy," said the elder Gist, "welcome to the very edge of civilization. What news from the South?"

"Not good I'm afraid." Nate explained how he had recruited several hundred Cherokees, many of whom he had traded with before. They were north bound when a South Carolina trader, one Richard Pearis, met them along the path. Because of prior business dealings, Nate knew him to be an unscrupulous trader, purveyor of liquor, and antagonistic toward the Gists. Caring nothing for the fate of Virginia and Pennsylvania, he began trading his immense store of whiskey to the Indians for anything he could get, including future promises of furs. He seemed to delight in foiling the plans of the English army to enlist the Cherokee by spreading lies about the Ohio Company. They had plans, he said, to move into the western portions of the Carolinas to steal Indian lands. Within several hours, most of the Indians were out of their minds with no thought of a northerly journey. Besides that, Pearis asked where was Nathaniel's letter of authority to recruit them? Where was the Governor's seal of approval? Nathaniel had none. His orders had been verbal. He waited several days for the Cherokees to sober up, which they did, but Pearis' words had hardened their hearts against fighting for the English.

The news was indeed disheartening. There would be no Cherokee and no Delaware or Shawnee. Braddock was livid. His anger made him easily swayed by Colonel Innis, commander of Fort Cumberland, who recommended employ no more than ten Indians as scouts.

"Mr. Croghan," Braddock demanded, "is it true these Indians eat twice as much as any soldier?"

"Now General, that be true, but ye see, sir, they also sees many starvin' times and so eat a plenty when it's convenient. Beggin' your pardon sir, but Colonel Innis don't have an ounce worth of knowledge 'bout Injen affairs. Your secretary has even said how they be managed much better since we took over."

"Shirley said!" The General raised his brow along with his voice. "What in hell would he know of such matters?"

"But sir, we need as many Injens as we can get to scout ahead and keep us from surprise attacks. And now without the Cherokees . . ."

"Damn the Cherokees!" roared Braddock. "I have neither wagons nor horses enough to carry the proper provisions for my own army, much less a band of insatiable Indians. I say no more than ten of your Iroquois warriors can go as scouts. You are to send the rest home and damn me if my life won't be much simplified!!"

On a cold May 29th morning Colonel Sir John St. Clair and his carpenters began cutting a twelve-foot swath along an Indian path up Will's Mountain. But it was soon evident that the mountain was too steep for wagons and artillery. Even with the help of Lieutenant Spendelowe and half a dozen seamen to work block and tackle, three wagons slid off the path and splintered on the rocks below. Another way was found – the "Narrows"– a corridor between Will's Creek and the mountain. It was rough, swampy and impassable in wet weather. But the drought rendered it usable and St. Clair's men spent several days on that road. On June 6th Colonel Sir Peter Halket marched his regiment from Fort Cumberland. Four days later General Braddock, his staff, and a mounted body guard of Virginia militia rode out.

But the army of 2300 men crawled slower than a slug. With not enough horses for all the cannon, wagons and packs, those that were supplied by Virginia and Pennsylvania comprised the dregs of the equine world – old, weak and sway-backed. Braddock suggested each officer, who often kept several, restrict himself to one horse. That freed up an additional one hundred. George Washington's suggestion of more packhorses and fewer wagons was adopted. Still, the pace was agonizing. The entire army, four soldiers abreast on a twelve foot road, stretched nearly four miles. More than once the rear camped where the front had been the night before. Braddock sent back some of the artillery and more of the wives, but it made little difference.

On the evening of June 16th the General called Christopher Gist into his tent for one of their usual meetings about what ground lay ahead. This time, however, he asked a new question.

"Mr. Gist," he began, "no doubt we have managed, with the utmost difficulty, to march a grand total of twenty-two miles in ten days. With ninety miles more of this wretched wilderness to Fort Duquesne . . . well . . . you can see how long this campaign would take."

Gist nodded. The General was telling him nothing he did not already know.

He continued. "Every intelligence we have tells us that Fort Duquesne is expecting reinforcements. Remember Governor Morris' message several weeks ago of thirty batteau passing Oswego on Lake Ontario? And several apparent Delaware deserters, or spies, have spoken of the same. We know with this drought that those forces, however many they be, cannot float down the river route to the Fort."

Gist again nodded.

"Our young Virginian, Mr. Washington, has suggested we split our force, marching faster with our best men and officers and light artillery, while the bulk of wagons, baggage and heavy artillery follow along behind. We would cut the time by half. You've been over the route. What think you on these matters?"

Gist felt this was his best opportunity to advise the General on how to fight Indians. He thought it quite presumptuous of Washington to be advising on military matters. He, himself, felt qualified to advise on Indians, but he was no tactician.

"Well sir, I have no eye for matters military and could not presume . . ."

"Come, come now Gist," Braddock interrupted. "I have the benefit of the best and worst advice from my officers. I shall seek that in good time. I do not hold you in any way responsible for our debacle on Will's Mountain. You were asked to scout which routes were in existence. Not having seen British engineers and seamen in action before, you could not have known our capabilities. No, I had poor advice from those who should have known better. I ask you this precisely because you are not military. Never let it be said that I do not seek alternatives before I make a decision."

"Thank you sir," Gist remarked at not being blamed for the mess, although he never considered himself culpable. "Seems to me Washington is correct in figuring your march time will be cut in half. The route gets worse with the several mountains to cross, and with less of a force you'll get there faster. One thing though, by taking the best of everything for yourself and leaving the worst for the rear detachment, the distance between will increase daily. If something goes wrong, they won't be able to help."

"Thank you Mr. Gist."

"One more thing, General, Croghan's Indians will leave soon and the Cherokee have not come. This leaves us with but eleven scouts, including me and my boys, to reconnoiter our approach. But since the marching army is several miles long, our flanks will be open to ambuscades. Why not let the Virginians and other Colonials guard the flanks? I know some of them are inexperienced . . ."

"And I witnessed that inexperience on the parade ground at Fort Cumberland. No Mr. Gist, this requires trained troops with discipline. Rest assured we'll have small parties marching on our flanks to examine all hedges, copses and ditches for enemy concealment."

"Sir, with all due respect, your troops are trained to stand in a line and fire on command, which they do very well. But in an ambuscade the Indians will be concealed behind trees, aiming at a dozen bright red coats all in a row. Their training and discipline will be for naught; they'll be dead. We need to train your soldiers to look for the nearest tree when the shooting starts."

"Mr. Gist, your exaggerated scenario will not hold up under scrutiny. The flanking parties will hear the enemy approaching and be at the ready. Furthermore, I'll not have Britain's "finest" cowering behind rocks and trees, hiding from ragged savages.

"Sir, I assure you that I can sneak up on your soldiers without being heard and the Indians are better at it than I. With Colonials patrolling your flanks, that won't happen. And they won't be cowering; they'll be picking their shots and making each one count."

"Zounds man, we can't have Colonials tramping around in the woods! My troops would think they were the enemy and fire on them. I'll tell you the same thing I told Franklin and anyone who questions the fighting tactics of my army. These savages may indeed be a formidable enemy to your raw Americans, but upon the King's regulars and disciplined troops, it is impossible they should make any impression."

"General, sir," Gist stood. "If we're attacked, you condemn your men to certain death at the hands of Indians who'll not stop at your surrender, but rush in and hack . . ."

"Mr. Gist," Braddock barked, "you are insubordinate! I'll hear no more! Dismissed!"

On June 19th after much reorganization and re-packing, Washington's plan was implemented. Thirty-five days of provisions were packed onto horses, the number of wagons was reduced to thirty while the number of horses per wagon was increased. Thirteen hundred of the best troops were picked. In addition the artillery was reduced to four howitzers, four twelve-pounders and two six-pounders. One entire wagon carried presents for any Indians they may meet.

Colonels Halket, St. Clair and Gage, Lieutenant Gates and others were included in the 1300. Colonel Thomas Dunbar commanded the second half of the army following in the rear. One man, however anxious as he was to ride at the front, stayed behind. George Washington, aide-de-camp to the General, whose idea it was to split the force, had been laid prostrate with the bloody flux. Braddock left him along the road several miles from Dunbar's camp with a guard and his own personal physician. The Colonel let it be known that he intended to be present at the taking of the fort. That enthusiasm was inspiring to some and foolhardy to others. Gist, knowing the young man better than anyone, felt these sentiments to be more self-serving in his continual effort to achieve notoriety in his military career.

In spite of problems and holdups and whatever else would go wrong, the army affected a slow slither through the woods on its way to liberate the frontier from the French. Soon, Gist thought to himself, he could resume his quest for property and position.

CHAPTER XXIII

June 27, 1755

Christopher Gist knew this path well. It led from Redstone Old Fort on Monongahela fifteen miles to his settlement, or what used to be his settlement. In the twilight hours he stood on that path on the hill overlooking the stump-covered valley. The smoky haze of hundreds of British campfires partially bscured the burned out ruins of the three houses he had helped build, but he knew where to look. The firelight reflected off the soot-covered logs left standing. One of those homes had been his. He remembered the special care with which he had picked the straightest logs to be hewn square, and fit the dovetail joints to perfection at the corners. It was to have been a showplace for the Company and the final home for himself and his family. Once the rival land claims were settled, there would have been 500,000 acres to find settlers for, an Indian trade to supervise, and so many other activities that he would be busy the rest of his life.

But the French had torched his dreams. With renewed bitterness he reflected upon the events that preceded their crime one year ago, almost to the day. After his meeting with Governor Dinwiddie, he and Croghan returned to Washington's camp at the Great Meadows and led the ragged Colonial army to his Settlement. Washington's men tore down his hand-hewn log barn and erected palisades for protection from the French, who were sure to arrive soon. Other soldiers began widening the Nemacolin Path that he had helped clear two years earlier. It led east from his home, thirteen miles up and over Chestnut Ridge, back to the Great Meadows. For Washington to make a stand, that path, their supply line, had to be reliable.

"Here, Colonel Washington, take my horses, my wagons and any of my supplies you need," Gist had offered. "We must defend at all costs what we and the Company have worked so hard to build."

Washington agreed, that is until his Indian scouts reported 800 French soldiers within hours of reaching Gist's Settlement well before he could complete his defenses. With grave reluctance, Washington and his officers made an unanimous decision to remove over the difficult Chestnut Ridge path to the Great Meadows. Here they reinforced an existing supply shack with a circular palisade and called it Fort Necessity.

Tanacharison and his few Indian followers, however, refused to fight for

Washington. The fort was indefensible, they said, out there in a small depression surrounded by forest, some of which was well within firing range. Gist had urged Washington, as had others, to move to a more defensible position, but that same stubbornness that surfaced in their Fort Le Boeuf mission closed his ears to any advice. So they hunkered down and awaited the French. And it began to rain. The newly dug trenches filled with water and the scant earthworks turned into heaps of mud. Then the French and their Indian allies began firing from behind the trees closest to the fort. Every cow and horse, many of which were his, every camp cur – his own pet hounds among them – were successfully targeted. In a few hours all their transportation and meat supply lay lifeless in the mud. The ensuing torrential downpour soaked their remaining gunpowder. And the bodies of the dead and wounded piled higher.

Washington had no choice but to accept the French offer of surrender the next day. So on July 4th Washington marched his tattered army back to Will's Creek. The articles of capitulation, which granted them the honors of war, also forbade the English from reentering the area, even crossing the mountains, for one year.

Now, as he stood overlooking the army, it was one week short of that year and the English were here in full force to send the French back to New France where they belonged. Many officers from Washington's fateful campaign were behind him now on this very path. All were captains now: George Croghan, Adam Stephen, Thomas Waggoner, Andrew Lewis and Peter Hog among others. Tonight they were volunteers, temporarily attached to Captain Robert Dobson of His Majesty's Forty-Eighth Regiment of Foot, leading a detachment of eighty men, most of whom were from the Virginia Independent Companies.

Earlier that day several miles ahead of Braddock's army, Monacatoocha had discovered an enemy camp at the base of a high rocky hill where the Nemacolin Path forked. Over 150 French and Indians had camped there for weeks. The number of warm campfire ashes and sheer volume of boot and moccasin tracks told of their recent occupation. Yet the affront given by the enemy's proximity to superior numbers was not enough. The Indians had stripped the bark off some of the surrounding chestnut trees. In red paint they had drawn many figures representing themselves in the taking of scalps and prisoners. Explicit taunts, threats and abusive French phrases accompanied the Indian pictographs.

"I remember this place," said Captain Adam Stephen, the thirty-year-old Scotsman who had been a surgeon on one of His Majesty's hospital ships during the wars with France in the 1740's. A captain called a break and the Virginia regiment dispersed to view the pictographs. Stephen spoke in a low, dramatic voice with a gentle brogue as Gist and several Virginians gathered around.

"Half-King's Rocks, some calls it. 'Twas under these very rocks we met the Half-King and planned the attack on that bla'guard Jumonville an' his frog-eatin' band o' spies. May last, it 'twas. There was forty of us, joined we was by the Half-King, Monacatoocha an' five other Iroquois all painted fierce, they was. We begins to sneak up on 'em an' surround 'em durin' the blackest night ye ever did see. Why, 'twas so black we lost seven men on our way to these rocks. Never did find 'em."

The men laughed at the obvious joke calculated to relieve the tension a bit before proceeding. Stephen resumed the story.

"Now, at first light, one o' them Frenchies sees us movin' about an' fires his gun, whereupon Washington yells 'fire,' which we do. 'Tweren't long 'fore a dozen French lay on the ground dead or writhin', an' the soldiers runnin' about tryin' ta find their guns, an' the Injens attackin' with their screeches an' blood curdlin' screams. Aye, but 'twas a wonderful sight ta behold, I tell ye."

Gist was silent, as was every other spectator, imagining the scene described in vivid detail by Captain Stephen. Some began to drift away, believing the tale to have ended.

"Aye, but there's more," he said, and the drifters returned. "Ye see, when the Injens began attackin' those Frenchies, they all run back towards us wavin' their arms in the air an' callin' fer quarter, which we give. Now all twenty of 'em be standin' in a line an' Tanacharison walks up to their commander, Jumonville. Stands right in front of 'im, he does, an' asks if he's an Englishman. Well, Jumonville answers proudly that he's a Frenchman. Now I would not o' believed it if I'd not seen it with me own eyes, but Tanacharison takes his tomyhawk and just splits Jumonville's head right down the middle like me mother would a ripe melon."

Gist could feel the crowd wince.

Still not done, the Captain continued. "Then the Half-King bends down an takes out the brains, washes his hands with 'em an' proceeds to scalp the rotten bastard. He holds up the bloody hair in triumph and demands that all the French prisoners be turned over ta him ta be dispatched to avenge the death of his father, who'd been killed, boiled and eaten by the French."

At the last statement several rangers retreated in utter disbelief and voiced their opinions. Captain Stephen defended himself. "I tell ye lads that be the honest truth or may Tanacharison come back an' haunt me! Ask Captain Waggoner; ask Monacatoocha; they was there."

"What happened to this Half-King fellow?" Someone asked.

"Well, he took it personal, that Washington would not take his advice and move to a position more defensible than Fort Necessity. Went on home to Aughwick and died several months later. Remained loyal to the English ta the end, he did. Now that's admirable, I'd say."

"Or damn foolish," shouted someone in the crowd.

"Here, here," said another.

"Move out," the call echoed among the ranks. Amid grunts and groans, the Virginians raised themselves to the task of following the tracks of the French and Indians, who had taken the western fork toward the Monongahela. They hoped to engage the enemy and avenge the deaths of four soldiers and a wagoner several days before.

The expedition marched all night to the mouth of Redstone Creek on Monongahela. A semipermanent Indian camp greeted them, but they found no enemy. The party destroyed one bateau, several canoes and some food and retraced its steps until they intersected the path that led due east to the ruins of Gist's Settlement. Here it was that the pride of the British Army under the command of Major General Edward Braddock had arrived while the detachment was gone.

Gist, lead scout on the return trip, was some distance ahead of the company and took the opportunity to sit on a downed tree to wait for the Virginians. Since Braddock appointed him, he could come and go as he pleased, answerable only to the General. His job had been easy so far, compared to the past year as assistant commissary for Washington's army. What a terrible experience that had been. The Virginia legislature would not appropriate money for the war effort because of its feud with the Governor over the Pistole. So he had used some of his own meager funds to buy provisions for the troops and reimbursed himself when he did get funds. Was he not in the employ of Virginia? And when was the last time he had gotten paid? So he had "borrowed" against his future income on several occasions to satisfy some of his old debts that had caught up with him, intending to repay the Colony at a later date. Governor Sharpe of Maryland had accused him of embezzlement. Gist's friends, William Fairfax, Washington and even Governor Dinwiddie defended his integrity. The loyalty of his Ohio Company superiors diffused the heated situation, but Gist was never so glad as when, on May 27th, he was appointed by Braddock.

His own current duties involved meeting with the General every two or three days to discuss the terrain ahead and where the army might bivouac. The officers marked suggestions on the map and Gist would take his leave. The rest of the time he scouted ahead with Croghan and his Indians. He was proud of his third son, Thomas, who had joined the expedition and whose wilderness skills rivaled those of the Iroquois warriors his age. He spent much of his time living and scouting with them.

The army had encountered no resistance, that is if you did not count the five who were killed several days ago while looking for stray horses. He wondered if that would change as they progressed.

The sound of footsteps, branches brushing against leggins and occasional profanity let Gist know the company was near. Less than half the eighty volunteers had had any real wilderness experience. Some were good marksmen and well fit for endurance, but a stealth mission through the woods was an altogether different matter. He was not surprised they encountered no Indians, as the noise they made preceded them. But it gave them all an immediate purpose, something missing from the past several weeks of marching with Braddock.

"Aye, Mister Gist," called the familiar Irish voice of George Croghan from behind, "'Tis a splendid spot ye've picked to admire His Majesty's finest lobster-backs. To be sure, we're the perfect distance, I'd say; they're pretty to look at, but ye can't smell 'em." Croghan picked a convenient rock on which to sit as the Virginians began to pass.

Gist laughed. A thousand unwashed bodies below could put out quite an unpleasant signal of their approach.

"So what d'ye think, Gist? How will His Majesty's finest bear up against the French and their Injens?"

"Do you mean little men in bright red coats standing in a skirmish line out in the open against Indians behind trees?"

Croghan nodded, gazing out across the half-mile to the fires of the Redcoats. "Arrah now, Mister Gist, where would you rather be?"

"You can be sure I'll pick myself the biggest tree I can find."

"Methinks since we far outnumber 'em, that may not make such a difference," Croghan replied. "With this drought, 'tis sure the French cannot get reinforcements."

"I was thinking about fear. I've noticed it coming on since that dance your Indians did at Fort Cumberland. The Colonials have been filling British heads with tales of scalping and torture and every manner of evil the Indians have ever committed. And since those men were killed, we have sentries shooting at their own shadows."

"Don't look now," Croghan said, "but your competition just walked up."

"Gist looked around to see Captain Andrew Lewis, a former surveyor for the Blair Company, whose grant conflicted with that of the Ohio Company.

"So what ye be thinkin' there Gist?" Lewis was another Irishman like Croghan with a penchant for jocularity. "When the French an' British have done with their fightin' over this land, will there be anythin' left fer us ta fight over?"

Gist smiled. "I was just wondering what George here promised you in return for not including his Iroquois land grant in your company's survey. Can't recall that I got anything."

"Now, that'll be between us," he winked in Croghan's direction.

"Now Chris, I cannot believe you disremember me own gift," said Croghan. "Why, I sparred ye an 'orrible death at the hands of them Injens. Imagine them learnin' your true designs on that first trip five years ago. They most likely would've cut ye up into pieces too small for bait." Croghan grinned.

"Then I wouldn't have to sit here and listen to your blarney and bullshit." Gist knew, however, there was truth in Croghan's words.

The volunteers quieted at the approach of Captain Dobson, who looked out of place in his scarlet coat, white breeches and tan garters alongside the blue uniforms of the Virginians.

"Blimey, I sees you blokes is too tired to march any farther, ay, and what wit you beein' an example to all these fine troops an' all? Well, that's all right wit me 'cause assistant commissary Leslie's ta doll out the last o' the rum ration this very night and I do means ta be there, I do."

"Better hurry then before it runs out," warned Gist. "I hear the sutler's charge four shillings a pint."

"Aye," replied Dobson. "Who can afford that, I wonder? Pleasant trot through the wood, ay?"

As the Captain strode away the officers spoke of how he was so amiable with the Colonials, congenial and pleasant, lacking the haughtiness of many British officers.

"Aye, he may be all that." The new voice of one who had just walked up on the conversation, belonged to Peter Hog, the grizzled, fifty-two-year-old Scotsman, who had fought with the Jacobites against the British nine years earlier. "But I cannot forget the British regiments who slaughtered us at Culloden. The Forty-eighth right down there were one of 'em." He pointed to Captain Dobson's regiment in the British camp below, "Mind ye now lads, after they beat us and the Highlanders, no quarter was given ta the wounded; and there was many. Butchered 'em where they lay."

Gist could see his eyes glaze over and his lip curl as he continued to described the events.

"They didn't stop there, no sir. They was ordered to lay waste all the land for fifty miles 'round; every house and barn burned, every animal shot and every woman defiled in the most ruthless manner. And 'twas men like Captain Dobson there and Braddock, hisself, that laid aside all shrouds of decency when so ordered. I've got far less feelin's against these Injens who torture and scalp and rape and eat the flesh of their victims 'cause they've never known different. But the British – them bloody bastards I cannot forgive nor forget."

There was total silence. Gist could feel the hate emanating from this bearded man, who was his age, but looked so much older.

Peter Hog, himself, changed the mood. "Cannot tell ye which be worse, that bein' the battle yell o' them savage Highlanders or the screechin' an' hollerin' o' these here Injens."

"Aye, puts the fear o God into a body," remarked Lewis. "Especially the women among us who fear debauchery at the hands of the Injens."

"Well," Croghan jumped in, "that's one thing they needn't fear. 'Tis a crime they despise and the only one punishable by death."

"What about murder?" asked Stephen.

"Murder is a crime avenged by the family, but rape brings tribal punishment."

"Well, I've heard different," Peter Hog countered.

"Then ye've heard it from men who know they'd gladly do it themselves if given the chance an' therefore expect the Injens to do it also. But it ain't so. I've lived and traveled among the red men for fifteen years an' never once heard of a white woman captive bein' raped. Now there be a reason. The Injens purify themselves in sweat lodges and take no carnal pleasures for three days and nights before and after a battle or raid. To do so, they believe, would bring bad luck and even their own death."

"And besides," Gist added, "most of the captured women are adopted into the tribe. Some marry warriors like that Mary Harris over in White Women's Town."

"Ahem," Captain Lewis cleared his throat, "has anyone noticed our troops have passed us by an' we're up here all alone. We may be Virginia's finest rangers, but wouldn't we be safer down there?" He pointed toward the British army below.

"Ye've nothin' to worry bout lads," Peter Hog promised, "I've kept some sentries posted. Besides, if in twenty hours o' marchin' we couldn't find a single Injen, you think they'll show up now?"

"Well, I do believe the fastest way to find the bastards would be to venture out here by meself," Lewis said. "Be just our luck to get ambushed after seeing nary an Injen tonight."

"Speakin' of ambuscades," spoke Croghan after some silence, "Franklin's warnin' to the General 'bout bein' ambushed on the march has not come to pass."

"I know, but we're still fifty miles from the fort." Gist offered. "Indian raiding parties have bypassed us and attacked all the settlers around Fort Cumberland. Colonel Innes doesn't have enough troops to protect anyone but himself. The last courier from the fort told how twenty settlers had been killed or captured. But those raiders will be on their way back soon and may start hitting our column. We'll not be hard to find. They'll just walk up the road we've made until they reach the rear guard."

"Aye, but ye know that the rear guard may not give us much protection, don't ye?" Croghan asked.

Gist gave a knowing glance and nodded his head. "The rear guard is just there to catch the deserters."

They all laughed at the clever joke that was by no means new.

Gist continued, "Well, I just had a thought, given the soldiers' knack for desertion. Maybe the General is right not to consider teaching the Redcoats to fight wilderness style. If he were to let them sort of fade into the woods behind the trees, he soon may be without his army."

Laughter faded into a silence that signaled the time to retire. They rose, called in the pickets, and headed down the path toward the army.

Croghan and waited for Gist. "Ahem, now Chris, I'd not yet found the right time to tell ye, but I was dreadful sorry to hear of your wife's passin'." Croghan hesitated as if not knowing whether to continue. "I never met the lass, but by all accounts she was a fine woman."

Sarah had never recovered from her sickness and died at their Opeekon home several months after he left her in Nancy's care. It had taken two weeks for the news to reach him and since she would have long been buried, he saw no reason to go home.

"That she was."

"And how did her passin' come about, if I might ask?"

The death messenger had not said. The short missive penned by their daughter, Nancy, had just mentioned "passing on." But he knew of her sickness; had heard of it before. It was the sickness of a strange, detached melancholy that overcomes a body when it no longer cares to live, like a prisoner with no hope of release. Perhaps she felt like a prisoner in a wilderness world of pain and drudgery. It might have been different had she been raised in that world, but she was not. How to convey that in a few words to Croghan, he did not know.

And how could he express his own guilt in the matter? In spite of the circumstances, he alone felt responsible for his failure in business and their subsequent move from Baltimore, where Sarah had been so vibrant and loving. He had tried to fashion a comfortable home for her on the frontier, and for a while it seemed to work. He had, though, cast his lot with the Company. He thought he was doing it for Sarah – a better life and more of the comforts to which she was accustomed. But he could kid himself only so long. He was trying to regain his family's status while satisfying his own frontier desires. Sarah got left behind. He knew he was the cause of her decline and death, and he could never atone for it.

"She died," he stopped. "She died of a broken spirit, if that's something you can die of George. Or maybe the Lord just called her home. Anyway, I'm sure she's a lot happier now than ever she was out here in this woods."

"Aye, it'll either make ye or break ye, I've heard it said. No offence intended."

"None taken. That's the way it is. And the weak shall perish and the strong shall survive."

"Sure now, but that sounds Biblical?

"No, I just thought it up, or maybe read it somewhere."

"No matter, sounds good."

"Yea."

CHAPTER XXIV

July 6, 1755

The moon tried to illuminate his path, but dark clouds loitered on their way across the night sky. Recent thunderstorm threats had kept the air close and damp, while a rising mist on its way to becoming a fog, conspired to trick his senses. It bounced his own footsteps, breathing and even his heartbeat right back at him. Often he would step off the narrow path and crouch in stillness, listening to the sounds of the forest, assuring himself that he was alone. Christopher Gist knew these sounds well: the screaming panther, wolves howling, chirping crickets, owls hooting. As long as this cacophony continued uninterrupted, he felt safe. But if the rhythm changed, the noise level diminished, or if one of the critter calls sounded artificial, he could be in trouble. For several miles he thought he detected one or the other, but the mist distorted the sounds. But there, just then, it was unmistakable; all three happened at once. He was being stalked.

Now, puzzling sounds he had heard earlier made sense – the gentle slap of a twig against a moving leg. He was sure of it. Again he pulled off the path to listen. Through the constant mosquito hum and the shrill cicada drone, he detected the lower pitched pattern of human movement. It was not like the careless bumpings of the Virginia Companies, but a more subtle disturbance of the natural rhythms of the forest. Absolute silence of motion in the woods was possible, but it took a great deal of time. A stalking team in a hurry would compromise some of that silence for speed and few white men would be aware of it.

For a moment he considered his predicament. He was twenty miles from the British army, almost within sight of the French fort. Could the stalkers be two of Croghan's Iroquois warriors; what were their names, Cashuwayon and Frason? Both had been sent ahead to determine the strength and whereabouts of the enemy. General Braddock, himself, had asked him to make his own reconnaissance unbeknownst to the two Indians. Colonel Washington convinced him that Indian intelligence could be suspect. This was sometimes true, given the Indians' tendency toward exaggeration. However, during the past month of scouting and living with "Croghan's Indians," as they were called, Gist had gained a respect for their accuracy, as well as their ability to track and stalk their prey. These two were good and would have known Gist by his moccasin print. Why would they be following him?

No, it must be Indians aligned with the French. The whole way to the fort he had seen no fresh human tracks. Several miles back a single wisp of smoke – the smell of a campfire – had alerted him to what he suspected was a raiding party bypassing the British army. Wanting nothing to detract from his mission, he gave the area a wide berth. Had he been followed since then?

Fear propelled him into action. Not a panic, but a firm realization that to linger longer could result in his own capture or worse. As he quickened his pace to a jog, the fog tightened its grasp on the surrounding hills and rock formations. The path was obscured. Trees and rocks loomed just steps ahead, forcing him to guess to which side the path led. He felt more than heard his pursuers as every sense cried out for clues: which way to go, how to evade, where to hide! His rifle switched hands; the tumpline pressed against his expanding chest; sweat blurred his vision; muscles strained against linen and leather. He was running now, running for life. Strange, he thought, that he had not yet seen the threat. Speeding toward a tree of tremendous girth, he ran to the right and found himself stumbling up a rocky incline that he felt was not part of the path. Like a chameleon, he blended with the rocks, hoping the Indians did not make the same mistake. Fighting to quiet his breathing and control his pounding heart, it was not thirty seconds before he heard the soft pat, pat, pat of moccasined feet on the dirt path. They raced by to his left, which meant the path must have turned sharply in that direction while he went in the other direction at a more oblique angle onto these rocks. Soon they would realize their error and retrace their steps.

He pushed himself out of the rocks and began a hasty retreat. Running hard on the straightaways and slowing for the turns, he made sure he could find the path and not get lost in the fog. After several miles he felt safe and slowed his pace. The fog eased back into mist as he continued. The closer he got to the Forks, the foggier it had become. Upon his return to higher ground away from the rivers and low-lying swamps, the less dense it was. He knew that this stroke of luck had saved his life; he could not have outrun two seasoned warriors.

Gist had no illusions about his warrior capabilities. He was a man of peace. He loved "the chase," as the Indians called hunting. To track and stalk game was the best of challenges and he was accomplished at it. Yet the thought of ambushing and killing Indians did not come easy. During his ranger days he had seen several skirmishes against Iroquois raiding parties and knew he had shot a few of them at a distance. Some died, but that was twenty years ago. Since then he had been a hunter, trapper, fur trader, businessman, and farmer – not a warrior.

He had made good time on the path, but he now felt it prudent to make his own way through the woods in case his antagonists decided to check all the way back along the path. At the next creek he waded up stream for several hundred yards and exited at a convenient spring so it would be more difficult to find where his wet moccasins left the creek.

It took time to leave as little evidence of passing as possible and for several miles he did so. But the closer he got to the army the less time he spent covering his tracks. He concentrated instead on detecting possible Indian raiding parties intent upon ambushing unsuspecting soldiers attending to their evening necessities. He detected no visitors this morning.

Being downwind of the army, Gist located it a half mile away and adjusted his course. As he neared what he thought to be the center of the column about where the General would be, he heard a loud, rapid BA-BOOM-snap! He knew this to be an unsuccessful attempt at firing several guns in unison, the snap being the misfire of one obstinate Brown Bess. Upon approaching the picket he made no noise to frighten him into firing a shot into the woods. "Ho there to the sentry," he yelled, "this is Christopher Gist just come from reconnaissance at the French Fort. Let me pass!"

"Ho yourself there Mr. Gist," replied the soldier, whom he recognized as one of the privates who had become friends with his son, Nathaniel. "Come on in," he called. As Gist came closer, the soldier stopped him. "Ah, Mr. Gist sir, you see I'm supposed to ask for the parole or I can't let you in."

Annoyed at the obvious absurdity, Gist answered, "look son, I left yesterday before that parole was issued. I have important intelligence for the General and there's no time for this." Gist could see the dilemma register on the man's face as he fought for a way out. "Why not just whisper the word in my ear, then I can give it to you?"

"Well, I guess that would work, but you won't tell anybody, will you?"

"No son, I promise."

With that, the private leaned over and whispered the parole in Gist's ear.

"Colchester," repeated Gist and thus gained entry to the camp, thankful that was all it took to outwit the private. As the actual "camp" was several miles long – 1300 men and wagons, horses, cannon, ammunition caissons, cattle and attendants within a twelve-foot wide roadway – Gist hurried past row upon row of tents like so many neat white mountain peaks in the dark.

As he drew near, he was surprised to see a fresh mound of dirt in a man-made clearing just off the edge of the road near Braddock's quarters. Along side the grave stood Croghan, his son, Thomas, Monacatoocha and several other Iroquois, two of whom he could see were wounded. A respectful silence enveloped the mourners and made Gist halt his approach. Croghan saw him and went over to explain.

"'Tis a terrible sadness that's come over us all now; young Dinwiddie's been shot."

Gist gasped. "Oh God." It was all he could say. Dinwiddie was Monacatoocha's only son. "And the chief?"

"Why, the man can hardly speak. The death would have been bad enough, were the deed done by the enemy, but 'twas by our own hand – men from the Virginia rangers."

The shock paralyzed Gist and he lowered himself until he knelt on the ground. Head bowed, he fought to keep his composure until his feelings welled up into the back of his throat. He was unable to speak. All he could picture in his mind was the face of that thirteen-year-old boy who had brightened the lives of so many he had met. He found it difficult to ask how it happened.

Croghan kneeled beside him. "'Twas like this. This mornin', them damn Ottawas attacked our baggage in the rear and killed two soldiers and a woman. Several hours later, Monacatoocha and his warriors startled those same bandits out ahead of the road cutters and commenced shootin'. So beein' all excited an' itchin' for revenge, the rangers rushed up to the fray, mistook our Injens for Ottawas, and fired. Dinwiddie was shot on the first volley as was them two over there, Kah-uk-to-don and All-scheeo-katha."

"I see," said Gist through his hands. "And the General gave him a proper burial and musket salute?"

"Aye, ye must have heard it on your way in."

"And what happened to the Ottawa war party?" Gist had regained his composure.

"Arrah now, that's disappointin' too. We sent the rangers to follow a blood trail quite some ways. Two spears and other accouterments was found, but no bodies."

"So, there's nothing more to be done," Gist said. He got up, leaving Croghan where he knelt, and walked over to Monacatoocha. Together they stood in silence looking down at the final resting place of the young warrior.

"I am remembering," Gist began, "the Winchester Conference two years ago when you and your wife brought this pride of Oneida youth to be christened. We all agreed on the name 'Dinwiddie' after the Governor. I was honored to be chosen his godfather, a promise to raise him as my own should any harm befall his parents. Like his father, he was a good man. I will miss him."

The old man was silent. Gist did not expect an answer and turned to go.

"Annosanah," the voice of sadness beckoned him to stop. "Did you know that my son took his first scalp this morning?"

Gist continued toward Braddock's tent. He was ushered inside ahead of several others awaiting orders for the next day. The General sat at a portable desk reading a stack of papers.

"May I offer you a libation?" He pointed to a decanter and glass on the desk. Gist poured himself whatever was in the bottle without a thought.

"Regrettable incident that." Braddock gestured toward the vicinity of the grave that could be seen through the tent flaps. Monacatoocha kept a lone vigil. "Can't understand bringin' a mere boy along to do the work of men."

"With respect sir, but that boy took his first scalp this morning."

"Yes, well, I myself received my first commission in the Coldstream at sixteen," Braddock said with pride. "And life is a bit more wild out here in the Colonies requiring a younger warrior, I suppose. Do sit and tell me all about your mission."

Gist did so, omitting no details.

"Well, that sounds like quite a harrowing experience." Braddock lifted a pinch of snuff to his left nostril and took a short sniff, spilling some on his white weskit. A long gray smudge was further reinforced where he attempted to brush it away. "Luckily this cursed damp heat has done someone good."

"Yes, sir." Gist did not feel much like conversation.

"Your reconnoiter has confirmed what Croghan's scouts reported. There seems to be no enemy build-up of troops or Indians to meet our invasion. These two got within sight of the fort, killed a French officer out hunting and brought me the scalp. I'm having it mounted even as we speak. Good men these Indians, yes, good men, but I needed your report too, of course. Can't be too careful, you know. Those French seem not to have the stomach for a fight. Have you anything else to report?"

"No, sir," replied Gist.

"You've been out there for twenty-four hours I'd guess, so get some sleep. Come and see me when you've arisen. Mr. Shirley!" The General yelled to his secretary. "Mr. Shirley!"

The young Shirley entered and faced the General. Gist had the feeling he had stepped into the middle of a quarrel. It was no secret the general and his secretary did not get along.

"Now Mr. Shirley," he said, "kindly write Mr. Gist here up for a citation. He will supply you with the details of his most recent mission against the French. And he's to be paid whatever we agreed upon. You are both dismissed."

Gist followed the young Shirley into another tent close by. Leaning on his rifle, he watched while the young secretary sat at his desk and retrieved paper, a quill and an inkwell. He did not look at Gist, but said, "Please give me the basic details of your mission, Mr. Gist." He was polite and aloof. Gist suspected Shirley thought of him as being on Braddock's side and therefore unworthy of any degree of friendliness.

Gist complied and began to relay the episode while Shirley took notes. Yet the young officer could not hide the wide-eyed astonishment as the details unfolded. Amid excited questions of "what did you do next?" and "how did they find you?" Gist got the tale told.

"I am in total admiration, sir, of your extraordinary feats on this mission. Were it me, I say, my fear would have immobilized me and I should have been captured and put to death under the same knife that would then have removed my scalp seconds later . . ."

"Mr. Shirley, sir," interrupted Gist, "Mr. Shirley, I am quite sure you would have behaved with honor. You see, sir, only a fool has no fear. It's how you use that fear that is important."

"You mean you were scared?"

"No doubt it's what propelled me off my arse and started me running in the first place." Gist said as he began to laugh in comic relief from the tension of his experience. Shirley also began laughing and Gist knew they had torn down the barrier between them. "But don't forget," Gist continued in all seriousness, "I never completed my mission. It was a failure."

"Yes, I do understand that, but that fact does not seem so important now does it? The necessary intelligence was obtained and you are still alive."

Gist had to admit that, but he did not feel comfortable with the admiration for a failed mission. Perhaps, he thought, some men like young Shirley were so starved for adventure that a rather insignificant escapade seemed heroic.

"Mr. Gist," Shirley began, "do you think the French and Indians will challenge us?"

"Mr. Shirley, I don't know for sure. I didn't see the fort myself, but all our intelligence points to a bare minimum garrison at Fort Duquesne unable to be reinforced. And since there are so few French soldiers, the Indians will not make a stand because they can't be sure to win."

"So you think we'll win without a fight?"

"I believe on our final approach we'll hear a mighty explosion as the French blow their magazine and set fire to the fort. They'll run away up the path to Le Boeuf never to be heard from again."

"So all the bad blood between the General and Colonel Halket, St Clair and others will have been for naught. You know Colonel Halket has pressed for keeping our forces together and building forts along the way to house supplies in case of our necessary retreat."

"Oh, I'm well aware of all the disagreements. I've argued that one with the General myself. But what do I know of affairs military, except that to err on the side of caution is rarely a mistake."

"Well, Mr. Gist, I hope you are right about all this, because it makes me nervous and I am not the only one."

"I think we can relax, but you know there will be one negative consequence if we take the fort unopposed."

"And what is that?"

"The General will be so full of himself, he'll be impossible to live with."

Both smiled and bid each other a good night. Gist took his leave as he heard Braddock yell for Mr. Shirley again. Finding his tent, he crawled inside. As he drifted off to a much needed sleep, he wondered how much that young Shirley had to endure because of his last name. Nice young man; doesn't belong out here.

CHAPTER XXV

July 9, 1755
Morning

Braddock's lead guide stood on the high, sandy east bank of the Monongahela. Behind him lay the burned out ruins of John Frazier's log cabin and trading house. He shivered as he remembered the exposure Washington and he had endured the night after the Major's now famous, frigid swim eighteen months ago. That cabin had saved their lives.

The army had completed its first crossing and now he leaned on his rifle watching the proud, confident British soldiers begin their second. Brilliant crimson coats burned like a forest fire against the dark green foliage behind them. Now the soldiers did a left oblique to begin their descent, four abreast, down the man-made incline to the west edge of the river some 300 yards away. Led by a company of light horse and Colonel Sir Peter Halket's Forty-fourth under the Union Jack and the regimental colors, the army marched to the drum beat while the fifes played a lively tune.

Ah yes, that incline. Amid curses and oaths directed at the guides for not choosing an easier crossing, one hundred men with picks and shovels took two extra hours to carve a substantial ramp, parallel to the river and wide enough for wagons and artillery. The twelve-foot perpendicular banks on both sides of the river posed problems. Earlier that morning Gist heard that Sir John had maligned him for misleading the General into choosing this route with its two river crossings. That was so patently false that he could not understand St. Clair's motivation for saying it. Gist had scouted Sir John's alternate path that would have had the army following the east bank of the river along a narrow, two-mile strip of land with high cliffs to the right; that route would have required much more than a two-hour preparation.

They could not have followed the Nemocolin Path – the one he had helped lay out three years earlier. That trail ran to the east of their current position and intersected Turtle Creek at the bottom of a 300-foot forested canyon. The path down and up the steep gorge was passable only on foot or horseback, not with wagons and artillery. He had explained to Braddock, Croghan concurred, that there was no other choice. The army was to proceed as Gist had suggested.

So that morning at two o'clock he had risen with Lieutenant Colonel

Thomas Gage's two grenadier companies, Captain Horatio Gates' New York Independent Company, two six-pound cannon and the Indian scouts led by Croghan and Montour – 350 men in all. Their orders were to march forward and secure both Monongahela fords against possible ambuscades. Of course the men were slow. Packing and organizing took hours, so it was after daybreak when they began the five miles to the first crossing. A short time later St. Clair arrived with his 250 road builders and carpenters. Gist knew Braddock would follow soon with the remaining force, wagons, pack animals, cattle and artillery. Somewhere close to Braddock was young Washington, having recovered from the bloody flux. For eighteen days he had been incapacitated. A lesser man, Gist thought, would have stayed down until he was stronger. But not George, who would rather have died than miss today's crossing.

Gist took out a small brass compass, pointed it north and flipped up the miniature sundial marker. The brilliant sun cast its shadow somewhere near the two o'clock mark; time to resume his duties and catch up with the lead. Now that the river was crossed, the best spot for an ambuscade was passed, or would be soon. Earlier that morning he, Croghan and his scouts had scared up thirty Indians between the army camp and the first crossing. They fled without firing. He expected no more resistance.

He turned and began jogging up the foot-printed path noting that he was gaining on Gage's men marching in files four deep. St. Clair's unit was ready to march. Out on the flanks, the grenadier companies traveled in groups of twenty. He was happy; no, elated was more like it. The tension of the last several days had been thick with the expectation of surprise attacks at their most vulnerable river crossings. The light of British confidence that had slowly extinguished over the weeks of wilderness darkness and foreboding was suddenly bright, as if a cork had been popped from a dark bottle.

Then the pipers changed melodies to one he recognized. He was so elated that he began to whistle, a rare endeavor for him because the best he could do was blow a melody through his lips, emitting tones purely by accident. He could not remember where he learned the song, but as he blew, he mentally recited the words.

Some talk of Alexander, and some of Hercules,
Of Hector and Lysander, and such brave men as these.
But of all the world's brave heroes,
There's none that can compare,
With a tow . . row . . row . . row,
The British Gren-a-diers.

These feelings of relief, joy and safety, his very emotions, had spread among the troops since the crossing, like water seeking its own level. They raised the spirits of the lowest, dismal private to equality with those of the highest ranking officer. He could see it in the faces of the soldiers he passed; could feel it in their step.

Having passed Gage's advance party, Gist came upon Harry Gordon and his engineers, busily blazing the trees necessary to be felled by St. Clair's carpenters for the road. These particular woods, unlike much of the last hundred miles since Fort Cumberland, were open with large walnuts, hickories and oaks and little underbrush. Now he passed some of Captain Stewart's Virginia Light Horse, trotting their mounts back and forth, peering ahead into the forest. They gave their fellow Virginian, at least in their eyes, a friendly wave.

Gist's thoughts turned to the Ohio Company and his role in its plans for the future. With the French gone by tomorrow, only months would elapse before he could rebuild his plantation and resume settling the Company lands. Rival land grants aside, there was room enough out here for everyone, he thought, in response to Croghan's unanswered question the other day. Wasn't it amazing how a change in mood could alter your point of view?

Fifty yards ahead, he could see the backs of some of Croghan's Indians, stripped to their breech clouts, picking their way through the open forest with caution, eyes alert for any movement ahead. He knew Thomas would be among them. And there was Croghan, eyes glued to the ground, careful to avoid stumbling. Not much of a woodsman, Gist smiled. His own son, Nate, the only guide on horseback, scanned every tree for signs of the enemy. And way out in front of them all by 200 yards was the lone Monacatoocha, ever the master of stealth, perhaps hoping to sneak up on the enemy and dispatch a few to avenge the death of his son. Birds chirped, squirrels chattered in chastisement from the tree limbs and the afternoon humidity rose. It did not matter. Had not the General claimed they would sup in the fort the next day? Having marched nearly a mile of steady upgrade, there were still six miles to the fort. Soon three o'clock would come and they would halt as ordered. To his right he noted a hillock beginning its rise and he wondered if military procedure would require Colonel Gage to send a detachment to occupy the knoll. Then again, he considered, was it really necessary given the circumstances?

CHAPTER XXVI

July 9, 1755
Afternoon

"The enemy, the enemy!" Monacatoocha and two guides came sprinting toward Gist. He saw them stop where Croghan stood, point forward, and continue toward Gage's soldiers, shouting, the words that were both exhilarating and frightening. Harry Gordon, the engineer, sped past Gist on horseback toward the Indians' position, stopped his steed, and peered ahead. At the same moment Nathaniel galloped in toward Gage's outfit shouting, "the Injens is upon us!" Gist was wishing he was on horseback, but even without the advantage of height he could see ahead what looked to be several hundred painted Indians stripped down to breech clouts speeding toward him. The French officer in the lead was clad as an Indian with a large, silver gorget about his neck. Now the enemy was a hundred yards from his position. He saw the officer doff his hat and motion his Indians to run along both flanks of the British column. War whoops filled the air.

Gist was awestruck; stuck in his tracks. This was not happening. Surely he was wrapped in his blanket somewhere having a nightmare from which he could not awaken. He heard the command for the front file of grenadiers to kneel. "Fire!" BOOM-M-M! The fusillade echoed through the valley. He was jolted into action and dove for the ground. "Fire!" BOOM-M-M! – went the sound of eight Brown Bess muskets exploding in unison. These eight then moved back to reload and eight more stepped up – all to officer commands. "Fire!" BOOM-M-M! Like a cannon retort it reverberated. Through the acrid black powder smoke Gist could see the Indians in some confusion. "Fire!" BOOM-M-M! The French commander with the gorget fell, as did others Gist could see. His anger at them for changing the mood of the day, for burning his home, for causing the death of Dinwiddie, propelled him toward the objects of his fury.

He got as far as the first downed tree and began looking for targets, but behind every other tree was an Indian whose aim was accurate. The Redcoats' volleys, executed with the finest British precision possible, were pointed straight ahead where the Indians were first sighted. But those Indians were gone, having melted away into the trees to begin firing on the right and left flanks of the British. Those brilliant scarlet coats that had shone like fire that morning, now glowed like coals in the smokey haze. Would that he had such a target. Gist waited for a puff of smoke by a bush or a tree and aimed his longrifle in that direction until he saw a head or an arm. A gentle squeeze of his trigger, a flash and a boom – he was lethal up to 100 yards and there were plenty of hidden Indians within that radius.

Redcoat bodies fell not twenty feet away. Within ten minutes of the first volley, half the officers he could see were dismounted, killed or wounded. At least fifty men lay sprawled on the ground within his immediate vision. Those who could, withdrew. Gist saved his shot and made a calculated break backward with them. A shot passed close to his head. In turning around, he was almost bowled over by an Indian bent on scalping a dead soldier. Gist shot the warrior as he flew past. While his rifle was empty, more of the enemy rushed by to do the same.

Soldier bodies lay in his path. He had to step on them to follow the retreating soldiers. The tall, pointy hats of the grenadiers with the large "GR" on the front lay everywhere, along with muskets, cartridge boxes and haversacks.

Several officers managed to halt the retreat to begin a skirmish line and continue the volleys. Just then several flanking parties of wounded and frightened grenadiers, having been overwhelmed by enemy fire, rushed in from the sides and crashed into the column, throwing the men into further disorder. Gist stepped behind a tree to reload. He had heard of woodsmen who could load and fire on the run, but he had not had the proper incentive to develop that skill. Maybe today would be the day. He fired another well-aimed ball at an Indian scalping a still conscious soldier. He considered shooting the soldier, but changed his mind. The soldier would die soon enough. He remembered Croghan's words about how the Indians would take risks and scalp their victims early in a battle only if they were unsure of victory. Gist hoped this was a good omen.

Enemy firing down along the flanks of the British column increased as the French and Indians followed their withdrawal. Frightened Redcoats retreated another fifty paces to where a few remaining officers again tried to form a resistance. Another subaltern, issuing the beginning firing sequence, fell from his horse. A company officer plunged forward in his saddle. The horse reared against a tree breaking the cinch allowing the dead officer to hit the ground. Like a cannon shot a young warrior jumped from behind a tree not six feet from the horrified soldiers and scalped the officer. Gist shot him. Colonel Gage was untouched. He could not, however, prevail upon the huddling grenadiers to form up or do anything but load and waste their shot into the woods. Gist looked into their eyes, glazed over, un-seeing, fixed in a stare, seldom blinking.

Then someone shouted that Indians had attacked the baggage at the rear. The soldiers heard shots in that direction. Two cannon, which Gist knew to be Gage's six-pounder now in the hands of St. Clair's men, went off. That did it. Gage's panic-stricken regulars fled full tilt back the road with Gist following. What could he do? Not being able to remain out there all alone, he maintained an irregular cover fire from the rear, trying to load while he ran. Somewhere along the road he met Nathaniel, still unscathed. His horse had been shot. Gist had not had time to wonder about him, but was relieved to see him. Nate had not seen Thomas.

Gage's men, however, could retreat only so far before they collided with St. Clair's carpenters. The jumbled, falling mass of Redcoats presented an even bigger target than before and, amid the horrible cries and scalp halloos, were picked off one by one. No longer able to restrain his men, St. Clair's entire command was swept away in the flood of Gage's routed soldiers. They abandoned the six-pounders and ran the entire 300 yards of open road until they careened into Lieutenant Colonel Burton's vanguard on its way to reinforce Gage. Gist saw young Shirley galloping toward him, presumably sent ahead by Braddock to ascertain the status of the battle. The next instant his boyish face registered a look of pain and he fell from the saddle. A soldier crawled across his path, groping, unable to see, a bloody mass of flesh where his eyes used to be. Another soldier, dazed, sauntered against the retreating masses toward the carnage wrought by the Indians. Christopher and Nathaniel fought with hundreds of other soldiers to negotiate that same road, sidestepping and jumping over bodies of dead and wounded. As he and Nate neared the collision zone at a jog, the tangle of men – grenadiers, Virginia rangers, carpenters, officers on horseback – presented a formidable obstacle. Enemy firing from the flanks did not diminish. Along the exposed front and sides, men fell.

"It's getting bad, no matter where you look, Nate," Gist said with concern. "These damn soldiers are so scared, they'll fire at anything."

"Let's just bypass this mess and find our own trees."

It was a task easier said than done, soldiers kept piling into each another. The enemy shot those who ran on either side of the column. The Gists were careful to run crouching from tree to tree, stopping to fire as often as they could find a target. They managed to place themselves behind one of St. Clair's felled trees facing the hillock from which enemy fire was coming.

Gist uncorked his powder horn to pour some down the barrel. "Damn, I'm out of powder. This loading on the run makes me use more."

"Thought you couldn't do that," Nate said as he fired off a shot. "Got him! Let's see, that makes seven"

"First time I tried it, I got too much powder and damn near blew my rifle apart. I learned mighty quick though, but I'm afraid I spilled a lot doing it. I'll just leave my rifle here. Back in a minute."

Gist had no idea where powder was. Since all the soldiers had cartridges, dead Redcoats could not help him. He spied a dead ranger and removed his powder horn. Returning in several minutes, he was horrified to witness a red-coated soldier swinging the rifle, which he had just left, at a tree, splintering the stock and bending the barrel beyond possible repair. Nate was nearby, but busy firing and loading, firing and loading.

"What in hell are you doing?" Yelled Gist as he ran and tackled soldier. "That's my rifle you son-of-a-bitch," he began pummeling the man with his fists until the soldier wriggled away and cowered up against a tree.

"Aye an', I'm sorry, I'm sorry," he cringed at Gist's anger. "I saw this fancy gun and just broke it up, bein' as how I sees it layin' there an' me not wantin' it ta be found by the Injuns." He rose from the ground, straightening himself, acting nervous. "But it's alright, 'cause if we ever git outta this alive, I'll buy ye a new gun." He continued running back toward the rear guard before Gist could react.

Gist did not have long to ponder the event as a ball whistled past his head and rekindled his survival instinct. Before he ducked, however, he saw a puff of smoke from behind a large walnut tree. "Nate," Gist called, "over there. I got no gun." Gist pointed the marksman out and Nate shot him.

"Nine!" Nate shouted.

Gist observed the sad situation had gotten no better during the rifle incident. The few remaining officers had been unable to untangle and organize the mass of soldiers. He and Nathaniel resumed fighting their way, moving as before from tree to tree back along the column. Gist found a rifle and ball pouch with matching caliber balls.

The minutes it had taken to travel down the column seemed like hours. Time was distorted within the envelope of barely breathable black powder smoke, screams of wounded, hideous ululations of Indians, slippery bloody ground, terror on the faces of panic-stricken men. It was not real. Somewhere along this line of worthless Redcoats, Gist felt someone had to be organized and ready to fight an effective counter attack. How far did he have to go back to find it?

As if in answer to a prayer, Braddock appeared on horseback. Alongside him rode George Washington, grimacing face wracked with pain as his emaciated body bounced up and down on the cushions tied to his saddle. Up there on his horse, making a bit less conspicuous target than the General in red, Gist could see several musket ball holes through his Colonial blue coat and tricorn.

The father and son team, hoping the savior had arrived, took up positions just off the main road behind another of St. Clair's felled trees. He could tell, however, the General was confused at the mass of cowering soldier flesh and unsure of the remedy. Before a moment had passed, Sir John, blood staining the side of his white weskit, staggered up to the General. The din of battle obscured most of his words, but "take the hill" was unmistakable. Sir John, however, collapsed, and Braddock looked around for the nearest officer –

Captain Thomas Waggoner. Words were spoken and the Captain shouted to his men. One by one, fifty rangers followed Waggoner up the hill. Gist nudged his son and the two joined the Virginians. They lodged themselves behind a rotting log halfway up the hill and began directing a lethal fire toward the enemy.

It was a total shock when a ranger to his right was hit from behind and fell screaming in pain. Again it happened. He turned around with his rifle pointed toward a possible foe only to find it leveled at the line of Redcoats some thirty yards away. Other rangers fired at the soldiers in anger and disbelief, but the "thud" of rifle balls hitting ranger bodies made them hug the earth, unable to continue. What could the rangers do but slink down and crawl back to the red ribbon of huddled humanity? Whether the British mistook them for the French or thought they were attempting to flee, Gist did not know, but the damage was done. Thirty of the Virginians, many of whom were wounded, made it back. Gist was livid and the tempers of other rangers were uncontrollable. Fights broke out between soldiers and rangers. Still, the enemy fired.

So much for attempts to help save the embroiled British Army, Gist thought. His own anger was rising. This was crazy. The mighty invincible British Army was a joke, a farce, a haven for the cowards and dregs of humanity. It was then that Gist vowed he would quit the battle as soon as possible. He would no longer risk his life for a lost cause. Everywhere he looked were dead and wounded bodies of men, horses and stray cows from the herd lying side by side, one silent, one screaming, one bellowing. The cacophony was so intense and ear splitting that an eerie silence emerged. Mouths opened to yell with no sound; guns discharged with no boom; movement stopped for one man and began for another. Motion slowed. Soldiers huddled and cursed and cried and shit themselves and lost control and shot each other. He saw a musket ball enter the ear of a soldier; the opposite side of his head exploded, spewing brains, tissue, blood and bone upon the red coat of the soldier beside him. The reds clashed.

He was jerked back to reality by Sir Peter Halket galloping up from the direction of the rear guard. He shouted orders at his officers above the noise of the battle. Having just discharged his piece at a now immobile foe, Gist observed a disabled Indian sitting near the road aiming his musket at Sir Peter on horseback. Gist tried to reload in time. "Nate!" He called, but he too was occupied with reloading. BOOM . . . and Colonel Halket fell. A split second late but loaded nonetheless, Gist blew the Indian's brains against a nearby wagon. Several men crowded around Halket's body to determine the extent of his wounds, among them Sir Peter's aged servant. Amid his tears and screams of disbelief, a second enemy ball tore through his temple.

Braddock by now was a madman. Mounted, racing back and forth, he prodded and poked enmeshed soldiers with his saber, shouting orders for them to form a skirmish line. Any soldier who ran to the forest edge to fall behind a tree was beaten back with the flat of the General's sword. "Cowards!" He roared. But the spectacle proved too big a target. The General's horse faltered as a ball ripped through its brain. Down like lead weights went the pair. Braddock's servant, Bishop, brought another and he began to mount. But the movement put him in direct line with another speeding projectile that pierced his upper arm and lodged itself in his chest. Down went the rider, unable to rise. Without a command, a protective shield of officers surrounded the fallen General. Washington dismounted and knelt beside his mentor. Others began clearing a human path to carry him away from the battle. Again Bishop was there pulling off Braddock's eight foot red sash to use for its intended purpose, a stretcher. Still conscious and in command, mouthing bloody air bubbles, he pulled Washington close. Whatever Braddock said, Gist saw Washington motion the officers toward the wagons scattered along the road. In the midst of chaos, Christopher rushed to Washington's side and offered his help. Already Bishop, Captain Robert Stewart and Colonel Gage were carrying him away from danger. A wagon with team still attached stood near. With what gentleness the circumstances allowed, they placed him upon it and headed back down the road from whence they came. The drums beat "retreat."

CHAPTER XXVII

July 9, 1755
Evening

In spite of the action surrounding them, Braddock's escorts were still able to choose a calculated withdrawal. Leading the horse-drawn wagon with the wounded General, they snaked in and out of the many abandoned wagons along the road. Christopher, Nathaniel and some of the soldiers lingered, laying a cover fire to aid the retreat. Most of the soldiers Gist observed were retreating in a manner that could only be called a rout, running full out toward the river, bumping into others, knocking them down, throwing away their muskets and any accouterments that might weigh them down.

For a quarter of a mile the entourage of mounted retreating officers and foot soldiers braved the enemy fire as they headed for the South Carolina Regiment at the rear. These Colonials had plenty of time to prepare and had already repelled one enemy attack. Shooting was sparse here, but the sounds of battle up front did not diminish. Soldiers, some wounded, some not, stood around the wagons describing the horrors they had seen to the remaining wagoners and each other. They were silenced by the approaching officers with the wounded General. Those who had hats, removed them. Whispers could be heard and one private asked of the General's condition.

Washington answered that he would be fine, but is was plain no one believed him. With a lead ball lodged in his lung, everyone, including the General, knew this was fatal; the question was when. Washington spotted a one-horse cart that he thought would be more comfortable and faster than the cumbersome supply wagon. Mindful of the approaching battle noises, they transferred the gasping General to the cart.

At that moment Croghan appeared and Braddock spied a brace of pistols protruding from his sash. "Captain Croghan," he pleaded through rapid, shallow breaths, "I'd be obliged if you'd lend me your pistols so that I might die as an old Roman. Then leave me and look to yourself."

"Aye, now General dear," Croghan answered with as much levity as he could muster. "I would now, but neither be loaded and I've no more balls for 'em. Just be still, and we'll have ye out of harm's way faster'n ye can scalp a dead Injen."

Just then a deafening outburst of musket fire erupted from the hillock to the east and was accompanied by the fiendish hoops of their red foes. As if on cue, the soldiers abandoned their moment of respect and began cutting the horses from their traces; wagoners yelled powerless protests. Others ran. Wagoners unhitched their own teams and galloped away toward the crossing. More foot soldiers, having cast everything aside, sped past the officers. Wounded men hobbled on inverted musket crutches. Others sat or lay in heaps begging for help. Blind combatants staggered, arms outstretched, calling for mates or mercy.

Gist, still acting as a "rear guard" for the officers, was in disbelief. He felt pity for the abandoned wounded and disgust for those passing by who would not help them. Yet he could not help them either. Stop looking at their pleading eyes; don't listen to their pathetic calls for help, he told himself. Harden your heart to them and their plight. The Indians will soon envelop them and they would cry no more. In a river of drowning men he could only save one. All he could do now was help the General and his officers affect a dignified retreat across the river. He took cover behind a tree and despatched another Indian attempting to scalp another dead soldier. The river crossing was just a few yards away.

By this time others retreating in an orderly manner had joined them. Captain Dobson had collected a number from the Virginia Regiments and Colonel Burton had gathered a hundred-man contingent of the Forty-eighth. Some of the wounded were being helped to the river. Gist looked at the ramp, choked with masses of screaming, maddened Redcoats crawling over one another to get down first. Somehow the masses moved to admit the General's horse cart. Enemy fire increased as they reached the water's edge; war hoops and scalp halloos resounded through the woods and across the meadow around Frazier's cabin.

From fifty yards out into the river, already stained red with English blood, Gist looked back to see shrieking savages tomahawking or wrestling with the wounded on shore. Several women near the wagons were struggling with as many warriors. He held his breath as Harry Gordon on a bridleless horse slid down the river bank with painted savages pursuing. Though he was hit, he managed to keep his saddle and ride on.

Halfway across the river, the breeze changed. Screams, cries and unidentifiable human sounds wafted over the waters toward him. Redmen, entire bodies painted vermillion or black, jumped the twelve foot banks into the water atop the fleeing, wounded soldiers, seizing on their sloth, delighting in the chase, reveling in their fear. Several shots from Gist and others tried to discourage Indian pursuit, but it was unnecessary. The predator had enough prey.

Upon reaching the far side, Washington chose a small hill, a defensible position for the night, a full quarter of a mile farther along as a rallying point for the wounded. Colonel Gage organized eighty Redcoats; Colonel Burton positioned his men. Pickets were posted, but the soldiers would not stay. Their fear of what lurked in the woods less than a mile away was too great and they slipped away. By sunset few soldiers remained. Braddock, in too much pain to ride a springless cart, was hand carried by his officers down the hill and along the road toward Dunbar's camp forty miles away. Gist took his turn, along with his son, but none of the soldiers would help.

The General wheezed and gurgled, sometimes moaning, but only during a fitful sleep. When he coughed, his entire body would heave as if to writhe away from the pain. In moments of consciousness he would repeat, "who would have thought it?" Shortly after sundown, Gist overheard Braddock and Washington talking. Between shallow breaths the dying General spoke short phrases. "Oh my dear . . . had I been governed . . . by your advice . . . we never should have . . . come to this. But we shall know . . . better how to deal . . . with them another time." His eyes, the eyes of a man who knew his own demise, pleaded for acknowledgment. "You must," he continued with the same breathy pauses, "ride to Colonel Dunbar and appraise him of our situation. I fear our wounded, arriving there before us, may give a wrong accounting of our plight. Order Dunbar to send as many wagons and provisions as possible back here for the wounded."

It was then that Gist learned the General had four horses shot from under him and was mounting his fifth when the debilitating shot struck. It was hard not to admire him for his courage and resolution. Braddock in command had reminded Gist of a bull dog, short, thickset, well shouldered. Now, folded up in his sash, he looked small and feeble, echoing the status of his once great army.

Washington looked at Gist. "You will accompany me, will you not?"

Gist nodded, "and my son?" He still had not found Thomas.

"Of course."

That journey, moonless, black as ink, was an endless nightmare. A mere twelve-foot slice through the woods barely cracked the leafy canopy overhead to allow any rays of starlight. But the forest was not quiet. Anguished wails of woe, uncontrollable sobbing, whimpering, agonized screams of pain were everywhere unseen in the blackness. They grew louder at their approach and faded, rising and falling in concert, a symphony of sadness. The messengers could do nothing but ride on. Who would you pick to help? Who among the invisible pariah would you choose? Some called out the most vile and cursed oaths at their passing, while their mounts side stepped dead and dying bodies.

It was surprising how far the most determined had made it along the road, but at some point the sounds of the sick and suffering were silent. The darkness was oppressive. More than once Gist had to climb down and feel around on the ground for stumps or wagon ruts. They rode on in silence, accompanied by the rumblings of their hungry horses and the shrill chirps of the cicadas. Gist entered a weird realm of half-sleep, plodding along, rocking back and forth, fraught with nightmarish visions from which he would be jerked awake by some unknown force.

The gray dawn of June 10th saw the three riders not far apart. They had no provisions, except some parched corn and jerked beef the Gists happened to have. The beef they ate; the corn went to the horses. Gist recognized a previous camp site and reported they had ten miles to go.

Late that morning the forty grueling miles to Dunbar's camp near Jumonville Glen, now being called Rock Fort, was over. Dunbar reappraised his decision to pack up and retreat after first hearing impassioned reports from fleeing soldiers that the Indians were only hours behind them. As Braddock ordered, Dunbar sent out the wagons and supplies while the three messengers slept. That evening the General arrived on horseback, grimacing with each hoof beat, unable to talk, move or breathe without pain. He had, they said, become too heavy to carry.

Finally Braddock gave the order to organize a withdrawal to Fort Cumberland. They found enough wagons to transport the worst of the 400 wounded and hitched the available horses to them. Excess wagons, numbering over 150, were slated to be burned. Powder casks were emptied; cannon shells broken with sledge hammers; food dumped on the ground. Since the work was not completed by the time the General was ready to leave on the 13th, a rear guard was detailed to finish the job.

Braddock's condition continued to deteriorate during the march and that afternoon he transferred command to Colonel Dunbar. Later that evening the army called a halt to camp within a gunshot of the rotting Fort Necessity. The Gists made a small fire and ate their rations. About nine o'clock Croghan, who had been attending the General along with other officers, came to Gist's camp and informed him of the General's death.

Feeling the need to be alone, Christopher got up and walked toward the fort. He had been depressed when the French had overrun his Settlement. But the rumors of a British counter offensive turned into reality and despair became hope. Gist had been on a mission. He was there to free his land for opportunity. The British were there because of their orders. Washington was there, at least in part, to further his career. But they all sought the same end – the removal of the French. Now with the finest army since the Roman Centurions in shambles, those hopes and dreams were extinguished, like water poured on a blazing fire. The French would not be driven out, he would not rebuild "Gist's Settlement" and he would never regain his family's fortune.

As far as he was concerned, with Braddock dead, his job with the British Army was over. He still had the coins Mr. Shirley had paid him just one week ago. He imagined it was all he would get, though he would petition for his pay. But Braddock's war chest, with over £4000 sterling, had been left on the field of battle and he reasoned it would be some time, if ever, before he got any pay. There was nothing in the settlements for him. His brother and the other families he had brought from North Carolina were all farmers, a life style unappealing to himself. It was just he and his son Nate. And what a fine man he had become. Thank God he had survived the battle. Dare he hope the same of Thomas?

So what was he to do? Where would he go? Well, he surmised, this territory will be overrun with Indians attacking settlers clear to the tidewater. There would be militia units raised that would need leaders familiar with the country. He would live off the land and whatever he could get from Virginia. Past debts would go unpaid and he would die a warrior. It was funny how that young Washington would be willing to give his life for a profession he, himself, was so reluctant to accept. He would bet that the recent aide-de-camp would be in command of Virginia's military forces in its attempt to fight off the French and their Indian allies. Maybe at some point the British would again try to reclaim their land. In any case, Gist vowed he would continue to be part of that effort until he was no longer able.

CHAPTER XXVIII

October 1755

The Crooked Billet stood on the wharf above Chestnut Street. Christopher would have called it an "ordinary" in Virginia, but here in Philadelphia it was an "inn." Weathered, wooden siding and warped porch floorboards told of its age. A steady rain had turned the dusty streets to mud and filled wagon and buggy ruts with brown water; darkness made it impossible to see them. His boots were saturated and mud splattered to their knee-high tops. Nathaniel's had faired no better. Their boots were the first purchases made with an advance from Colonel Washington for journeying to meet with Governor Morris, Secretary Richard Peters and Benjamin Franklin. The former gentlemen having already been seen, Franklin was to meet them at the inn.

"Oh, good evening Christopher, Nathaniel, how good of you to come." A well-dressed, bespeckled man, sitting at a table in a dark corner of the main room, rose to greet them. His smile was genuine and handshake firm.

"It's a pleasure to meet you again Mr. Franklin," Christopher said. "We did not get to talk much at your last visit to the General several months ago."

"Well, you had your duties and we did not have much to talk about then, did we?" Franklin called for flagons of ale for each of them and continued, "I'm delighted you agreed to meet me here instead of my small house or the Assembly Hall. Some say this inn is beneath my current social standing, but when first I came to this city in '23, 'twas here I stayed. I come here often, as it offers me a familiar surrounding in which to write."

Franklin's damask weskit and ruffled shirt did not outshine the look of the Gists by much. Christopher had stored most of his fashionable clothing at his Opeekon home, thus escaping the fate of his belongings at the Settlement. Over ten years old, frayed and moth-eaten in some places, the quality of his clothing spoke of his old Baltimore social connections. Nathaniel being the same size, wore his father's clothes. Yet in marked contrast to the weathered, hardened features of the Gists, Franklin's tendency toward corpulence spoke of a more comfortable living. His fleshy, smooth skin gave him a youthful appearance. Gist was surprised to learn they were the same age.

Franklin moved his notebook aside. "Just some notes for my next

Almanac." He paused, deep in thought. "You know, I began publishing Poor Richard twenty-three years ago, before I had the wisdom to understand the power of the pen. But after all this time of writing, I still cannot find the words to express the depth of my sorrow. The tragedy at Monongahela was truly Shakespearian. The senseless depredation and loss of life are appalling and the maddening thing is – it was avoidable. He spoke with such sincerity and sadness, Gist was reluctant to begin a new topic. Franklin interrupted his thoughts, "but I digress. What news from the Virginia frontier?"

"The Indians daily attack somewhere along the several hundred miles of frontier, killing or capturing settlers in the most unspeakable ways," Christopher reported. "Some have built blockhouses and a few forts exist, but those inside are too scared to venture out to harvest their crops or hunt. Meanwhile, the Indians just bypass the forts. Colonel Innis at Fort Cumberland is presently cut off from Winchester. The last messenger said the smoke was so thick from burning settlers' cabins that you couldn't see Will's Mountain."

"If that cowardly Dunbar had stayed at Fort Cumberland like the Governors had asked, those troops would be protecting the settlers. Instead he brought them here to winter quarters, in August!" Nathaniel's exasperation and contempt were apparent.

"Who can know his true reasons, though he has voiced enough false justification for it." Franklin stopped to take a sip of ale. "I've just been informed that he left for Albany to confer with General Shirley. Where he may go thereafter no one knows, but there are those who wish his soul to, shall we say, heaven." He held out his glass for his guests to toast, which they did, and continued to enumerate the Colonel's failings.

"You know," Franklin changed the subject, "this inn has wonderful food and it would be a crime to spend hours in conversation and deny ourselves the pleasures of the palate. It'll be my treat, what do you say?"

The Gists agreed. Franklin ordered a feast of roast beef, ham, cabbage, various greens, Madeira and desserts of mince pie and Moravian apple cake. Neither Christopher nor Nathaniel could do justice to the meal. Months of army rations and years of frontier living had shrunk their stomachs to accommodate little more than the necessary sustenance. Franklin, accustomed to several full meals a day, had no trouble filling himself.

Between bites and chews Franklin told them of his latest crises. The hundreds of farmers, who had contributed wagons and horses to the Braddock expedition, had come to him and demanded compensation. Since he had given his own bonds for their safe return, he faced financial ruin. He appealed to General Shirley, who had replaced Braddock as the commander of British forces in America, to release the necessary funds. After agonizing weeks of inaction, nearly £20,000 had been paid and he was spared.

Several moments of silence elapsed, only disturbed by mouth noises and an occasional belch. It was Nathaniel who ended the lull. "Curious really, Mr Franklin, but we've been here less than a week and everywhere we go people come up to us with a welcome or some encouraging word. At night in the taverns they want to know all about the battle and how the Colonials fought and did the British really cower in masses and a hundred other questions. They inquire after Washington and other officers. I must say, all this attention is embarrassingly pleasant."

"That is as it should be," Franklin opined. "You are heroes to them. They must live vicariously through you, since they could not themselves be there. Enjoy it while it lasts. Not often do we stand in the light of public approval without candle snuffers all about."

"Speaking of Washington," Christopher began, "the Colonel has sent me to ask of Pennsylvania's military readiness to mount another campaign against Fort Duquesne. Or, if not an offensive plan, then defensive actions against Indian attacks that surely must come soon, since they're numerous in Virginia. Both the Governor and Secretary say they've done all they can and it's now up to the Assembly. Will your pacifist Quaker Assembly vote money for the cause?"

"Quakers!" Franklin spat. "Those stiff rumps gave us trouble to no end by not voting funds for a fort at the Forks – a condition Virginia took full advantage of, I might add," Franklin pointed his fork at Christopher. "Though many of us would have the Quakers retire to more celestial matters and leave the business of government to those more worldly, they are not now the problem. The Assembly, upon learning of Braddock's defeat, met the next day and voted £50,000 for the defense of the colony; this money to be raised by a tax on all real property. Why, this is unprecedented and we were elated.

"But before the ink was dry Governor Morris vetoed it. We were shocked when it came back three days later proposing that the Proprietary Estates be exempted from the tax. That's over half the Colony. The Penns, of course, instruct the Governor not to allow any property taxes on their estates, even in dire circumstances where they are in danger of losing them. We've been arguing ever since, neither side willing to budge."

"I've heard," Christopher said, "that these months of inaction have forced the Delaware, Shannoah and Wyandot to go over to the French. These are the same people who befriended me on my expeditions for the Ohio Company five years ago."

"To quote Monacatoocha," Franklin interjected, "'you can't live in the woods and stay neutral.' As we cannot protect them from the French, the French are ever ready to enlist them against the English. The Assembly meets now and as a dutiful member I occupy my days seeking reconciliation with the Governor on this matter. I fear it will take some calamity to persuade them to cease this stalemate."

Conversation turned to Virginia's preparations and problems. The new Commander-in-Chief of the Virginia Regiment, George Washington, had as of yet no regiment. At the very least, recruiting had been minimal and then only among the dregs of humanity. The county militias, prone to cowardice and desertion, could not be relied upon. So the first priority was to recruit soldiers to fill the regiments.

"I know of no better man to lead Virginia's military effort than young George Washington. If he were to write me, formally outlining the property damage and murder of settlers due to Braddock's defeat and request our assistance, he would get it faster than any other man in America."

Dinner plates having been removed, three glasses of Madeira remained, frequently drained and constantly filled. As discussions are prone to rehash earlier points, this one returned to the Battle of Monongahela. Long into the night, each man gave his opinion on how the outcome could have been changed and how and when, and what must be corrected on the next attempt, whenever that may be. What had the Colonies learned from the experience?

"My dear sirs," Franklin's speech was slurred at this point, "I will tell you what we learned. Prior to the battle we thought the British Army invincible. They rule their possessions in part by fear of reprisal – an elaborate web they weave to protect themselves on their small island. We have witnessed a rent in that web. The French won, you see, but we in America did not lose. Our mettle is yet to be tested."

After the melodramatic ending, the Gists departed for their own inn on the outskirts of town where rooms were less expensive. Franklin offered to pay their bills for the entire week-long stay and promised to send blankets, stockings and shoes for Washington's new recruits.

"Surely the man talks enough for two people," observed Nathaniel as they rode away.

"Well son," Christopher paused, "he has a lot to say."

CHAPTER XXIX

October 11, 1755

The road from Philadelphia west to Lancaster was well traveled with many farms, several settlements, and no shortage of inns to stay the night. Somewhat less traveled was the road from Lancaster to York, twenty-five miles to the southwest. From there the Monocacy Path led southwest a hundred miles to Winchester.

Slippery, muddy clay and swift currents on swollen streams conspired to rob the horses of their footage. The journey back to Opeekon took six days, a day longer than normal because of excessive rains. A letter from Colonel Washington awaited them. Nathaniel built a fire in the massive fireplace. As the house began to warm, damp, moldy smells receded into the corners. Christopher sat near the blaze beside three candles and began reading the letter. He was tired and wet from the hard trip and thought about waiting until tomorrow to tackle the Colonel's sometimes long and wordy messages. But Nate was out back chopping wood and the fire soothed him. He felt good about his meetings, especially the one with Franklin. The others had been formal and short, with that feigned friendliness and forced smile so common to the aristocracy. Tomorrow he must write to Washington of these meetings, but for now the letter wanted reading. He pulled out a small pair of reading glasses, recently purchased in Philadelphia. Their twin oval frames stared back at him as a reminder of that demon, age, that had sapped his focus on things less than a foot away. Skipping over the opening lines, he read:

> Before I got to Williamsburg, the Commissions were chiefly disposed of: yet, having you strangely in mind (which occasioned an earnest solicitation), I succeeded in procuring the only commission that was vacant, i.e. to be Captain of a Company of Scouts.

This Company was a new creation as far as he knew and he wondered how it would integrate with the others. The normal foundation of a Colony's fighting ability was its militia. All able-bodied free men between the ages of eighteen and sixty were called during emergencies and paid for their duration of service. The Governor, often a man of no military experience, was the commander-in-chief, who appointed his officers from gentlemen council members more at home chasing the fox than the Indian. Christopher had seen no militia units trained as fighters. They were farmers and settlers or mill owners and shopkeepers, unaccustomed to the rigors of training, discipline and wilderness warfare. Who could blame them for their fear and desertion?

Another of the Colony's protectors, one with which Gist had personal experience in Maryland, was the ranger. As volunteers, Gist and his fellow rangers had lived in the general area they patrolled and were quite familiar with the terrain. Their primary object was to protect their own homes and families. This was practicable because Maryland's frontier was not large. But Virginia was so enormous – more than 400 miles of undefendable mountain ranges – that the sparse population could not support enough rangers to be effective. If you tried to move them to locations far from their families, they would desert. Since there was no permanent garrison of British Regulars stationed in Virginia, She had to recruit, train and equip her own regiments. Gist's Company of Scouts would be one of sixteen total companies.

Nathaniel entered the room with an armload of logs. "Sure wish Gabriel was still with us. Made life a damn sight easier when it came to things like this."

"That was what, two years ago, just before I went to Fort Le Boeuf with Washington?"

"That's right. Never did get the full story, but you sent him to me with medicine for my ague. He brought it to me at the mouth of Conococheague, but he'd been shot and was half dead. He died later that night. Never had a clue who done it, but if I ever find out, you can bet they'll pay."

"Probably some bounty hunters thinking they'd seen a runaway slave. Gabriel was a slave, or perhaps more of a servant, but there's not a man anywhere that I would praise more highly than he, with the possible exception of yourself. I never did tell you that I'm proud of the way you handled yourself at Monongahela. You rode into the depths of Hell with the rest of us and walked out with honor. Not too many can say that."

"And thank God Thomas made it through. When the tide of battle turned for the worse, he melted away into the woods with Monacatoocha's Indians. "He's in hog heaven up there at Fort Cumberland chasin' Injens," Nate placed new logs on burning coals.

"And right good at it, I'll say. His unit has the most skirmishes with the enemy, last I heard," replied Christopher. "Anyway back to this letter. Washington says this commission, listen to this, and I quote, 'is attended with equal honor, rank and profit with the other captains, but will be accompanied with more fatigue, which you will not regard, as you are greatly inured to it.'"

"So my father is greatly inured to fatigue, physical pain and discomfort. Even I noticed that." He laughed.

"Well, he thinks that about me, though it's getting harder to live up to that reputation as I get older. Two years ago, when he was green as a tree frog, he was easy to impress. I wonder what he'd think if he ever knew I wasn't sure we'd make it back from Le Boeuf."

"None the less of you, I'm sure. From what I've read of Washington's Journal, I'm glad I was sick. That letter say anything about me?" Nathaniel came over to sit by his father.

"I believe so," he skimmed a line, "here it is 'you may be assured that I shall endeavor to provide for your son in the same Company.'"

"He'll probably set me to shoveling shit holes for the militia."

"On the contrary, he'll have a lieutenancy for you. He thinks well of you. You're still blaming yourself for not being able to bring the Cherokees to fight for Braddock. I've told you before. You got in the middle of an old quarrel between me and that rascal Pearis."

"But if I'd been more forceful, or challenged him directly, maybe I could have reasoned with the Indians . . ."

"Nate!" Christopher chastised, "You can't reason with a drunken Indian! It's not your fault. Maybe if I'd gone instead, Pearis wouldn't have interfered. I bested him once and I'd have done it again." He frowned as he remembered their altercation nine years ago. When he first came to North Carolina he wanted someone to take him around to the Indian villages; Pearis was at hand. They had a gentleman's agreement to split the profits of their trading venture. But Pearis liked to get the Indians drunk with rum made more powerful by certain drugs. Then when weighing their furs, he knew how to slip the scales, cheating the unsuspecting Indians. Gist confronted him. Pearis, who was drunk, began the fight that Gist finished. Pearis had hated him since.

"Maybe you're right, but I felt about two feet tall that day I rode into Fort Cumberland with no one but myself. Anyway, what else does that letter say?"

"It asks us to determine the disposition of certain Indian tribes and get their aid if possible. I'm to inquire of Andrew Montour, Monacatoocha, and Conrad Weiser. And we've been ordered to begin recruiting for our company. He sends along a copy of his instructions to recruiting officers issued last month to all the other captains."

"He don't want much does he? Where do we go for all these activities?"

"Philadelphia! We got a rousing response from all we met. A week ago they were willing to venture under Washington's command and learn how to fight in the Indian way. Now, lets go see if they were just fartin' in the wind."

CHAPTER XXX

November 1755

By November 1st the Gists were back in Philadelphia to meet again with Governor Morris. One purpose of the visit was to obtain Indian allies for the Virginia cause; he hoped for the same ones who had scouted for Braddock in July, as well as "Croghan's Indians" dismissed by the general before the campaign. Governor Morris suggested he consult Conrad Weiser at his home in Heidleburg twenty miles west of Reading on the road to Harris' Ferry, and even gave Christopher a packet of letters to deliver.

Yet, the Governor asked, why bother trying to get these Indians to fight for Virginia when they were so committed to Pennsylvania? In fact, he had a captain's commission in the Pennsylvania Militia with Christopher's name on it, and he expected the disagreement between himself and the Assembly to be resolved soon. The Colony would then be wanting experienced Indian fighters to train an army. Christopher was honored, but he declined, explaining his position in the Virginia Regiment.

Gist would have left the next morning had the Governor not sent him a message informing him of a letter from Montour and Monacatoocha. The missive requested Conrad Weiser and the Governor to come to John Harris' Ferry for a council at once. They had important intelligence from the north. Enemy Indians were at Shamokin, just fifty miles from Reading; an attack was expected in three days; a French fort was to be erected soon thereafter. The frontier was alive and it was time to act. Settlers must organize and attack at once. The Governor should hurry to send guns and powder.

The mood of frontier Pennsylvania had changed in the intervening weeks while the Gists were away. On October 16th a Delaware war party, led by none other than Kick-ena-pau-lin, attacked and massacred the German settlers along Penn's Creek near Selinsgrove. The terror lasted two days, during which thirteen settlers were killed and twenty-eight presumed captured. Several days later the Indians continued their attacks down the Susquehanna, killing the farmers from Thomas McKee's residence down to Hunters Mill. Then on October 31st one hundred Delaware and Shawnee under the leadership of Shingas, obliterated all the Scotch-Irish settlements in Big Cove and surrounding areas in Fulton and Franklin Counties along the Maryland border; forty-seven were killed or captured.

These attacks marked the first Indian violence in Pennsylvania since William Penn's treaty with the Delaware chief, Sassoonan in 1682. What gave the depredations a particularly ironic twist was that most of the Indians, especially at Penn's Creek, were known to the settlers; had eaten and drank with them; been intimate playmates with them and their children; had befriended them on many occasions, and had that friendship reciprocated.

By this time news of the failed British attacks on Canada had also arrived. Colonel William Johnson's expedition to Crown Point, while including a victory against French troops, ended without taking the fort. He withdrew to Albany. And General Shirley's campaign against Fort Niagra got no farther than Fort Oswego, when for lack of supplies and reinforcements, he too retreated to winter quarters in Albany.

Along with these realities was the rumor that 1500 French and Indians had marched out of Fort Duquesne and were racing toward the settlements. It was enough to fill the frontier towns with hollow-eyed refugees, forced to leave their cabins at a moment's notice with nothing but the clothes on their backs. Others, having had more time, carried a few belongings on horseback or in wagons. Carlisle, York, Reading and others, including Lancaster, became massive refugee camps with temporary shelters everywhere, full of hungry frontier farmers ill prepared for the coming Winter.

Gist was ready to go to Harris' Ferry for the conference to ask the Indians to join Virginia. He knew the Governor was right about their sentiments, but if Pennsylvania could not mount a defense, then he could offer an alternative. It was one hundred miles to Harris' Ferry and although a good wagon road connected the two cities, it was a journey not to be taken without some assurances. Gist sent a message to Andrew Montour saying he and his son would go there as soon as the exact date of the conference was established.

They were fortunate not to have rushed to Harris' Ferry. On November 7th the Governor informed Gist that Conrad Weiser was to arrive the next day with Monacatoocha, Montour and others. It was imperative that they address the Governor, the Assembly and the people of the city. So, in the State House at three o'clock that afternoon, before the important men of Philadelphia and many of its citizens, Monacatoocha made an impassioned appeal. Christopher and Nathaniel observed.

"Brethren, I am returned from my journey where I went as far up the Susquehanna as where the Nanticokes live. I told them that I had undertaken that journey to appraise them of the approach of very heavy storms. I bid them to rouse and awake to the noise all around them and if they did not now awake, the first noise they would hear would be that of the tomahawk upon their heads. I went in this manner to all the Indians on that river and I know their sentiments. I must now know yours. I must know if you will stand by us – to be plain – if you will fight or not. Be persuaded that we are determined to know the certainty of your measures before we take any ourselves.

"Brethren of Pennsylvania, the enemy have crossed the Blue Mountains and the River Susquehanna. Many of your people are dead and still you sleep like bear in the winter. We urge you English to act like men and be no longer like women, pursuing weak measures that rendered their names despicable. We urge you to take up the hatchet and join the Six Nations and the Indians on the Susquehanna against the French."

Monacatoocha then took two wampum belts tied together to represent the union of the Six Nations with their tributaries on the Susquehanna and threw them on the table. With this action he demanded an immediate response.

The Governor thanked Monacatoocha, but regretted he could not give a reply. The Assembly, to whom he had requested a return to its house to make a decision, did so, but adjourned without a commitment.

In private, Montour informed Gist that if the impasse between the Governor and the Assembly could not be resolved soon, it would mean the loss of all the Susquehanna Indians to the French. As for coming to help Virginia, both Monacatoocha and Montour felt a more urgent mission to journey to Onondoga to propose they exert their control over their wayward nephews, the Delaware and Shawnee.

Gist now had no choice but to implement the second purpose for his trip – recruiting. If Pennsylvania were not yet ready to have its own army, he would enlist as many of their best men as he could. Where to start? Everyone suggested Lancaster Town.

The Great Conestoga Road led from Philadelphia to Lancaster Town past neat little farms with fields of winter rye and apple orchards. Brindle colored cattle with their long horns hooked backwards, white breasts gleaming in the rare November sun, grazed in pasture. Large, dark draft horses dotted the landscape. Mule teams pulled fifteen-foot Conestoga wagons, their boat-like bodies rolling on ironclad wheels, bringing supplies and finished goods between the two cities.

Twenty-five years ago a businessman, James Hamilton, planned Lancaster to be a haven for artisans, merchants and professionals and encouraged their freedom to pursue their business without government regulation. By the time Gist rode into town, it was one of the largest inland colonial cities with more than 1000 inhabitants in 400 houses, a dozen churches and at least as many taverns. A three-story, stone prison, complete with attached workhouse, was home to a growing criminal element plus a rising number of citizens plagued by unpayable debt. As with other frontier towns, the streets were clogged with refugees from the hinterlands, some having lost homes and loved ones to Indian attacks, others only willing to lose their homes.

With its production of guns, wagons, clothing and military accouterments, Lancaster Town had been the center for supply to Braddock's army and was readying itself to accouter the Pennsylvania Militia as soon as the Governor and the Assembly could settle their differences.

The Gists lodged at The Swan, a three-story, brick inn on Queen Street, bounded on the north by Center Square. On the southwest corner of the Square was Joseph Simon's trading house, attached to his residence. Simon was one of only a dozen Jews in the town. He owned two Torahs and an Ark, which he used in services held in his home. Christopher and Nathaniel recruited in all the inns at various times, but his favorite spot was Simon's store, because of the high volume of customers. Simon liked the idea too, as the now famous frontiersmen were quite a draw. Also, Gist knew he could borrow money from him if necessary, with Virginia's IOU as collateral.

It was in Joseph's crowded store, amid the smells of wool blankets, brick teas, gun oil, beaver and deer pelts and wood smoke from the new Ben Franklin stove, that Christopher set up his recruiting station. With an empty barrel as a desk, he sat before six young perspectives.

"So you've come to enlist in my Company of the Virginia Regiment, is that right?" Christopher asked the short, young man who stood before him. Five others stood around him waiting their turn.

"Well, sir, we heer'd 'bout Mr. Washington wantin' t' fight Injun style an' we done studied on it an' figured we'z ready an' able. Mr. Gist, everyone knows you're in town, an' besides we met yer son, Nate, last night over t' the Blackhorse an' he told us all 'bout it. We know it pays two pistole to join and a shillin' a day after that for six or eight months dependin' on when the war of expedition is over."

"Nate says you an' he was both with Braddock when his army was ambushed," an older man spoke up. "Says you helped bring the General out after he was wounded."

"Well boys, I was the head guide for the whole army. If we had run into an ambush, I believe I would have known. No sir, we were most assuredly never caught in an ambuscade, though most folks still believe that. You see, the French and their Indians were on their way to surprise us as we crossed the Monongahela, the perfect place to do so. They just got there too late and we ran smack into them on their way." He continued to tell about the battle, and responded to related questions.

All was silent after his tale, each spectator picturing the battle and the carnage, the acts of heroism and cowardice. The nearest recruit broke the silence. "And you'll train us how to fight Injens?"

"You bet," Nathaniel answered. "We'll teach you to track 'em, kill 'em an' scalp 'em just like an Injen. And you'll meet all the heroes of Virginia who fought in that battle."

With that, the natural hubbub of half a hundred men resumed and Gist continued his task. "Sounds like you boys are ready then. What's your name, son?" Gist addressed the young recruit.

"Cornelius Henley, from right here in Lancaster."

"Age?" Gist read from a short list of questions and penned the answers.

"Twenty . . . one yesterday," he halted, as if not quite sure.

"Aye Corney, we'll call you Corney, lived long enough to start forgetting, ey? Well congratulations there, this'll be one hell of a birthday present. Say, how tall are you anyway?"

"I'm five foot and three inches without m' boots."

"Well, we'll just keep them boots and add an inch. Regulations say you got to be five foot four, so we're going to make you all at least that tall if it takes a pair of stilts." Gist got a chuckle from two other men whom he was sure were shorter.

"Last question, what's your trade?"

"Why, I'm a hunter, sir. I'll hunt for whoever'll pay me t' hunt. I been huntin' since I'z a shaver."

"Well, you'll be perfect for the job. We need men with knowledge of the woods who can track game and shoot straight. Your skills will be honed like the edge of a knife to find the trails of Indians and follow them. Now, can you sign your name?"

"No sir, never did learn writin'."

"No matter. You just make your mark here and I'll print your name under it." Gist did not explain that his recruits would be expected to endure more fatigue, hardship and danger than men in the normal regiments.

He took the same information from the other five recruits. They ranged in age from twenty-one to thirty-one, in height from five foot four to five foot eight and included one hunter, two soldiers, a sailor, a blacksmith, and two of unsure occupation.

He felt this was a good beginning. It was November 19th and since he began on the tenth, he had sent twenty good recruits down to Fort Cumberland. Their monetary incentives spent, he was forced to borrow from Joseph Simon just to get back to that fort, get more money and continue recruiting.

Christopher and Nathaniel spent only a week at the Fort, where they began training twenty-five recruits in the ways of wilderness warfare. Soon the training was given over to Captain Robert Stewart and the Gists rode to Alexandria to rendezvous with Colonel Washington. They collected £100 for past and future expenses and returned to winter in Lancaster Town.

But things had again changed in Pennsylvania. More Indian attacks, this time west of Reading, had inflamed the surrounding people. In fact the citizenry from the towns around Philadelphia marched in an angry mob, threatening the Governor and Assembly if they did not pass a militia law. Had Thomas Penn, the Proprietor in London, not sent a letter to the Assembly offering a gift of £5000 for the defense of the province, who knows what the mob might have done. But on November 25th the Assembly passed Benjamin Franklin's Militia law and appropriated £60,000 for its implementation, without taxing the Proprietors. The organization of Pennsylvania's army had begun.

CHAPTER XXXI

December 1755 – March 1756

Recruiting was slow after his return from Alexandria. Gist surmised that Pennsylvania's enlistment was cutting into his own. Coming back to Lancaster Town had been a waste of time; he might as well have stayed and trained his troops. Washington, however, told him that he had already enlisted more men than all the other captains put together. In fact, since the Gists were such accomplished recruiters, they were to continue through the first of March. Winter snows would close the passes through the Appalachians, putting a temporary stop to the Indian attacks. Indians wintered in the villages with their families and were supplied by the French in payment for their services against the English. Washington hoped enough recruits could be trained to counter the new wave of attacks in the spring.

Since his enlistments in Lancaster Town were so meager, Gist decided to try Fredericksburg, and if he could gain assurances from his creditors not to prosecute, move on to Baltimore Town. They split up in Fredericksburg; Christopher remained and Nathaniel continued on to sound out the creditors.

The £100 Washington had given him at the beginning of the month was dwindling. It had paid Joseph Simon, the bill at the inn, and other debts that accumulated as he bought drinks for prospective enlistees, as well as meals for himself, Nathaniel and sometimes a recruit. There was more to do and he was about to head straight for the lion's den – Maryland – wherein lay the bulk of his debt. He knew he had always found it difficult to refuse a creditor who came face to face and asked for his money. If he had it, the man got it. While Christopher was sitting in Simon's store considering his financial woes, in walked none other than the Prince of Pennsylvania Traders.

My God, what a surprise, Gist and Croghan both said in their own ways. Croghan had about fifty men with him, all now settling down at the various inns around town. They had been recruited by him to build four forts in Cumberland County west of Carlisle, one of which was to be a stockaded fortress at his own home in Aughwick.

Croghan brought his friend up to date on Pennsylvania's preparations and his personal triumphs. "There I was, holed up in me little stockade with forty men both red and white, and me havin' the best intelligence on the enemy of any man on the frontier. But the Governor would not heed a word I said."

"So I wrote a letter to ex-Governor Hamilton, who always did solicit me humble opinion on Injen affairs. I told him of me plight. Not bein' able to appear in Philadelphia for fear of bein' thrown in jail due to me rather extensive financial encumbrances, and me home bein' always surrounded by Injens, I could not be consulted.

"Hamilton put in a good word, so Governor Morris signed a bill submitted by the Assembly to forbid those creditors from throwin' me in the debtor's prison. Mind ye now, this is for the next ten years."

"Well, the Lord works in strange ways, doesn't He? That's the very thing I've been wrestling with by returning to Baltimore Town to recruit for Washington. Most of my debts are small, except for the British Fur Company. I've spread small sums among several; the big one still haunts me."

"Aye, 'tis a terrible burden, this debt, what renders a man incapable of endeavors to better hisself. An' should ye be so unlucky as to see the inside of a jail, how would ye ever pay off the debt? The sense of it escapes me."

"Well, I'm likely to find out about all that. I can't get any more of your Pennsylvanians to enlist, even when I mention the famous George Washington. I guess they would rather fight for you."

"No matter. Ye've no doubt snatched up the best we have to offer, to be leavin' me with nothin' but shitsacks and whisky bait."

"I have no doubt you'll be able to whip them into shape."

Croghan, now with the government's full credit behind him, bought £50 worth of trade silver as presents for the Indians, as well as supplies and accouterments for his men. The next day the Prince pulled out, leaving the town thankful that steps for the defense had begun at last.

Gist knew they had to leave, but he procrastinated another week, hoping things would get better. On January 7th one last man signed up. Alexander Turnbull, age thirty-four listed his occupation as "soldier." Perhaps he was one of Braddock's soldiers whose enlistment was up, or a deserter with no home in this country, yet not wanting to reenter the service of the King. And who could blame him? Several of his recruits had listed this occupation and no questions were asked. It did not matter what they had done. Even the best of men on that fateful day at Monongahela would have crumbled. What mattered was how, with the proper training, they would act from now on.

March 1756

The change in Baltimore Town was dramatic since Christopher had departed eleven years earlier for the Yadkin River. Then it was a tobacco port along with many other small towns on the Patapsco River and its tributaries. Since any overland journey was damaging to the dried tobacco leaves in their respective hogsheads, water routes were required. Baltimore Town provided a water access.

The village proper contained but twenty buildings including one church, two ordinaries and 150 inhabitants. An Indian scare some years back had prompted the erection of a stockade wall around the town; a rotting vestige could still be seen.

During the next ten years, however, the countryside, with the help of a young Irishman, Dr. John Stevenson, learned it could make more money growing wheat and shipping the flour to Ireland and Scotland. Settlers from these countries began to sail for Maryland.

William Fell had begun building his "Chesapeake Bay Ketches" at Fell's Point a short distance east of the town. While the Patapsco River at Baltimore Town was shallow, the water at the Point was deep enough to harbor ocean going ships coming to trade for the wheat.

The Baltimore Town Christopher Gist rode into that February was packed with people. For the past three years Swiss and German immigrants, gravitated to Maryland, many of whom landed here. A further influx of foreigners came in the form of French Acadians from Nova Scotia. These unfortunate refugees were deported last October for refusing to swear allegiance to the British King and were scattered throughout many of the Colonies. Baltimore Town drew its share. They mingled with the many back-country settlers made homeless by Indian attacks. Baltimore, like Lancaster with its flood of diverse people and rapid growth, was a haven for the recruiter.

The Gists rode down Baltimore Street, past a dozen one-and-a-half story hip-roofed houses painted blue, yellow or white, to a tavern not quite two years old owned by Valentine Larsch. Christopher informed the owner they would be staying there and recruiting from time to time. The two other ordinaries in town, Payne's Tavern and Rogers' just down Calvert Street as well as Dr. John's own store, would all make fine places for enlistment.

Christopher and Nathaniel spent some time visiting old friends, family and Sarah's parents, the Howards. Christopher's own two brothers still had plantations in the area. But while Nathaniel was off drumming up potential recruits, Christopher's first visit was with Violetta's father-in-law, William Cromwell, Esquire, with whom he had assigned his property ten years earlier.

"Well, you've become quite the subject of conversation. Everyone claims to have been your closest friend." The lawyer's bulk filled the chair in the law offices of Cromwell and Stansbury, not far from Larsch's tavern. "My son has written us from time to time of your adventures."

"Yes, a lot has happened since I left," Christopher said. "Anyway, I thank you for persuading my creditors to allow me entrance into the town."

"Well, this is the King's business and you must get an army together. Even though you recruit for Virginia, She makes up much of our frontier. Besides, Fort Cumberland is in Maryland and you are garrisoned there."

"I've sent my recruits there for training and when I'm done I'll report there, unless the Colonel wishes otherwise."

"Not to change the subject," Mr. Cromwell interjected, "but as you've become famous, we here in Baltimore Town have achieved some notoriety ourselves. Do you know this is one of the few places in all the Colonies where you can get protection from the smallpox? The good Dr. Thomas Stevenson, that would be Dr. John's brother, has learned that if you give a man the mild disease called cowpox, thereafter he cannot become sick with its more serious cousin. We have not had a smallpox outbreak in seven or eight years. I see you have not had the pleasure." Cromwell said studying Christopher's un-pocked face. "Perhaps you should visit Dr. Thomas."

"In all my fifty years I've remained free of the pox, though I've been close to it. So I'm not too worried about it."

"The choice is yours, of course. I hope you will reconsider. This insidious disease has caused so much sorrow among our people. Yet we Marylanders, as do all colonists, have much to thank the smallpox for. Why it has wiped out more of the red savages than wars and spirituous liquors combined. The Indians of the Eastern Shore are a case in point."

"Yes, my father and I used to trade with them. What has become of their reservations?"

"Oh, there are only two of them left I think – Chicone on the Nanticoke River and Locust Neck on the Choptank. I'll bet there aren't 200 Indians left. Most have gone north to the Six Nations."

"These Choptanks and Nanticokes and the other tribes around here were always good to the whites. They never made trouble for us and were treated fairly well. They've been on the reservation since my grandfather's day."

"You forget when the Shawnee came in '42 and tried to start an uprising. Our militia put it down, thank God."

"I guess I do remember all that but I was off in the western parts much of the time," Gist admitted.

"Ever since then, they've had rough treatment from the planters around them; settlers cutting their timber without permission, burning down their cabins and stealing their belongings when they go hunting. The poor miscreants submit constant grievance petitions before the Council. The proper inquiries are ordered and the Indian's rights are upheld, but nothing ever changes. Greed is too great. Planters want the land, simple as that."

"Not much uncultivated land over there I guess."

"Right. Since wheat farming replaced tobacco, not as much land lies fallow and more gets planted in wheat. The planters want that land to expand their plantations; that will happen. The Nanticokes and Choptanks will move out and everyone will be happy."

"Everyone except the Nanticokes and Choptanks," Gist added.

PART FOUR

"We expect to live on these Lands we now possess During our Time here, for when the Great Man Above made us he also made our forefathers and us of this Colour and Hue; he also fixed our forefathers and us here and to inherit this Land and Ever since we Lived after our manner and fashion."
Nopkehe – Eractasswa of Catawba Nation
(King Hagler)

CHAPTER XXXII

April 16, 1757

"Injens! Injens!" Came the cry from a sentry atop the west stockade wall of Fort Cumberland.

"What d'ye see?" shouted the corporal of the guard.

"At the tree line off to the west, twenty or thirty of 'em chasin' two of our 'tawba scouts."

Amid a hail of orders, and not without some confusion, the gates opened and two hundred anxious and overzealous soldiers poured onto the stump-covered ground toward a grizzly scene. Not 150 yards from the fort lay the mutilated bodies of the two Catawba warriors, messengers from a small reconnaissance patrol. For the rest of the day scouting parties scoured the area in search of the enemy's trail. Gist heard the cries and witnessed the confusion. He was not asked, nor did he volunteer his services in tracking the war party. It would have been a waste of time. He doubted anyone could pick up the trail, now obliterated by 200 sets of boot and moccasin tracks.

This was the normal course of events. If an Indian's trail ever were found, it proved too old to lead to their foe. When Indians did attack one of the few settlers left in the area, soldiers would rush out to the scene only to find dead, mutilated bodies and a burned cabin. Attempts to track the marauders were rarely successful, because the war parties were small and fast with a good head start. The frustration level of the regiment was high and fear of ambush real. During the past year Washington's troops along the frontier had fought in twenty engagements and lost 100 men. Gist reflected on these conditions as he sat in Washington's tent wondering, as he did so often, what they could do to catch the Indian assailants. Despite his recruiting promise to teach his men the art of tracking, they had not had sufficient time to acquire the skills necessary to find and follow their enemy. His own Company of Scouts had been recruited with an assault on Fort Duquesne in mind. They would have scouted ahead of the marching column along with Indian allies. But no expedition had commenced. Nearly half the garrison at Fort Maidstone, where he now spent much time, had been recruited by the Gists. Many were from Maryland. Convinced that they were being held long past their promised enlistment period, they allowed themselves to be persuaded by friends and relatives to desert across the Potomac. Hidden by

Maryland residents, all attempts to apprehend the deserters were unsuccessful. Washington appealed to Governor Sharp, but colonial powers could not change a public view of sympathy for soldiers living under harsh conditions and brutal punishment.

Leaving those problems behind, Christopher was here at the Maryland fort to confer with his commander. The Colonel was complaining about being quartered in a tent. It seemed that Captain Dagworthy of the Maryland Militia and his subalterns occupied all the quarters not already containing Virginia Regimental officers. Gist had heard Washington's tirades against the Maryland commander and his previous King's commission many times and was not listening until he detected a change of subject.

"It is official," the Colonel was saying, "that Maryland will take over Fort Cumberland. For two years I have petitioned Governor Dinwiddie to abandon it, but for naught. 'It is the King's fort,' he would say, 'and we must continue to provide troops and provisions until a royal officer is appointed.' So now he has, in the form of Dagworthy."

"When will this happen?" Gist asked.

"Within the next several months we must redistribute our garrison and supplies. The Assembly meets as we speak and I have been called to Williamsburg to submit my Bill of Particulars and hear their plans for restructuring the Regiment."

"So the rumor about reducing the number of companies is correct. I had a suspicion the Regiment couldn't go on like it was – too many officers drawing too much pay and not enough enlisted men to fill sixteen companies. What'll become of those officers who lose their companies?"

"They'll be demoted and that is why I wanted to talk to you. You will be asked to take a lieutenancy."

Gist remained stoic, jaw muscles working back and forth.

"I know this will not sit well with you, but know that you are not alone in your vexation. The Assembly has given financial control of the Regiment to the Governor, who, in a fit of frugality, has cut my pay and eliminated certain perquisites on which I have come to rely." Washington's voice rose in anger "He even presumes to dictate where I am to garrison my troops."

Gist felt his anger and frustration and could only nod in sympathy.

"You know," the Colonel continued in a more relaxed tone, "I have all but begged the Governor that some person of sense and probity, with a tolerable share of knowledge of Indian customs, be appointed to transact the Indian affairs of Virginia."

"Yes," replied Gist, "and that person, one Edmund Atkin, arrived in New York in October last and has been following Lord Loudoun around lo these past months, trying to obtain orders, for what I'm not sure. If his job is Indian agent, then he should be here. Loudoun knows nothing of Indians, so how could he give any pertinent orders?"

"I quite agree, yet Atkin will take over the management of Indian affairs at some point and he will need an assistant. I believe that man should be you. I am authorizing you to go to Williamsburg now and present this idea to Governor Dinwiddie for his approval. He may then recommend it to Mr. Atkin. Should the Governor approve, I will write the appropriate official letters of recommendation."

"But Colonel, might I remind you that I can neither speak the language of the Cherokee nor the Catawba, which compose most of the Indians we deal with."

"No matter. I know of no man more sensitive to their customs and manners than you. Your constant intervention has helped smooth their ruffled feathers and allowed us to remain friendly. We'll just get you an interpreter."

The two continued to talk about this probable new position and its attendant duties. Christopher had already been managing the Cherokee and Catawba who came to Fort Loudoun and Maidstone. Through interpreters he would divide them into bands of thirty, equip them with whatever presents and war necessities Washington had on hand, if any, and send them out against the French. In cases where no presents were available, they would wait around until a shipment arrived. Their drinking and gaming with the soldiers often caused conflict that Gist would have to mediate. Sometimes the Indians would turn around and go home, grumbling about empty promises and what liars the Virginians were.

Yet all these unpleasantries were expected and Annosanah was good at dealing with Indians. He could see that as assistant to the Indian Agent he would spend his total energies as liaison to them. In the role as Annosanah, speaker of true words, perhaps he could help insure Indian participation in the coming expedition against the French, whenever that might be.

CHAPTER XXXIII

June 1757

To Gist, as he rode along the all too familiar path toward civilization, this trip was unnecessary. Why not have them sent by express? He looked down at the leather bag containing the official letters of recommendation Washington had written to Governor Dinwiddie and Speaker of the House, Robinson. His journey to Williamsburg two months ago to speak with the Governor had been fruitful. His Honor was receptive to the suggestion that he be Atkin's assistant, because of his loyalty to the Ohio Company and the interests of Virginia. Having returned to Fort Loudoun, he was again bound for the capital.

Why the Governor could not have written the letters when he was there before, was beyond him. But no, he had to make a verbal suggestion, get an approval, go back and get Washington's "official" recommendation, return for the Governor's "official" recommendation, find Atkin to get his "official" appointment so it can be "officially" approved by the House of Burgesses. Maybe he was being too cynical; this was the way it was done. The Colonel insisted these letters were too important for some messenger boy. Besides, the more the settlers saw him and knew about his mission, the better chances would be for smooth relations between the Virginia Regiment and the public. If this were the case, he reasoned, then relations ought to be pretty damn good, since this was his third trip to Williamsburg this year. And had he not made several the year before?

He was happy to leave the monotony of fort existence. It was not always safe to stay at his home in Opeekon a few miles away, so he stayed at Fort Loudoun in Winchester. Lord Fairfax had granted him a lot in town four years ago in recognition of his explorations into Ohio. If his new duties required his presence there, he would have it surveyed and build a house.

For now, each step of his horse carried him that much closer to his new position as Indian agent. Oh, he knew he was a "deputy" agent, but rumor had it that Edmund Atkin would be in Virginia just long enough to begin his plan of action and then move on to the Carolinas. Gist would be in charge. The position was perfect for him and he wanted it. He felt that what had been a long series of personal failures and misfortunes was about to change. He did not yet know Atkin's plan, nor the full scope of his own duties. But they had to include the type of work he had already been doing with the Cherokee and Catawba. His success had been marginal, but then he had no control over the amount of presents to give the Indians or who should go on scouting ventures. He was like a patch for a birchbark canoe. At each leak in Indian-white relations, he was rushed to plug the hole. Perhaps he could work with Atkins to build a whole new canoe.

It was clear something needed to be done. Each Indian encounter reinforced Washington's already dim view of them. To him they were undisciplined, churlish, individualistic, greedy and too mercenary. They complained about insufficient presents and refused to go out against the French until properly supplied. Gist knew these presents were necessary payment for their services against the French. Had they remained home hunting and trapping, they could trade for the goods they needed with their furs and hides. Having given up the chase, how else were they to be supplied? The argument made perfect sense to him, who as assistant superintendent would be in a much better position to fulfill their needs . . . he hoped.

Gist arrived in Williamsburg on June 7th. The blistering heat slowed his horse, browned the grass, withered the trees and dried up the runs. How he missed the cool mountain air.

The Governor, having suffered at the end of March a most violent cold and fever that incapacitated him for six weeks, was worse than when Gist last saw him. What had once been a robust and fleshy figure was now pale and thin.

"I must confess, Gist, that this sickness, which has flat got the better of me, and this constant frustration with matters of state . . ," a violent liquid cough erupted and forced him to cease. "Pardon me, but I have no control over it."

Gist nodded in sympathy.

"It angers me incredibly," he pounded on the table with a thin hand, "that Lord Loudoun will not come down to Virginia to inspect our frontier. He's quite taken with an invasion of Canada at Louisbourg and wants only a defensive posture for us. There'll be no campaign against Fort Duquesne this year." The Governor continued, amid bouts of coughing, to complain of Loudoun's inaction and then switched the subject to the new superintendent of Indian affairs. "He arrived here in April and no amount of prodding or persuasion on my part could move him to go to Winchester where the Indians are."

"I've heard he is partial to his comforts and likes to cook his own meals." Gist offered the rumor he had heard. "How did the appointment of Indian agent fell on one so unfamiliar with Indians."

Dinwiddie related how Atkin had for years been a merchant in Charles Town, South Carolina and grew familiar with the Indian trade on that front. As a member of that Colony's Council, he became very dissatisfied with its Indian policy. He then sailed to England and wrote a massive treatise to the

Board of Trade, giving a detailed account of the history of southern Indian relations. The Board was impressed, allowing Atkin to solicit his present appointment.

"Finally I was able to persuade him to go to Winchester by promising him £150 for expenses. You know, Loudoun did not grant him one farthing for his office. He ordered the Colonies to support him. I told him he had to go there, because the Cherokee had learned of a new agent and wanted to meet him. So with much groaning and complaining, he departed. You should have passed him on the way."

Gist could not recall passing anyone on his way in, but there were several paths leading to Winchester for part of the way.

"Oh, as I was saying, with all these problems and my sickness, I have, with the deepest regrets, applied to be relieved of my duties and return to England. No reply yet, but I simply cannot continue . . ," another bout of coughing cut his sentence short.

Gist was silent. This was sad news indeed. The Virginia war effort could not have a more ardent supporter. A new governor would not be versed in frontier affairs, nor be sympathetic to the designs of the Ohio Company.

Christopher Gist now carried the requisite letters of recommendation to Atkin from Dinwiddie and Robinson on his way back to Fort Loudoun. Upon his arrival he found, of all people, George Croghan engaged in serious debate with a man who could only be Edmund Atkin. A dozen Cherokee warriors stood around a pile of blankets, scalping knives, hatchets, and various other materials found among presents to the Indians. Gist kept his distance for some time until the negotiations were over. Croghan was speaking with the Cherokee through an interpreter while Atkin was jotting down figures in an accounting ledger.

"You must be Superintendent Atkin," Gist said as he walked over and introduced himself.

"Captain Gist," Atkin answered, "your reputation precedes you. I have heard so much about you from the good Governor and your esteemed Colonel Washington. I will be wanting to speak with you this afternoon. May we count on that?"

Gist acknowledged the request and decided to present the letters at that time, since Mr. Atkin turned and walked away without another word. Croghan interrupted his entertainment of the Cherokees to turn and greet his friend. They threw their arms around each other, slapping their backs.

Gist spoke first as they stood and watched the Cherokee collect their presents and begin packing them for transportation on horses. "Never thought I'd see you here. Aren't you supposed to be in New York working for Sir William Johnson?"

"Aye, and but for the seein' of yourself, how I'd much rather be in that country. Hotter'n the seven brass hinges of Hell it be down here and that Atkin laddie's not got all his buttons."

"So I've heard. But what brings you here and what's this all about?" Gist gestured toward the Indians.

"Arrah now, 'tis a long story, but I've nothin' else that requires me." He cleared his throat, "last month these here Cherokee," he pointed to the warriors nearby, "chased a Shawonese war party into Pennsylvania and did, mind ye with some difficulty, manage to terminate their earthly rambles. Sure but I'm after rewardin' 'em with a handsome £100 present approved by the new Governor Denny of Pennsylvania. In searchin' for 'em to give the gift, my messenger finds 'em here askin' for presents from Atkin. Well, my man summons them to our own Fort Loudoun to collect their bounty."

"Yes, I noticed that even the mighty Penns have to kiss the arse of the Earl of Loudoun once in a while," Gist interrupted.

"Aye, we can't allow Virginia to be the only Colony with a fort named after him now can we? Anyway, where was I? Oh, two days later Atkin's letter finds me, rantin' and ravin' he is, about the importance of himself givin' the presents and that all gifts to southern Indians must pass through him or his power will be diminished. Then he orders me to Winchester. Well now, the nerve of him orderin' me to do anythin'! But in the interests of keepin' the peace I came down. Then I find out he hasn't got any money to buy presents, or damn little. So those presents ye be seein' there are supplied by meself, makin' Atkin seem like the cock o' the walk. Now d'ye think I'd get a 'thankee Mr. Croghan' from the bugger? Ha! When the Devil goes blind, and then maybe." Croghan answered his own question.

Gist told the Irishman all he knew of his new position and how Atkin would move on to the Carolinas leaving him in charge of Virginia's Indian affairs. Croghan related how Sir William Johnson and he were negotiating peace with the Delaware and Shawnee.

"If you're successful," remarked Gist, "we'd better not let the Cherokee find out or all hell will break loose. They've been bitter enemies so long none of them can remember why."

The two friends talked for some time of frontier issues until Gist remembered his promise to call on the Superintendent. They agreed to resume their conversation that evening.

At Atkin's headquarters, a wall tent outside the gates of the fort, Gist caught him with pen in hand, scribing ferociously to some inner deadline. Gist relinquished his letters and waited for an invitation to sit. One never came. Atkin commenced a tedious reading of the recommendations and put them aside. Gist felt as if he should be at attention.

"Well, Captain Gist, you come most highly recommended by everyone to whom I have spoken. I have little choice but to approve your appointment as my deputy. I shall not belabor your duties at this time, as I have been occupied in the most delicate negotiations with our friends the Cherokee, Catawba, Tuscarawa and others. You will be distributing the necessary accouterments of war to the various raiding parties; this to be done with great attention to detail and full accounting of each item. Upon their return, you will reward them with certain presents according to their success, which presents must also be accounted for. Most importantly, you will arrange escorts and issue passports for these bands to travel to and from the frontier, taking the utmost care to keep them away from the settlements, away from the liquor sellers, and away from the unscrupulous traders who would rob them of their presents for a few drams of rum.

"Now, as to the matter of your legislature passing a law on the 8th instant allowing a bounty of £45 for every enemy captured and £40 for everyone killed; the killing of them cannot be proved but by the taking of scalps, of which the Cherokee in particular have discovered the art of making four out of one. And since they demand to keep them from a point of honor, they are free to produce the same scalps again and again. You will, therefore, encourage them to keep their trophies and reward them in proportion to their contributions.

"Oh, one more thing. You must be sure the Indians obtain fresh meat instead of salted meat. The consumption of salted meat is one reason the colonials are such heavy drinkers and our relations with these tribes cannot afford the same behavior in them."

Gist cleared his throat. "Those sound like very logical details necessary for an organized and efficient management system. I'll do my best to fulfill them." Gist bid Atkin good day and exited the tent in a state of shock. Croghan was right; this man belonged anywhere but in the woods managing Indians. Gist could see trying to keep the Indians on the mountain trails away from the settlements. He could even understand not buying scalps. But trying to force a system of passports on people, who often could not tell you what they would do tomorrow, was ludicrous. Atkin was trying to impose British precision on a people who were by nature impulsive, individualistic and not given to following regulations. You might as well try to make a heard of elk line up for dinner. Oh, what had he gotten himself into?

Gist prayed the man would soon make the appointment official and then be off to impose his madness on Carolina Indian affairs. Gist, however was not discouraged. His task would be to facilitate the Indian actions against the French and her allies until an offensive against Fort Duquesne could be mounted. He hoped it would be soon.

CHAPTER XXXIV

June 1757

"I don't know George," Gist shook his head as he and Croghan sat illuminated by the fire. He took a drink of warm rum from a pewter flagon; he took another. "He claims to know Indians. So how can he expect to reroute them away from the settlements and stick to a system of passports?"

"Arrah now laddie, d'ye know what Sir William Johnson would do?" Croghan upended his cup. "Why, he'd dress in a breech clout, he would, dab on war paint and dance from dusk till dawn, just gettin' them Injens all riled up with the drum beatin' an' the fire too high for a giant to jump. Then he'd hand out passports to every Injen there," Croghan chuckled. Gist smiled at the image. "'Course, His Majesty the King's a bit more generous with money and Injen presents for Johnson than he is with Atkin." Croghan raised his own container.

"What money Atkin gets for Virginia comes from Virginia, not His Majesty." Gist drank deeply and motioned for Croghan to come nearer. "Did you know that he chased Loudoun around the Colonies for five months," Gist couldn't help snickering. "First, he went to New York and the Lord had just left, then to Albany and back to New York, each time missing him by a day. Then at Boston Loudoun wouldn't see him so he followed him back to New York." By now both men were laughing hysterically. "Shh, shh," Gist motioned with a finger over his lips. "Atkin finally caught him in Philadelphia to get written orders on what he's supposed to do."

"Begorrah, he's Injen Agent and he's not got a hint of what to do?"

Schoolboy laughter was all that could be heard.

"Aye, could be that the Lords in London saw through him and decided too much authority could put him out of control." Gist took another sip.

"Can't you just picture Atkin out on the road from here to Cumberland with a big, wooden gate, asking each Injen raiding party for their passport before they can go through?"

Silence. Then the night was pierced by an uncontrollable laughter that rendered its originators incapacitated. At length Gist got control of himself. His sides hurt; his face hurt. "I've got to turn in, George. I rose before dawn, rode forty miles and this merriment is more than I can stand." He stood yawning and stretching.

To their surprise an express rider trotted his horse over to them and asked for Colonel Washington. Gist pointed toward the house in town that the commander called headquarters. Gist and Croghan looked at each other– a midnight messenger was unusual– and sat back down to await developments. Half an hour later Ensign William Crawford came to their fire. The Colonel, he said, had called a Council of War for 2:00 A.M.

The sour smell of new oak pervaded the air of the new officers' barracks. A gentle breeze flowed through the open windows and flickered the candle flames. Besides Gist, the room held eight officers. Some sat on nail casks or temporary benches while others leaned on the new wall. Washington stood behind an empty hogshead on which two pieces of parchment shone amber in the candlelight.

"Gentlemen," whispers and fidgeting stopped as their commander spoke. "I am in receipt of two letters: one from Dagworthy and another from Major Livingston, both from Fort Cumberland written two days ago. Dagworthy's reads as follows: 'Six Cherokee Indians, who just came from Fort Duquesne, say that six days ago they saw a large body of troops march from that garrison with a number of wagons and a train of artillery, and by their route, must intend an attack on this garrison, 'meaning Fort Cumberland. Livingston's letter concurs and says the six Indians were from Captain Spotswood's expedition. Regrettably, they report, the Captain and his men," he paused, "did not make it back." Washington's voice lowered. "I have no details at this time."

The silence became oppressive as sadness filled the room. Each man looked down at the floor or over at the wall, trying not to show the emotion felt by all. Spotswood was well liked.

"Any confirmation by white soldiers?" asked Captain Thomas Waggoner after clearing his throat several times.

"The Major takes great care to say this report is solely based on Indian intelligence." Washington tried to repress a smile, but others snickered at what they considered a humorous contradiction. The comic relief gave them something else to focus on. "Major Livingston believes the report to be credible. Now I have two questions. Number one: should our Virginia Regiment make haste to Fort Cumberland for its defense against a possible French invasion? And number two: should we work to assemble a more sufficient force of men here at Fort Loudoun to make it more defensible?"

"That would mean abandoning some of the other frontier forts and bringing their garrisons here," reasoned Captain Stewart.

"Correct," stated the Colonel. "We'd have more soldiers to finish this fort in a timely manner."

"Here, here," someone shouted in agreement and others joined in the expression.

"What if the Indians are wrong?" Gist shouted over the noise. Everyone was quiet. "It's happened before. A large force splits into many smaller raiding parties as they reach our settlements. What if there is no artillery?"

"Gist is right," Stewart again spoke. "If we can't trust this report, we must send our own reconnaissance before we uproot our own defenses."

"Besides," Gist continued, "it's a four-day journey from Fort Duquesne, plus the two it took this message to get here. We just don't have time to gather our scattered troops and march to Fort Cumberland before the place becomes invested."

Washington agreed to send Major Andrew Lewis on a scouting mission to determine the veracity of the Indian account. If it were true, he would round up the smaller garrisons and bring them to Winchester. They sent copies of the letters to Williamsburg and dispatched messengers for the nearby counties requesting their militias. Finally they increased the hours of construction on the fort to twenty-four.

Gist met Croghan outside the barracks and acquainted him with the news. They walked together toward Gist's tent and came upon Lieutenant James Baker, normally stationed at Pearsall's Fort thirty-five miles northeast of Winchester. He was here with a band of Cherokee to deliver a French prisoner captured on a recent raid to Fort Duquesne. Gist did not know him well, only that he was one of the few officers capable of leading an Indian raiding party into enemy territory. This elite corps wore breech clouts and leggins, slept, ate and traveled in Indian style and often spoke enough of several Indian languages to be understood.

Gist greeted the Lieutenant. Having heard sketchy details of the excursion, he asked him to fill them in. Baker indulged their request and began to relate how on June 1st he led a party of fifteen Cherokee and five Virginians toward Fort Duquesne. They intended to gather intelligence, acquire scalp trophies and capture French prisoners. Four days later and twenty miles from the Fort, they discovered tracks and followed them for ten miles until their lead scout spied a patrol of French soldiers.

"There's only ten of 'em, see, so we sets up an ambuscade," Baker continued, "and when they gets close, they spies us. We's all naked, 'cept fer breechclouts, an' they calls to us; asks who we is." The Lieutenant leaned on his rifle, spit a trail of tobacco juice, and renewed his stance. "Now we don't give no answer, but we all rise up and fires on 'em, which they return. So we rush in with hawks an' knives an' make the French run away. Our Injens outrun 'em, kill two, wound two an' two others give up. The rest get away." Baker showed no emotion. He seemed to stare off into the distance as he spoke, twitching his head to one side. "When we return to the place of our first shots, we find our best scout, Swallow Warrior, shot dead by a ball to the head. The Injens go crazy, kill the wounded and one other prisoner. I'm able to save only one; Ensign Velistre is his name. The Colonel orders me to send him and the Injens here, but that I should stay at Pearsall's if there's no particular reason to the contrary. But they wouldn't come without me." Baker made sure they understood this so there would be no accusation of disobeying orders.

"But that's not all," Baker brightened up a bit. "In that first volley, Swallow Warrior's young son is shot through both thighs," he pointed to mid-thigh on himself. "So one of my boys hoists him on his back and carries him 'til he wears out. Then another does the same, and another and so on until we're far enough away. He's hurtin' real bad, so we make a bier to carry him on 'til we get to Fort Cumberland. Those four days we et naught but wild onions, bein' afraid as we are of pursuit."

The three men talked awhile of personal experiences against Indians over the years. Baker was invited to their fire, but declined in order to camp with his Indians.

"Arrah now," Croghan said to Baker before he left, "ye must know that Superintendent Atkin has no presents for your Injens. But Colonel Stanwix, the British commander at Lancaster Town, can certainly use 'em. Why not let me take 'em to Pennsylvania? I'll supply 'em with presents and outfit 'em for more raids. You look good, Virginia'll look good and I'll have more Cherokee to throw at the enemy."

Baker said he would talk it over with his Indians and went on his way. Later, after a long time staring into the fire, Gist commented. "Carrying Swallow's son on their backs and a bier for 100 miles is truly an act of heroism and compassion. Why can't there be more cooperation like this between Indians and whites?"

"Aye, ye are right about that bein' heroism, but methinks 'twas an act born of camaraderie between men who've fought together an' watched friends die. Put that same soldier on his farm where Swallow an' his son are stealin' his horse an' killin' his cow an' mutilatin' his wife an' child, an' I'll guarantee he'll be an Injen hater."

Gist stared into the fire without a word. He knew this.

Croghan continued, "I know you want to believe that whites an' Injens can live together in peace an' harmony. Hell, I'll even allow it might be possible in some places. But mostly out here where the two meet, there's hate, blind, evil hate. No offense to your experiences, which may tell ye different, but over at Aughwick there's always a hundred or more Injens camped. I see 'em every day; I talk to 'em, hell, I know their own tongue, an' I listen. Now I'll be tellin' ye it's always about the white man takin' the land. That's why so many tribes who once was on the Delaware is now livin' on the Ohio." Croghan gesticulated with excitement. "D'ye think the Colonies are gonna stop expandin'; stop sending surveyors like yourself and what you was doin' when we met? Settlers follow the surveyors an' they won't be goin' east! The Shawonese and Delaware can't go much further west, 'cause that be Miami country. They'll fight first!"

Croghan relaxed after his brief outburst. He grabbed a coal between two sticks and held it above his pipe. The flame illuminated a small scar above his left eye.

"Well George, you haven't told me anything I don't already know. But now that I'm in a position to make things smoother between our two people, maybe there's something I can do, like explain the Indian's viewpoint to the leaders of the Company."

"Arrah now Chris, maybe so, and maybe that'll bode well for them Injens dealin' with your Company, but ye cannot stop the change," the Irishman softened his tone. "Ye can speed it up or slow it down a bit, but she cannot be stopped. Ye can only influence your Company. You, yourself, have said there's six other land companies who'll bring in more settlers, an' ye cannot affect the likes of them. Some day this land'll be parceled out clear to the Mississippi and not a single Injen in sight. Me, I just do the best I can an' try to be on the winnin' side, like most of the Injens I know."

The next morning the two friends parted company. Atkin had little choice but to approve Croghan's suggestion about Baker's Cherokee. Croghan left leading twenty warriors up the path toward Pennsylvania.

Anxiety was high at Winchester for the next three days. On June 20th, however, an express arrived from Dagworthy. He admitted that the six Cherokee who had reported sighting the invasion force were young warriors frightened enough to imagine wagons and artillery. Further intelligence reported the force splintering into many smaller raiding parties as Gist had suspected.

The following day, to everyone's surprise, 170 militiamen from three counties arrived. They had been called, of course, but militia were not known to be that reliable. As always, their arrival was a mixed blessing. Over half were without arms and ammunition. They would not work to improve the fort's defenses; would not take orders from Washington's officers; could not be trusted to stand guard duty without abandoning their post. Many times Gist had heard the Colonel rave against the Militia. "Obstinate and perverse," he called them. And although they managed to answer their call in record time, they might as well not have come at all.

CHAPTER XXXV

July 1757

The double gallows stood forty feet high on the parade ground within the walls of the incomplete Fort Loudoun. When June's Indian scare was over, work on the fort was redirected and the tower appeared almost overnight. The Assembly had renewed the mutiny act, giving Washington the power to execute deserters, but this time without the prior approval of the Governor.

As the hammers rang out on the construction site, Gist was resigning his commission from the Regiment. The soon- to-be Deputy Indian Agent began his duties before his official appointment by escorting 129 Catawbas, Tuscarawas, and Nataways to Fort Cumberland. A small contingent of Cherokee were supposed to accompany him, but were absent with no explanation. He returned to find the new Indian Agent already in trouble.

"Come in Captain," Washington called upon seeing him at the door to his house. "I am glad you are back. We have another disagreeable situation, due this time to our new Superintendent."

"May I remind you, sir, I'm no longer a Captain," Gist said with a smile.

"Yes, of course, but I suppose I shall refer to you as Captain for some time. One develops habits, you know. Now this business with the Indians: six days ago ten Indians, some Cherokee and Mingo, came here from the Cherokee Nation. Apparently they could give no good account of their intentions and the Superintendent took them for spies. He had them confined to the public jail and there they remain." He threw up his hands in disgust.

Gist sat on a bench, not quite believing this. "What are the other Cherokees in town doing about this?"

"A dozen, and greatly exasperated I might add, say they know the prisoners and obliged Atkin to send an express to the South Branch for their chief, Outassity, to come here and clear up the matter. But the chief, being very sick, has not yet arrived."

"That explains why the Cherokee were not with me when I escorted the others to Fort Cumberland. Outassity is the one they call Mankiller. He was here last month with a dozen warriors, promising to send many more?"

"Indeed, I do wonder that you can keep them all straight, but I remember musing whether they would wait for Atkin's passport or come on their own."

Gist chuckled at Washington's sarcasm. "Sir, Outassity is regarded as the

King of the Cherokee Nation and his support is imperative for the success of our war effort. This incident could jeopardize that."

"Well, to make matters worse, a diet of food to which they are unaccustomed has led to the flux among them. Do you think there is anything you can do? I cannot order Atkin about, as he is under the command of Lord Loudoun."

"I don't know what I can do. I've not yet got an official appointment."

"Yes, the man is quite dilatory at every turn," Washington commented, "but please try to prevail upon his sensibilities to release the poor devils. It simply will not do to have them die on us."

"By the way," Gist turned as he pushed open the door, "I thought we were shooting deserters."

"Yes, but I believe the hemp will provide more of a deterrent than the shot. You know that desertion occurs at such an appalling rate. We have been plagued with it from the beginning and I have been powerless to act beyond lashing. By the time I could ever have gotten the Governor's permission to execute a deserter, the urgency would have been gone, you understand. We have lost a quarter of our latest recruits. So now, on whatever day our newest recruits march to their various stations, I will commence the hanging for all to see."

Gist wished the Colonel success with his new power over life and death and went to see Edmund Atkin. The Cherokee situation was indeed critical. These were some of the warriors with whom he would work in his new position and this was not a smooth beginning. Atkin considered himself an expert on Indians and Gist knew not what he could say to change his mind. But he would try. He decided to visit the inmates.

The public jail in Winchester was a small cabin of logs with two cells, each having a small barred window in its thick wooden door and rear wall. With little circulation the July heat was oppressive. The stench of ten unwashed bodies and the unmistakable odor of the flux was almost unbearable. The place was not designed for this many inmates. The jailor, though sympathetic, was powerless to help them.

Gist went inside to look through the small windows at the prisoners sitting on the floor leaning against the wall. Some looked toward him and spoke a few unintelligible words. They were pitiful to behold, these once proud warriors, and Atkin's stupidity made him seethe with anger. He recognized none.

Atkin, however, could not to be found. No one had seen him or knew where he might be. So Gist enlisted Richard Smith, the interpreter, to learn the facts from the Indians. Their story was simple. They had left Choto weeks ago to fight for the Virginians and were promised many presents for their services by 'The Bird,' the reference being to William Byrd who was recruiting Indians for Virginia. When they arrived here, they requested their presents from an important Englishman and were told those gifts had not yet arrived. They should, he said, proceed on their scouting mission and collect the goods upon their return. The Indians refused and became outspoken in their demands to be outfitted as promised. Too great a distance, they said, had been traversed for them to be treated with such rancor. Their captain, a Mingo warrior, spoke through an interpreter to the Englishman, who retaliated with anger and then threw them in jail. They did not know why.

Gist brought a change of clothing, breech clouts and shirts, for each and made sure they had fresh meat instead of the soldiers' ration of salted beef. Having done all he could, he returned to his tent to find a letter on his desk.

> July 25, 1757
> Edmund Atkin, Esqr. Agent for and Superintendent of the Affairs of his Majesty's Allies the Several Nations of Indians inhabiting the Frontiers of the Colonies of Virginia, North & South Carolina & Georgia.
>
> To Christopher Gist Esquire
>
> WHEREAS the Welfare and Security of this Colony in particular stands in need at this time of the constant aid & Assistance of Parties of the Indians living in Friendship with his Majesty's Subjects, against the French Subjects & their Indian Allies.

He skipped down the page, wondering whether the sole mission of a university was to teach students how to say in a profusion of verbiage what could more easily be said with brevity.

> And Whereas the honorable Robert Dinwiddie, Esqr. Lieutenant Governor & Commander-in-Chief of the said Colony hath deemed me to nominate a person to act for me in my absence, I therefore reposing Trust & Confidence in your Loyalty, Fidelity, & Ability, do hereby constitute & appoint you to be my Deputy Agent for the purposes aforesaid.

Ah! There it was. His appointment was official! Now what were the purposes aforesaid? He skimmed the words before the last sentence to see if there were any surprises. He read out loud the part referring to parties of Indians living in friendship, "to direct them, their Conductors or Leaders, Interpreters, etc., to subsist and distribute Presents to them and generally manage and transact whatever relates to them."

Did this mean he could take charge of the Indian prisoners since Atkin could not be found? He considered it, but decided it would not bode well for him to defy his superior his first day on the job. Tomorrow he would again search for Atkin and persuade him to free the prisoners.

The next afternoon Gist found Atkin at his headquarters tent again writing in his ledger. He asked how the Indians came to their confinement.

"Well, when these savages came before me," Atkin gasped, "they spoke to me in the Mingo tongue by an interpreter, declaring their desire to fight against the French. They then demanded to be fitted for battle. They demanded, I tell you, as if I were their lowly servant. The Virginia Assembly has appropriated funds for presents but they have not yet arrived. I suggested they leave for some scouting mission and collect their goods upon return. They refused. Their captain became exceedingly rude and churlish, so I had them incarcerated."

"Colonel Washington has explained the consequences of jailing these Indians. You know, sir, there is a group of twenty Cherokees in town. They have sent runners to their Nation and to Carlisle, where many others are camped, saying the English have fallen upon their brethren and with help will defend them." Gist's voice was rising.

"I was not aware of that development." Atkin looked worried. "But it changes nothing. I believe those Mingoes are French spies and I'll not release them until proven otherwise."

"What about the Cherokees with them. Are they also spies?"

"They are guilty by association and cannot be exempt."

"Mr. Atkin, Sir," Gist was stern, "are you prepared to jeopardize Virginia's treaty with the Cherokee? By holding these men prisoner, that's exactly what you're doing. I've spoken to them and got no clue they were more than they seem."

"And they seem to me to be spies!" Atkin raised his voice as he looked Gist in the eye. Gist stared back but was silent. "When I have moved on to the Carolinas," his voice returned to normal, "you may handle Indian affairs as you see fit. But while I am here, we will do as I say. I am the one who hired you and if we cannot agree, I will have another deputy."

"Mr. Atkin, sir," Gist bristled, "if this causes a break with the Cherokee, you won't even have this position."

Gist turned and left the tent with a force that pulled on the flaps and rocked the canvas. He could not decide if he were more angry with Atkin or with himself for resorting to threats. Perhaps gentle reasoning would have worked better. No, not with a man who believed himself infallible. The little man lived in his own world and went about doing those things he believed he had to do, without anyone's approval.

What could he do? If more Cherokee came from afar and joined the twenty who had sent the runners, they would confront Atkin. With his stubbornness and temper, that could be dangerous. He could be injured or killed. Washington would have to call in his troops. He shuddered to think of that outcome. But what if Atkin were bypassed? He must speak to Washington.

Gist caught the Colonel in his tent writing letters. "You cannot imagine, Captain, how much of my time is spent keeping correspondence. There lies a letter from the Governor that needs answered," he pointed to his desk with neat piles of paper. "Colonel Stanwix requires one also and the Earl of Loudoun must be kept abreast of Virginia's military readiness for a campaign against the French."

Gist wondered if Washington were complaining or airing his own importance. "Colonel, regarding the Indian prisoners," Gist began as the commander continued writing. "If there should be any . . . a . . . show of force by friends of these Indians, what would be the obligation of the Regiment?"

Washington stopped writing and tilted his head to reveal one eye. He paused for a moment and offered a measured response. "Captain, the Cherokee are our allies. Any show of force by friends to aid their brethren in distress would have the full support of the Regiment."

That was just what he wanted to hear. He knew the regiment would not interfere. Now he needed an interpreter. That evening he and Richard Smith entered the Cherokee camp and sought their captain. Many of their brethren, he said, were coming from Carlisle and would arrive on the morrow. This was perfect. There would be enough warriors to be intimidating. He suggested they wait until nightfall and walk to the jail en mass to demand the prisoners be freed. Gist instructed them not to hurt the jailer, who was a good man and in sympathy with them. Now that things were set, he would have to quell his anxiety and wait until the next evening. First . . . the hanging.

The morning sun warmed the 100 new recruits lined up in companies bound for various frontier posts. News of the hanging had circulated for weeks, but no one knew until yesterday that it would be staged for the benefit of the new soldiers. Of the 400 draftees from Fredericksburg and Winchester early that month, 114 had deserted. Thirty of these escapees from Winchester had been captured. Among them were Ignatius Edwards, a three-time deserter, and William Smith, whom the Colonel claimed was "one of the greatest villains on the continent." Gist agreed. Washington decided to make an example of these two men.

The townspeople and soldiers crowded into the fort to watch them being led up to the platform. Washington had dispensed with the hoods. Ropes were placed around necks, brief charges of desertion read and the lever pulled. Both bodies fell together and jerked at the end of the rope. Necks broke, eyes bulged, tongues protruded, body functions released and hanging forms wiggled as life drained away. The crowd was silent.

"Look at 'em dancin' 'round up there, 'ay Mr. Gist," said a young soldier whom he had recruited; the smile on his face left little doubt he was enjoying the affair.

Gist watched without expression. He had seen a few hangings while growing up in Maryland, usually involving slaves. But the fact that these two men may have deserved the punishment did not alter his feeling of disgust at the practice. How could hanging be a deterrent to desertion when the deserter would not see himself getting caught? The death warrant was just a way to rid the population of unwanted miscreants. Any other reason was mere rationalization. Washington could not see this, having coveted for so long this power that he believed would curb this maddening epidemic.

In a similar vein, he knew jailing these Indians was counterproductive and dangerous. Even if they were spies, which he doubted, was it worth damaging the Cherokee alliance to incarcerate these few? He was quite sure there were some Indian spies among the many who filtered through Winchester. So what could another spy tell the enemy it did not already know?

It was necessary that this rescue happen without violence. Gist and Smith stood in the shadows where they could observe and be ready to intervene if necessary. Almost in silence, forty tawny warriors dressed and painted for battle appeared in front of the jail. The jailor was easily convinced to release the prisoners. With this simple act the crisis abated, nerves calmed, tensions relaxed.

The following day Atkin demanded an audience with the Indian perpetrators. After their predictable refusal, they sought the intervention of Colonel Washington. All afternoon the commander, Gist and Smith tried to assuage the Indians' anger. The claim that the arrest was a gross misunderstanding fell on deaf ears. They had more success, however, at convincing Atkin to apologize and bestow a generous amount of presents upon the wronged warriors – it seemed he did have some in reserve. In exchange, the Cherokee sent runners to their homeland proclaiming the incident settled. This, they said, would assure that white traders among their villages would not be harmed in retaliation.

Later at an opportune time the Superintendent cornered his deputy. "By any chance did you have a part in that scheme last night?" There was a tense silence.

"What, you don't believe them capable of acting on their own initiative?"

"Mr. Gist, if ever I find out you put them up to this, I will have you arrested."

Gist leaned close to the Indian agent, met his eyes and smiled. "Mr. Atkin, if you ever do that to our Indians again," he warned, "I'll personally make a space in that jail for you along with them." The frontiersman held his stare for a moment and ceased the grin. Atkin lowered his eyes.

Gist smiled as he walked away. During his first four days as Deputy Indian Agent, he had done more to further the war effort than he had in the past six months, while at the same time alienating his superior. What an exciting job this would be.

CHAPTER XXXVI

December 1758

It was quiet in Winchester. The enlistment period of the Forbes Campaign draftees was up December 1st, none too soon for them. And by some coincidence an express from Forbes had arrived yesterday exclaiming that the victory over Fort Duquesne – the victory Virginia had prayed for since July 9th three and a half years ago – was theirs.

Seasoned Deputy Indian Agent Christopher Gist sat in McGuire's Tavern drinking a fresh mug of spruce beer. The door opened to admit a cloaked patron dripping water across the plank floor. It had rained for weeks for hundreds of miles around, a condition that must have made Forbes' march miserable. He was glad to have stayed behind; to leave the adventure to others more energetic. He was tired and the good news of the victory could not rouse his spirits.

Unending arrows of depressing events struck him as if shot by an unseen enemy. On the grand scale, during his first month as Indian Agent, Lord Loudoun had shelved plans for a Fort Duquesne campaign in favor of a massive invasion of Canada at Louisburg. It failed. The same month the Marquis de Montcalm sacked Fort William Henry on Lake George.

These were devastating blows to both the regiment's morale and that of his own. Even in the aftermath of two minor victories earlier that year, William Pitt, England's new, aggressive Secretary of State, began by recalling the incompetent Loudoun and installing his second, Major General James Abercromby, in his stead. Fort Duquesne again became a serious venture and Pitt chose Brigadier General John Forbes for the task. Spirits rose, only to be shot down again. On another July 9th, Montcalm vanquished Abercromby at the French Fort Carillon on a promontory point the Iroquois called Ticonderoga.

Neither were events more promising at home. In January Dinwiddie sailed for England leaving John Blair, President of the Council, as acting head of state awaiting a new Governor. Blair and the Virginia Assembly were slow to fill Gist's requisitions for Indian presents. He was at times without supplies to outfit Indians for war and reward them upon their return.

It got worse. In spite of Washington's continued insubordinate pleas to use Braddock's Road, General Forbes cut a new road from Rays Town west toward Fort Duquesne. This was damaging news to the Ohio Company and other Virginians, who knew that a thoroughfare through the wilderness would draw centers for settlement, trade and commerce in the coming decades. Virginia wanted that road to cross Virginia. To Gist it meant the loss of, or at least a major delay to, much he had worked for with the Company. To Virginia it would mean a major investment to reopen the road. After four years of disuse, Braddock's road was virtually unusable.

On another matter, Atkin's premature appeal to the Cherokee for the upcoming campaign brought 650 warriors to Winchester by March 1st. To Gist's relief, the British contributed heavily to their supplies and presents. Yet while the Indians waited to be outfitted, hundreds flowed into the settled parts of Maryland and Pennsylvania. Some stole horses, cows, pigs, chickens. Armed conflict ensued, resulting in the deaths on both sides. Gist could do nothing. He was one man doing a job difficult enough for ten. Other warriors, impatient for the campaign to begin, took their presents and went home. By the time the army marched in September only a few Cherokee and Catawba remained. Gist conducted a small band of Catawba and Cherokee to Rays Town and awaited their departure. He was, however, a handy scapegoat for their mass desertions. The General and his second, Colonel Bouquet, blamed him. Many times had he tried to persuade the Indians to wait, but they were stubborn. He knew he could not have done more.

The event, however, that made the lump in his throat almost unbearable, was the loss of his youngest son. On September 13th Forbes dispatched Major James Grant and 750 men to reconnoiter the area around Fort Duquesne. The details were not yet clear, but they had encountered a superior force of French and Indians, who captured Ensign Thomas Gist – fate unknown. Try as he may, his mind could not purge the picture of a slow, painful torture and lingering death for his twenty-three-year-old son. Years of hardening his heart to adversity and disappointment would not let him shed a tear.

Gist's depression was interrupted by half a dozen noisy Virginia soldiers entering the inn, drenched and dirty from an arduous journey. Upon seeing Gist the sergeant, whom he knew to be a rough and cruel man, came over. His tone was challenging and his Irish brogue irritating and rough.

"Aye Capt'n an' ye'll never be guessin' who's the red nigger we brung here in irons, and on the Gen'ral's orders, ye can bet."

Gist was curious and concerned, but not given to show it. These boys could make short work of one Indian. "And who might this Indian be?"

"He might be an acquaintance o' yours," the sergeant said, a sinister smile showed yellow, uneven teeth. "D'ye 'member the Little Carpenter?"

Gist looked up, giving away his interest and concern. This was none other than Attakullakulla, nephew of Old Hop, the current "Emperor" of the Cherokee Nation.

"Sure now, but I've raised a hair or two, 'aven't I?" His smile widened.

"Sergeant, if you and your men harmed him in any way, I'll see you brought up before the Colonel . . ."

"Now, now, Capt'n," the sergeant interrupted, hands raised in mock protection, "he was used no worse by the journey than we. Cowardly he was though, aye. 'Twas but two days from the French fort and him and nine of his heathen brothers desertin'." The sergeant shook his head in disgust.

"And where is he now?"

"Aye now, and after the good Gen'ral's orders, he's countin' bars in Winchester jail, he is. Sure, and we hang deserters here, don't we?"

"Well, sergeant, if you'll excuse me, I think I'll see to our distinguished guest. Our 'deserter' has been to London for an audience with King George and deserves better treatment than that, don't you think? Perhaps the General didn't know that."

The sergeant maintained his sinister grin.

"And I'll bet he was not informed of this 'coward's six years in a Canadian prison for his loyalty to the English."

The sergeant's face became a question mark.

As Gist reached the door, he turned to the sergeant. "Maybe we'll have the Little Carpenter make his own coffin to save Virginia the expense." It was a cheap joke, but he thought he would beat the sergeant to it.

Gist, of course, knew Attakullakulla from the several times he outfitted him for war during the past year and a half. When last they met, it was October and the chief was leading thirty warriors to join Forbes. It was then he learned the English had given him the name "Little Carpenter" because of his diplomatic skills. Like a carpenter, he could make every tongue and groove of a dispute fit together smoothly. He was loyal to the British and fierce in battle. So how could this charge of desertion have any credibility?

The Deputy Agent found Richard Smith and went to visit the chief. He knew he would not use the same tactics with this Indian that he did with the ten Cherokee so many months before. Attakullakulla was here by the General's orders, but he was beyond caring.

Accommodations at Winchester jail had not changed since its last Cherokee inhabitants, though now in December it was cold and wet. Wrapped in a blanket and sitting on the floor the famed leader whispered a song as he faced the rear wall and tilted his head toward the little barred window. Gist ordered the jailer to release the prisoner into his custody. Three figures hurried, bowed against the pelting sleet, to Gist's home not far away.

The one-story log house, like all the other houses in town, was small and crowded. Built last spring the aroma of new cut timber was refreshing. Gist's younger daughter Nancy, now twenty-four, waited on them inside. After a new set of clothes and a hot meal without speaking, Gist introduced

Nancy and told of his wife's death four years ago.

The chief spoke in Cherokee to Smith, who translated, "you must miss her very much, for your daughter is like the wild rose in the forest."

Nancy acknowledged the compliment and retired to a corner of the room to listen. Through the interpreter Attakullakulla told of his service to the army.

"I and my nine brethren scouted many times for the Lying- Down-General." He referred to General Forbes, whose debilitating flux confined him to a litter strung between two horses. "We brought back much knowledge of the path ahead and the whereabouts of the enemy." The chief used his hands to indicate the direction ahead and the positions of enemy Indians. "Then we heard of the peace signed between Pennsylvania and the people of the Shawnee and Delaware Nations. Soldiers tell us this." He referred to the Treaty of Easton that Gist had advised to keep from the Cherokee. "Our ears would not believe this thing which we had heard, but we ourselves saw our enemies leaving the French fort. We were greatly angered by this sudden treaty with a people who have been our enemy since before the white man came. Then a curious thing happened. The French soldiers took the coverings from the tops of their houses and laid them around the fort, by which they meant to light it on fire. We then believed our ears. The English fight with the French is over, we said, and we left, taking our presents with us, for we had earned them by all that we did."

Gist listened. This was no crime. He knew what must have happened. Little Carpenter had made himself obnoxious in demands for presents from General Forbes, as he had done to Gist, himself, at their first meeting. Then, when he left before the expected fight, the General ordered his capture, an action exacerbated by the desertion of hundreds of his countrymen. This chief was the one to push Forbes beyond his limit.

"Brother Attakullakulla," Gist began, "do not let this incident blind your eyes to the friendship of our people. Little bird say the General, being sick, sometimes act without knowledge and speak without thought.

"I know you have several times met with the Governor to ask that Virginia traders be sent to your home. Each time they have promised and each time that promise has not been kept. We now have a new Governor, Francis Fauquier, who desires to be closer to our Cherokee brothers.

"I will send you with Richard Smith and a letter of introduction, telling the Governor of your disagreement with the General and the circumstances of your departure."

When Gist was done, the chief's ego was restored and his expectations for a successful audience with Fauquier high.

"Brother Annosanah," the chief called him, "in the light of friendship you make a long shadow and I will remember you always."

The chief stayed with Gist that night and left with the interpreter and fourteen other warriors in the morning. The Deputy Agent watched them go, wishing he too were along. Something about Little Carpenter made him want to know the famous Indian diplomat better. How could he suffer the indignities of his arrest by Forbes and the journey with the intolerable soldiers and remain loyal to the English? A man like that was worth knowing.

When the party was gone, Gist prepared again to go to Carlisle. The General had ordered him there to receive instructions concerning the Indian service for the next year. He had expected to supervise trading missions to the distant Cherokee land. But relations between Virginia and that nation were spiraling downward and would have to be settled. Maybe he would be asked to help negotiate a treaty between the two peoples. He would soon find out.

CHAPTER XXXVII

July 1759

Christopher Gist sat in the shade at his camp alongside the road several miles west of Williamsburg. Yesterday he visited the town for personal supplies and now awaited the coming of King Hagler, principal chief of the Catawba Nation, and his warriors. The interpreter, Thomas Rutherford, often escorted the Catawbas alone. But this time Gist had accounts to settle in the capitol and thought he would then meet the Indians on his return to Winchester. From there he would outfit them for scouting parties against Francophile Indians still attacking the Virginia frontier. The removal of the French from Fort Duquesne did not stop these depredations and Virginia still required help from southern Indians.

The Deputy Indian Agent, therefore, was spending the latter part of the morning engaging in the rare luxury of relaxation in the company of his interpreter.

"And Governor Fauquier," Gist related, "claimed that all the past differences were adjusted and that trade between the Virginians and Cherokee would begin in the Spring."

"Which Spring, 1760? It's already Summer," Rutherford asked. "He told Attakullakulla this?"

"Smith told me Little Carpenter left Williamsburg believing it would happen. But you know how Fauquier can put on that act and have anyone believing him sincere?"

"Aye and for that very reason I'm doubtin' it," the translator said. "There's too many incidents of Cherokees extractin' tribute from Virginia settlers along the way to and from the war. Then the settlers retaliate. Too much bad blood's been shed for differences bein' adjusted so easily."

"And how many times has Virginia promised to set up a trade with the Cherokee? A year and a half ago the Assembly appointed five men as Trustees of the Indian factory. They appropriated £5000 for presents and supplies to open trade with them. Dinwiddie promised. Wonder what happened to that money."

"We'll just have to rely more on the Catawbas until the war ends. Won't break my heart though. Them Cherokees are a whole lot more troublesome."

Meanwhile, the war dragged on. General Forbes died in March and was succeeded by Brigadier General John Stanwix. Even now Brigadier General John Prideaux, along with Sir William Johnson and his Iroquois, were sailing against Fort Niagara and there was talk of an offensive against Quebec in the fall. But Gist did not care much about that. He was no longer confident the Ohio Company would prevail after the war, whenever that would be. He had found his niche as Deputy Indian Agent and would likely remain as long as there were Indians.

The Catawbas had proved to be steadfast allies throughout their involvement in the war. It would be good to renew his burgeoning friendship with King Hagler. In September of last year, on his journey to join General Forbes' expedition, the chief had stayed in Winchester for several days and had become better acquainted with Gist.

"Here comes a boy who looks like he's got somethin' to say," Rutherford nodded his head toward the oncoming messenger.

"Father Gist," the young Catawba said to him, "Nopkehe come." He knew the reference to the man the English called King Hagler– Eractasswa of the Catawba Nation. A loyal friend to South Carolina for years, he was more recently acquainted with the Virginians, whose need to protect its frontier came at an opportune time. The Catawba needed the support.

If King Hagler's intent were to make an impression, he was successful. Mounted before half a hundred warriors, the entourage rode into Gist's camp. Their dark complexions contrasted with the many buckskins and grays ridden by the tattooed warriors.

Their pigtailed hair and naked bodies shone with bear grease as they rode in. Gist and the Rutherford marched up to Hagler on the lead horse. The King brought one leg over his horse's withers and dropped to the ground to exchanged handshakes and amenities.

"We will rest here tonight and on the morrow head toward Winchester, if that is agreeable to you and your warriors."

Rutherford translated the reply, "we are truly honored to be escorted by one so esteemed as Annosanah."

Gist knew of Hagler's reputation for flattery and smiled at the address. No wonder he was so popular among the whites.

Gist asked Rutherford to translate. "Nopkehe, my brother, we have known of each other a short time and have talked only once. I invite you to my fire. We shall learn one another's hearts. Take this gift, a token of my respect and admiration." Gist handed the Indian a soft leather bag containing a pair of engraved silver arm bands and matching gorget. Hagler beamed at the present and accepted the invitation. He spoke a few words to Rutherford, who left to join the warriors.

Sitting cross-legged on the ground with the fire between them, Hagler filled a long-stemmed pipe with a bowl carved from a red stone in the shape of a bird. The stem was wrapped in deer hide with two eagle feathers hanging from it. They smoked for a long time in silence. Gist wondered how they were going to communicate. His own sign language was good for small talk, but his reliance on interpreters had not equipped him for an extended conversation.

"Father Gist, An-no-sa-nah," the chief pronounced the Indian name, emphasizing each syllable. "If you speak true words, tell me what is in the heart of Virginia?"

Surprised at Hagler's command of English, Gist did not show it. He puffed awhile and thought of his reply. "Just as the King surrounds in smoke his skill with English speech, so does Virginia encircle her heart with a cloak, which she opens on occasion for some to view." The fire felt warm and enveloping as it heated the damp, cool evening air.

"I must guard my English as the quail protects her nest, lest the fox come to steal her young."

Gist considered the metaphor. By withholding his knowledge of English from the whites, he could assure words were translated with their original intent. Thus he could lessen the chances of his people being cheated and losing something of great value. Now he knew he must respond in kind about Virginia. He figured that the astute King sensed the Colony's motives. He would know the truth.

True to his name, Annosanah began. "Listen my brother and I will tell something of my past. For sometime I served important men in Virginia. They wanted me to buy land from the Indian people, build a settlement and bring trade. I was to survey that land into parcels to sell to other white men. The Indian people only wanted us to build a fort to protect them from the French. But the important men said the cost was too much for them to bear. The great King across the water must pay for it, they said. We did nothing and the Indians made friends with the French. Some of these very Indians attack our frontier, even though the Lying-Down-General, the one we called Forbes, drove the French out.

"At this time we are building a fort at the Forks of Ohio. My people will say that we have fought for this land and will not give it back to the Indian people who live there. You see, Nopkehe, the truth, and this truth you must know, is that my people desire land; they must have land. Our creator commanded us to be fruitful and multiply, fill the earth and conquer it."

Nopkehe was silent. The truth teller wondered if he had said too much. Could he be risking the alliance Virginia had with the Catawba? No. Deep down, everyone knew these things, but few whites voiced them.

King Hagler sucked on the pipe. Smoke escaped from his mouth as he removed the calumet and passed it to Annosanah. "Before the white people," Nopkehe began, "we had no instruments to support our living but bows, which we completed with stones. Of knives, we had chipped stone. Our axes were of stone. We bled ourselves with fish teeth. Our clothing was skin and fur, instead of the cloth we now enjoy, which we got from the white people. Ever since they first came among us, we have enjoyed all those things that we were then destitute of, for which we thank the white people."

"Do the Catawba still remember how to make the bow and the stone axe?" Gist asked.

"It is true we cannot make these. The English can make clothes to supply those we wear out and we cannot do so. We must trade with the white people to live. We cannot go back to the time before the white man came among us." He sucked from the pipe, blew a long column of smoke and continued.

"But as for our lands, we expect to live on these lands we now possess during our time here, for when the Great Man Above made us, he also fixed our forefathers and us here to inherit this land. Ever since, we have lived after our manner and fashion."

"Nopkehe has my sincere hope that his people can hold onto their land, but it will be hard. Many whites behave meanly and despise the Indian. I, myself, do not understand this hatred."

"Ever since the white people first came among us, we have lived in brotherly love and peace with them and it is our earnest desire that the love and friendship, which has so long remained, should ever continue. We have little choice. There are so few of us and so many white people."

"Your choices are difficult. With so many whites, it must be hard to remain Catawba."

"We cannot be what we are not. When the Great Man Above made us he also made our forefathers and us of this color and hue," he exposed his hands and chest to demonstrate his point, "and this we cannot change. We may ride the white man's horse and wear the white man's clothes, and live in the white man's log house, but we will never," he was emphatic, "take the white man's religion and we will never give up our lands. The ground we live on was our forefathers' and we shall live there too. Last year when the snow melted from the mountains, the Governor of South Carolina sent men to build a log house complete with chimney. He desired me to live in it. He also desires all Catawba to live on our land in the white man's way."

Gist wondered that Governor Lyttelton would go to the trouble to appease the Catawba King in such a way. But etiquette would not allow him to question further. "It will be hard for the Catawba to abandon their ways and live as the white man."

"Annosanah, my brother, we will do what we must. I now go to my camp and speak with my warriors. We will leave tomorrow with you as our conductor. But first, take this," he handed Gist the pipe they had been smoking. "It was given to me by one of our wise, old men ten summers ago. Many prayers have found their way to the Great Man Above through its smoke."

The Indian rose and departed, leaving Gist with the pipe. It was a wonderful gift, but a rather abrupt end to their meeting. He wondered if he had said something wrong, or offended him in any way. It would take several days to reach Winchester, plenty of time to pursue further conversation.

For two days the entourage poked along, despite Gist's attempts at quickening the pace. Slaves working in large tobacco fields soon gave way to white farmers working in their own fields. Indian bands traveling this road on foot had been commonplace for several years, but even the sight of so many on horses barely turned a head.

On the second night King Hagler came to Gist's fire. Gist pulled out the pipe, filled it with tobacco and lit it with a hot coal. He sucked on the stem and handed it to Nopkehe. The Indian took a mouthful of smoke and blew out seven rings, each smaller than the last.

"Nopkehe's talents are many," said the Indian Agent.

"It is a gift from the Great Man Above that reminds me to humble myself before truly wise men. Annosanah, my brother, to you who speak true words, I am ashamed that I did not do the same. Two nights ago my speech was as one given to important white men who must be told what they want to hear. I have thought for many hours and now realize your words and your thoughts are not of those men. I will now tell you some things we talk about only among ourselves and to no other white man."

Gist was silent. He forced himself to relax and hear what secrets this revered chief was about to reveal.

The King proceeded to recite to Gist the Nation's oral history from the time of first contact with the Spanish. Seeking the precious yellow mineral, the ruthless Conquistadors tortured and burned alive their warriors in order to learn its whereabouts. They burned villages, violated their women and sent fierce war dogs to tear the People to pieces. When the Spanish could find no gold, they left. Later, an era of peace and prosperity with the English of South Carolina began. Their traders brought goods that improved the lives of the People. But the People became dependent on the traders, who grew mean and cheated them and stole from them. Their Nation and other Indians rose up against such treatment, but were defeated because of a lack of supplies on which they had come to rely. Then came the white man's diseases to take their toll. What were once many villages of separate tribes scattered through the land, were now crowded into several towns along the Catawba River.

"The white people are now so numerous around us and our once plentiful hunting lands belong to them. We are forced to journey a long distance to find food. We no longer have skins to trade and therefore the traders never come among us.

"And the white people are no longer polite to us; the head men of Charleston give fewer presents and do not listen to us as they once did.

White people come onto our land and do mischief and we have no one who will hear our cries for help. All we are good for, they say, is to keep enemy Indians away from the Colony and to frighten their slaves from escaping."

Nopkehe's story was quite moving and far more of a tale of woe than he had expected. The Indians' side of relations between the two peoples was never verbalized. And the tone of Nopkehe's delivery left no doubt of his unfeigned passion for his people.

"Nopkehe, my heart is sad to hear these terrible things done to you by my people. I do not have words to express my sorrow, only a pain in my heart and a lump in my throat. It should not be this way. Why did the Great Man Above allow this to happen? How could he?"

"Father Gist, Annosanah, do not concern yourself so much with our condition. We are still a people; we are still Catawba. Many who have met the white people are no more. Even now our head men debate whether to ask South Carolina to measure out our lands and put this on paper. In this way we can stop white farmers from pushing themselves over onto our land. They will not be stopped, for they say they will continue to do so unless we show them a paper to restrain them."

"You will then have the white people's law on your side, but what of the churlish treatment to your people and the broken promises? How will you stand up against your white neighbors, being so outnumbered as you are?"

King Hagler was silent for a moment and then said, "we Catawba view the white people as a flock of tame fowls. A flock of such birds will more easily accept strangers if they resemble themselves. With each passing year we adopt more of the white people's ways. Soon we will resemble the flock enough that we will be accepted. But in our hearts we will always be Catawba."

CHAPTER XXXVIII

July 1759

Drizzling! It had drizzled all night and showed no signs of clearing. The Indians lingered in camp to await a change in the weather. Gist broke off dead tree limbs; wet on one side, they made a smoky fire until the water boiled off. The lean-to he and Rutherford had made the night before was leaking and required attention. But he was chilled. Instead of fixing the leaks, he wrapped himself in his blanket and sat cross-legged, comforted by the heat of his fire. He took out the pipe Nopkehe had given him and lit the sweet-smelling tobacco. A puff on the pipe and a sip of fire-warmed rum relaxed him. The rum was smooth and caused immediate warmth to radiate throughout his body. He dozed. Rutherford was off hunting. His turn; time to have the younger generation wait on the veterans for a change. Anyway, he was tired; a short rest was all he needed.

He was aroused by soft of moccasin steps. "Father Gist."

It felt good to hear those words. Only he and the Governor were honored with this term of respect. He did not need to see to know it was Nopkehe. "Come and sit by my fire," he invited, leaving his eyes closed.

"You sleep?" asked Nopkehe. "At first I think Annosanah talks with the Great Man Above, but then I hear sleep noises."

Gist smiled. "Nopkehe, I don't speak with the Great One anymore." He opened his eyes. It was growing dark. How long had he dozed?

"Forgive me, Annosanah, if I have offended you."

"No, no, it's fine. You haven't. You see . . . it's just that . . . four years ago my wife passed on and I was away. I was always away; gone hunting, trading, exploring. We argued much about it. She wanted me to be a farmer." With a hollow smile, he stared up at Nopkehe.

"I used to be religious," he continued, and told the story of how he acquired his Indian name. "But since Sarah died, I've been unable to pray."

The rain continued; darkness engulfed the eerie shapes of tangled tree limbs and grapevines. The fuzzy sound of light rain filled the silence.

"Annosanah, it is sad to lose a loved one. When the pox visited our People, I lost many relations. I, myself, was afflicted. I was angry with the Great Man Above for allowing His People to suffer and die. And I was angry with the white man for bringing the sickness among us. Then I thought this must be a sign to us that we had done bad things. Maybe it was to punish us for giving up our old ways. I thought The Great One was saying, 'if you want to live like the white man, then you must learn to die like him.'

"For a long time I could not talk to He-Who-Never-Sleeps," Nopkehe paused. He gazed into the coals. "One day I heard our old men tell stories of our past. I was reminded that our People suffered the smallpox brought by the Spanish long before we thought about taking up the white man's ways. The pox was a terrible burden on our People, but the Great Man Above provided those things necessary to overcome the hardships. We must always pray for guidance. These things our wise men have told me. It was then that I began offering my prayers through the smoke from the pipe which you now have."

Gist relit the pipe and handed it to the wise leader. "I envy you, my brother. You have a peace I will never find. I've watched my Indian brothers – Wyandot, Shannoah, Delaware and now the Cherokee – pushed by my own people to the point of war because they have no choice. And it's not because the French and English fight for the same ground. No. It's because of the greed of my own people. How can I pray to a God who gives license to that appetite by commanding us to multiply and conquer? How can I pray to that God?"

They sat in silence, passing the pipe, listening to the rain, gazing into the fire and out into the jet black night.

"Nopkehe, do you believe the Great Man Above and the white man's God are the same?"

After many moments Nopkehe spoke. "I do not know if the white man's God and the Great Man Above are the same and if they are different, I would not wish to offend either. I have no knowledge of gods, but I do know this of men: the white man feels with his head, which tells him he wants this thing or that thing. Then he takes it. The Indian feels with his heart. The heart tells him how to live with his brothers. The heart tells him what he must have and he asks the Great Man Above to provide. You, Father Gist, feel with the heart."

Gist remained silent and reflected upon the accolade. It was not how he felt. Those things that his white man's head told him he wanted – land, wealth, the old family standing in a new land – had been unobtainable, his efforts thwarted at every turn. His attitude toward the Indians was fashioned after his father's. He did not see what his heart had to do with it.

Nopkehe took a large skin container hanging at his side and offered it to Gist, who removed the cork and took a sip. It was the watered rum most often traded to the Indians, but just then it tasted good and warmed his insides.

Nopkehe sipped from the skin and replaced the cork. "This pouch is made from the stomach of the buffalo, who once were plenty here. Now they are not so many. It is the same with my People, who fall to the white man's sickness and the guns of our enemies."

"I've heard," Gist offered, "there are vast lands across the Mother of All Rivers toward the sun-setting that no white man has ever seen. This land, other Indians have told me, has great snowy mountains, wide grassy plains and hot dry deserts. There are more buffalo than fish in the river." Hagler nodded while Gist continued, "why not lead your people there away from the whites?"

Hagler took a long pull on the pipe and let the smoke trail out his nostrils. "I too have heard of these lands. Travelers from other Indian Nations as far away as the Great Western Sea have told us. Their stories make this land sound good, but I fear we would trade one problem for another. We are a small People and many enemies lie between here and there. Besides, we have come to need the white man's trade goods and could not easily return to our old ways. No, my brother, He-Who-Never-Sleeps has put us here. It is our home and here we shall stay."

The two men shook hands and King Hagler walked off through the rain. Thunder rolled in the distance as Annosanah fingered the pipe. He felt sleepy and chilled. Reaching for several dead branches, he stoked his fire, wrapped himself in his blanket and lay down.

He knew why he had stopped talking to God. He felt responsible for Sarah's misery and resulting death. Then there was Wau-thee-wee-la so many years ago. Unworthiness plagued his thought, like the pox of Nopkehe's past. But unlike Nopkehe, his situation was his own doing. He could not speak to the white man's God, but perhaps the Great Man Above would hear him. He would have to think about that later, for now he was so sleepy and his muscles ached. He closed his eyes. Maybe just a good night's rest . . .

CHAPTER XXXIX

July 20, 1759

Thunder crashed as lightning rent the sky, like an axe splitting wood, and then it was gone, and again it chopped while another cannonade of thunder boomed, sequential, synchronic, then random. And rain inundated from above. It bowed his pine boughed roof, drowned his fire and streamed through his bower.

Into this chaos he awoke, but it was not a normal awakening. Drenched in sweat, he shivered violently, teeth chattering, muscles taught against some unseen shaker. Joints moved with rusty resistance. Rising with the barrage of thunder, his pulse pounded as it threatened to blast through the top of his head.

Fumbling in his knapsack for his pouch of Cinchona Bark and herbs – mind foggy – he realized his fire was out. Switching to locate a tin container of char cloth, and leather bag of flint and steel, he shivered uncontrollably. He found them, removed the items and began striking. But between his shaking body and throbbing head, he kept missing the flint. He thought of using the lock on his rifle, but it was loaded and he doubted he had the energy to remove the charge.

"What's happening to me?" He heard himself say the words between chattering teeth and trembling lips.

He tried fire starting again, but his body erupted into a fury of uncontrollable vibrations that tore the tools from his hands. He tasted blood and searched with his tongue to find a chunk of meat missing from inside his cheek. He grabbed his blanket, but its wetness felt like ice as the cold water wicked through his shirt to touch his fevered skin.

Lightning flashed an image of tangled vegetation, green and twisted around grapevines and tree limbs. Another round of thunder clapped. The earth shook.

Could this be his ague acting up? No, it never began with this intensity. Besides, this was the wrong month. But if it were, he must start a fire and make the tea and take the herbs. He found the flint and steel, but the char cloth was soaked. Retrieving some tow from his patch box, he braced himself for another quivering episode. He pulled himself deep within the fibers of his wet, wool blanket as a blinding white lightning bolt exploded in a nearby treetop. The deafening detonation muted his hearing to a fuzzy, high-pitched drone.

When the shaking ceased, he took a cloth from his pack, dipped it in rain water and dabbed his sweating brow. Like a madman he clawed out of his shirt and lay down on the wet floor of his shelter. His fever cooled as he listened to the fading thunder of the passing storm. The momentary relief from his heat was welcome and he thought about renewing his fire starting efforts. If only he could lay here a little while longer . . . But what is that music? A violinist taking a high-pitched drone and resolving it into a playful melody; a cello bowing a low harmony while a second violin counters; the trio played on, happy, relaxed, free of the daily burdens and thoughts of . . .

"Mr. Gist."

"Go away Rutherford," he croaked. The music was so soothing and the interpreter could be obnoxious at times.

"Gist! Gist!" The words sounded so far away. "My God, he's burning up. Let's cool him down. Put him in that creek over there."

Gist opened his eyes to see two Catawbas at his feet while he felt two others supporting his shoulders. His head pulsated as they jostled him about, but the coolness of the water flow eased his discomfort. "Water," he mumbled and tried to rise. "Must start my fire . . . must take the bark . . ."

"The bark! What're ye doin' with the ague in July?" asked the interpreter. "Here, drink this."

The water was cool going down, but left his thirst unquenched. He drank more and lay back in the flowing stream. Then a sudden, violent cramp doubled him up, forcing him to spew forth the entire contents of his stomach. And when he had ejected his own juices, his body kept heaving.

He awoke to the crackling of a fire and rustling of someone nearby. Rutherford's raspy tones registered just outside his lean-to; ". . . second day," the voice was saying. "Smallpox all right." Smallpox!! Gist strained through his haze to hear better. "When I had it," Rutherford continued, muffled, ". . . eighteen and strong as a bull buffalo . . . mild sort . . . bad enough. Gist has the vilest kind."

"How is this?" Inquired the voice of King Hagler.

Gist heard someone rise and feed the fire. When Rutherford resumed, his voice was more pronounced than before. "Well, I ain't no doctor, but I seen enough of it to know. Common pox has round, yellow, puss-filled sacks that scab over and fall off. But this 'confluent' sort gives a body big, patches filled with brown puss. It's awful. They've started on his arms already."

Gist opened his eyes, but was too weak to lift an arm.

"Your eyes swell shut," Rutherford continued, "and your face and then your throat. Most folks, who don't die of the high fever, just suffocate. I've seen two epidemics and there's some that live. He could survive this."

Gist looked up to see an old Catawba woman with a cratered face. She smiled and applied cold deer hide compresses to his body. He lay naked on a soft bed of pine boughs overlaid with a wool blanket.

"We Catawbas have a water cure for this pox," Nopkehe was saying, "and we are building a sweat lodge for him now. First you go in there and sweat out the bad fluids; then the stream washes the evil away."

The woman called for someone outside. Rutherford appeared.
"I see you're still with us," he said as he crawled into the lean-to. "I'm sorry to say it's the pox. Lucky for me and these Injens, we've all had it before." Rutherford's tone was soft, "it'll be a bit rough I'm afraid sir, but I and the Injens'll help ye through it. Try to drink this." Gist's head was lifted and an unidentifiable, warm liquid was dribbled down his throat. Its earthy, bitter taste made him gag. "Gettin' ye ready for the Catawba water cure. You'll be better soon."

He closed his eyes and felt the cooling touch of the old woman. His mind filled with random thoughts. Jesus, how could he have gotten the smallpox? He tried to think where he could have become infected – Williamsburg, Carlisle, Rays Town – he did not know. He was sure he had been around infected people before while remaining unscathed, but maybe not. One thing was certain: if this water cure really worked, there would be more Indians alive to tell about it. They will do it anyway. Besides he was powerless to stop it. Damnation, why had he refused that vaccine? Must be stubbornness – pure, blatant, ornery, goddamn stubbornness.

Then it struck him for the first time that he might die. To have been so close to death from the elements and the war, and then to die of a disease he could have prevented, was hard to believe. Well if this killed him, would he meet He-Who-Never-Sleeps, or God, or The Great Man Above? Perhaps, but he did not want to die. There was so much to do . . .

"Annosanah," someone called from a distance. He opened his eyes to find himself no longer beside the path to Winchester among the Catawbas. "Annosanah." There it was again. He walked toward the voice. His moccasined feet made no sound. Where was he? Looking around, he could find no familiar landmark, just a narrow path in the woods. "Annosanah, are you ready to come with us?"

Gist stood still and listened. He could not say why, but he sensed no threat. "Who are you?"

"Annosanah, you know who I am." An old Indian man stood before him. Naked, except for breechclout and moccasins, his gray hair fell below his waist.

"I'm not sure I deserve the name," Gist admitted. "When it was given to me, I was deceitful and did not reveal my true mission. In this way I was not truthful."

The man led him to a clearing and motioned for them to sit. "Let us smoke the sacred pipe." Brown wrinkled skin on the old man's knees smoothed over as he sat cross-legged on a grassy ground. He produced a plain red pipe and held a glowing coal to its bowl. After a deep inhale, he handed it to Gist.

"Annosanah, it is not what you were, but what you have become. I have watched you these past years as you have opened your heart to Indian People."

Surely this was a dream, but it was better than being painfully awake. "Why have you called me?"

"I did not cause your affliction, but since it has happened, I think that you will not live much longer. Look at yourself." The old man pointed a crooked, brown finger toward a small stream nearby. Gist could see a man being carried on a litter to an earthen sweat-house beside the creek. Nopkehe and others, brows furrowed, faces long, pulled the limp body through the opening to the inside. Gist looked closely; the body was his.

"They will roll the hot stones inside and pour water on them to bring the steam. Your body will give its fluids to the vapors. Then you will be removed and laid in the flowing water. It is there you will likely die. They often do. The water cure has no effect on the smallpox."

"Why do the People still use it?" He turned his attention to the old man and handed him the pipe.

"The People must have hope," countered the old man.

"And Rutherford was right about my having the worst kind?" He looked toward the stream, but the scene was gone.

"Your interpreter speaks rightly."

"What do you want of me?"

Gathering his hair behind his neck, he flipped it down the middle of his back. He relit the pipe and continued. "You have a rare quality among white people – a true love and respect for your Indian brothers. To you they are human beings."

"But I don't know their languages, nor all their customs. Nor do I always understand why they do what they do."

The old man shook his head, "this is not important. You could not possibly know this. You are white. Your gift is that you do not judge Indian People by white man's ways." He passed the pipe to Gist.

"I've sought the Indian's point of view in settling their many disputes with my people. This is what I do and it is for this very reason I'm not ready to go with you. Virginia will open trade with the Cherokee in the spring and the new Treaty of Easton will allow the Ohio tribes to restore commerce. I must oversee this transition."

"Annosanah, there are other white men to help Indian People through this time. You can be more useful elsewhere."

"How can I be useful if I'm dead?"

The old man was silent, as if considering how to answer. "Annosanah, Indian People must endure very bad times as the white man moves west. His land will be taken and he will be forced to live on barren tracts unfit for human beings. Each time the Indian resists, the white man will punish him."

"Old man, this cannot be. What of the reservations on the Eastern Shore and the many places where whites and Indians live in harmony?"

"Annosanah," the old man continued, "you speak of these things as you would have them be, not as they are. There is little harmony, mostly coexistence, and only that until there are so few Indians they are forced to sell their land for a mere token. Look and you shall see."

Christopher stood on a barren hilltop overlooking a scene so familiar, but for thousands of lights shining in the dusky evening as far as he could see. Could this be? It was; it was the unmistakable confluence of the three large rivers he knew so well, the Forks of Ohio. He could see the clear lights emanating from buildings, street lamps and carriages. A black cloud hung overhead, joined by billowing smoke from hundreds of tall chimneys along the river. Row after row of houses replaced the forest. White people in strange clothing scurried about everywhere, walking, riding horses or carriages.

"This is the white man's world," spoke the old man appearing beside him.

"This is a whole city where the fort used to be. And the forest is gone." He could not close his eyes to the strange scene. More lights appeared one by one.

"One of many across the land, more than you can count. Annosanah, in this time there are more of your people than stars in the sky. Now you must see the home of Indian People. In your time their land reached from the eastern mountains west to the Great Shining Sea. Indian People, as many as the animals in the forest, made up hundreds of tribes. Few white men had ever been to these Indian lands. But in the time you have just seen, Indian People are no longer there."

"They're all dead?" Annosanah's jaw dropped.

"Millions have died – war, pestilence, famine, genocide. But many remain. See for yourself."

Annosanah stood on a cracked, dirt path, bordered by a dozen dilapidated dwellings, some of log, some of earth. An oppressive heat baked the ground, withered the corn in the fields, blurred the horizon and burned his moccasined feet. Cadaver-like cattle fed on a few clumps of yellow grass.

People of obvious Indian descent shuffled about, hunched over, morose, dressed in dirty white man's rags. No joy or laughter graced the air, only weeping and moaning, dogs barking, babies crying. The old man walked up beside him. "Here are the Shawnee, the Delaware the Cherokee and other nations, whose forefathers you knew in your time."

Annosanah stared in disbelief. Tears streamed down his face. His chest heaved sighs of sorrow. No thought could ease the weight on his chest nor make him swallow more easily. Sweat beaded upon his brow and his clothing was soaked.

"Come Annosanah. Your friends call you."

Rough hands held him while the water flowed over his body. The fluid cold relieved his fever. He felt pulled back into a limp body of swelling and pain. Where the puss-filled vesicles rubbed together, raw flesh seared like fire and no water could cool the heat. Agony revived him.

"Capt'n Gist. He's coming to." Gist could distinguish Rutherford's voice. A flurry of activity splashed the water. Pains in his arms told him he had been bled with sharp fish teeth the Catawba used for that purpose. But he could not open his eyes. With all his diminished strength, he raised a hand to his face and felt his swelling. He pried one eye open, but it was mung encrusted and he could not see. To swallow was impossible. Wizened lungs labored to force air through a swollen passage.

"Been away a long time, haven't ye?" Rutherford said. "Welcome back. Most folks just give up, but I see you've no intentions of that. The Catawbas pray for your recovery and King Hagler keeps a twenty-four-hour vigil. He literally collapses from lack of sleep. We're all prayin' you can hang on a little longer."

He could feel himself being taken from the water and laid on the cool ground. A gentle hand lifted his head and placed a wooden bowl to his lips. A trickle of water ran down his parched throat. But with no stream of water to counter his rising fever, he soon lost consciousness.

CHAPTER XL

July 25, 1759

He was back in the forest sitting across from the old man. It was morning and the sun warmed his back.

"Annosanah," the old man said, "you are strong as sinew. You should be dead by now, and yet you cling to life."

"Forgive me, but it's the only life I've ever known and I'm reluctant to give it up. Besides, you never answered my question. What can I do for Indian People if I'm dead?"

He met the question with silence. Though Gist did not see it appear, the sage held in his hands a clay bowl full of water. "This represents the reservoir of life from which Indian People must draw strength." Without warning he poured half the contents into his cupped hand, allowing some to fall to the ground. "The coming years will be difficult for them, for just as the water is now low, so will Indian People nearly deplete this reservoir of its goodness." Then he held his hand over the bowl, allowing the fluid to flow back into it. "I can tell you that in the same way the water in my hand adds to that in the bowl, your rare qualities of understanding and compassion will enrich that reservoir from which the People will draw strength."

"How can I do this?"

"Annosanah, it is not necessary that you understand all that there is. You will not be alone. There are spirit guides, beings from the past who help those in the future. You will see."

Gist lowered his head in silence. After several moments he looked at the ancient one and asked, "how far into the future did I see?"

"Four generations."

"If you can show me this future, you must know the fate of the Indian Nations."

"Annosanah, it is not good to know the end, for the means loses its value and nothing is ventured. I can tell you this. Indian People are strong with a mighty will. With a healthy reserve of love and determination, they will rise again in ways we cannot imagine."

"Perhaps I can return and tell Nopkehe and others what I've seen, so they can be prepared to resist the white man's world."

"Your intentions are good, Annosanah. But there are already many who advise Indian People to resist. You cannot help in the present. You have done all you can in this life. Look at yourself."

His body lay on its back on the ground under the lean-to. The pock-marked Catawba woman continued to rinse the deer skin sheets in cold water and place them on his body. She lifted a large one from his chest. Gray hairs protruded from a solid mass of chocolate brown, pus-filled tissue. It covered his forehead; his face had swelled beyond recognition. His breath rasped.

"Your fever has been so high for so long, it is doubtful you would be the same man if you recovered. It is sad that such a fine man as yourself should succumb to such a horrible fate." The old man walked up beside Annosanah and looked at Christopher Gist's wasted body. "Are you ready to go with us now?"

"But the Gist lying there still sleeps. Besides, I must know if the Great Man Above, He-Who-Never-Sleeps and the white man's God are all the same being?"

The old man was silent for a moment. "The white man's sacred book says that the Creator made man in His own image, is this not so?"

"This is so," Annosanah replied.

"Could it be that man makes God into his own image?"

"According to what that man believes," he carried the thought to its logical extension. He considered this. "If that is true, then they are all one God, but appear distinct to different people." Annosanah looked the old man in the eye and held his gaze. In one timeless moment he saw a depth of sorrow and joy he had never seen. It was as if this ancient sage had experienced the total misery and heartbreak, as well as the combined pleasure and contentment of the entire human experience.

"You are the Great Man Above."

The old man remained silent.

"You appear before me in my own image according to my expectations."

"You would not understand otherwise."

He thought about all the questions to ask and the challenges to make and even critiques to give. Yet the single most important matter, the one sin for which he had not forgiven himself; this he must ask, "will I see Sarah again?"

"Annosanah, your time with her was in this life."

"Yes, and I squandered it."

"If you had not been among your Indian brothers, you would not have become the man you are."

"But there are things I must tell her."

He had been here before. It was the dense forest near their homestead on the Yadkin River as he and Sarah had first seen it. They had arrived in the early summer to a multi-shaded green wonderland laced with grapevines and ground ivy. They were happy here . . . for awhile. Amid the twittering of birds he thought he heard a woman humming. He listened and headed toward the tune that became more clear as he neared. Sarah used to hum that tune. He walked faster on the narrow trail toward the sound, heart pounding, thoughts racing and by some unexplained convention he found himself in the center of the approach to their home. Sarah rocked in a chair on the porch.

She looked as she had looked on that last day before he left for the Ohio country so long ago. She stood to meet him. They embraced for a long time. He held her at arms length and gazed into her eyes as he had so many years ago. "Are you real, or an image from my memory?"

"I am both." she smiled.

"What happens now?" He did not know quite what to say.

"What do you want to happen now?"

"The Great Man spoke of spirit guides and a reservoir of strength to aid Indian People. Shouldn't I get started?"

She laughed, "Chris Gist, I declare, you bring with you in death the same attributes you had in life – hurry up and get the job done. No wonder you kept so busy and got so much done."

"I hardly took the time for you, did I?"

"Your time was spent preparing for this moment."

"And the Shawnee girl?"

"She came at a time when you needed someone and I could not be there for you."

They were walking hand-in-hand now down the wide path through the forest, content, quiet.

"Do we remain together," he asked?

"No, I have my own tasks as you will have yours. I am here only to help you pass over."

"But there are so many questions I would ask."

"Annosanah, they are questions of the living." It was the old man speaking and it was the old man who now held his hand as they walked along. There was a tenderness in his voice that soothed his anxiety and removed his doubts.

"Then I am ready."

AFTERWORD

Who was Christopher Gist? It is a question that has fascinated me since I first read about him in Allan Eckert's Wilderness Empire some twenty years ago. Here is a frontiersman who does not hate Indians; a fur trader used to the company of rough and rowdy men, yet not one himself; a white man with whom most Indians felt comfortable.

Contemporary writers, Washington in particular, refer to him as knowledgeable about Indians and respected by them, hearty, indefatigable and loyal. The Colonel spent his time "in the bush", so his opinion on those matters would seem reliable. Not much more is direct. His three journals record much about the Ohio Valley, its geography, flora and fauna, and, most importantly, the Indian inhabitants. His correspondence to Washington, Governor Dinwiddie, and others is brief and to the point.

But unlike Washington, Franklin and Croghan, to some extent, Gist left no records about his feelings, beliefs, thoughts, or opinions. He was not endowed with the vanity of self promotion. The only direct evidence we get from the Indians of his relationship to them is that the Catawba called him "Father Gist," a term they reserved for whites they loved and respected. With all the unpleasant dealings the Indians had had with condescending, prejudiced whites over the years, it would have been impossible for a Christopher Gist to "fool them."

Kenneth Bailey explains how The Horn Papers attempt to fill in the gaps of Gist's life and personality, though they have been discredited as an elaborate forgery. In the interests of historical accuracy I have not referred to them, although certain scenes I have created to build Gist's character are consistent with that Christopher Gist. I wanted to reach my own conclusions. As a novelist I was then free, within the constraints of the historical record, to create the character I thought Christopher was most likely to have been.

Whether Gist was the man I have portrayed, or a figure less benevolent, he was certainly an important player in the French and Indian War. And it would be hard to argue that he did not exert a pivotal role in the character development of our nation's first president. But more than that, Christopher Gist exemplifies traits common to those responsible for our westward expansion. Allan Powell writes about Gist and his sons, who went on to fight in the Revolutionary War on the side of the colonists against Britain:

> "They were nurtured on the myths of self sufficiency and unfettered movement which figured greatly in the movement for independence. We are deeply indebted to them for their tenacity against the French, their energy in clearing the way for settlement of the transmontane region and for their sacrifices in securing our independence from England . . . Christopher Gist exemplifies this independent restless spirit. He contributed greatly to independence and westward expansion and as a consequence deserves a place in history on a footing with more famous frontiersmen such as Boone, Kenton, Croghan and Cresap."

CHAPTER NOTES

Prologue

Thomas Cresap and Hugh Parker, both Indian traders from Maryland, were hired to deliver this first load of trade goods to the Indians and to search for suitable tracts of land for settlement. Their efforts were unsuccessful. (Bailey Ohio Company 70) Although no reason is given for their failure, this meeting with the Shawnee is a plausible outcome. Parker later became a member, but died in 1751.

Parker's account of the scalping knife incident. (Hanna II 353)

King George's War, called the War of Austrian Succession in Europe, broke out in 1744 between France and England and ended with the Treaty of Aix-la-Chapelle in October of 1748. This was one of four major conflicts between the two superpowers, beginning with King William's War (1689-1697), Queen Anne's War (1702-1713), King George's War, and The French and Indian War (1755-1762). (Peckham)

Richard Peters, secretary to Pennsylvania's Council, wrote Thomas Penn on July 28, 1748 about "that vile fellow Cresap who had suggested a scheme to Colonel Lee and other great men of Virginia to make trading houses at Allegehny." (James 13)

The conflict between Maryland and Pennsylvania was over a strip of land several miles wide that ran the entire length of their common border. Called the Conojacular War from 1730-1736, it finally ended with Cresap's capture and removal from the area. The dispute was settled with the survey made by Mason and Dixon from 1763-1767. (Wroth 14-16; Bailey Cresap 31-55)

The Board of Trade granted the Ohio Company 500,000 acres in two increments. The second 300,000 acres was contingent upon a settlement of 100 families and a stockaded fort within two years.

"Wills Creek" referred not only to the actual creek, but the area where it flows into the Potomac at present day Cumberland, MD.

Redstone Old Fort was at present day Brownsville, PA was a prehistoric Indian ruin located where Redstone Creek flowed into the Monongahela.

Description of Shawnee warriors as seen by Nicholas Cresswell on his travels through Virginia and Ohio, 1774-1777. (O'Neil 46-47)

"Shauwanoa" is one of the many early pronunciations of what was later spelled and pronounced "Shawnee." I have used the spelling of Trowbridge, Written references from the time hint of this pronunciation, e.g. Shau-wan-oa, Sha-wa-no and the French spelling Chaou-an-on. In this time, when spelling was often phonetic, there were other forms in use. George Croghan, in a journal of 1751, spells (says) "Shawonese." Gist spells (says) "The Shanaws" and "Shannoah" in his journal. See Hanna for many other spellings, 448. I have chosen to have each individual pronounce (spell) the word as he has written and use "Shawnee" in the narrative.

The matchcoat was a wool blanket-like covering about four or five feet square, which tied around the waist and came up over the shoulders to be pinned at the chest, giving the wearer a hood, shoulder cover and leg protection. They were commonly worn on the frontier by whites and Indians alike. Historical trekker Mike Alton demonstrates how they were worn in Mark Baker's Pioneering Long Hunter Video Series Vol III.

Chapter I

Shortly after Cromwell was deposed by Charles II in 1660, one Christopher Guest, a distant relative of Cromwell, emigrated to Maryland. His son, Richard, who changed the spelling to "Gist," was the father of Christopher Gist. (Bailey Gist 12-13)

The entire text of Gist's instructions. (Darlington 31-32)

Gist's home was on the north shore of the Yadkin River, on the west side of a stream called Small Saw Mill Creek, near and west of the Reddies River, near present day Wilkesboro, North Carolina. *(Ibid.* 24)

Gist left no account of his delivery of trade goods, but he was employed to do so on March 29, 1750. (James 34)

Assarquoa is an Onondoga word meaning "Big Knife" or "Long Knife." It was first applied by the Iroquois to Lord Howard, Governor of Virginia in 1684, when he wore a cutlass to a treaty ceremony. It became a metaphor for all Virginians and, in time, for all Americans. (Hanna I 318)

The word "plantation" at this time did not carry with it the connotation it did 100 years later, i.e. a large operation of hundreds of acres for tobacco or cotton. It was then another word for "farm."

Chapter II

Interstate 220 from Covington, VA to Cumberland, MD lies on or near the portion of the Great Warrior Path followed by Gist.

Oldtown is about 14 miles southeast of Cumberland, MD.

Cresap's "Long Meadows" was near present day Hagerstown, MD.

Cresap had a gigantic slave named Goliath. (Bailey Cresap)

Barnaby Curran had worked as a trader for George Croghan prior to his employment with the Ohio Company. (Bailey Gist 159) As early as the fall of 1749, the Indians reported that "Barny Currant, a hired man of Mr. Parker," (Hugh Parker was then working for the Ohio Company) brought them a message that the Company's goods were cheaper than those from Pennsylvania. (Hanna I 347)

This Journal entry concerning Gist's start from Cresap's. (Darlington 32)

Chapter III

Warrior Mountain, just north of Old Town, MD, is still called that today.

As far as I can determine, our sole reference to Gist's companion being a young black slave is implied from his journal entry of February 12th. "Having left my Boy to take Care of my Horses . . ." (Darlington 46) All the authorities agree this could not have been one of his sons. Gist was recorded as having at least one indentured servant in 1739. (Dorsey 11) In May of 1745 he "conveyed to William Cromwell . . . his slaves, furniture, etc. (Dorsey 12) He could have had more or acquired one. I have chosen to follow the convention and give him the name of Gabriel, since Gist did not name him. Many whites named their slaves after heavenly bodies or biblical characters. His background is borrowed from "The Life of Olaudah Equiano," himself an escaped slave brought to America by slavers in 1759 from Guinea. His speech is patterned after West African Pidgin English. (Dillard 73-93)

Malaria (bad air) at that time was believed to be caused by swamp exhalations. It was often contracted around newly cleared land that left many pools of stagnant water in which mosquitoes could breed. Today, we know it is caused by five or more species of parasitic protozoans that are transferred to human blood by mosquitoes (genus Anopheles). They occupy and destroy red blood corpuscles. Webster.

Peruvian Bark, from the Cinchona tree of South America, contained quinine. It was also called Jesuit's Bark. (Meyer 125-127) It could be bought in Williamsburg at McKenzie's Apothecary Shop (1732-1755).

The "Trader's Road" was also the "Rays Town Path."

"Shawana Cabbins" was located one-half mile east of present day Schellsburg, PA. (Hanna I 281)

The "Edmund's Swamp" campsite sat two and one-half miles north of Buckstown, Somerset Co., PA. It was named for Edmund Cartlidge, who began trading with the Delaware as early as 1727. (*Ibid.* 281)

Chapter IV

The site along the Quemahoning Creek is now submerged by the Quemahoning Reservoir.

Kick-ena-pau-lin (Kickeney Paulin, Kechkinnyperlin). His cabin stood on a tributary of Quemahoning Creek now known as Picking's Run near Jenner Cross Roads, Jenner twp., Somerset Co. (Hanna I, 282) I have hyphenated many of the Indian names to aid the reader in pronunciation. Most Indian names were recorded by white observers who attempted to spell phonetically what they heard. But since they heard many sounds differently, there are always many spellings for each name.

Loyalhanna is the present site of Ligonier, PA, the location of Fort Ligonier, built by General Forbes in 1758.

Cock-Eye's Cabin, was on Bushy Run, a branch of Turtle Creek, near the site of the Battle of Bushy Run. (Hanna I 288)

Shannopin's Town is now in Pittsburgh, PA, two miles up the Allegheny from the Forks. (*Ibid.* 289)

Logstown was near present day Economy, PA. (*Ibid.* 289, 352-383)

Chapter V

For details on Croghan, see Wainwright and Volwiler.

The Lower Shawnee Town was at present day Portsmouth, OH.

Lewis Evans' map of 1755 locates the town of "Tuscarawas" just north of present day Bolivar, OH. (Hanna I 334; II 145; Wheeler - Voegelin 55-56)

Conchake on the Muskingum River, now called the Tuscarawas River, sat at the northeast end of what is now Coshocton, OH.(Hanna II 188-189)

John Patten was arrested November 20, 1750.

The Miami fort was located near present day Fort Wayne, IN.

The details of Croghan's land grant from the Iroquois is in Wainwright, 28. Why else would Croghan be so helpful to Gist? Surely he felt the Marylander might help him secure the grant?

Chapter VI

Falkner, an employee of Teafe along with Erwin, one of Croghan's traders, were taken by the French at Sandusky Bay in September 1750 and sent to France. (Hanna I 332-333)

Montour's biography. (Darlington 152-175)

The Cherokee Milky Way – Gil' Li Utsun. (Underwood 8-9)

Chapter VII

All three passages of Gist's Christmas message are taken from the Homilies of the Church of England. (Leith 230-266)

Gist's sermon. (Darlington37-39) I searched in vain to find the meaning of "Annosanah", beyond the interpreter's mention that it was the "name of a good man that had formerly lived among them." In view of Gist's account that so many Wyandots came up to him after his sermon believing that he spoke the truth about so many things, "speaker of true words" was a logical translation. Ted Franklin Belue offers "the go-between" as a translation, but gives no reference.(Beleu Hunters 47)

The killing of the woman and speech to the Wyandot. (Darlington 39-41)

Chapter VIII

White Woman's Creek, called Walkending by the Wyandot, is today called the Walhonding. Her village was opposite the mouth of present day Killbuck Creek. Mary Harris was captured in the Deerfield raid in 1704. Soon after Gist's meeting, her husband and Mary Harris did indeed repair to

French Canada. In 1756 one Robert Eastburn, a New York tradesman, was captured by French Indians and taken to Canada. For a time he was held at the town of Cohnewago, where he was lodged in the house of an Indian "Captain" and his wife Mary Harris. (VanDerBeets 167-168)

Hockhockin was near present day Lancaster, OH. You can still climb Ach-sin-sink, now called Mt. Pleasant, in Rising Park within the city limits.

Hockhocking River is the Hocking today. (Darlington 116)

Maguck was located about three and one-half miles south of present day Circleville, OH on the Pickaway Plain. The small rising in the middle, called Black Mountain by the Indians, was an ancient mound.

Sciento is the present day Scioto River. (Darlington, 118)

The account of the Delaware council. (Darlington 43-44)

Chapter IX

The spelling of Tshil-i-kau-thee. (Trowbridge 8) He names the five prominent divisions (clans, tribes) of the Shauwanoa Nation as follows: Tshilikauthee, Maakoatshaa, Pickaways, Kishpookoo, and Thawikila.

The history of the Lower Shawnee Town – Tshil-i-kau-thee, Chillicothe. (Hanna II 125-162) That it was called Tshil-i-kau-thee by the Shawnee. (129) The names of the Shawnee chiefs are taken from this chapter and Gist's journal and were likely there at the time of Gist's visit.

The deposition of Morris Turner and Ralph Kilgore. (Hanna II 265-267)

Details of the Shawnee council. (Darlington 45-46)

Description of the council house. (Howard 80, 362 author's drawing)

These are the speeches received by us from your great men." Big Hominy's reference here is to strings of wampum, within which different colored beads would remind the tribe historian of important points of the particular speech represented by that string. This was their record of treaties, agreements and speeches, as true to them as writing was to the whites. At an early age, special boys were trained to become memorizers for this task.

Gist's account of the Shawnee divorce and remarriage ceremony. (Mercer Papers 121-122) It should be noted that the Shawnee historian, T.W. Alford, calls Gist's account "apocryphal" and adds that a "close search of Shawnee literature and tradition has failed to verify this procedure as a custom of this nation." James Howard, an Anthropologist and author of Shawnee, boldly states that "Gist's purpose in disseminating this patently false account was probably to discredit the Shawnee as moral human beings, and hence to justify the expulsion of these 'savages' from their lands by white frontiersmen." (340-341) That scenario obviously does not fit with the Christopher Gist I am writing about, or the Gist upon which Kenneth Bailey based his biography, or the contemporary opinions of George Washington and Governor Dinwiddie and others.

That the Shawnee do not tell their own names. (Trowbridge 27)

Chapter X

Wau-thee-wee-la was a name I picked from Trowbridge's list. (Trowbridge 27) The suggestion that Gist had a relationship with an Indian Woman can be found in The Horn Papers. This account has Gist's wife dying in 1747, marrying a half-Indian woman named White Rose the next year.(226-227) This publication, which appeared in 1937, contained much new information about Gist and other historical figures of frontier Virginia. The work, however, was determined to be an elaborate forgery. Though some of the new information may have been true, none of it could be verified and so must remain suspect. (William and Mary Quarterly October 1947)

Though Bright Horn, Wau-thee-wee-la, is fictional, she represents a custom widely practiced by Indians and traders during that time. No hint of an episode like this can be found in Gist's Journals, but the opportunity surely presented itself and this is how he might have responded.

Vocabulary words come from Trowbridge.

Chapter XI

Pickawillany stood at the site of the abandoned village of the Pickawa tribe of the Shawnee on the west bank of the Great Miami River at the mouth of Loramie Creek about 2½ miles north of present day Piqua, OH. (Anson, 47) This was not the site of the Shawnee village of Upper Piqua destroyed by George Rogers Clark in 1780 and where Tecumseh was born in 1768. That location is about 7 miles west of Springfield on the Mad River near present day George Rogers Clark Park.

According to Allan Eckert, Unekenemi's actual name was Unemakemi Quilehtse, which translates "Thunder Bug" or "Thunder Fly" – Dragonfly. The French called him Demoiselle, meaning Dragonfly. (Eckert 624 note 9)

Most of the details on the Miami Indians comes from Anson.

Gist's Journal entry. (Darlington 47)

All councils and speeches. *(Ibid.* 49-55)

Acquenackqua was the father of Little Turtle. (Anson 44-55)

All Miami Indians mentioned come from Anson and were probably there at the time of Gist's visit.

Chapter XII

The trail south from Pickawillany crossed the Mad River near present day Springfield, OH and intersected the Little Miami River near Yellow Springs.

The Miami Feather Dance is describes by Gist. (Darlington 53-54)

Gist's Paroquete was most likely the Carolina Parakeet, one of a large species of the Parrot family, plentiful in Ohio and the East in general until the late 1800's. They became extinct due to over hunting for their beautiful feathers. Their fondness for corn also made them a target for pest control.

For details on the buffalo east of the Mississippi, see Belue. Basically these buffalo were the same species as those in the west, indeed came from there, and slowly spread eastward. They never attained the numbers they did in the west. Period accounts rarely report herds of more than one hundred.

Chapter XIII

The account of Gist's journey from near the Falls of the Ohio, present day Louisville, KY, to his home on the Yadkin. (Darlington 59-66) Though Gist believed at the time he was the first to explore Kentucky, Dr. Thomas Walker beat him by 11 months, leading an expedition through the Cumberland Gap in April of 1750. (Beleu Hunters 19 - 33)

Gist states at the end of his journey, of finding "his Wife and Family away to Roanoke about 35 M nearer in among the inhabitants." This could not have been Roanoke, VA, which is more like 115 miles away and was called "Big Lick" until 1882. Gist could have referred to a settlement on a tributary of the Roanoke River to the north. Alternatively, some time in 1752 Rowan County was formed with its County seat at Rowan Court House, a settlement that eventually became Salisbury. This is about 45 miles from Gist's. Is it possible that the settlement of Rowan, which would not yet have been "Court House," is where Gist's family went, and was miscopied from Gist's journal later to read "Roanoke"?

Gist's encounter with Joshua and his answer to the Delaware chiefs. (Darlington 78) The suggestion that Gist's reply was patterned after that of William Penn. (Jennings 19)

Chapter XIV

Tanacharison (Tanagrisson, Tanngrishon, Thanagiesan, etc.) was the Seneca chief sent by the Onondoga Council to watch over the Mingos in the Ohio Valley. Mulkearn suggests he may have won the position because of his skills in diplomacy, rather than on the battlefield. (Mulkearn 65) Sipe calls him an Oneida chief born about 1700, sent by Onondoga as vice-regent over the Delaware. He lived at Logstown. (Sipe 179) Jennings says he was Seneca, overseeing all the Ohio Indians aligned with the English. (Jennings 29) Joncaire says Tanacharison is originally from the "Lake of the Two Mountains," meaning from a Christianized French Mohawk village north of Montreal. (Kent 47)

In the "Treaty of Loggs Town, 1752," speech by Tanacharison, the "hill on the other side of the Allegheny hill" means the Blue Ridge Mountains. The entire proceedings in Mercer Papers.

This Warrior's Path is called "The Great Road from the Yadkin River thro Virginia to Philadelphia" on the Fry & Jefferson map of 1755. Also marked "Indian road by the Treaty of Lancaster." It is an eastern fork of the one Gist traveled from his home on the Yadkin to Cresap's place in 1750.

For an excellent account of the Lancaster Treaty of 1744 and its repercussions for the Logstown Treaty eight years later. (Lewis 59-60)

The description of Croghan's Pine Creek. (Wainwright 50)

Chapter XV

In Tanacharison's speech, "Lead" is a reference is to Celeran de

Blainville, who buried the lead plates which proclaimed the Ohio for France.

This speech by Tanacharison. (The Journal of Major George Washington Facsimile Edition 7-8) I have changed some of the wording to make it more readable. This, of course, is the Half-King's version of the September 1753 meeting with General Marin at Presque Isle. Marin's version shows less hostility, but a refusal of Tanacharison's "requests" all the same. Marin had received a letter from Joncaire before the meeting saying that the Half-King had little support from the Ohio Indians: none from the Shawnee or Delaware, only from some of the Ohio Iroquois. Later he was chastised by the Onondoga Council for his stand against the French. (Kent 49-50)

The Wampum Belt is the French Speech belt – the Indians' record of their treaty with the French and the accompanying speeches

A fusil fin is a French trade gun.

Monacatoocha was the Oneida chief sent by the Onondaga Council as liaison to the Shawnee.

Chapter XVI

Venango was located on the present site of Franklin, PA.

The River au Boeuf – River of the Buffalo or Beeves. Apparently Washington called it French Creek, because he did not know the name of it. The Delaware name was Toranadachka. (Donehoo 243)

John Frazier, a Scotsman who came to the Colonies in 1735, first located his trading post at Venango as early as 1741. He was known as "the blacksmith" and repaired guns for the traders and Indians. After he was ousted, he removed to the mouth of Turtle Creek on the Monongahela several miles south of the Forks. Washington and Gist stopped there on the way to Logstown.

Captain Joncaire, son of a French Indian agent, was an adopted member of the Seneca tribe and was quite influential among the French Indians.

Young William Fairfax was the son of the William Fairfax who came to Virginia and built the Belvior estate. Fairfax Sr. was the agent for Lord Thomas Fairfax of London, who actually owned the massive estate. Fairfax Jr. being born to his station, befriended Washington, who was still in his late teens. (Lewis Chapter 1)

Washington did court Nancy Gist for a short time. (Bailey Gist 171)

Chapter XVII

Lewis convincingly develops the theme of Washington's feelings toward Indians. "In addition to the highest virtues of an emerging nation, he would also come to embody [one] of its most glaring and persistent failings – its contempt for people of other races..." (Lewis 9, 23-25, 75)

Much of the phrasing and many of the words of this chapter are taken from Washington's journal. Gist also kept a journal of the trip, but much less dramatic. (Washington 19)

Chapter XVIII

The phrase "allez vous faire foutre" comes from profanities written on a 1780's French billeting map of Colonial Williamsburg. (Simpson 12-13)

Chapter XIX

Murdering town in Washington's journal, but Murthering Town in Gist's. Gist places the town about fifteen miles from Logstown on a branch of the "Great Beaver Creek." On Gist's map of 1753 , the town at this place is marked "Minacing Town." Christian Frederick Post calls it "Conoquenessing" on his 1758 map. (Donehoo 123)

In Gist's journal, the Indian met them at the town and acted as their guide until he fired on them. Washington has himself and Gist being "ambushed" by a "party of French Indians, who had lain in wait for us: one of them fired at Mr. Gist and me, not 15 steps, but fortunately missed." Washington, 21; Darlington 84-86) If we remember that Washington's Journal was edited by George himself for publication, a task recommended by Governor Dinwiddie it seems that he may have embellished his version a little. Gist had no reason to alter his account.

Chapter XX

I have taken Washington's description of the "immersion story," which is quite detailed, for this chapter. (Washington 21-22) Gist barely mentions it. "The Major having fallen in from off the raft, and my fingers frost-bitten, and the sun down, and very cold, we contented ourselves to encamp on the island." (Darlington 86)

Chapter XXI

William Trent was a Pennsylvania Scotsman employed by the Ohio Company. He was born in 1713 in Philadelphia. His part in history becomes more pronounced during the fall of Ft. Prince George, later Ft. Duquesne, later Ft. Pitt. (Slick)

Sewell Slick, in his 1947 biography of William Trent, says when Ensign Ward was asked by Contrecoeur whether he could buy the Company's carpentry tools, he replied no because "he loved his King and Country too well to part with any of them." He does not cite a source. (Slick 56) Sipe states that the French Commander permitted Ward to "take his tools with him." (Sipe, 154) Francis Jennings, though, says that Contrecoeur had Ward as a dinner guest the night of the capitulation and sold the tools, "with which the French resumed the building of the fort." He cites a deposition made by Ward three years later. (Jennings 65)

Chapter XXII

Seven of the eight Indians brought by Croghan from Aughwick and stayed to scout for Braddock are as follows: Monacatoocha (Scarooyadi), Cashuwayon, Frason, Kahuktodon, Allscheeokatha, Dyoquario, and Kesh-wugh-daniuto. (Lowdermilk 127)

The eighth one was Monacatoocha's son, unnamed in Lowdermilk. But on Sunday, September 16, 1753, at the Winchester Conference, Monacatoocha had his son Christened. Commissioners William Fairfax, and Christopher Gist shared the honor of being Godfather and re-named him "Dinwiddie." He was 11 years old. (Koontz, Dinwiddie 141 footnote# 162)

Braddock's replies to Gist about the Redcoats fighting the Indians are taken from the General's reply to Franklin in Frederick MD in April, 1755. (McCardell 174-175)

There has been some confusion about the proper name for "Will's Mountain." Every source I checked refers to the mountain directly north of Fort Cumberland as Will's Mountain. (Sargent, Freeman, Albert, Bailey, James, McCardell). Lowdermilk, in his history of Cumberland, states "Caiuctucuc Creek and the great mountain which forms the northern boundary of the city of Cumberland were baptised [sic] by the earliest settlers here, as 'Will's Creek,' and 'Will's Mountain.'" "Will" was the Indian after whom all this was named.(Lowdermilk 21) Today it is still called "Will's Mountain." Haystack Mountain lies to the southwest across Will's Creek.

Chapter XXIII

I have stated here that Gist viewed the burned out ruins of three houses. George Mercer in the Ohio Company Papers states that twenty families had settled on the land. If so, they must have settled on other parts of the grant. The French described Gist's Settlement as consisting of three houses and some outbuildings. (Trimble 19-26)

The Fort Necessity capitulation was signed on July 4, 1754. De Villers, the French commander, burned Gist's Settlement the next day. (Baily Gist 89)

When Governor Duquesne of New France read the capitulation, he severely chastised De Villers and reprimanded Contrecoeur, the commander of Ft. Duquesne, for not communicating to his officers the official policy. The Ohio Valley belonged to the French. No Englishmen were permitted to settle on it, trade in it, or barter for it ever. (Trudel 6-7)

McCardell, on page 231 seems to confuse the enemy camp of barked trees at the base of a cliff called Half-King's Rocks with Jumonville Glen. The glen, which can still be visited today near Fort Necessity, is two miles further north and one-half mile east. This glen is where George Washington's band of forty militia and Tanacharison's dozen warriors attacked the French on the morning of May 30, 1754, resulting in the death of Jumonville. This event was believed by many at the time to have been the direct cause of the French and Indian War. (Freeman I 371-372; Tiberg 8)

The standard story of the Jumonville Affair has Washington being tricked into admitting he assassinated the French commander, who was on a diplomatic mission to deliver an ultimatum to the English, in much the same way Washington executed his diplomatic mission with Gist in the winter of 1753/54. Jumonville fell during the first volley, or at least that's the story adopted by American history books. Jennings includes an excerpt from a period newspaper stating that the Half King tomahawked Jumonville. (Jennings 65-90; Freeman I 370-376; Lewis 142-144)

Statements that Eastern Woodland Indians did not rape white female captives can be found in numerous sources, both period and scholarly. (Axtel 181-183; Drimmer 12-13; Walace 50; Withers 33-34; Derounian-Stodola xvi)

I did not wish to become bogged down in Gist's commissary problems, nor all of his financial difficulties. There is some allegation, no existing proof, no self-defense and precious few details. For more explanation. (Baily Gist 96-103)

The bit of humor about the rear guard I borrowed from Kopperman 10.

Bailey gives no information on Sarah's death. (Bailey Gist 64)

Chapter XXIV

Gist's actual citation reads thus: "This is to certify that Mr. Christopher Gist executed the Office of head Guide with great Sobriety Prudence & Fidelity to which Office he was appointed by Genl Braddock the 27th of May 1755. And I do farther certify that he was sent to bring intelligence from the French Fort which Service he performed with great Risk being for a long time pursued. Upon his return the Genl being very well satisfied with his behavior ordered Mr. Shirley the Secretary to pay him his 50 thirty six Shilling Pieces." (Bailey Gist 92)

The story of friendly fire killing Monacatoocha's (Scarouady's) son. (Sipe 184-185; Sargent 350)

Chapter XXV

The incline (McCardell 245-246; Lewis 178; Freeman 64-67)

The fifes played "The Grenadier's March." (McCardell 246)

Chapter XXIV

My account of the Braddock's Defeat is taken from numerous sources: Lewis, McCardell, Freeman, Sargent, Kopperman, Hamilton, and others. Especially interesting is Kopperman, who reviews every period account of the battle and gages its possible accuracy. The scout who came back shouting "the Indiens is upon us" is not named, but could have been Nathaniel Gist. (Kopperman, 55) One French account says they heard cannon fired during the first volleys from the English, yet Gordon had no artillery up front.(57) He suggests elsewhere that this could have been eight Brown Bess muskets fired simultaneously. Croghan's words that Indians would scalp their victims early if unsure of victory,(165 and 185). The anecdote where the father of the father-son team (unnamed) has his rifle destroyed,(182-183). It could have been the Gists. Thomas Waggoner's Virginians taking friendly fire, (174). Sir Halket's death really did involve Gist,(172).

Chapter XXVII

The story of Braddock wanting Croghan's pistols was a rumor that circulated after the battle. (Kopperman 87)

Braddock ordered Washington to ride to Dunbar's camp the night of the battle. Washington had two guides with him. (Freeman II 78) These guides are unidentified, but could have been the Gists.

Apart from the fact that Christopher was surely among the scouts who first saw the French, and the anecdote of Halket's death, his movements are undocumented.

Chapter XXVIII

The Crooked Billet was first visited by Franklin in 1723. (Lathrop 171)

For a detailed account of Pennsylvania's problems and its Indian relations. (Wallace Weiser 390-416)

Christopher Gist's movements during this time are deduced from correspondence to and from Washington and others. (Bailey Gist 104-110)

Chapter XXIX

The journey from Philadelphia to York would have been accomplished via a fairly well developed wagon road. Gist writes Washington on November 24, 1755 from Lancaster, that he had sent twenty recruits to York Towne (York, PA), and would follow them the next day. (Bailey, Gist, 108). From York the path followed a branch of the Monocacy Path, passing through Gettysburg, Hagerstown, MD and Winchester, VA. This path later became The Wilderness Road, which followed Virginia State Route 11 (and now Interstate 81) on down to Abingdon, VA and west to the Cumberland Gap. This was the same road Daniel Boone took his party of settlers to Kentucky in 1775. (Walace Paths 105)

Letter from Washington to Gist dated October 10, 1755. (Bailey Gist 106)

The incident with Richard Pearis is alluded to by Bailey. He mentions business dealings between the Gists and Pearis and how they became "bitter enemies." Then according to Nathaniel, the first thing Pearis does with the Cherokees on the way to join Braddock, is give them liquor. (Bailey Gist 89)

The idea of rum laced with certain strengthening drugs and slipping the scales comes from Major Robert Rodgers' play, Ponteach Act I scene 1.

Chapter XXX

More details of the massacres of November and December 1755 in Pennsylvania. (Sipe Chapter VII)

For a day-by-day account of these times after Braddock's defeat in Pennsylvania, see Paul Wallace's Conrad Weiser. He often tells the story through period correspondence. (Specifically 384-427)

On November 1st Gist wrote to Washington from Philadelphia explaining his plans to meet Monacatoocha and Montour at Harris' Ferry (Harrisburg) and of his offered commission by the Governor. (Bailey Gist 108)

The Conrad Weiser homestead is in present day Womelsdorf on U S

Route 422, twenty miles west of Reading. It is open to the public.

Monacatoocha's speech is a compilation of details from Paul Wallace with some of his and my own paraphrasing. (Wallace Weiser 407-408) His speech in the Pennsylvania Colonial Records Volume VI 685-687.

The information on old Lancaster Towne. (Klein)

On December 3rd Washington wrote that three days earlier ten of his officers had brought in only twenty recruits among them. This exceeded, by one man only, the number Christopher Gist had already sent to Fort Cumberland for his Company of Scouts. (Freeman II 143)

That Gist was in Alexandria for several days in early December, 1755. (Dorsey 19) This source gives many excerpts of letters to and from Gist, which place him in all the different locations throughout this book.

Chapter XXXI

For an interpretation of these many problems that gives Gist the benefit of the doubt. (Powell Gist 48-53)

Croghan was at Joseph Simon's store in Lancaster on December 22, 1755 to purchase "silver truck" worth £50 for Indian gifts and other supplies for the government, meaning his troops. On December 27 he paid a tavern keeper £8 "for soulgers expenses for dayet and loging 3 days." Since one shilling a day per man would have been standard, this amount would have paid for about fifty men. Before January Croghan led 180 recruits from the settlements to Cumberland County. (Wainwright, 103)

I have no factual basis for the conclusion that recruits who listed "soldier" as occupation were from Braddock's army. But of the 68 on the roll for Gist's Company of Scouts dated July 13, 1756, we find 8 soldiers, one sailor and 22 who list no occupation. It makes sense for at least some of them to have been British soldiers whose period of enlistment was over, or perhaps a deserter. (Bailey Gist 197-199)

Again, referring to Gist's roster of July 13, 1756, from January 16 to March 30 the recruiting locations jump back and forth between Baltimore and Fredericksburg. Some recruits were enlisted on the same day from both locations. Christopher and Nathaniel had to have split up. *(Ibid.* 199)

Baltimore Town was surveyed in 1730 by seven commissioners appointed for the project, one of whom was Richard Gist, Christopher's father. Though Baltimore was a "tobacco town", not much tobacco was ever exported from there. (Owens 30-31)

These Swiss and German immigrants, Protestant Palatines, were the descendants of inhabitants along the Rhine and the Necker Rivers who had been displaced to Holland during the Wars of Louis XIV. About 3000 settled in Maryland between 1752 and 1755. (Edgar 96)

The Acadians, 14,000 strong, happy French people, were ripped from their homes and loaded onto ships. The first sailing was on October 8, 1755. Half of them were dispersed from Massachusetts to Georgia. Without belongings, money, supplies, and without much compassion from the colonists, many perished. Those who were sent to Baltimore faired better, being welcomed into individual homes. In the climate of growth, many found jobs and eventually established Frenchtown, an area just outside the limits of the town on the southwestern corner of the harbor. (*Ibid.* 83-93)

Dr. Stevenson had actually discovered the smallpox vaccination and it was in use at that time.

The history of the Eastern Shore Indians is complex and not pertinent to this book. It does establish that the system of reservations for Indians was existent during Gist's time and was a topic of conversation. In 1798 the Maryland Assembly voted to purchase the remaining Choptank reservation lands from the five Indians still living there. The next year saw the sale of Locust Neck. (Roundtree and Davidson 124-160)

Chapter XXXII

This minor skirmish at Fort Cumberland is mentioned in Lewis 233. Washington had just come from Philadelphia where he had met Lord Loudoun, new Commander-in-Chief of British forces in America. Washington was at the fort on the 20th,possibly earlier, but in Williamsburg by the 27th for a conference with the Assembly.

The "Roll of Capt. Christopher Gist's Company, July 13, 1756" shows recruits from Baltimore having enlisted through April 7, 1756 with one from Fredericksburg on June 3rd. (Bailey Gist 199) Yet Washington ordered Captain Gist to Conocheague (Fort Maidstone) on April 7th for supplies. (Ansel 135) It is probable that Gist returned from recruiting shortly after March 1st as originally ordered and left Nathaniel to finish the job.

Colonel James Innis, who had been appointed Governor (commander) of Fort Cumberland by General Braddock, had gone to North Carolina on personal business in September 1755. In his place he named Adam Stephen, the senior Virginia officer at this fort, which was built, supplied and mostly garrisoned by Virginia, though located across the Potomac in Maryland. Shortly thereafter, one John Dagworthy marched a contingent of Maryland Militia to the fort and took over its operation on no one's authority but his own. He claimed seniority to provincial officers of any rank by virtue of a King's commission he held in the last war, which ended in 1744. Trading his commission for a lifetime pension three years earlier, he now re-commissioned himself a Captain and assumed command. In March 1756, Washington visited Governor Shirley, commander of British forces at the time, and appealed for a ruling on Dagworthy's legitimacy. Shirley ruled the Dagworthy commission provincial, not royal, and therefore under Washington's command. But on Washington's visit to Lord Loudoun the following year, he was ordered to give command of the fort to Dagworthv and remove Virginia's forces back to Virginia. (Lewis 200-201)

Washington received a 2% commission on public money. (*Ibid.* 233)

Fort Maidenstone was situated on the south side of the Potomac across from the mouth of Conococheague Creek in present Berkely County, West Virginia. It was located on the Great Warrior Trail leading south from Pennsylvania up the Shenandoah Valley to Winchester and beyond.

Washington's Bill of Particulars the year before included more authority to punish deserters, more money, more supplies, etc. (Ansel 131-136)

Gist was in Williamsburg soliciting Dinwiddie's approval. On April 21st Speaker of the House, John Robinson wrote Washington that he had already spoken to Atkin on Gist's behalf. Then the end of May Gist again traveled to Williamsburg carrying Washington's letters of official recommendations to Dinwiddie and Robinson. (Trimble "Indian Service" 144-145)

Chapter XXXIII

The word "express" was commonly used to signify a courier.

Atkin was appointed by the Board of Trade in the spring of 1756 as "Agent for and Superintendent of" the southern District. (Atkin Report xxii)

It was 200 miles from Williamsburg to Winchester. At thirty miles per day it would take six good days of travel for someone like Gist. Edmund Atkin left Williamsburg about May 23rd and arrived the evening of June 2nd or morning of June 3rd. (Freeman II 248). That makes eleven or twelve days, which is consistent with his reputation for sloth. Gist left Winchester May 30th or 31st for Williamsburg and was back in time to attend Washington's war council 2:00 June 16th. (Trimble, "Indian Service" 146; Koontz Virginia 108)

Croghan did show up for this incident June 12th and departed for Fort Loudoun on or about June 16th. (Wainwright 125-127)

Croghan used this spelling of Shawnee in his journal of 1756. By 1765 he had changed it to "Shawnese." (Thwaites 86, 134) Maybe this shows a change in pronunciation?

Sir William Johnson was the Superintendent of Indian affairs of the northern Colonies, primarily their liaison with the Iroquois.

William Denny was appointed new governor of Pennsylvania in June 1756 to replace Morris. He arrived in August.

James Campbell, fourth Earl of Loudoun in 1756 was appointed titular Governor of Virginia (Dinwiddie actually being Lieutenant Governor) and Commander-in-Chief of all British forces in North America. (Baily Gist 189)

Detailed written instructions to Gist. (*Ibid.* 128-138)

Chapter XXXIV

Sir William Johnson did indeed dress, eat and dance like the Iroquois. When necessary. He spoke their language and as Warraghiyagey, an adopted Mohawk, acted as liaison between the British and Iroquois. Alan Eckert's Wilderness Empire is devoted largely to the life of Johnson.

Washington rented a house in Winchester from Captain William Cocke. Here he entertained and lived as much as he could on the frontier the life of a Virginia gentlemen. (Freeman II 199)

This is the same William Crawford, who was to be burned at the stake by the Delaware Indians twenty-five years later.

Dagworthy's letter. (Freeman II 251)

Major James Livingston was from the Maryland Regiment stationed at Fort Cumberland.

Fort Loudoun was begun by Washington May, 1756, 200 yards from the north end of the town of Winchester and not completed until Spring of 1758. (Powell Loudoun 25-35)

Captains Thomas Waggoner, John McNeill, Robert Stewart, Christopher Gist; Lieutenants John Campbell, Mordecai Buckner; and Ensigns William Crawford, James Roy and Henry Russell were at this Council of War Thursday June 16, 1757 2:00 PM. (Koontz Virginia 108)

Details of this Council of War. (Hamilton 94-95)

Washington did not see the value of sending out offensive guerilla bands led by whites. Good officers like Baker, Lewis, Spotswood were hard to find. But while Washington was in Williamsburg in May, these three officers organized raids. Washington preferred the defensive until a major campaign could be organized against Fort Duquesne. (Freeman II 249-252).

Baker's own story is cited in his letter to Washington. (Hamilton 89-90) Added details are found in a letter from Washington to Colonel Stanwix. (Fitzpatrick 60-62)

Colonel John Stanwix was Commander-in-Chief of the middle colonies.

Chapter XXXV

The story of Atkin's jailing the Cherokees. (Fitzpatrick 97-98, 115; Freeman II 256; Lewis 236-237.

Gist writes to Forbes on July 6th of the Catawbas, Nataways and Tuscarawas saying that "there was a report of a large party of Indians and some white men in western Augusta and Halifax [counties]. I suppose it was Little Carpenter and if so, will wait for them and escort them to Fort Cumberland also." (James, Forbes 128-129) But it was Outacity, not Little Carpenter. The two Cherokee leaders were confused with one another in some modern writings (Franklin) and they were apparently confused then also. Gist must have found out that neither Little Carpenter nor Outacity were coming and decided to escort the others to the fort. I have him arriving after the Indians were jailed, because I cannot believe the incident would have happened had he been present. The documented rescue does not mention Gist, but it is likely he was there. For the whereabouts of Little Carpenter. (James Forbes 142, 228, 231, 233, 241)

Outassity (Outacite, Outacity, Autoscity, Ustonecka), was one of the most noted chiefs of the Cherokee, known as early as 1721 as "king" of the lower and middle Cherokee settlements. He visited London in 1730 along with two others. (Fitzpatrick, 98)

The English translation of "Outacity" was "Mankiller." It was a military title as well as that of a conjurer, who could make an illness worse or shoot an invisible arrow toward the enemy. This Outacity joined a Cherokee delegation visiting London in 1762. (Mankiller xxi, 2-13)

In the Eighteenth Century they felt the flux (dysentery) was caused by poor diet.

For months in 1757, Washington had tried to get the death penalty without so much what we would call red tape – approval from the Governor, etc. Finally he got it, but within two months was no longer convinced it provided a deterrent to desertion. (Freeman 260)

The "Bird" is Colonel William Byrd III, who in 1756 concluded a treaty with the Cherokee and Catawba whereby they agreed to send warriors to assist the English against the French. He promised presents, arms, ammunition, clothing, provisions. (Bailey Gist 129)

Chapter XXXVI

Spruce beer was brewed by boiling the tender sprigs of the spruce tree for three hours. The broth was mixed with molasses (six gallons broth to one quart molasses) and allowed to ferment for twelve days in wooden kegs. (Powell Loudoun 37)

McGuire's Tavern opened in 1755 and remained so for 150 years. (Guide to Old Dominion 332)

Thomas Gist was wounded and taken to Canada. After a year of great hardship he escaped and returned to his Virginia regiment. (Powell Gist 67)

The details of Grant's skirmish. (Freeman II 339-349) Briefly, Grant disobeyed orders and, seeking glory for himself, tried to lure the French and Indians out of the fort and into a trap. It backfired.

Attakullakulla, Little Carpenter, sailed to England with two other Cherokee chiefs in 1730. From 1741-1747 he was prisoner of the French in Canada. He was named "Emperor" of the Cherokee in 1770. (Bailey Gist 147, 193; Woodward 85)

Dragging Canoe, the famous Cherokee leader during the American Revolution and son of Attakullakulla, said that one day nothing of the Native People would remain but their "names imperfectly recorded." Since all the names of 17th and 18th century Cherokees were recorded by whites barely familiar with the language, the author concludes Dragging Canoe was correct. Cherokee historians who know the language conclude that Attakullakulla' s name was more properly pronounced Ada-gal'kala. (Conley viii)

Frederick Christian Post notes that by November 21st, when Forbes was still fifteen miles from Fort Duquesne, the roofs of the houses were made ready to burn. Post was at the fort to inform the Ohio Indians of the results of the Easton Treaty in October. (Post's journal, Rupp 140, 109 Appendix)

Letter from Forbes to Bouquet October 13, 1758: "30 Catawbas from Winchester joined me two days ago as did Little Carpenter and about 30

Cherokee. They are very demanding, bullying us into a mean countenance or determined to leave and go home...King Hagler stayed in Winchester but have hopes to get him up." (James Forbes 231)

Forbes to Abercromby October 16, 1758: "Little Carpenter and about sixty warriors here from Winchester. He is a great rascal to the full...In place of going out to war with me or persuading others to stay, he has strengthened them in their extravagant demands by making his own more reasonable.

"If I have any Indians, it'll cost me dear and yet should anything fail the Cause [it] may be attributed the want of them, whose presence I [might] have lost for saving a few hundred pounds after foolishly spending thousands. But a little good luck often justifies the worst of measures and stupidest of actions." (*Ibid.* 241)

In 1752 Little Carpenter was in Williamsburg appealing to Dinwiddie. In 1756 he attended a conference in North Carolina where Virginia delegates sought a military alliance with the Cherokees. Again trade was discussed. In January 1759 Little Carpenter was in Williamsburg appealing to the new Governor. (Franklin "Cherokee Trade" 21-27; Reesse I 135, 139)

Chapter XXXVII

King Hagler kept his ability to speak English secret. (Merrell Indians 48)

Two articles by W. Neil Franklin detail Virginia and the Cherokee Indian trade from 1673-1775. ("East Tennessee Historical Society" V 26-28)

Fort Niagara fell on July 25, 1759.

Thomas Rutherford was well respected among the Catawba. Bailey says he remained one of Gist's assistants at least through the fall of 1758. Dinwiddie referred to him as "agent" to the tribe. (Bailey Gist 191-192)

By Hagler's day the custom of riding horses was prevalent throughout the nation. No Catawba went anywhere on foot. (Merrell Catawbas 57)

Hagler's speeches to Gist are taken from actual speeches and statements he made to the white men throughout his years as chief. The terms "Great Man Above" and "He-Who-Never-Sleeps" come directly from him. (Merrell Indians 88; Merrell Catawbas 13)

Governor James Glen of South Carolina and Christopher Gist were the only two white men who earned the right to be called "Father." (Merrell Indian 148)

By 1755 there were 500 white families within 30 miles and this particular chapter is set 4 years later. (*Ibid.* 198-199)

Cabin being built, (*Ibid.* 188)

In 1540 the Spanish explorer Hernando de Soto led 600 soldiers through the southern Piedmont region. Twenty years later Juan Pardo followed. (Merrell Catawbas 13-14)

Charleston was founded in 1670 and soon Carolina fur traders headed for the interior to trade with the Catawba. (*Ibid.* 42)

"Their Nation (Catawba) and other Indians rose up against such treatment" is a brief reference to the Yamasee War 1715-1717, which involved almost every Indian tribe that traded with the English in Carolina. (Merrell Indians 42)

Finally in February 1764, after eight years of asking for a reservation, 144,000 acres were surveyed and deeded to the Catawba. (*Ibid.* 198-199)

Chapter XXXVIII

The smallpox epidemic to which Nopkehe refers was 1738. One of every two Cherokees died and it may have affected the Catawbas. (*Ibid.* 136)

Chapter XXXIX

Information on smallpox found in Baker, Book of Remedies, printed in 1832, 153. "Confluent" was the worst strain.

The water cure worked well for many diseases other than smallpox, but the Indians tried it often, because they had no other choice. "During the height of the scourge twenty-five corpses were being pulled from the Catawba River every day, sad evidence of the failure of traditional water cures to do more than hasten the end."(Merrell Indians 193; "South Carolina Gazette" Dec. 15, 1759; Conley 12)

This event where Gist contracts smallpox is one incident in the outbreak of another major epidemic among the Catawba. The South Carolina Gazettes of November and December 1759 speak of fully one-half the Catawba Nation dying in that year. (Bailey Gist 194 n43)

Chapter XL

Lest the reader think it implausible for Gist or anyone to question religious beliefs in the 1700's, you have only to look at the work of the Baron de Lahontan, who in 1703 published a dialogue between himself and an educated Huron Indian he calls Adario. This Jesuit educated Huron rejects Christianity and articulates what he believes to be gross inaccuracies and inconsistencies in the French brand of it. Adario asks pointed questions that Baron de Lahontan, the defender of Christianity, never is able to defend in a convincing way. In this way the Baron levels a critique of Christianity. (Lahontan)

On the road from Williamsburg to Winchester Gist died conducting sixty-two Catawbas to help guard the western frontier of Virginia. (Dorsey, 28)

In July of 1759 more than sixty Catawba warriors, "probably 20 percent of the total number the Nation could muster," were headed north to help the British fight France. "Closer to home, Hagler and twenty-three others traveled through South Carolina on something of a goodwill tour, lobbying their friends for supplies and protection." (Merrell Indians 192)

Probably Merrell is correct about the Catawba band escorted by Gist going north to aid the British and not the Virginia frontier. So Hagler was not really with Gist at his death. It was easier, however, to have him there to speak on such a personal level with Gist, since it can be inferred they were friends. It also helped that so much of Nopkehe's words are on record.

Captain James Gunn of the Virginia Regiment wrote of Gist's death on

July 31, 1759. "I thought it proper to advise you that Capt Gist Deputy agent for Indian affairs here, died on the Road from Williamsburg 25th. Instant with Small Pox." (Bailey Gist 150)

On August 12, George Mercer wrote General Stanwix. "...I...was detained by a Message from the Catawbas with whom I was personally acquainted who desired to speak to me. I met Them early this Morning near the Town which i would not allow Them to enter upon Account of the Small Pox, and have been very much perplexed, til 8 o'clock P.M., with their trifling arguments and Excuses, insisting [that] as...their Father Capt. Gist, as they called him, was dead, it was better to return Home, as the Presents they were promised were not ready for them here." (*Ibid.* 150)

BIBLIOGRAPHY

Alden, John Richard, Robert Dinwiddie: Servant of the Crown. Williamsburg Colonial Williamsburg Press, 1973.

Ansel, William H Jr, Frontier Forts Along The Potomac And Its Tributaries. Parsons, WV: McClain Printing Co, 1984. Reprint, Romney, WV: Fort Pearsall, Inc, 1995.

Anson, Bert, The Miami Indians. University of Oklahoma Press, 1970.

Axtell, James, The European and the Indian. New York: Oxford University Press Paperback, 1982.

Bailey, Kenneth P, Christopher Gist. Archon Books, 1976.

-----, The Ohio Company of Virginia: A Chapter in the History of the Westward Movement 1748-1792. Glendale, CA: Arthur H Clark Co, 1938.

-----, Thomas Cresap, Maryland Frontiersman. Boston: Christopher Publish ing House, 1944.

Baker, Joseph, Natural Physician's Book of Remedies Containing a Patent Right for Doctoring. Chillicothe, OH, 1832.

Baker, Mark, Pioneering, The Long Hunter Series Volume III. Bowling Green, KY: American Pioneer Video, 1995.

Belue, Ted Franklin, The Long Hunt. Mechanicsburg, PA: Stackpole Books,1996.

-----, The Hunters of Kentucky. Mechanicsburg, PA: Stackpole Books, 2003.

Conley, Robert J, Cherokee Dragon: A Novel of the Real People. New York: St Martin's Press, 2000.

Darlington, William, ed, Christopher Gist's Journals, with Historical, Geographical, and Ethnological Notes. Pittsburgh: J R Weldon & Co, 1893. Reprint, Salem, NH: Ayer Company Publishers, Inc, 1991.

Dillard, J L, Black English. New York: Vintage Books, 1973.

Donehoo, George P. Indian Villages and Place Names in Pennsylvania. Harrisburg, PA: Telegraph Press, 1928.

Dorsey, Jean Muir & Dorsey, Maxwell Jay, Christopher Gist of Maryland and Some of His Descendants 1679-1957. Chicago: John S Swift Co, 1969.

Drimmer, Frederick, ed, Captured By Indians. New York: Dover Publications, 1961.

Eckert, Allan, Wilderness Empire. Boston: Little, Brown & Company, 1969.

Edgar, Lady, A Colonial Governor in Maryland: Horatio Sharpe and His Times 1753-1773. London: Longmans, Green, and Co, 1912.

Equiano, Olaudah, The Interesting Narrative of the Olaudah Equiano, or Gustavus Vassa, the African. In The Classic Slave Narratives. Ed, Gates, Henry Louis Jr, New York: Mentor Paperback published by Penguin Group, 1987.

Fitzpatrick, John C, ed, The Writings of George Washington. Vol II 1757-1769. Washington DC: US Government Printing Office, 1931.

Franklin, Neil W, "Virginia and the Cherokee Indian Trade 1753-1755," East Tennessee Historical Society's Publications. Vol 5, 1933.

-----, "Pennsylvania-Virginia Rivalry for the Indian Trade of the Ohio Valley," Mississippi Valley Historical Review. Vol 20, Mar 1934.

Freeman, Douglas Southall, George Washington: A Biography. Volumes I and II. New York: Charles Scribner's Sons, 1948.

Hamilton, Stanislaus M, ed, Letters to Washington and Accompanying Papers. Vol II, 1756-1758. New York: Houghton, Mifflin and Company, 1899.

Hanna, Charles A, The Wilderness Trail: Or The Ventures, and Adventures of the Pennsylvania Traders on the Allegheny Path, With Some New Annals of the Old West, and the Records of Some Strong Men and Some Bad Ones. New York: AMS Press, 1911.

Horn, W F, The Horn Papers: Early Westward Movement on the Monongahela and Upper Ohio 1765-1795. Vol I. Scottsdale, PA: Herald Press. 1945. (Found to be an elaborate forgery)

Howard, James H, Shawnee Athens, OH: Ohio University Press, 1981.

Howe, Henry, Historical Collections of Ohio. Cincinnati: E Morgan and Company, 1857

Hulbert, Archer Butler, "The Indian Thoroughfares." Ohio Archaeological and Historical Publications, Vol III, Columbus, 1900.

Jacobs, Wilbur R, The Appalachian Indian Frontier: The Edmund Atkin Report and Plan of 1755. Lincoln, NE: University of Nebraska Press, 1967.

------, Wilderness Politics and Indian Gifts: The Northern Indian Frontier, 1748-1763. Lincoln, NE: University of Nebraska Press, 1967.

James, Alford P, The Ohio Company, It's Inner History. University of Pittsburgh, 1959.

-----, ed, Writings of General Forbes. Menasha, WI: The Collegiate Press, 1938.

Jennings, Francis, Empire of Fortune. New York: W W Norton and Company, 1988.

Kent, Donald H, ed, Contrecoeur's Copy of George Washington's Journal for 1754. Eastern National Park and Monument Association, 1989.

-----, The French Invasion of Western Pennsylvania. Harrisburg: Pennsylva-

nia Historical and Museum Commission, 1991.
Kinietz, Vernon and Voegelin, Ermine W, ed, Shawnese Traditions: C C Trowbridge's Account. Ann Arbor: University of Michigan Press, 1939.
Klein, Frederick S, Old Lancaster: Historic Pennsylvania Community, From Its Beginnings to 1865. Lancaster, PA: Early American Series, Inc, 1964.
Koontz, Louis K, The Virginia Frontier. Baltimore: Johns Hopkins Press, 1925. Facsimile Reprint, Heritage Press, 1992.
-----, Robert Dinwiddie: His Career in American Colonial Government and Westward Expansion. Glendale, CA: Arthur H Clark Company, 1941.
Kopperman, Paul E, Braddock at the Monongahela. University of Pittsburgh Press. 1977.
Lathrop, Elsie, Early American Inns and Taverns. New York: Robert M McBride and Company, 1926.
Lewis, Thomas A, For King and Country: The Maturing of George Washington, 1748-1760. New York: Harper Collins Publishers, 1993.
Leith, John H, ed, Creeds of the Churches. Atlanta: John Knox Press, 1963.
Lowdermilk, Will H, History of Cumberland Maryland. Washington DC: James Anglim, 1878.
Mankiller, Wilma and Wallace, Michael, Mankiller: A Chief and Her People. New York: St Martin's Press, 2000.
Merrell, James H, The Catawbas. New York: Chelsea House Publishers, 1989.
-----, The Indians' New World: Catawbas and Their Neighbors from European Contact Through The Era of Removal. Chapel Hill, NC: University of North Carolina Press, 1989.
Meyer, Clarence, American Folk Medicine. Glenwood. IL: Meyerbooks Publisher, 1973.
McCardell, Lee, Ill-Starred General: Braddock of the Coldstream Guards. University of Pittsburgh Press, 1958. Reprint paperback, 1986.
Middleton, Arthur Pierce and Adair, Douglas, "The Mystery of the Horn Papers," William And Mary Quarterly. Vol IV Oct, 1947.
Mulkearn, Lois, George Mercer Papers Relating to the Ohio Company of Virginia. University of Pittsburgh Press, 1954.
-----, ed, George Mercer Papers. University of Pittsburgh, 1954.
O'Neill, James F II, ed, Their Bearing Is Noble and Proud. Dayton: JTGS Publishing, 1995.
Orrill, Lawrence A, "Christopher Gist and His Sons," The Western Historical Magazine. Vol 15. August, 1932.
Peckham, Howard H, The Colonial Wars 1689-1762. University of Chicago Press, 1964.
Pennsylvania Colonial Records. Vol VI, Apr 1754-Jan 1756.
Powell, Allan, Christopher Gist Frontier Scout. Shippensburg, PA: Beidel Printing Company, 1992.

-----, Fort Cumberland. Parsons, WV: McClain Printing Company, 1989.

-----, Fort Loudoun: Winchester's Defense in the French and Indian War. Parson's, WV: McClain Publishing Company, 1990.

Reese, George, ed, The Official Papers of Francis Fauquier, Lieutenant Governor of Virginia 1758-1768. Vol I. Charlottesville, VA: University Press of Virginia, 1980.

Roundtree, Helen C and Davidson, Thomas E, Eastern Shore Indians of Virginia and Maryland. Charlottesville, VA: University Press of Virginia, 1997.

Rodgers, Robert, Ponteach: Or the Savages of America. A Tragedy. London: J Millan, opposite the Admiralty, Whitehall, 1766.

Rupp, I D, Early History of Western Pennsylvania. Harrisburg, PA: Daniel W Kauffman, Publisher, 1846. Reprint. Lewisburg, PA: Wennawoods Publishing, 1995.

Sargent, Winthrop, The History Of An Expedition Against Fort Du Quesne In 1755 Under Major-General Edward Braddock. Philadelphia: Historical Society of Pennsylvania, 1855. Reprint. Lewisburg, PA: Wennawoods Publishing , 1997.

Simpson, Alan, The Mysteries of the "Frenchman's Map" of Williamsburg, Virginia. Colonial Williamsburg Foundation, 1984.

Sipe, C Hale, The Indian Chiefs of Pennsylvania. Butler, PA: Historical Society of Western Pennsylvania, 1927. Reprint. Lewisburg, PA: Wennawoods Publishing, 1994.

Slick, Sewell E, William Trent And The West. Harrisburg, PA: Archives Publishing Company of Pennsylvania, Inc, 1947.

Smith, James, Scoouwa: James Smith's Indian Captivity Narrative. Ohio Historical Society, 1978.

Tilberg, Frederick, Fort Necessity. Washington DC: National Parks Service, 1954.

Trimble, David B, "Christopher Gist and the Indian Service in Virginia, 1757-1759." Virginia Magazine of History and Biography. Vol 64, April, 1956.

-----, "Christopher Gist and the Settlements on the Monongahela, 1752-1754." Virginia Magazine of History and Biography. Vol 63, January 1955.

Trowbridge, C C, Shawnese Traditions. Vernon Kinietz and Ermine Voegelin. Ann Arbor: University of Michigan Press, 1939.

Trudel, Marcel, The Jumonville Affair. Eastern National Park and Monument Association, 1989

Thwaites, Reuben Gold, ed, Early Western Journals 1748-1765. Vol I of 32, Cleveland, 1904. Reprint. Lewisburg, PA: Wennawoods Publishing, 1998.

-----, ed., New Voyages to North America by the Baron Lahontan. Vol II, Chicago: AC McClurg & Company, 1905. Reprinted from the English edition of 1703.

Underwood, Thomas Bryan, Cherokee Legends and the Trail of Tears. Cherokee, NC: Cherokee Publications, 1956. Twentieth printing 1993.

VanDerBeets, Richard, Held Captive by Indians: Selected Narratives, 1642-1836. Knoxville: University of Tennessee Press, 1973. Revised Edition, 1994.

Volweiler, A T, George Croghan and the Westward Movement 1741-1782. Cleveland: Arthur H Clark Oc, 1926. Reprint. Lewisburg, PA: Wennawoods Publishing, 2000.

Wallace, Paul A W, Conrad Weiser 1696-1760: Friend of Colonist and Mohawk. Philadelphia: University of Pennsylvania Press, 1945. Reprint. Lewisburg, PA: Wennawoods Publishing, 1996.

-----, Indian Paths of Pennsylvania. Harrisburg: Pennsylvania Historical and Museum Commission, 1987.

Wainwright, Nicholas B, George Croghan, Wilderness Diplomat. Chapel Hill, NC: University of North Carolina Press, 1959.

Ward, Harry M, Major General Adam Stephen and the Cause of American Liberty. Charlottesville, VA: University Press of Virginia, 1989.

Washington, George, The Journal of Major George Washington. Williamsburg: Colonial Williamsburg Foundation Facsimile Edition, 1959. Ninth Printing, 1990.

Wheeler-Voegelin, Ermine, Indians of Northern Ohio and Southern Michigan. New York: Garland Publishing Company, 1974.

Wilcox, Frank, Ohio Indian Trails. Cleveland: Gates Press, 1933.

Withers, Alexander Scott, Chronicles of Border Warfare. Cincinnati: Robert Clark Company, 1895.

Woodward, Grace Steele, The Cherokees. Norman, OK: University of Oklahoma Press, 1963.

Wroth, Lawrence C, The Story of Thomas Cresap, A Maryland Pioneer. Columbus, OH: The Cresap Society, 1928.

Photograph by Leslie Heath

About the Author

In "what seems like another life," Christian Wig was a US Marine, allowing him to obtain a BA degree in 1975 from Kent State University with a double major in Anthropology and Political Philosophy. Since then he has been a farmhand, folk musician, luthier, insurance agent, square dance fiddler, fur trade era rendezvous musician and aficionado of the French and Indian War. Two of his articles on Christopher Gist have been published in Muzzleloader magazine. Currently he and his significant other make Southwestern style jewelry and sell at national level arts and craft shows across the country. In some of these shows, garbed in period clothing, they demonstrate and tell about the history of their craft. They live in the hills of east central Ohio. Mr. Wig's interest in Old Time music as a fiddler and banjoist leads him to attend music festivals and collect Appalachian fiddle tunes.